A Smile in His Lifetime

Also by Joseph Hansen

A Smile in His Lifetime

JOSEPH HANSEN

 HOLT, RINEHART AND WINSTON
NEW YORK

Published by Holt, Rinehart and Winston,
383 Madison Avenue, New York, New York 10017.

Published simultaneously in Canada by Holt, Rinehart and Winston of Canada, Limited.

Library of Congress Cataloging in Publication Data
Hansen, Joseph, 1923-
A smile in his lifetime.
I. Title.
PS3558.A513S6   813'.54   80–21420
ISBN 0–03–056064–0

First Edition

Designer: Lucy Castelluccio
Printed in the United States of America
1 3 5 7 9 10 8 6 4 2

Acknowledgments

My thanks to the National Endowment for the Arts, whose 1974 grant let me get a start on this novel, and to William Harry Harding, who saw to it that I finished it. My thanks also to John Harris and Joe McCrindle, in whose magazines *Bachy* and *Transatlantic Review* chapters of the novel, in forms since changed, first appeared.

—J.H.

For Jane, with love

FIRST PART:
Dell

Ah how stupid I am, I see what it is, they must be loving each other,
that must be how it is done.

—Samuel Beckett, *Malone Dies*

Horse

He waits for mail, not hopefully—dully, ready for disappointment. Coffee mug in one hand, cigarette in the other, he sits in worn Levi's on paintless back steps and stares vacantly across the canyon. It is in the hills back of Los Angeles: dry brush and rocks, red flares of geranium, clumps of ragged eucalyptus trees, shacky houses propped on posts. The sun is already hot on his thin naked arms and on his scalp where the hair is thin. Not that he is old. He just feels old this morning. He's sat here too many times waiting for mail not hopefully.

He tilts up the mug to finish off the coffee. He likes it small-boy style, white with cream, candy-sweet with sugar. It is cold. He pulls the last smoke from the cigarette, snubs it out on the step between his bare feet, blue-veined, white. He drops the butt among scraggly chrysanthemums beside the steps. He moves to stand up, then doesn't because something stirs at the far foot of the shrubby yard where a pittosporum spreads mottled leaves, shiny as new frogs.

The pittosporum is a broad, squat parasol, fed by weepers from the cesspool. Beyond the pittosporum the land drops sharply. Down there, in the canyon bottom, among abandoned chicken runs and jungles of morning glory and wild cucumber vine, lives Mrs. Grieve.

3

She comes through the pittosporum now, tall and gaunt. She wears an old cotton print dress and a brown cardigan. Sighting him, she extends a bony hand. She can't expect him to take it over a distance of fifty yards, but she keeps it held out as she climbs, leaning forward stiffly, gray head bent, watching her long feet in faded red tennis shoes. The climb is steep. He gets off the steps to meet her, take her hand, help her the remaining distance. But when the hand is almost within his grasp, she withdraws it and halts, looking up at him, cheerless.

"Miz Miller's not here, I guess," she says.

"Teaching," he says. "Summer session. Coffee?"

"She'd want to know." Mrs. Grieve doesn't budge. "Guess you'll have to tell her. Path's kind of steep for me to climb twice. And I don't like to tell her on the phone. Not about a death."

The coffee churns in his stomach. "A death?"

Her false teeth smile. "Not human. Made it sound like a person, didn't I? Didn't mean that." The smile goes. She never keeps them long. "But Miz Miller loved that fool horse—Sergeant. He's dead. Letter came from the folks who bought him off Kenny. He fell. There's a ravine through the place up there. Fell in it, some way, broke his neck."

Whit nods. "She'll be sorry." He digs a cigarette from his pocket. His hands shake. He has trouble scratching a paper match on its limp folder. "He was a real character. How old was he?"

"Not old—maybe fifteen. He could have lived a lot longer. Accident was all. Nobody riding him. Just out there by himself. I thought Miz Miller'd want to know."

"Thanks. I'll tell her. Sure you won't have a cup of coffee?" But she turns and goes. She doesn't like him. He knows why but that isn't on his mind now. He is shaken. He tries and again fails to light the cigarette. In the kitchen, which is half a cave dug out of yellow hillside rock, he slops the coffee, pouring it. Outside the open door again, his knees give too soon and set his bony ass down hard on the step. His nerves are shot. *It isn't Kenny,* he tells himself, *it's only the horse.*

4

Eight years ago, a shirttail relative of Dell's left her a little money. They wanted a place of their own. This one wasn't much, studs and shiplap, windows loose in their frames, the boxed-in board steps between the two levels always crumbly underfoot from the sift of grit, the roof leaky. When winter came, they slept to the drip of water into pans. But they were young, the winters were short, and the price was low. They liked the stone fireplace and the way the house crouched, dowdy as a bird's nest, under tattered trees out of sight of the road.

Dell said it would be a good place for him to write. He said it would be a good place for her to have a horse. She'd grown up with horses, and he blamed himself because she didn't have one. But the first house payment and the price of an old car to take him to work used up the legacy. His wages fed them dried beans and clothed them at thrift shops and army-surplus stores. They had no savings because they bought too many books. The magazines that now and then printed his poems seldom paid. The book of his poems that Sandy Fine printed nobody bought. So a horse seemed unlikely.

But she got it. When it rained, she crouched on the roof, wet hair in her face, swearing and patching the leaks with black mastic and a putty knife. But did luck send her a new roof? No—it sent her a horse. On a morning like this, maybe six months after they moved in, Mrs. Grieve stood on these steps. She looked like an Indian, not a squaw, a sour old brave. Whit, startled at the breakfast table, half expected her to wave a scalping knife. But Dell knew her. Dell knew all the neighbors, still strangers to him. Mrs. Grieve sat down on a rickety but bravely painted yellow chair, and took a letter from her apron pocket.

It was from her son Kenny. The army had crooked its finger at him. He was herding cattle in Wyoming. Did cowboys still exist? Was Mrs. Grieve young enough to have a draft-age son? Evidently they did and she was. Kenny owned a horse. He didn't want to sell it and he didn't trust anyone he knew in Wyoming not to use it to death. Would his mother board it?

The letter was in ball-point on blue-lined pulp paper from a ten-cent Indian Head tablet. She folded it and tucked it away.

"Now, Miz Miller, you know horses. If I write him back yes, will you look after it, ride it?"

Miz Miller would. She was sober as a second wedding—until Mrs. Grieve left. Then she cheered. Whit wasn't ready for the hug. She could be sudden and rough. Reflex made him dodge. Her chin hit his nose. It spurted blood. His chair went over backward. They sprawled together on the green-painted floorboards, laughing. She kissed him hard. They pulled each other's jeans off and fucked on the floor, bloody but happy. A few days later, Kenny brought the horse. With Dell's help, he built a paddock next to the disused Grieve garage, and a stall inside. He left for training camp. Whit didn't meet him. Whit was at work.

He did meet Sergeant. To Dell, the horse was a six-year-old bay gelding, fifteen hands high, in good condition, handsome and gentle. To Whit he was an ice-age hide stuffed clumsily with gut and muscle. Dell coaxed Whit into the saddle. He rode a few stiff-backed yards down the pitted blacktop road behind Grieve's. "You're a born rider," she called. "You sit him beautifully." He said, "It's my sacroiliac." He didn't know what the horse was thinking. A hoof slipped an inch on a scatter of gravel. It would be far to fall. He got down.

On a day when Dell was somewhere with the car, Whit answered the phone. "Your wife's horse is out here on Barrymore Drive. He's gonna get hit." Whit didn't know what to do but he went to do it—down the dirt path, down the narrow paved trail that was cold under big Japanese pines. Barrymore Drive was a high shelf of sun-white cement lofted to fit the bends and thrusts of the hills. Sergeant stood there gazing out across the San Fernando Valley that lay under smog brown as an army blanket. He looked lost but he would look lost anywhere. Whit let startled cars crawl past, then took the bridle and led the horse home.

The paddock gate hung open. Its latch was broken. He didn't try to fix it. He knew better. When they had first got the

6

house, he'd started sawing boards for bookshelves. Dell had begun to yell at him. He had yelled back. She threw a scrap of wood at his head. He stamped off. When he got home again, she was building the shelves and happy. He picked up a hammer to help. "No," she said, "you'll hurt your hands." There was no answer for that—he always did. "Go write," she said. Later, the sink trap had clogged. She had taken the wrench away from him, damn near hit him with it. The wiring had shorted. They were *her* screwdriver, *her* pliers. Anyway, he'd electrocute himself. So he tied the paddock gate shut with clothesline. Dell would fix it.

He felt protective and sad about Sergeant after that. He still wouldn't ride him. The beast was clumsy as hell—he would kill them both. But he sometimes stood at the foot of the yard and talked to him, Sergeant rumbling answers through his big sinuses from the paddock below. The sound filled Whit with tenderness and despair, as for a huge idiot child. Unless you knew the right place to stand, brush and trees made it hard to see the paddock. Sandy Fine, who in those days seldom came around, thought Whit was crazy when he found him talking loudly but alone down by the pittosporum.

"I'm conversing with Dell's horse."

"Ah." Solemn nod. "That, of course, is not crazy."

Whit grins for a second, remembering. But the grin turns bleak. *Just out there by himself.* Sergeant pokes his dark, soft muzzle at a clump of grass that shows a little green. The earth breaks away under his hooves. The bare brown hills tilt upward. He snorts and his eyes roll white. He treads dry air, comes down. A foreleg snaps. He screams and pitches forward on a shoulder, somersaults to a crackle of vertabrae and, with a thick drum sound, lands on his side in the dry creek bed. A rear leg kicks once, twice. He lies still. The dust of his falling settles on his open eyes.

Whit stands quickly and carries the coffee mug indoors where it is dim and still cool, so that his sun-warm skin pebbles and he shivers slightly. His ten-dollar drugstore wristwatch is upstairs somewhere but he knows it's still too early to hike down the trail to the mailbox. He has to move, though. Away from Sergeant's death. He can try to write—his morning chore. He abandons the mug and starts upstairs. But he comes back down. He will wash the dishes—his afternoon chore.

Those from last night are on the drainboard, those from breakfast still on the yellow table. He gathers them, noisily, dropping a fork. The rush of hot water into the chipped sink kicks up soap powder. He sneezes. His hands are wet. He wipes his nose on his forearm. It reminds him of when he met Kenny. And that reminds him of Sergeant's death, which he has forgotten for ten seconds. And he tells himself it could have been worse. Kenny goes there sometimes. Kenny might have been riding him. Kenny might have been crushed, broken, killed. As Dell might have been when Sergeant was here. He shoves a dishmop into a glass and turns it and sets the glass aside.

That was a good time for her and not for him. The job he had was numbing. He typed bills of lading at a film-processing lab. He needed to make love in the afternoon when he got home from work. They didn't drink in those days, couldn't afford it. They could afford to fuck. But that stopped when Sergeant came. Dell rode. These hills had wide and empty spaces then, bulldozed and built on now. He used to come into the darkening house and worry that she'd been thrown and was lying out there somewhere hurt or dead. He would go down and mope around Grieve's in the dying daylight. Homecoming cars would grind gears up the steep little trails. Children would laugh, dogs bark, screen doors slap, and women call their young to supper.

His worry gave way to loneliness. He would climb the paddock fence and sit hunched forward, elbows on knees, hands dangling, staring into the gathering dusk. Crickets rasped in the weeds. Up the canyon slope, owls screamed, staking out hunting grounds in the brush. Here and there windows began to glow yellow. And his loneliness gave way to self-pity. Which changed to anger when she came, swaying to the slow clop of Sergeant's hooves, the easy creak of leather,

8

up the dark lane out of the looming shadows of the trees. Hell, she wasn't hurt. She was happy. Her contentment was cast iron. Sulk, grumble, shout—he couldn't dent it.

Where that saddle had been all afternoon was the only place he wanted to be. He couldn't hate the horse but he couldn't like the saddle. Maybe she knew that. She wouldn't let him lift it down off Sergeant for her. It weighed forty pounds but, thanks, she'd handle it herself. *Remember your sacroiliac.* She always gave the saddle an affectionate slap when it was balanced on its sawhorse in the dark garage. The first times, she walked ahead of him up the path in the cutbank. Later he made sure to lead, because watching her neat little butt in the worn dungarees gave him a hard-on. And there couldn't be sex now. There had to be supper if he was going to write.

And he was going to write, wasn't he? He was ready to give up. She wasn't ready to let him. She wasn't ready even to listen to him argue about it. Now, seven years later, hands in soapy water, he feels his face grow hot, remembering how he stood crying that first week Sergeant came, standing without his pants, begging her. And how she'd given in. It had been no good, no good at all. She just lay there. She'd never done that before. He never wanted it to happen again. It scared him. No—he was going to write.

Every night, by the bandaged light of a junk-shop gooseneck lamp, he poked away at his gummy old portable, sorting words and looking up to see his thin, pretty child face in the dark window of the coffin-width porch of pine boards where he had, where he has, his desk. And when he got up, back stiff, brain stunned, at midnight, she was asleep, wearing one of his ragged sweatshirts, her boy face half buried in the pillow, lamp still on, copies of *The Nation* strewn on the raveled blanket. Writing against the odds of not knowing how had left him sexed up. But he couldn't make himself wake her. He'd wake early. They could make it in the morning.

But he didn't wake early and she wouldn't wake him, sorry for how hard he was working, moved by how he slept like a chopped tree. And he didn't know how to tell her. Not after

9

that bad, bad suppertime fuck. He could put together the words in his head, but he couldn't speak them. He took to jacking off after writing, spilling his urgency down the rusty little bathroom basin. *I love you,* he sometimes said, and kissed his own mouth in the soap-speckled mirror—while out in the sage-smelling darkness of the canyon bottom, Sergeant stood in shaggy sleep, a lucky gelding.

Miz Miller loved that fool horse.

Rain

The dishes are all in the rack next to the sink now and dripping suds. He fills a pan with hot water and sloshes it over them. He turns them gingerly and repeats the action. They steam. He finds a cloth and starts to dry them. The crockery is chipped, the glasses ten cents each, but Dell hates them to show streaks from being left to drain dry. He opens a cupboard of whitewashed orange crates fitted into the rotten rock wall. A mouse, for whom Dell leaves broken spaghetti there, scampers out of sight. Whit speaks to it, sets a dry glass on the gritty shelf, walks back to the sink for another. He thinks about Kenny. It's a bad way to start the day. But he can't stop himself.

A crooked path climbs maybe fifty yards to the house from the road where he parks the car under a red gum in whose thick humanoid trunk the bumper has dug a crease like a belt mark in a belly. When it rains, the path is a trough. The day he met Kenny, it rained. His shoes slipped on the path. Water seeped into them. A fence of whitewashed lath leans beside the path. Tall geraniums reach through and over the fence. Their mitten leaves dabbed water on his thin windbreaker and denims. Red petals stuck to him like crepe paper to a kindergarten window. A droop of peppertree leaves licked his forehead, cold. When

11

he reached the top of the path, he saw Dell on the roof with her putty knife and can of mastic. A black smear was on her cheek. She wore an old yellow slicker of his he'd tried to throw out because it was ripped at the shoulder. It was too big for her but she'd turned the cuffs back. She pointed with the sludgy blade.

"Go down and help Kenny with the hay."

She'd saved money buying a truckload. It was piled in blocky wired bales under a winter-stripped walnut tree back of Grieve's. If it got soaked it would mildew. He muddied his hands when he slipped on the cutbank path. A bleak slot of electric light shone under the roller shade upstairs in the house but the yard looked empty. The paddock was a pockmarked pond. So Sergeant was dry in his stall. The feed was covered by a tarpaulin anchored at the corners by broken bricks. He started to turn back.

But something moved behind the stacked bales. He wiped rain out of his eyes. It moved again—a shovel throwing dirt. He splashed toward it. Kenny was digging a runoff trench. Rain plastered a brown shirt to his back, pouch-pocketed fatigue pants to his flanks, black hair to a skull like Sitting Bull's in that old photo. Whit stood and stared. Then Kenny saw him, flicked him half a smile, nodded at a second shovel on the ground. Whit picked it up and began digging alongside the stack. When the trench was finished he had blisters and was covered with sweat that made him cold.

Kenny took the shovel away from him. "Come in."

Whit shivered. "I want to get in a hot tub."

"Have a drink first." Kenny walked off with the shovels, threw them under the house that was tall and plain and not finished. Somebody had stopped siding it a long time ago. There were extensive shows of lath, tar paper, chicken wire. Kenny climbed steep back steps. "I don't want to drink alone." Whit pulled his feet loose from the mud and went after him. For the drink, he told himself. He assumed drink meant whiskey and he didn't get whiskey very much these days.

They passed through a tall, murky kitchen where cupboard

doors hung open and dirty dishes glinted dully by a sink with unplated steel faucets. They climbed long stairs where no one had ever got to plastering. The upstairs hallway was plastered, though, and even papered—on one side. "My old lady and my old man," Kenny said, "couldn't agree on anything."

"Where is she?" Whit asked.

"At my sister's in Dago. New baby." Kenny opened a wrecking-yard door to the room Whit had seen light from. It was a big room with four windows but three had been boarded over. The light came from a single bulb dangling from a cord out of a snaky metal conduit that crawled along a naked rafter. The walls here were neatly sheathed in plasterboard but the labels and nailheads showed. A gas heater hissed. It was old, with flutings and acanthus leaves in tarnished brass. It was sending out warmth but it was also leaking. There was a stink of gas.

"That's dangerous," Whit said.

Kenny crouched, turned it off, went and sat on an old iron cot spread with a sleeping bag. He dragged from under the cot a knapsack. From the knapsack he dug a flat pint bottle of whiskey. Comic books came out with it and whispered to the floor. Kenny didn't notice. He went to a dresser of peeling veneer, cracked the bottle cap, and poured into spotty glasses that stood there. Leaving wet boot tracks in the floor dust, he brought the glasses, gave one to Whit, looked into Whit's eyes, and drank. Then he returned to the cot, set his drink on the floor, and took off his boots. "They always wanted something different from each other." He drank again, set the glass down again, and stripped off his shirt. "That's why the house never got finished." He lifted his butt, pushed down the soggy pants, and kicked them away. "You better get out of that wet stuff."

Kenny was naked. He was the color of those brown eggs they charge extra for at supermarkets, and so smooth and hard he seemed carved. Whit couldn't look at him. He looked at pictures thumbtacked to the wallboard above the cot. They were childish pencil and wax-crayon drawings of horses and cowboys, a smoking .45, a coiled lasso. They were signed, KENNY G. GRADE 7A. Kenny went to the dresser and took blankets from a drawer. He wrapped one around himself and held one out to Whit.

Whit tried for a smile and shook his head. "I'll just finish this and get back up home. Dell will be wondering what happened to me."

"You need a new roof." Kenny pushed the folded blanket into Whit's hand. It smelled of camphor and it felt bristly. *The rough male kiss of blankets.* It was a faggoty line but he would go to his grave with it. Kenny stooped to pick up his glass and the blanket slipped off his shoulders. He stood holding it bunched closed at his waist. It made him look very Indian. He had the heavy brow ridge, the jutting nose, the broad cheekbones. All he lacked for an 1880 dry plate was a bear-claw necklace.

Whit told him, "Sears did us an estimate. They'll roof the place for a hundred dollars, labor and materials. We just never seem to have the hundred dollars."

"Keep your money," Kenny said. "I've got bundles of shingles under the house. Been there a long time but you can't hurt asbestos." He drank off the whiskey. "Me and you can do it ourself. When the rain quits."

Whit shook his head. "Dell and you. I type. She does the man's work."

Kenny watched him for a second without speaking, then went back to the whiskey bottle. He knocked it flat trying to unscrew it with one hand, then used both hands and the blanket dropped. A wavy oval mirror over the dresser showed Whit his nakedness. He stared, and Kenny looked up and caught him at it while he was pouring into his glass. He moved the corners of his mouth but not quite enough to call it a smile. He left his glass on the dresser and brought the bottle to Whit. "Drink up," he said. He stood there without anything on as if he didn't know the difference.

Whit's hand rattled the edge of the glass on his teeth when he drank and rattled the glass against the bottle neck when he

14

held the glass out for Kenny to put whiskey into it. Kenny frowned.

"You hurt your hand."

"Blisters," Whit said. "I didn't do half the work you did but I got blisters." With a suddenness that surprised him, he tucked the blanket under his arm, took Kenny's hand and turned it over. It was a small hand but thick and square. It felt tough.

"Calluses," Kenny said. "That's the army. Jesus, man, you feel frozen." He went out the door and down the hall, bare heels thumping bare boards. Someplace, water began to splash. He came back and leaned in the doorway. The whiskey bottle was still in his hand. He drank from it. His lifted throat was thick and smooth. So was his cock, which had stretched and swollen. Hadn't it? So, was he all that easy about going naked? Whit turned sharply away. And there lay the comic books on the floor. He laughed at himself. Kenny wasn't feeling anything or thinking anything Whit was attributing to him. Whit crouched and picked up the comic books. POW! said the fist of a blue giant on one cover. BLAM! said a gangster's automatic on another.

"This is junk," Whit said.

"The shower's hot now," Kenny said. "Steam's coming out. You're so cold you're shaking. Go get in the shower. I'll give you dry clothes afterward. And you can borrow my rubber poncho. One size fits all."

"Thanks, but I better just go." Whit dropped the bright magazines and stood. This was too much like the way it had started with Dell and him. Rain. Undress. Bath. Dry clothes. But this wasn't the start of anything. Kenny wasn't Dell. Far from it. He gulped the last of the whiskey and set the glass on the dresser. The whiskey balled sour in his stomach. Was he going to cap this stupid episode by throwing up? "Is that all you read—comic books?"

"I buy them mostly for the drawings." In the looking glass, Whit watched him pick them up and drop them on the cot. "I used to think I was going to be an artist."

15

The whiskey settled. "It's not art," Whit said, "and the stories are lies. Guns and muscles—that's not how we cope with life. You know that."

Kenny shrugged, grinned. "I just keep moving."

Whit picked up Kenny's blanket that lay at his feet. He took it to him and held it out prayerfully. Kenny shook his head.

"I'm for that shower," he said. Before Whit could dodge, Kenny zipped open his jacket. "Come on. There's plenty of room. My old man made it so we could all three kids use it at once. He was always saving on us. My old lady asked for a separate room for the girls. He built it, okay, but with no door, no windows. He was nuts." Kenny slid a hand down Whit's sleeve. It came away dripping. "So are you. Strip, man. That shower will feel great."

Whit shuddered. "What happened to your father?"

"She threw him out after we left, my sisters and me. Made him live in a chicken house down in the ravine there. Said he had dirty habits. After while, he went back to the reservation. Man, your teeth are chattering."

"Is your mother Indian too?" Whit asked.

"I guess he picked her because she looked like it. She's German. He's Ute. I'm what John Wayne used to call a 'breed.' At Republic Pictures, Indians were bad but breeds were worse." Kenny nodded at the iron cot. "If you don't want to shower, get in the sleeping bag."

"I don't need sleep," Whit said. "I need to go home. If you'll let me." He sneezed. Kenny stepped out of the doorway. Whit told him, "Thanks for the whiskey," and went down the shadowy hallway that was filling with steam. The wet leather of his loafers was rubbing his feet raw.

Kenny called after him, "I've got a week's leave. When it stops raining—"

Halfway down the narrow staircase with its warping wooden ribs, Whit sneezed again, very hard sneezes. The clammy windbreaker sleeve smeared mucus across his cheek. Wet gravel clogged his throat. He had begun to ache.

Kenny went on, "—get a couple days off from your job and we'll nail that roof on."

Whit turned. At the stair top, in luminous steam, Kenny idly scratched his crotch. Whit shut his eyes on that. He stumbled down to the dark, cold kitchen. "Dell," he called back, heading for the door. "The roof is Dell's department." He pulled the door open.

"Yeah, well—" Kenny called. He sounded doubtful.

Whit shut the door behind him. And through the rain the beam of a flashlight caught him in the face. He winced.

"Where have you been?" It was Dell. "What happened?"

"Nothing happened. Could you stop shining that light in my eyes?" The light swung away. She stood by the hay bales in the torn yellow slicker. He went down the steps and slogged to her. "We dug a runoff trench. Then Kenny asked me in to have a drink with him."

"I can smell it," she said. The flashlight ran its beam over him. "Good God, darling, you're soaking."

"I want to get in a hot tub and never get out."

She put her arm around him, kissed his ear, led him through the flashlit puddles like somebody wounded on the six o'clock news. "You're going to have an awful cold."

She was right. She'd bedded him down here on a buttsprung old couch he'd tried to get rid of when they moved but that she'd decided they would need. There were fewer roof leaks down here. For a week he lay sweating and shivering, sneezing and hacking, aching in his bones, groggy from pills, starey-eyed from inhaling Benzedrine, drunk on the dope in the cough syrup, half awake, half dead, while the rain kept on.

Before it quit, Kenny went back to the army.

Roof

He hangs the dish rack under the sink, wipes the drainboard, wipes the table, squeezes out the cellulose sponge, and sticks it between the faucets. A square of mirror in a white wood frame hangs above the sink. He winces into it. He needs a shave, has needed a shave for two days, three. This keeps happening when he is writing. The problems in the book are enough. Poking into his shirt pocket for a cigarette, he climbs the crunchy stairs. The living room is nearly all there is to the upper level of the house. It's walled in pine boards and bookshelves.

The rug is woolly with dust. There are slued stacks of magazines everywhere. The ashtrays brim over. Empty coffee mugs are on the tables. In a corner, beds are unmade, his under windows, hers under a Chinese painting of a girl standing with a horse beneath a tree on a rocky hillside. A breeze flutters the horse's mane, the girl's sashes. She's a legend who went off to war in her dead brother's clothes. The picture belongs to Dell. The glass on it needs washing.

Dell hasn't noticed and won't—not that, not the unmade beds, none of the neglect. He is the housekeeper and not a very good one. The odds are against him. She won't throw anything away. She won't even let him buy a vacuum cleaner.

The noise hurts her ears. She warned him before they were married—she hated housekeeping and wouldn't do it. It didn't faze him. She could have said she liked to keep the house crawling with rattlesnakes. That would have been all right. Making her bed, now, he smells the good warm smell of her, honest as fresh-baked bread, and he knows if he met her tomorrow it would be the same.

He finishes her bed, his bed, boxy rep covers making them into places to sit. He leans cushions along their backs against the pine boards. He empties the ashtrays, wipes them out with tissues. *Clean ashtrays make a clean room.* Was it Sandy Fine who said that? Some faggot he knew. He picks up his watch, winds it, straps it on. Nine o'clock. Still too early for mail. He gathers up the cups, takes them down, and sets them in the sink. He stands at the back door in speckled shade and smokes another cigarette. Then he sighs and goes back upstairs.

His desk waits at the end of the narrow porch. An electric typewriter squats on it. The gummy old portable was two typewriters back. He gets paid for what he writes now—not well, but paid. A sheet of yellow paper with words on it sticks out of the machine. The coffee churns in his stomach again and he turns away. There's the bathroom. He pisses noisily. *Common,* his mother called that, *coarse.* And he agreed with her, nice little girl that he was. Until he learned that his cock was Jesus, Bach, Michelangelo, Shakespeare, earth, air, fire, water, the sun by day and the moon by night. Pissing noisily cheers him up. His cigarette goes *sput* in the yellow suds. He pushes the flush lever, admires his cock, strokes it, feels it begin to grow. Thinks of Kenny, frowns, tucks his cock away, buttons the Levi's. Locking up the insane.

He flips the switch on the typewriter. Its hum comforts him. He reads the last words on the paper, runs the carriage back, crosses out half a line, and rattles new words to say it better than the old. But he doesn't know how to go on. He lights a fresh cigarette and stares out across the treetops, down the canyon, to farther, higher hills. Red tile roofs show through the leafage. Sunlight glints off the brightwork of a climbing car.

19

A blue jay squawks. His hand drops to his lap. His cock is still half hard. But he is not going to jack off remembering Kenny. Seven years of that is enough.

He switches off the typewriter, pushes the chair back on its little wheels, edges his thin body past the bulk of the heirloom chest of drawers that is Dell's and half filled with yellowing and priceless handmade lace and moldering and equally priceless patchwork quilts made by generations of Everetts past—goes right across the living room and out the front door. But the path hurts his bare feet. He returns for his grubby rubber thongs. He shuts the door firmly after him. Tall, shaggy children in beads and feathers roam these hills, trying to forget where they came from, going nowhere. They have blurred ideas of what is theirs for the taking. He heads down the path at a trot, trying to get away from Kenny. It's no use.

Seven months after the rain, Kenny stood outside the back door. At whatever barracks he'd been assigned—in Korea, Guam, the Philippines?—a buddy saw him blow smoke out through his ears and told him he could get a medical discharge. He got it. Bundles of asbestos shingles were piled at his feet, green shingles, faded around the edges. A brown paper sack had spilled onto the ground nails with broad heads that looked soft. Hammers were hooked in the loops of Kenny's fatigues. Dell stood on the back steps with another hammer, her hammer, in her hand. A rolled bandanna bound her hair. She wore a work shirt with the tails out over her jeans. Whit lurked indoors, perched on a corner of the yellow table, staring unhappily into an empty coffee mug.

Dell said, "He'll hurt his hands. He always does."

"Yeah, well," Kenny said, "he could roll off and break his neck too. Nothing you can do about that."

"Not let him go up there," Dell said.

"He wants to roof his house," Kenny said. "It's not too dignified for a man in front of some other man for his wife to tell him, 'You can't do that.'"

Dell said, "You're impertinent." It was Boston talking. Whit saw her grip tighten on the hammer, the knuckles grow white.

20

He also heard something in her voice that said she was near tears. That hardly ever happened and it alarmed him. Kenny said:

"Yes, ma'am," and picked up the long ladder he'd dragged up from the Grieve place. He leaned it against the edge of the roof, next to the drooping greenery of an old peppertree that curtained the bathroom window. He picked up a bundle of shingles and began to climb the ladder. He halted halfway. "If he can't, and you have to, that's okay," he said. "I guess we'll all live through it. Only let's get started."

"You take your goddamn shingles," Dell shouted, "and get the hell out of here." That was not Boston, that was Texas, where Dell had spent the other half of her childhood. She turned, red-faced, eyes wet, pushed past Whit, and ran up the stairs. He took a step after her, reached out, said her name. She didn't answer, didn't stop. The door at the top of the stairs slammed. Then the front door. Last came the slam of the car door down on the trail, the engine revving into life. Whit set down the mug and went outside.

Kenny was still up the ladder. "Shall I do what she said? Or do I even need to ask that?"

"She's just worried about me," Whit said.

"She could get up here tomorrow and pull all the nails out again," Kenny said.

"We need the roof." Whit crouched to pick up a bundle of shingles. "She's grateful to you. Honest."

"You're going to do it with me, then?" Kenny asked. "Not scared to go against her? She's a scary lady."

Whit lodged the bundle in the crook of an arm and put a foot and a hand on the ladder. He grinned up at Kenny. "Just don't let me fall off. She'll kill you."

"I believe it," Kenny said.

The work wasn't hard to learn. Even if he made it his trade, he'd never be as fast at it as Kenny, but he was more help at this than he'd been at digging the runoff trench. By noon they'd shingled almost half the sun-scorched south slope of the roof. He was soaked with sweat. His knees were raw. He had blisters again. His muscles ached. But he was pleased with himself.

Kenny had long since peeled off his T-shirt and flung it into the peppertree, where it hung out of reach. Whit followed him down the ladder and got beer from the refrigerator. He punctured the cans, dripped the excess foam into the sink, and turned to find Kenny sprawled on the old couch, naked. He stretched a lazy hand out and Whit put a can into it—scowling.

Kenny sat up. "Something wrong?"

"Do you have to do that all the time?" Whit walked to the door and stared out. "Take off your pants?"

"I don't do it all the time," Kenny said. "They're hot. The other time they were wet."

"What if Dell walks in?" Whit said.

"It's not her you're worried about," Kenny said. "It's you. You get uptight. The last time, in the rain—you should have seen the look on your face."

"So"—Whit turned—"you do it to make me uncomfortable. Why? What did I ever do to you?"

Kenny studied him from under black brows for a long minute, mouth thin and tight. Then he sighed, set the can on the floor, picked up the crumpled fatigues, stood and pulled them on. He jerked up the zipper. He sat on one of the stiff yellow chairs, took a long pull from his beer, wiped his mouth with the back of a hand. Then he gave Whit a lovely, open smile. "Forget it. Okay?"

Whit smiled back but what he felt like was sitting down on the floor and crying. Instead, he made peanut butter sandwiches because that was what there was. They washed these down with second cans of beer, then climbed the ladder and nailed on more shingles. Dell showed up sometime at the top of the path with grocery sacks. She gave them a cheery hello. He worked happier after that. But the time came when he couldn't lift the hammer anymore. Anyway, the sun had lost itself beyond the ridge. He and Kenny crawled down the ladder. Dell had washed the dishes. She'd laid gay straw mats on the table. The chipped plates and secondhand silver gleamed. Good smells came from the oven. She said:

"Kenny, you're to stay for dinner."

"I'm filthy," he said. "Got to clean up."

"All right, but if you don't come back, I'll think you haven't forgiven me. I'm sorry, really. It's just that I know Whit. Physical work is very hard on him."

"He did fine." Kenny said it to her but he was looking at Whit. What was in his eyes, Whit couldn't put a name to. "All we need's about two more days."

"I really can't thank you enough," she said.

He shrugged. "You looked after Sergeant." He went off down the long yard to that bleak, ugly house, the shower big enough for three. Whit sank tired into deep, steamy water in the tub below the window that opened out into the peppertree. Kenny's T-shirt hung there ghostly in the dying light. After a while, he couldn't see it anymore. Later he heard Kenny's voice below, Dell's voice. He couldn't make out the words but the sound was sad. And he began to cry. He cried silently for a long time.

"Whit?" Dell tapped the door, put her head in, backlit but not brightly. "Darling? Are you all right?"

"Fine," he said. "Be right down."

"Don't you want the light on?"

"No need. Just leave the door open. Thanks."

She went away slowly, doubtful. But at last he heard her steps on the stairs. He pulled the plug, wound the chain around the faucets, got out of the tepid water. After he'd toweled himself, he turned on the light. In the mirror, his eyes were red-rimmed, bloodshot, the lids swollen. That would be fun to explain. He dug jeans and a sweatshirt from a drawer, put them on, and went downstairs. There was nowhere else he could go.

The pot roast Dell had fixed was heady with herbs, tender with new vegetables. They hadn't had a meal like this in months. And he could hardly swallow. Dell didn't make it easier. She kept giving him worried looks, puzzled. Her eyes asked questions. Kenny watched him too, while he ate. He put the food away fast, the way he dug ditches and nailed shingles. Then he said to Dell:

"You were right about him. He looks sick."

"Oh, for Christ's sake!" Whit flung his chair back and lunged out the door. He stood under the peppertree, hugging himself, sucking in deep, shuddering breaths. He heard them get up from the table. He knew they were watching him. Dell came down the steps and touched him.

"I'm not sick," he said. "Don't let me break up the party. I just want to be alone for a while—okay?"

"I should have stopped you," she said.

"It's not that," he said. "Please? Leave me alone?"

She went back inside and shut the door. They washed the dishes. He heard the splash and rattle. The light went out and they climbed the stairs. He sat on the back steps and lit a cigarette but the crying had left salt in his mouth that made the smoke taste bad. He ground out the cigarette. The night was warm. His eyes kept falling shut. But he couldn't make himself go inside. He leaned against the doorframe. He must have slept. A hand shook his sore shoulder. Kenny bent over him.

"Hey, I'm going to sack out. You better too. We ought to get started early tomorrow."

Whit rubbed a hand over his face. "Where's Dell?"

"Upstairs. She's been showing me art books. She's a very intelligent lady."

Whit stood up. "Let me tell her where I'll be."

"Where's that?" Kenny asked.

Whit drew a deep, slow breath. "With you," he said.

"Jesus," Kenny said.

24

Burr

He is wearing a work shirt with sleeves and collar torn off. He has sweated it. And the pine shadow of the trail has chilled him a little. He stands in a slot of sunlight at the foot of the trail, panting from the useless run, waiting for cars to pass so he can cross Barrymore Drive to the mailboxes that lean in a row on scaly posts in a stand of Spanish broom. A Santa Ana wind blows his thin hair. He tries to comb it back with his fingers. He must look like a lost wino standing here unshaven in his rags. To hell with it. Nothing to do about it now.

   He's not here anyway. He is suddenly lying again in a dark rooftop workroom on one of those beds that comes out of a couch. Big white canvases sleep on the walls. A dirty skylight is pale overhead. It's years after that night with Kenny. Burr Mattox has met Whit at the Brackett House office Christmas party and taken him away. From San Fernando they wheel along miles of twilit freeway in Burr's rackety old MG into Hollywood. In Babushka's, a little Russian restaurant where a zither twangs among gingham table cloths and candles, Burr praises Whit's books. Brackett House is a publisher of sleazy paperbacks. Burr tells him he's too good a writer for them— which Whit already knows.

Then, fuzzy from martinis before dinner, wine with dinner, brandy with coffee after dinner, they are leaving the MG down a side street off Melrose. It's ten o'clock. They're walking with Burr's arm through his along Melrose, they're leaving the streetlights and neons and going quiet down a brick passage into a yard with dimly lit plantings. They climb wooden outside stairs. Burr goes softly, all six-feet-five of him. On the duckboards crossing the roof Whit stumbles and Burr shushes him. Then there are drafting tables, big color transparencies, lights out.

Whit has never been treated so tenderly. It's like extra Christmases for a dying child. Burr gives him three of them. By two o'clock they're simply lying naked side by side in the dark, talking. He talks. It's always that way. When he's happy, he talks. He's been telling the story of Kenny. It's run like a loop of film in his memory, run so often that if it were real film, the sprockets would have torn, it would be only a streak of light. He's never told it aloud. He recites it in the dark. He is disastrously happy with no idea there's going to be a disaster.

Burr said, "You don't expect me to believe that." He propped himself on an elbow and blinked down at Whit. "Baby, you have got to be putting me on."

Whit grinned. "I said, 'It's what you want, isn't it?' And Kenny said, 'I thought you'd never catch on.' "

"That's all right." Burr rolled away, coughed, sat on the bed edge. He got his cigarettes off a low white chest that held drawing papers. "I know his type. They're thick on the ground. Who I don't know is the man that's going to walk in and tell his wife he won't be home tonight because he's got an appointment to suck some boy's cock." He chuckled. "No way." A lighter clicked. The flame threw his shadow large and fitful up into the skylight. "Don't put that in one of your books, baby Nobody is going to print that." He set a lighted cigarette in Whit's mouth and lit one for himself. The lighter rattled on the chest. He stretched out beside Whit again. Big white teeth gleamed in his black face. "Go on. Tell me the rest. What did she say?"

26

His tone was wrong. But it had changed too fast. Whit's guard was down. He normally answered questions. He didn't know how to lie. Dell had tried to teach him to say nothing when in doubt. Or to change the subject. But he wasn't in doubt. He felt safe with Burr. He could do that—confuse nakedness with total trust. He rolled onto his front and groped the vinyl tiles next to the bed for an ashtray he'd set there. He mumbled into the rumpled sheet: "She said, 'You should be very pretty together.' "

Burr snorted. "Shee-it."

Whit stopped moving. He'd been warm enough till now, even if it was December. He hadn't thought about being a stranger in a strange room with a stranger. He felt cold now. And alone. He got out of bed and went into the little washroom where the basin was streaked with ink and paint. He pissed without joy in a blinding tile dazzle of light. He switched the light off, came out, found his clothes on a high stool. He pulled on his shorts.

"What's happening?" Burr asked.

"I'm going home," Whit said. "It was very nice but it's not nice anymore." His T-shirt smelled of spray-can deodorant when he pulled it over his head. The bed squeaked. Burr loomed in front of him, bulky against steel-frame, push-out windows whose wired opaque glass netted wan light from someplace. Whit turned his back, flapped into his shirt. "Home to my wife, who is none of your goddamn business."

"I never said she was," Burr said.

"You said 'shit.' Don't say 'shit' to me." Whit fumbled, working at the shirt buttons. His voice shook. "She and I made an agreement. And I don't want to hear 'shit' to this. Before we got married. Her idea—not mine. I didn't have the sense. I was young. She was my first woman. I was out of my skull in love with her. We were fucking up a storm. I thought it would never end." He kicked into his pants, zipped the fly so hard he almost broke the tab. "It was so much better than"—he gestured at the bed—"than this. I'd had years of that, since I was sixteen. This with Dell was the real thing."

27

"Are you telling me you been faking tonight?" Burr said. "With me? You have to be kidding."

"Apples and oranges." Whit sat on the floor to put on his socks. "I said it was good. You know how good it was."

"But she knew you'd get fed up with apples? Knew you'd have to have oranges again sometime?"

"What the fuck did I do with my shoes?" Whit groped around on hands and knees. Burr put the shoes into his hands. "Thanks." They were loafers. He stood and jammed his feet into them. "Where do you keep the phone, please? I need a taxi."

"Forget it." Burr went into the shadows. "I'll drive you." Cotton knit fluttered in the dark. There was a show of eye whites. Small breathy grunts as he dressed. The clink of a belt buckle. "So, how the agreement went was," he said, "when you wanted some dude, you told her, and she smiled and said something graceful."

"Kenny was the first. Dell and I had been fine for three years." Whit worked a spring lock, pulled open the door. The duckboard walk went dim across the rooftop where neat young trees stood in boxes—the outlines of neat young trees. "That was why I didn't touch him when I knew he wanted me to—the time I met him in the rain, the time we shingled the roof. That was why I cried. Because I knew I was going to take him. And it was some kind of end." He was the doomed Christmas child again: daddy Burr helped him into his jacket, put a big gentle hand on his back, eased him out and followed, shutting the door on the room where Whit had been so happy for so short a time. "I didn't want it to be the end."

Burr went ahead of him, massive in a corduroy car coat with a sheepskin collar, across the deck, moving again like the last of the Mohicans—no snapping twigs. At the foot of the stairs he said softly, "How did you feel, telling her? Going to mama for permission?"

"Fuck you!" Whit whispered it and ran out the brick passage to Melrose, early-morning dark and quiet. He turned the other way from where they'd left the car and his legs pumped fast.

28

But Burr had longer legs. Burr caught him in front of a photographer's shop where tinted children leered. Caught him in rough hands. Burr shook him.

"You crazy? How old are you?"

"Sixteen," Whit panted, "luckily for you."

"But not for you." Burr kept a grip on his arm and walked him along the street like a cop with a war protester to the MG waiting down the cold side street on its big rusty wire wheels. He yanked open the little door and shoved Whit inside and slammed the door. "Not for you, baby." He got in and prodded the asthmatic little engine into life. He ground the gears, the car went forward in jerks to the corner, where orange signal lights winked at nothing. He tugged the wheel left. They swung west on Melrose. The snarl of pistons was loud off the blank night building fronts.

"What do you want from me?" Whit asked.

"Not much," Burr said. "Just to love you forever."

"Keep it up," Whit said. "Shake me till my teeth rattle, drag me down streets, maybe knock me on my ass a few times. Most of all, say 'shee-it' when I tell you the truth. But save it till I'm really happy. Pleased with the sex we've had, you know? In a good mood. Thinking you're great." He fought to light a cigarette in the wind streaming over the front glass of the little car. "You'll win my heart completely. You asshole."

" 'Black,' " Burr said. "You omitted the adjective."

"Shee-it," Whit said.

Burr braked the car and steered it to the curb. Whit looked at him. Burr raised his eyebrows. "Light your cigarette," he said, "and we'll get on where we're going."

"We're not going anyplace." Whit pushed the door lever and got out. "We've been where we're going."

Burr took a deep breath and blew it out. He stared along the empty street. Then he turned and smiled. "All right. Whatever you say. Just one question. Before that night, she cut your balls off, didn't she?"

Whit turned, jammed hands into pockets, and began to walk. Remembering Sergeant, remembering the midnight

29

washbasin, the mirror cold to his kisses. Burr inched the little car along beside the curb. He said:

"Yeah, right. Because, face it, Mr. Miller, honey, you fuck like a mink. Just no end to it. Which is ace with me. But no woman is going to put up with that forever."

"I was using her," Whit shouted, "like a fist." Dell had flung that at him during that terrible suppertime fight.

Burr said, "Sure, that's what they all say. Only she was smart. She left herself an out. That agreement."

"She knew I was bent," Whit said. "It was generous."

"Who to? You were the one who sat in the bathtub and cried. All she did was make a pretty speech."

Whit began to run. Burr let the car out a notch.

"Listen," he said, "I want you and I need you. And you *know* I can handle it, all of it, all the time. That's my only condition. I get it all. I split you with nobody." He lifted a hand and the MG roared off. "Phone me when you get your head together."

Whit stumbled up the path at 3:20. It had taken time to get that taxi. A phone booth had been miles to find. And there'd been only one savage dispatch woman on the switchboard. He halted. Something dark and bulky leaned beside the front door. Burr? He squinted and took a step. He breathed. A Christmas tree, trussed in supermarket twine. He pushed open the door.

Dell stirred. "Are you all right?"

"I don't think so," he said. "I doubt that I have ever been less all right." He threw his clothes off and sat on her bed. On a book, cold, with sharp corners. He wanted to hurl it across the room. He only laid it on the floor. He touched her face. "Love me?"

"It's very late," she said.

"I don't want to know what time it is," he said.

She sat up sleepily and kissed him. Her mouth was fine and firm. It had a slightly stale taste from sleep. He liked the intimacy of that, the old knowing, the comfortableness. He

30

took her in his arms. How slight she was and soft. *Man and wife,* he thought. Maybe it was the idea he kissed, the safeness. He kissed it hard till Dell gasped, laughed, turned her head. "Get up," she whispered. He did. She folded back the blankets. He sat again.

She gave her little pleased murmur when her hand found his cock. Out of old habit, he echoed the sound. His cock stood stiff. Inside his head, Burr mocked him: *Another hard-on? Tonight? Baby, you are too much.* Forget Burr. Whit slid his legs under the blankets and pressed against Dell. She wore an old shirt of his, plaid cotton flannel. He undid the top buttons and buried his face between her breasts. She opened to him, her hand guided him in. His hips thrust. He nuzzled her hair, traced with his tongue the crispness of her ear. His hips thrust. It was all right. Burr was the father of lies.

Dell cried out and came with him. That was how it always was. Well, almost always. They were good together. But he slipped out of her small into the cold night again. He left her asleep and breathing untroubled, her face to the pine board wall. He found his old robe and went downstairs. In the half-cave kitchen, where the whitewash on the rough planks and beams made him wince when he turned on the light, he located whiskey. They could afford it by then—Brackett House and Golden Bough paid him for his books. He worked part-time for Sandy Fine. And Dell had a job—not teaching yet, but a job. He sat at the yellow table and drank, hoping it would stone him to sleep. It didn't work. Instead, the room started turning.

He lurched outside and threw up, came back inside, switched off the light, and fell onto the couch that had a new slipcover but was still buttsprung. In the dark it spun slowly like something jettisoned in space. He staggered outdoors again, threw up again. Finally nothing but bile. He hung on hands and knees over his vomit. He spat and wiped his mouth. He climbed to his feet and, stumbling, falling, made his way down the long yard and the cutbank path. The house stood

31

gaunt against a sky full of hard stars. He picked up a handful of gravel and with a wide, drunken swing of his arm, threw it at the upper window.

"Kenny!" he shouted. "Kenny!"

A light went on downstairs. Mrs. Grieve appeared in a cotton nightdress at the back door. She was poking bony arms into a bathrobe.

"He's not here." She blinkered her eyes with her hands and peered into the dark. "Oh, it's you. You must be drunk. If he was here, you'd know it before I did."

Whit realized his robe was open and he was naked under it. He pulled it shut and groped for the sash. He'd lost it, probably snagged it on a bush, getting down here. "Where is he?"

"Up north," she said, "with that Doreen woman and her kids. You know that. It's five o'clock in the morning, Mr. Miller. Why don't you go home to bed?"

"I want Kenny," he said.

"Your poor wife," she said, and shut the door.

Stripes

There is a break in the traffic and he lopes across to the mailboxes. He drops the tin door marked MILLER. It hangs and squeaks with the wind pushing it. Inside the box is a Jiffy bag, a plump one, the kind batches of paperbacks come in. *Ganymede Press, New York.* It's a surprise, welcome enough, but not the one he wants. He uses a thumbnail to pry up the wire staples. He digs out a book. Good. The cover art is fair this time. Not as good as Burr used to design for Brackett House. But Brackett House went bankrupt. And Burr? Burr just went. Wind whipping his hair, Whit tucks the Jiffy bag under an arm and flips pages with a thumb. A typesetter's mistake makes him wince. When will he get a decent publisher?

He stuffs the book into a hip pocket and pokes into the mailbox again. There is a thick stack of envelopes. His heart beats faster. He shuffles them. Phone bill. Bank statement. A plea from CARE. They keep coming when you've answered one. He won't look at the pictures of starving children in the leaflet. He will send a check for five dollars, knowing that if it helps these starving children grow up, they'll produce twice as many starving children in their turn. And knowing that five dollars is too much for him and Dell right now.

The reason why is that lately he wasted half a year on a book that, when he sat down to write it, he knew Ganymede wouldn't publish. It doesn't have a dozen fuck scenes in it. It doesn't have one. He is sick of them—not in life but on paper. Yet Ganymede is what stands between Mr. and Mrs. Whit Miller and the dried beans he gags to think of going back to, or Rainbow Labs, which he also gags to think of going back to. Dell wouldn't mind starving again. She means it. Nine novels for Brackett House, Golden Bough, Ganymede, are enough. He has a fine talent. Sometimes she calls it genius. It's time he broke away from pornography peddlers. He gives his head a sour shake. Neither of them has any common sense.

The next envelope holds an ad for a record club. Addressed to Dell. It's a waste. Dell thinks only 78s are records, and they don't make 78s anymore. An ad for *Foreign Affairs*. Dell would like that. He can skip CARE this time, let someone else feed the Biafran babies. Dell won't read *Foreign Affairs*. She'll save it, along with all the other magazines, for the day when she has time. He doesn't know what that means after ten years and she doesn't know either. Or it's too complicated to explain. When she isn't looking, he lugs the stacks of magazines to the cobweb cave under the house that is the cellar. It's damn near full.

The other envelopes out of the mailbox aren't what he was waiting for either. He shuts the flapping door, dodges cars across the pavement, climbs the trail glumly, rubber soles flapping. They slip on rusty pine needles. For surer footing he finds the middle of the scabby blacktop. Watching his feet, he hears himself called and jerks his head up. Phil Farmer squats in the green ground ivy that covers the steep drop from his house to the road. Wild oats and ragweed poke through it. He is pulling these up. He is about forty, wears thick, rimless glasses, a brush haircut, and a brown jumpsuit.

"How's it going, kid?" He grins.

"As long as real sex scares people"—Whit squints up into splinters of sun through pine boughs—"there'll be a market for pornography."

"Putting down our talent today, are we?" Farmer is a salesman. Charm comes natural to him. Men like Farmer

34

remind Whit of his own dead father, whom he loved. Farmer stands up. His glasses wink down at Whit. "Is that your new one, there?"

"I'll bring a copy over." Whit always says this and never does it. Farmer has leftish political views that jar with his glasses, haircut, dated suits and ties. But Whit doubts he's ready for the sexual revolution. Farmer never asks for the books a second time. There are, in fact, few books of any kind in Farmer's house. There are some good antiques, some well-chosen pictures, and many recordings. There is also expensive equipment to play them on.

Farmer and his wife Billie used to invite Whit and Dell over evenings to listen to records. And drink. The drinks were odd and often bad because Farmer has a bias for bargains and buys cases of off brands cheap—Mexican dry vermouth, that kind of thing. Whit drank them regardless. Dell smiled politely and shook her head. She loved the record sessions, though, and sometimes hauled over the ridge prized 78s of hers that sounded to Whit almost like music, played on what Farmer calls his lash-up. The Farmers also hosted parties Sunday afternoons under the big live oak on their flowery patio. Dell doesn't like parties but she sometimes went to these.

Then Billie left Phil and Dell wouldn't go near him. No more bathing in Beethoven, Bach, Bartok late into the night. No more tinkling ice and joky chatter on the patio. Dell and Phil Farmer look at politics the same way and can't rest away from it. They are serving together now on a citizens' committee to have a park built instead of light industry down below in Cahuenga Pass. But she can't stand the man. *And those awful, shiny advertising women he keeps nuzzling.* Whit still wanders over to the parties. Usually at least the booze cheers him up. He blinks at Farmer.

"What are you doing home on a weekday?"

"LBJ is flying into Century City for a fund-raising banquet at the Century Plaza Hotel." Farmer checks his watch. "Fifty thousand of us are going to walk around outside, bleating ineffectually against the war. You won't be there?"

35

"I confine my political action to throwing up," Whit says. "At regular intervals. Dell handles the marching. She'll be there. Listen, I've got to get to work." He starts on up the trail. Farmer calls after him:

"What about the Great American Novel?"

"No news again today." Whit pauses. "No publisher, no book club, no movie rights, no television interviews."

"They'll come," Farmer says. "You paid your dues."

But Whit is worried about paying the bills in his hand. He drops them on the coffee table in the pine room and goes to his desk on the porch. The book he's putting through the typewriter is for Ganymede. The one he took the big risk on may never sell. Something slant-eyed and hairy keeps slavering around the door. Hope won't drive it off. He switches on the machine, wheels out the chair, and sits. He reads again the passage on the yellow paper half typed through. A black activist is threatening the piano player in a gay bar for corrupting his young brother. There is a description of a paramilitary uniform.

And again Whit is back with Kenny. In that plasterboard room upstairs at the Grieve house. It had changed since that time in the rain. It had books in it now, real books, not comic books. Drawing materials were strewn around, color chalks, pencils, inks, Strathmore pads. To the walls were tacked reproductions of paintings Dell had bought for Kenny at the museum shop—Remington, Homer, Eakins. She was easing him along. She'd also chosen the books, starting Kenny like a seven-year-old, with Robin Hood stuff, King Arthur stuff. She quizzed him about them when Kenny came up for meals. Sometimes after supper, Kenny and Whit played chess. Whit taught him. With money borrowed from the Rainbow Lab credit union—it would make Christmas thin but he was too happy to care—Whit took Kenny to a ballet, an opera, grainy art films, Kabuki plays.

Kenny sat on a chair under that naked hanging bulb. Whit stopped in the doorway. Kenny had phoned and asked him to come down. When that happened, Kenny was always on the cot. The hot weather had held for three weeks. Since they'd done the roof. So Kenny was usually naked and always doing nothing. He always looked up and smiled. Now he was fully dressed. He was not on the cot. He was not smiling. He was even busy. One of his army shirts lay across his knees. With a razor blade he was taking off the corporal's stripes, stitch by stitch. Without looking up, he said:

"Sit down. We have to talk."

Whit had brought up cans of beer from Mrs. Grieve's palsied old refrigerator. What it mostly held these days was beer. Mrs. Grieve was spending a month with her older daughter, the one in Dallas. There were grandchildren for her to menace. The beer cans were chilling Whit's hands but he only stood staring. "Talk?" he said. "What about?"

"You better sit down," Kenny said to the shirt.

"I had in mind to lie down," Whit said. "Here. I brought beer." He walked to Kenny and held out a can. Kenny took it, set it on the floor, and went on with the razor blade. Whit put a kiss on his hair. Kenny shook his head. "No. Sit down and listen to me."

Whit straightened. "What do you mean—no?"

Kenny said, "I'm not going to do it anymore."

Beer ran over Whit's knuckles and splattered on the floor. He righted the can. "You're not going to do what anymore? Will you please stop that and look at me?" Kenny looked at him. Expressionless. Whit said, "You mean you're not going to love me anymore? You said you loved me."

"I do love you," Kenny said. "And Dell. You're the best people I've ever known. Nobody ever treated me like you have. But Whit, I can't—hell, you know what I mean."

"Oh, I know what you mean, all right," Whit said. "What I don't know is why. Why, all of a sudden?"

Kenny took another stitch out of the chevron. "Because I'm not queer."

Whit laughed. "Come on. Whose idea was it? Yours or mine? Or can't you remember?"

"Mine," Kenny said softly, picking out a thread. He looked

37

up. "I was horny, Whit. And the way you looked at me, I knew you wanted it. I couldn't see why you didn't take it—that day in the rain. Then, when I got back, you looked the same. So it happened. Great. But I mean, like, once, Whit—not on and on. I mean, it's not like you need it or something. You've got Dell."

"And who have you got?" Whit asked.

"Nobody, but—Whit, I am not that way."

"You've gone with men before. You told me."

"I did a lot of wrong things when I was a kid."

"What we have been doing is not wrong," Whit said.

"For me, Whit," Kenny said. "Only for me."

"You sure never showed it." Whit crouched in front of him. "You loved it. You sure as hell never just lay there. Come on, leave that alone and tell me the reason."

But Kenny went on with the shirt. "Will you please sit over there? I said we had to talk. We have to talk." Whit sat over there and Kenny, working on the stitches, watching his fingers, said, "I couldn't figure out how to stop. I didn't want to hurt you. Like I said, nobody was ever so good to me. Not my own folks. They never knew if I was around half the time. You and Dell—I never loved anybody like I love you two. And I was afraid—"

He threw down the shirt. The razor blade made a frail tinkle on the dusty boards. He went to the window. Outside the sky had lost most of its light. He stood facing the last red streaks. He said, "I was afraid if I made you stop, you wouldn't love me anymore. I mean, it happens to me. Women, men. It's my cock they love, my muscles, right?" He turned, holding out his hands. "It's more with you, isn't it? We won't break up? I can still see you and Dell?" He began to cry. "I need that, Whit. I need it very much."

"You've got it." Numbly Whit set his beer can on the floor. "You'll always have it." He got off the chair and went to the room door. He turned back. "Only don't do this again, Kenny. To anybody. It's the wrong way to be kind." He made himself keep to a walk down the hall, down the long stairway, through the grim kitchen. He shut the screen door behind him, making no sound. He took the outside steps measured, head up, shoulders straight. He was halfway to the cutbank before he broke into a run.

After that, Kenny began to bring girls around.

Van

The typewriter waits for him. The motor pulses and waits for him. The neat keyboard with its white letters waits for him, the possible words. He folds his arms on the cold white enamel case and rests his chin on his arms. Smoke from the cigarette in the corner of his mouth stings his eyes. He squints. But not to see the dust-spotted window and treetops. Why didn't he tell Kenny to get lost? Why didn't he tell Kenny it would destroy him to have him around and not be free to get naked and hard and juicy in bed with him? That was the truth, wasn't it? No. He shakes his head quickly. The truth isn't what you think afterward. The truth is what you do at the time.

It hadn't destroyed him. Not quite. He thought it had. So did Dell. He lunged in the back door and fell, clutching his head, cramping into a fetal shape, howling. It was nineteenth-century Russian. No one would buy it now. But it happened. He rolled on the green-painted planks and howled. Dell was at the stove. She thought he'd been shot or stabbed. She came running. But there was no blood. She knelt and held him, stroked him, murmured pity for him, till he cried himself out. Then she led him, tear-blinded, upstairs, where she took off his clothes in the dark. She didn't take her own clothes off. He was the one who needed loving. She knelt over him. He feels her kiss cool

40

on his swollen mouth. Her hands move gently down his chest, ribs, his belly that still jerks with dry sobs. She lowers her shadow head and takes his cock that stands and throbs and never will know anything about grief.

He sits up sharply now and grinds out the cigarette in a big ashtray that overflows with butts beside the typewriter. He puts his fingers on the keys. But he doesn't write. He remembers what happened after that. She didn't let him lie and start to hurt again. *Come on, get dressed,* she said, and drove him to the beach. You could go there at night in those years. No one would mug you. They walked the sand. Sometime he'd told her the ocean could quiet him and she'd remembered. They walked a long way. It was kind of her—she hated walking. When they turned back, he was still shaky and wrung out, but he felt better. Until they neared the car, and he glimpsed in an empty brick area way below a pier, a small dog alone in the dark, fucking an empty gunny sack. He switches off the typewriter and gets away from the desk. He wants the telephone. He has to stop remembering.

After a snarling search, he locates the phone. Under open pages of the Sunday *New York Times.* This one Dell has read. He carries the phone to the open front door, receiver in the fist that pokes the finger that dials. He leans in the doorway, listening to the ring at the other end of the line, while he watches a squirrel carry a light bulb out on a eucalyptus branch and drop it. It explodes. The squirrel rubs little black hands together, jerks its tail, and looks at Whit with shiny eyes. He tells it, "Well done. Encore!" But he frowns at the phone. The number is ringing too long. Sandy Fine jumps to answer phones. He should be at his shop. Whit thumbs a button to disconnect and dials another number. Sandy's house. This time he gets an answer. But it doesn't help. It's the wrong voice. Whit says, "Sandy?"

"Who's calling, please?" The voice is hairy-chested.

"Whit Miller."

"Sandy's in the shower. I'll have him call you back."

"He never called anyone back in his life. I'll wait." Sandy

41

will come. Sandy never lets him down. Sandy comes, and Whit asks, "Is that a before or after shower?"

"After," Sandy says, "but there are exciting new developments. It looks like a long afternoon."

"That's not what looks long," Whit says. "Sandy, I need you." There's a pause. That's unnatural and it scares him. "What's wrong? He's only a trick. You can ease him out in an hour." Sandy still doesn't say anything. Whit reads his watch. It's not quite eleven. "Two hours?"

Sandy takes a breath. *"Chez vous ou chez moi?"*

"I have to get out of here," Whit says. "Cabin fever."

"And Dell has the car. So I'm to pick you up?"

"Please? I'll buy you lunch."

"If you think I'm the sort of girl that can be bribed," Sandy says, "you're right. I'll see you around one."

The receiver clicks and hums in Whit's ear. He sets it in place and puts the phone down. He stands in the leaf-rustling quiet, the sunstruck emptiness, and dreads the next two hours. Or more. Sandy is often late. A path cuts through a tangle of wild laurel up the ridge. He can climb it to Boulanger's and tell the major the fate of his outdoor light bulb. It will launch a string of stories that will kill time. Boulanger, in some far-off, possibly fictitious past, was a British army officer. He's been in films since the twenties. A tall, ruddy old man with vigorous white hair and a bristling mustache below a splendid nose, he pretends rage at the squirrels and is always threatening to wipe them out but he won't. He's too soft. Also they keep adding to his stock of anecdotes. Grinning, Whit takes a step out the door and stops. He has to shave and bathe first.

But when he gets to the narrow porch, he turns the other way, not toward the bathroom, toward the desk. Because he suddenly knows where the novel goes next. He switches on the typewriter and is stringing words along the page before his butt hits the chair. When he remembers where he is, what day it is, that he has to meet Sandy at the foot of the trail because Sandy's car isn't up to climbing to the top, his watch reads 12:40. Hot sunlight is banging through the south window. He is drenched in sweat. He has smoked all his cigarettes. His mouth feels as if someone has doused a bonfire inside it. He leans back in the little wheeled chair, wipes a hand down his face, dries it on his Levi's, picks up and lets fall back to the desk the sheets he has typed. Five. He laughs and shakes his head. He would never have believed it. He feels drained but happy. He stands up smiling, stretches, knees the chair out of the way, and heads for the bathroom, shedding his clothes.

But he hasn't shed Kenny. He's only pushed Kenny offstage for a while. Kenny is back when Whit lies in the tub soaking out the tiredness, gazing out the open window into the peppertree. Kenny is back with those clean, breakable-looking girls he kept bringing to meet the Millers. Nursing juniors, computer trainees, play-school helpers, they smelled of soap and Sunday schools. If Kenny was getting any sex, it wasn't with them. Before he'd stopped getting it with Whit, he'd found a job in a lumberyard. With the proceeds he'd bought a suit. It didn't fit right. Dressed up, he looked misshapen. And uncomfortable. The farm boy got up for a Saturday night movie in town. He sat in the book-lined lamplit room and admired Dell's talk about Roman history, Washington politics, Renaissance painters. He laughed at Whit's jokes. But all the time he looked as if he needed to scratch. And couldn't. Not in front of those wholesome girls. It was funny and puzzling. Kenny had told Whit about the women he'd been with— waitresses in dusty highway cafés, pickups in cheap bars, trailer-camp widows on the bottle, Laramie whores. This was a new chapter.

But not a long one. His mother told Kenny about the pay his brother-in-law was getting in a San Diego ice cream plant. And Kenny caught a Greyhound. It was a relief. It was a wrench. In January came a letter saying he was married. To his brother-in-law's sister. Then there was silence, a year of it. Whit ached for Kenny. He woke mornings speaking his name. He mumbled it into his pillow falling asleep at night. At crazy times, washing dishes, watching television, he cried. He'd never have got through it without Dell. She made him talk about it. She

43

loved him well and often. He can't remember her words, maybe there weren't words, but somehow she told him to find another male. He tried. Once. There was a youth with black hair and lashes and pale smooth skin in the shipping department at Rainbow Labs. He wore a wedding band. Whit had him in his car during a rainstorm in the parking lot. All it did was sicken him. He didn't want somebody. He wanted Kenny.

Then suddenly Kenny was back. *I just keep moving.* A Saturday morning in February, clouds making up in the south, black and low, wet warmth in the air. What was this about him and rain? A knock came on the back door. Whit was at the yellow table, drinking a third mug of coffee to delay going up to write. He can't remember now where Dell was. No one came to the back door but Mrs. Grieve and that was rare. He got up and pulled it open. Kenny tried for a smile and missed. Something had happened to him. It had smoothed and paled his features. He was going to look like that in his coffin.

"Can I come in?"

"You know the answer to that," Whit said.

Kenny clumped across the sill. He wore low boots with buckled straps. Dirty dungarees were tucked into them. His fake leather jacket was stained and scuffed. During the time of the girls, he'd used shiny cream hair lotion. Now his hair was dry and windblown. He needed a shave.

"Sit down." Whit went to the orange-crate cupboard for a mug. "I'm glad to see you. If I told you how glad, you'd get angry." At the stove, he tilted the coffeepot. There was exactly one mugful left. He set it on the table in front of where Kenny stood. He looked into the carved face. "I love you, and it's very painful."

"Yeah. I treated you like shit. I lied to you." Whit had turned to take his chair. Kenny caught his arm, pulled him back, kissed his mouth. Whit shut his eyes and jerked his head back.

"Don't do that," he said. "Not if that's all."

"It's not all." Kenny touched Whit's crotch.

"Ah, Christ." Whit sat on his chair and looked up at Kenny. "What lie?"

"That I didn't want you. Like that. Anymore. I did. Only I got scared." Kenny sat down too. He moved a spoon on the table, watching it. "At the lumberyard—it was 'cocksucker' this and 'cocksucker' that. And I kept thinking, what if they found out? About you and me. Those days when you came to pick me up in the car, I was scared shitless they'd guess."

"How?" Whit held out cigarettes. "Am I so obvious?"

"No, but—ah, hell, I don't know." Kenny took a cigarette and set it in his mouth. He got up and went to the stove for matches. "I was stupid, all right? Young and stupid and scared." He came to the table with the matchbox in his hand. He lit Whit's cigarette and his own. He dropped onto the chair again. "That day, when I told you I wouldn't do it anymore— what happened was, they caught Ernie in a shed doing the Mexican kid. They didn't beat him up or anything. It was what they said. The words. He ran out the gates into the street. Right into a car. Blood everyplace. I was scared, Whit. Really scared."

"Of liking it." Whit made this a statement.

Kenny nodded, watching the cigarette as he tapped it into a plate where egg yolk dried. "Too much. With you. I had to quit. I guess I thought it was—what the jerks at the lumber- yard thought." He shook his head, drank from his mug, set it down. "You been to gay bars? Those screaming queens. I didn't want to end up like that. Christ."

"You never could," Whit said.

Kenny looked at him for a few seconds, then went to the sink and drank water. "What about you? What if you didn't have Dell? Could you?"

"If I didn't have Dell, I'd be worse off than that," Whit said. "This year? Face down in the water."

"She loves you. Even your old clothes." Kenny stood behind Whit's chair, put hands on Whit's shoulders. "I know why. Ah, Whit"—his voice wobbled—"I'm so fucking miserable."

Whit pressed one of the hands. "Join the club."

The sound Kenny made was half laugh, half sob. He went to his chair again, eyes wet. "It's been a rotten year for me too. But I've learned from it. Have I ever! About love. What it is and what it isn't."

"I know what it is," Whit said. "What isn't it?"

Kenny's smile was bleak. "Some teenage chick who wants to get away from her parents and hooks into the first jerk that gets a hard-on for her in a drive-in movie and then says she's pregnant and makes him marry her and has the baby like seven months later and while he's at work makes out with the beer-belly slob next door."

Whit nodded. "I'd say you're right."

"I honest to God caught them—walked in and caught them. Early from work. Like you read about. I knew why. I know Jackie. Slob had a fucking Mercedes. Brand new." Kenny grinned savagely. "That night I cross-wired the son of a bitch and drove it into the ocean."

"Ah, Kenny," Whit said.

"Next day, I come home, empty closets. She's gone, the baby's gone. Not that it was mine. I didn't care whose it was. I loved it. Anyhow, the slob is gone too. Easy to figure." Kenny laughed, not happily. "My lousy brother-in-law blames me. She's his sister. So what else is new?" He crushed out his cigarette. "I need to be loved, Whit."

Whit ought to have said, *For how long?* He didn't say it. He didn't have the guts. He wanted Kenny too much. He'd wanted him too long. He felt sorry for him. He felt sorry for himself. He stood up. "Come on," he said.

Kenny stayed two months. He said, "I told her."

Whit sat up straight. "Your mother?"

"You said not to be ashamed of it. Dell knows."

"Yes, yes, but—"

That spring Kenny was working cattle in Wyoming again. He came down for two weeks before the fall roundup. He was with Whit and Dell for Christmas. One week. Whit gave him a white windbreaker jacket. It looked great against his brown

46

skin. In two days' time he'd lost it. He drove earthmovers grading highways out of Sacramento. He came to Whit for four days. On a Yamaha. Next time he arrived it was for a weekend. In a new pickup truck. Someone had backed a bulldozer over the motorbike. He logged in the Sierras and grew a beard. He came to Whit for a day and a night. *I just keep moving.* Whit kept hoping. When his hope about ran out, Kenny would grin in the doorway and kiss him.

Then came the van. Whit frowns, soap in his eyes, trying to remember why he was down at Grieve's. He can't but he was. And into the yard by the empty paddock—Sergeant long ago sold to the ranch in Topanga—jounced a new VW van. With shrill kids of four, five, six, Kenny at the wheel, a young woman next to him, prim, square-jawed, ash blonde, divorced. Kenny jumped down. He grinned, all right, but there was no kiss this time. Just a handshake.

"This is Doreen. Richie, Kevin, Gee-Gee." Later, up at the Millers'—Doreen and the kids down below with Mrs. Grieve —"I shouldn't marry her, should I?"

"You'd never stand still for it," Whit said.

Dell said, "You're not ready for the responsibility."

"Yeah." Kenny brooded for a while, drinking. "But I love those kids. Christ, how I love those kids."

They stayed for a few days and Whit watched him with them. He bossed them around all the time. They had to stand this way, holding a bat. They had to throw like this, catch like this, run like this. He sat them down with crayons and paper. They had to hold the crayons this way, put the colors back in the box this way. He corrected their pronunciation, their grammar, their table manners. He hadn't known damn-all about any of these things before Dell got to him. He was copying Dell. And enjoying it. He swaggered, bossing his little troop. Whit guessed he would marry Doreen, all right. And he did.

That was why, six months later, when Burr, towering like a black saint carried in procession, came to him through the pack of secretaries, stock clerks, copy editors, slopping their plastic glasses of cheap champagne and using loud voices against the

47

piped-in Percy Faith Christmas album, Whit went with him. *You're Whit Miller, right? I'm Burr Mattox. I like your books. I wanted to meet you. Now I've met you. I want to get it on with you. Let's go.* Here, today, Friday, June 23, 1967, in the tub, using a soapy washcloth on his right foot that he's propped on his left knee, he understands. He had thought Kenny was as lost and gone as Darling Clementine. All somebody had to do was ask him.

With his luck, it had to be Burr.

Weiss

Two things happened that Christmas. First, Burr sent a card.
Not off a drugstore rack. He'd made it himself. A black mink
and a white mink fucking in snow under pines. Lovely.
Obscene. Whit started to tear it up. Dell took it away from
him. *That was a lot of work,* she said. *You make a difference to
him.* Whit told her why. She still patched the card with Scotch
tape. Then it was Christmas Eve and Kenny was back—seven
months after he'd married Doreen, two days after he'd left her.
It was the same as before. *I need to be loved, Whit.* It was the
same as before. Whit couldn't make himself ask for how long.
It was maybe a week. Then a fat deputy sheriff came
chain-rattling up the path and Kenny went out the back door
not even stopping for his shoes.

Now a small yellow cat comes out of the leafage of the
peppertree, up the slope of roof to the open window, where it
regards Whit in the tub. It reaches down and puts a delicate
paw on the rim of the tub. Three more paws follow. The tub
rim is curved. This makes for a difficult balancing act. Whit sits
up in the soapy water.

"Polk," he says, "don't you remember?"

Polk pauses and eyes him.

"You always fall in, and you don't like that."

Polk makes a remark and takes two teetery steps. He is the last of the cats. Dell began collecting them about the time Kenny sold Sergeant. A cat got a saucer of milk on the back steps and moved in. Then another, and another. Kittens were born. There came to be eleven cats. Each, regardless of sex, was named for a president. In the rains of winter, the shut-up house got to smell bad because Dell insisted the cats live in. It did no good. One windy spring, enteritis wiped out all but the runt of the bunch, Polk. Dell quit taking on cats. So Polk has things his way. Now he slips on the tub rim and claws out wildly to save himself. Whit cringes to avoid the claws. Polk splashes, hysterical, scrabbling on the slippery porcelain. Whit risks a foot to hoist him to the window. Polk bullets off across the roof, scattering bright drops in the sun.

Whit calls after him, "I told you," and climbs out of the tub. He pulls the stopper and uses a hand to erase the soap ring. He towels himself, shakes a pressure can of shave cream, spurts foam from it onto his fingers, coats his beard, takes up a razor. It is old, corroded. It belonged to his father who gave it to him when he first needed to shave. That was late. He is very blond. Before he sprouted beard he was spurting semen. In his sleep. *What kind of practice,* his mother asked, *is going on with you at night?* She might have overlooked it, but his pajamas were red and the dye ran, staining the sheets. He was as shocked as she was, but he couldn't answer. Also he couldn't stop. He found a ragged pair of jockeys and wore them at night. In a week, they were stiff with dried jism. He washed them himself in the bathroom basin when she was out. Sleep was what did it to him. Night after night. There were no dreams, visions, desires. It was his physiology, right? It still is. In the Greece of the archaeologists, he'd have had horns, hooves, a whisk of tail. This is a subtler age. *Fine, but why me?* He wipes the steamy mirror and shaves.

Afterward, he splashes on cologne. For Sandy. Or is it? Rummaging for shorts and T-shirt in the top drawers of the old chest, he tells himself it is not for Sandy. Sandy doesn't give a damn. It is for Whit, who pretends he is being loved when he knows he is not. To Sandy, he could be any warm male body. He grimaces. He never thought he'd come to this, however many sad faggots he knew who did. Sex for the sake of sex. It's L*O*V*E he lives for. Which means? He drags the T-shirt on and goes back to brush his teeth.

Kenny said, "What kind of Christmas card is that?"

"It's a joke," Whit said, "in poor taste."

His watch says he's got to go. He kicks into clean denims, pulls on white gym socks, blue-and-white tennis shoes. For a date with Sandy? These are boy's clothes. Sandy likes grown men. What happens to Whit? He remembers a hot day with Sandy on some errand. They stopped at a greasy hot-dog stand and he ordered cream soda. Right straight back to age sixteen. Before Chang, even. Back to the days of Donnie Wright—first cigarettes, first alcohol, first fumblings on a narrow, boy-sweaty bed. Why? Puzzled and not pleased, he shakes his head.

Where has he left a cigarette burning? Nowhere—the empty pack lies twisted on the desk. He runs down to shut and lock the back door, runs upstairs again. What has he forgotten? He tugs another copy of the new book out of the Ganymede Jiffy bag. Sandy won't be able to keep it. Some one-night bedmate will go off with it after breakfast and a marmalade kiss. Still— Whit sets the front door lock and starts down the path.

His toe catches in a tree root and he stumbles. He doesn't fall, but Burr wouldn't have let him stumble. Burr put an arm under his when they crossed streets. Burr always drove him, no matter whose the car. Burr took his hand when they walked in dark places. He wasn't even sixteen with Burr. He was six. A frail six at that. He hadn't known he was going back to Burr. Not till he pushed open the doors of Brackett House one morning, after turning in a manuscript, and Burr was in the parking strip that fronted the plant, hauling a portfolio from behind the bucket seats of the MG. He straightened up, saw

51

Whit, and stopped. He held the portfolio at an awkward angle and stared at Whit over it. It was January, bright, clear, cold. He had on the sheepskin car coat. It was coming apart now at the seams.

Whit said, "I just finished a book. Let's have a drink." Saying it surprised him. Saying anything. Sometimes his cock used him like a ventriloquist's dummy. It didn't believe in hoping. It believed in taking. And this time, Kenny couldn't come back even if he wanted to. The law wanted money from him for Doreen's kids, more money than somebody like Kenny could earn.

Burr gave a tight little nod, dropped the portfolio back of the seats again, got into the MG, leaned across and opened the door on the passenger side. "Get in," he said. Whit said, "Go on. I'll follow you." Burr didn't stop anywhere for a drink. He drove straight to Melrose and left the MG down the same side street as before. Whit parked behind the MG. Together they went along Melrose and down the brick passageway into the garden yard.

Today a neatly dressed small old man in a Russian fur hat met them there. He was latching an aluminum screen door under the wood staircase that led up to Burr's rooftop. Cottage curtains in a window beside the door said the place he was leaving was an apartment. That was unexpected here. Shops, storage sheds, workshops were up and down the alley. Burr made a sound when the little man sighted them and smiled. It might have been a groan.

"Mr. Weiss," he said. "Mr. Miller. Advertising."

"I remember you." Weiss had very blue eyes and a hard handshake. "Once before, you were here. Late at night. One o'clock, two, maybe." He had an Old World accent, not strong, but there. "I sleep. When I get in bed I sleep. Insomnia I never had. I pray God I never will."

"It's worth a prayer," Whit said.

Mourning over Kenny, worrying about Kenny, where was he, what was he doing, Whit had been lying awake a lot lately.

After a week of this, he'd learned to go down to the white cave kitchen and wash down aspirins with stiff whiskeys. Then, when he climbed back up to bed, he passed out. It made waking hard and morning writing impossible.

"But my wife," Weiss said, "she hears all, sees all, never misses anything. She shakes me till I wake up. 'A prowler is in the yard,' she says. 'Go look.' "

"I'm harmless," Whit said.

"It's the nature of the job." Burr's voice was impatient. "Art does not keep business hours."

"Not banking hours, anyway," Weiss said, and left.

On the bed that made down out of the sofa, among the drafting tables, green tin supply cabinets, hanging T-squares, drifts of rough sketches on tracing paper strewn across the floor, Whit lay breathing paint smells, his back curved against the warm inward curve of Burr, Burr's arm across his middle.

"Advertising?" he murmured.

"Did you expect me to tell him what you were really doing up here that night?"

"I noticed you walked very softly." Whit grinned. They lay in silence. Whit started to slide into sleep, easy and content. Dangerously again. Burr said:

"How did she take it?"

Whit stiffened. "If you mean Dell, if you mean my wife— she is no one you and I are going to discuss. Ever."

Burr let go of him, rolled away from him. Cold January air went between them. Burr said to the skylight, "I told you my conditions. I'm not sharing you with her."

Whit said, "You agreed to have a drink with me. Bed was your idea. I liked it. Didn't you like it?" He turned over fast, threw a leg across Burr's legs, kissed Burr's shoulder, kissed Burr's ear. "I want to do it again today, maybe twice. And tomorrow and tomorrow and tomorrow." He slid a hand down to Burr's crotch. "What's wrong with that?" Burr slid away from him, got off the bed, pulled on a cotton kimono. "Where are you going?"

"To get you that drink. That's what you asked for, wasn't it? You wanted me to have a drink with you. We'll have that drink." He opened a file drawer and brought out a half-gone bottle of Old Crow. He reached into a closet where he had rigged a camera obscura and came out with glasses. He poured whiskey and added water from the painty washroom tap. He handed a glass to Whit. "And that is all we are going to have."

Whit sat up, swung his feet to the floor, set the drink on the floor. "Then I don't want it," he said, and pushed past Burr to get his clothes. Off the drafting table stool again. "This is starting to get monotonous."

"It won't happen again," Burr said.

"You didn't act like it bored you," Whit said. "You seemed to like it. A lot."

"Where I'd like it is in your bed," Burr said.

A leg in one leg of his corduroys, Whit stopped and stared. "All right. Fine."

Burr snorted. "You mean, she watches too? Is that part of the famous agreement?"

Whit dressed in silence after that. His red quilted jacket lay on a chair piled with magazines by the door. He moved to get it but Burr was there ahead of him. To help him on with it. Burr said:

"I want to be first in your life." He turned Whit around gently, spoke gently, pleading. "Can't you understand? I say to hell with Susan Hayward in *Back Street.*"

Whit worked the tough brass zipper of the jacket and pulled up the hood. He opened the door and stepped out onto the duckboard walk. Burr caught his arm. "Aren't you going to answer me?"

"I don't know how. I don't know anything about what you call love. All those ifs and buts. What kind of love is that?" Small birds fell out of an ice-blue sky into the rooftop saplings. "Love is like yes and no, Burr. Either it is, or it isn't. If you're afraid of it, then it isn't." He pushed his hands into the slash

54

pockets of the jacket, turned, looked into Burr's face. "I sure as hell could love you. If you'd let me."

Burr's wide shoulders were hunched up in the cold. He held the flimsy kimono shut at his chest with a big fist. He shivered and shifted from one bare foot to the other. He gave that same quick, tight little nod again. "Come back in," he said. "You don't understand a fucking thing. But come back in."

Key

Sandy's red hair shines in the sun. He sits in an old VW with its rag top down, beside the mailboxes. About five-feet-five, weighing maybe one-ten, he looks like the bad kid on the block in a hundred 1930s movies. He has propped a book against the steering wheel. Freckled hands hold it flat. Library plastic protects the jacket. Odds are, it's a new mystery. Sandy has read everything else. Whit lopes across Barrymore Drive, wrenches open a door, sits on a cracked, sun-hot, fake-leather seat, slams the door, takes the book out of Sandy's hand, and puts the new one from Ganymede in it.

"Ah," Sandy says. "The latest." He glances at the cover drawing, flips the pages, lays the book between the seats, and starts the car. "Good," he says.

"Are you okay?" Whit asks him.

Sandy's smile might mean anything or nothing. But he's not acting typical. There should be a graceful little paragraph of praise. Instead there is loud radio music. One of the big Mahlers, pouring *Weltschmertz* into the Los Angeles wind. The noisy car takes Barrymore to Mulholland, hedged by brush and rock, where Spanish-style mansions of forgotten film stars fall apart. The paving slants down to Cahuenga Pass and they follow Cahuenga past the recording studios to Sunset, and follow Sunset past whorehouse and hustler motels to Babushka's.

"I thought—" Whit begins.

"Lunch," Sandy says, "you promised me lunch."

Babushka's is dim and quiet at lunchtime. The walls are red with onion domes in white silhouette. You bring your own wine. Weekend evenings, the old woman in gaudy scarves who twangs the zither will read your palm if you're not careful. Sandy spends a lot of time at Babushka's, mainly after hours, playing bridge with desiccated queens who have been at it since the place first started in a Greenwich Village basement in 1933. The U.S. tilts. Everything not too square to roll ends up on the West Coast. Including Babushka herself, a bowlegged little woman with a face like Mrs. Punch. She is kind, giving away too many meals, hiring as waiters too many failed actors, painters, writers. She's funny, but you miss a lot of her jokes because she has some kind of accent and talks softly. In the kitchen, she's a genius. Half the faggots in L.A. know that. It was to Babushka's that Burr took Whit the day of the Brackett House Christmas party.

Today, almost anyplace else would have been better. Whit walks along a sun-bleached sidewalk now toward a liquor store for wine and cigarettes and remembers how hard he tried to make it work with Burr. Getting Burr into his own bed hadn't turned out to be the answer. Burr sulked in the pine plank room with all the books, the tall Chinese painting, the dusty and neglected Everett cut glass, the stacks of political magazines, shelves of 78 albums, cats peering at him wide-eyed or turning their backs to him and washing their tails.

He sat with his coat on, hunched up white around the perfect black globe of his skull, and sullenly leafed over an art book while Whit fetched him a drink from downstairs. On the way up to the house in a gray drizzle of February rain, Burr had sounded eager to see where Whit wrote his books. He never looked at it. Whit finally dragged the coat off him, the tie, the suit. The bed was too narrow, too short. But that had nothing to do with the outcome. The damp cold that kept them shivering when they got naked and lay together had nothing to do with it either. It was just plainly Dell's house. Whit didn't need telling. He saw it in Burr's eyes.

But daytimes were all they had. Whit needed evenings with Dell. He grew lonely for her in the gap between good-bye in the dark morning and supper, which he'd taken to cooking. Oh, there were evenings Dell filled with political action. Whit and Burr got it on then, once or twice, in Burr's workroom, keeping quiet for fear of the Weisses below. But mostly what they had was noons. And these came scarce. Burr too often had to drink lunches with people who might give him work. Whit was on call to Sandy Fine in those days, to mind the bookshop while Sandy was out hunting up new stock for the shelves.

The noons Whit and Burr did manage could be interrupted. By the phone. Or by droppers-in—men in wasp-waist Italian suits, high collars, shag haircuts; women sun-tanned, blonde-wigged, with dark glasses and clanking bracelets—ad-agency types, publishing types. Once, when Whit insisted it was raining too hard for anyone to come, they risked making down the bed. But footsteps sounded on the duckboards. They had to jam the bed back into the couch and scramble for their clothes. It was no way to make love.

A couple of days after that, Burr met him at the door of the studio, his coat already on. They drove in the MG down side streets to a new building with white gravel landscaping in front. Burr led Whit up stairs and along an outside gallery. He used a key on a door as personal as a hospital room's, and pushed him into a little apartment that smelled of fresh paint and carpet and no hope. Utility was the style throughout, blue-green utility. Burr nodded at a sharp-cornered little couch that faced a color television set.

"That makes down into a bed too," he said.

"What?" Whit gaped at him. "What is this?"

"This is where you're living. Where we can get it on together. Just you and me."

Whit walked into the kitchenette and opened and shut new

58

cupboard doors on stacks of plastic plates printed with daisies, on drinking glasses in electric blue. He turned a shiny new tap. Water drummed into a stainless-steel sink. The place would be easy to keep clean. With no one to be bothered by the noise of a vacuum cleaner. No stacks of *Newsweek* and *The New Republic*. Pictures he chose on the walls. Only his books on the shelves. No grown-up girl child to pick up after. "You must be out of your mind," he said.

"I told you"—Burr came in, reached over his shoulder, turned off the tap—"I ain't splittin' you with nobody."

"Black English doesn't excuse this." Whit tried to pass him. Burr pinned him by the shoulders against a new refrigerator that began to purr. Whit said, "Look—I am not going to trade Dell for a swinging-singles apartment. You bitched about Susan Hayward in *Back Street*. How the hell am I supposed to feel?"

"I won't be keeping you, man. I'm poor, you know that. I signed the lease but I haven't got that kind of bread. Weiss practically gives me that studio rent free. No, we each pay half on this." His smile coaxed. "Okay?"

"Negative," Whit said.

"Change, man," Burr said. "That's what life is. That shack on the hill—you've had that. You don't need that anymore. You said it—wrecks your writing day, coming clear down to the studio. Flow with it, baby. It's the next thing."

"What's the next thing? Will you let go of me?"

"I am the next thing. This place. Bring your typewriter, your clothes, your books. Here. Today. Mr. Miller, honey, this is the answer for you and me. Don't you recognize this place?" He waved a big hand. "This is our fucking vine-covered cottage in the woods."

Whit laughed. This was breaking his heart. "You crazy jig." He struggled, hoping Burr would hit him. "You rock-headed spade." He twisted free and lunged for the front door. But he was blind with tears. He fell over a chair and lay on the floor with his face in his hands. He wanted Burr to come and kick him. But Burr wasn't going to make it easy. He knelt and stroked Whit's back until the crying stopped. He brought toilet paper and dried Whit's face and made him blow his nose like a little kid. He kissed Whit's mouth.

"All right now?"

"No. Where the hell do you live?"

Burr looked away. "At the studio."

"There's no kitchen. No shower."

"I eat out. The Weisses let me use their bathroom."

"Christ." Whit pushed to his feet and walked to a window that was cheap, wavy glass clinched in a thin aluminum frame. He ran his look along a gray cement strip that led to a swimming pool he'd glimpsed from the kitchen. He heard Burr stand up. Whit said, "The shack on the hill isn't it. Dell and I have been together since I was nineteen. Burr, I can't just—" He didn't have the words to finish that. He said, "You're crowding me."

"I know what I want," Burr said.

"Yup." Whit brushed his mouth with a bleak kiss, went to the anonymous door, pulled it open. Cold came in. "Now I have to find out what I want, don't I?"

But Burr wasn't buying it. He was dragging open the couch. New blankets, new sheets, neatly made up, meaning he'd been here earlier. He shrugged out of the car coat and sat on the bed to take off his shoes. "You know," he said. "You already know."

With wine and cigarettes in a brown bag, Whit trudges along in the sun, back to Babushka's. That was the trouble. He didn't know. *The story of a man who could not make up his mind*—Olivier's voice, echoey, at the start of that artsy *Hamlet*. It was a near thing, so near that for once he didn't talk about it to Dell. She sensed he was in trouble. She asked him a couple of times and then quit when he fobbed her off with mumbles about a new book. She knew planning was tough for him, so maybe she believed him. Part of their agreement was to tell each other the truth. Up to now he had. Even about Burr, phase one. Burr, phase two, was different. But he knew what she would say:

60

Do what you have to. I'll miss you.

Even imagining it hurt. But he stood brooding over modular shelving at the lumberyard, picturing where he would put it up in the blue-green apartment. He saw a flower-painted Mexican pottery pig in a shop window and imagined it on the fake wood grain of the coffee table. He'd be able to look at Westerns on TV instead of the six o'clock news. The pocket radio he'd bought her wouldn't forever be buzzing with talk shows wherever she went in the house. There was heating. No more wet wind leaking in at every joint, having to pile on blankets till your legs cramped.

You must be out of your mind.

For a week he held Burr off and drank a lot, mostly down at the yellow table, when sleep backed away and wouldn't come out of the dark. Sometimes by daylight too, making what he wrote sloppy and unusable. Making him cry. Then he got a phone call from Carmen O'Shaughnessy, at Brackett House— about the book he'd brought in the morning he'd linked up with Burr again. She liked it. She'd bring him a contract and a check. They could have a drink.

In the half dark of a flossy Mexican restaurant on La Cienega, she asked, "How are you and Black Beauty getting along?"

He blinked at her. "Who do you mean?"

She threw back her head and laughed. It was theatrical. That was how she was. She was a handsome *señorita,* olive-skinned, brown-eyed, wore her hair in a bun at the side like Dolores del Rio in the late-night movies. She was a little thicker through the middle than Dolores del Rio. She ran to heavy-buckled wide belts and tall, zip-up boots with high heels. "You have to be kidding. Honey, everybody in the plant knows." She squeezed his hand on the starchy white tablecloth.

"Knows what?" Squares of gold-veined mirror tiled the wall back of her. He saw his face fake bewilderment.

"About you and Burr Mattox." She laughed again and tossed off a second margarita. "You are funny, aren't you? Transparent. And blushing too. How sweet. *Señor, por*

61

favor?" She held up her empty glass by its stem, cocking an eyebrow at the dimness. A red-jacketed man with an Aztec face took her glass and Whit's. She put her elbows on the table, her chin in her hands, and looked serious, ready to hear. He didn't know whether to trust her or not. But he was half drunk and he wasn't figuring out what to do by himself. He needed to air it. He took a deep breath and said:

"It's out of hand, Carmen. He wants me to leave my wife for him. He's, for Christ's sake, rented an apartment for me to sit around in in my makeup and my best frock, waiting for him to get home from work."

The glossy eyes with their thick claw lashes opened wide. She started to speak and changed her mind. She dug a cigarette from a big black patent-leather shoulder bag on the seat beside her. Whit lit the cigarette for her. She picked a shred of tobacco off her lacquered lips. She frowned at him through the smoke, then realized he didn't have a cigarette and found the pack again and shook it at him.

He said, "No thanks."

She laid the pack on the table. "He told you this?"

"He's got a key. He took me there. We had it on there. It's no fantasy."

"Oh, honey," she said sadly, "it is. I mean, Whit, you are so innocent. I mean, cling to that little woman of yours. You need somebody to call you in out of the rain."

The waiter set down another big margarita, another bad bar bourbon on the rocks, another tab, and went away.

"What rain?" Whit said.

"No." She gave her head a quick shake. "Come on. Forget that. We've both had enough." She slid out of the red tufted corner, stood, hung the bag on her shoulder. "Let's go."

He stared up at her. "What the hell is it you're trying to say?"

"I'm trying not to say it." She went off in her boots through the room's crafty shadows to hand the tabs and a credit card to a girl behind a discreet cash register—a *señorita* prettier than Carmen but with stupid eyes. Whit got his quilted jacket from

62

another red-coated Mexican and watched Carmen rattle red nails on a counter while the girl fixed up a receipt, ran it through a gadget, had Carmen sign it. She came to Whit and he pushed open the red plastic-padded door and they stepped out into drizzle. He gave her his jacket to cover her hair and they ran for the corner parking lot. In the car, he asked her again, and she said, "I'm not going to tell you. Let's talk about something else. Got an idea for a new book? Get me an outline and I'll get you a check."

"I can't write anything, for Christ's sake. I can't even think. Burr is driving me up the wall. I mean—he *means* this, Carmen, he means this. I'm supposed to throw away—" He gestured behind the gestures of the wipers on the runny windshield. "Either, slant, or." He shook his head grimly. "Shit. It's just too goddamn much."

"You knew it would come to this one day," she said. "You're gay. You're married. You knew."

"I hate it," he said, "and I can't talk to anybody about it and I'm losing my alleged mind. I love him, I need him, I don't want to hurt him. But he's asking too fucking much."

She moved the car across the intersection. "Dead right," she said. "Now, let's see. I get to the Pass by going over the bridge— correct?"

"Left," he said. "Next left and around." He moved his hand to show her. "If you know something about him I ought to know—" He stopped. Would it make any difference? What could he hear about Burr that would change anything?

She didn't offer it. She kept on about his book, going over praises she'd already used in the bar, then asked him again about his plans for the next novel, then veered off on a manuscript she'd accepted that day, then mentioned a couple of Brackett House authors he knew who between them cranked out a book a week using prefabricated sex scenes where all they changed was the hair and eye color. "This one's about gay brothers. I'm calling it *Twincest.* Nice, no?"

Then they were at the top of the trail and he was getting out in the rain, flapping into the hooded jacket. He thanked her and slammed the door and started up the spillway that was the winter path. He hadn't taken many steps when she tapped the horn. He turned and peered. She rolled down the window on the passenger side. He jogged back down to her. She poked a square of paper at him. Something was scrawled on it but it was too dark for him to read it. He tilted his head.

"You might want to look at that place, if you're thinking about shacking up with him." She gave him a brisk career-lady smile, rolled up the window, and drove off.

What was on the paper was an address. In the Valley. The next day was Saturday. Dell didn't need the car. He drove out there under a high blue sky that the rain had cleaned and polished. The district was one of old eucalyptus trees in shaggy, hulking clumps on corners, small, neat 1940s stucco houses with lawns and ivy geranium and chest-high chain-link fences. No sidewalks. Tin country mailboxes. The number Carmen had given him was on one of these. With the name MATTOX. In the yard, two little girls in jeans played with a shepherd pup that was awkward and soft. The girls were reedy. Coffee-color little girls, *café au lait.* He parked the car, got out, stood at the gate.

"Is your daddy home?" he called.

The girls paused, faced him, bright-eyed. They shook their heads. They wore stiff braids tied with red yarn. The pup worried their ankles. They pushed him off without turning their gaze from Whit.

"Your mommy, then?" he asked.

They nodded. The pup attacked again.

"Will your dog bite me?"

They grinned and shook their heads. Then, overcome by shyness, they ran around the house out of sight, giggling. Whit opened the gate and went up the walk. He thumbed a bell push. A youngish woman came to the door, drying her hands on paper towels. Her hair was fair, her eyes very blue, she was fine-boned. Whom did she remind him of? He couldn't think. "Burr Mattox?" he said.

64

"He isn't here." Nervous, she snapped a lock on the screen door. "I'm his wife. What is it?"

"Do you expect him?"

"Any minute." She stepped back, taking hold of the house door, ready to close it. "He's at work. He's a free-lance commercial artist."

"His studio's on Melrose," Whit said, "upstairs, at the back—right?"

That eased her wariness. She nodded, gave a little smile. "That's it." She wiped a damp strand of pale hair off her forehead and blew out breath. "Hot, isn't it? Look, shall I phone him for you? Tell him you're coming?"

"That's all right, thanks." He turned away, turned back. "Was your maiden name Weiss?"

"Yes," she said, surprised.

"You look like your father," he said.

Genes

Sandy has chosen a table halfway back. Out of the sun heat through the plate-glass window, out of the heat from the kitchen. Babushka has been talking to him. Wrapped in a cook's apron too long for her, she waddles away but at the kitchen door she glances back and sees Whit and returns to give him a hug. She is about chest high. The apron is smeared with blood and gravy. Good smells drift out of the kitchen. Whit kisses her thinning gray hair. Laughs at some joke he can't quite make out and, when she goes away, sits down on a red bentwood chair across from Sandy, who has fetched a corkscrew to the table. Whit sets the sack on the gingham cloth and Sandy takes the bottle out of it and starts opening it while Whit makes a stack of the cigarette packs at the table corner and neatly folds the sack and sits on it. Sandy sets the wine glasses right side up and pours from the bottle. The bottle is long, narrow, and green. The wine that comes out of it is almost as pale as water. The label says Wente Brothers. It is a little bit expensive.

"You have a nice sense of occasion," Sandy says.

Whit isn't sure what this means exactly. Is there a wanness to Sandy's smile as he lifts his glass? Whit touches the glass with

66

his own, says mechanically, "Cheers," and tastes the wine. "What's the occasion?"

"Your new book," Sandy says. "What else?"

"I don't know what else," Whit says, "but you do. When are you going to tell me?"

"It can wait," Sandy says. "How's Dell?"

Sandy and Dell were friends before Whit met either of them. Sandy's bookshop then had been in Cordova, the foothill town where Whit grew up, and where Dell taught at the junior college—no classes Whit took. Dell met Sandy in his shop. Whit met Sandy in a tavern that staggered along the beachfront at Laguna, room after bare-board room of faggots, the slim and young jostling the bald and potbellied, sand from tiny swim trunks brushing off on business suits. It was the summer of 1956. Chang had driven Whit down in the Dragon Restaurant's panel truck. In the bar, bulky Chang collided with Sandy in the press of bodies, and Sandy stuck out his hand to Whit. There was polite chat about Chang's last play—he directed at the Cordova Stage. But when Sandy drifted off with an aging youth brown and stringy as a buried pharaoh, Chang glared after him. He steered Whit roughly to a wet table by spotty plate glass facing the surf. Ordinarily a laughing Buddha, he scowled now like a demon in a bad temple painting of hell. He hissed, "You stay away from that one. He'll have you in bed in five minutes flat."

Chang had talent, but not for prediction. It would be years before Sandy had Whit in bed. They didn't meet again until the fall of 1957, when Sandy was part of a citizens' committee trying to get Dell her job back, after she'd been fired for telling a reporter that the Cordova schools were as tightly segregated as the schools in Little Rock, Arkansas—where the president had lately sent in troops so that black children could learn to read, write, and figure, alongside white children. And soon after that, Whit and Dell were married.

Dell not only didn't get her job back, but no other school district would hire her. The big New York publisher that had optioned Whit's first novel dropped it. The Millers were broke.

Sandy used to come around for drinks, bringing the bottles himself. He took them to Babushka's for meals. And when he moved his shop to West L.A., he not only published a book of Whit's poems, but he took Dell on part time to sweep out, answer the phone, type the bills, and feed the shop cat—a haughty Persian whose picture appeared in ads for a pet food she despised. Then Whit got the job at Rainbow Labs. But years later he too worked for Sandy on and off, to pad out the meager advances Brackett House paid its writers.

Sometimes Sandy would ring up with a spare ticket for an opera or ballet—at the Greek Theatre, the Philharmonic, Hollywood Bowl. Dell never went. She liked theaters the way she liked parties—even less, because she was convinced that to concerts she couldn't wear jeans. But Whit went every time. He knew the extra ticket had been bought for some youth Sandy hoped to sleep with, who had yawed off unexpectedly. It didn't matter. It was a chance to sit among plush and gilt shadows and drown in music. Or words. He never forgot anything that happened in a theater. He was a true faggot.

He was still licking his wounds in a corner after the Burr affair when Sandy wheeled him off to a non-plush-and-gilt little theater on La Cienega to see a Strindberg play. An old actor with a middle-European accent ripped up the first act so badly that they left as soon as the dingy house lights flickered on. They were sitting in a weedy parking lot where the headlights shone on blown trash piled against a chain-link fence, waiting for the corroded valves of Sandy's VW to chime in harmony, when Sandy laid a hand in Whit's lap and gently squeezed.

"I'm dreaming," Whit said. "Why now?"

"Why not now?" Sandy said with a smile.

"It wouldn't work," Whit said. "Two negatively charged particles. Ask Edward Teller."

"I will," Sandy said, "if we ever meet."

"I believe it," Whit said. He remembered a wry comment by an old friend of Sandy's at some party. The discussion had been with a young painter whom Sandy had asked for a picture. *Give it to him,* the old friend had said. *More people*

68

will see it hanging over Sandy Fine's bed than in any gallery.
Sandy hasn't slept with more men than he can remember but
that's only because he has a remarkable memory. When Chang
told Whit this at age eighteen, it revolted him. If Sandy had
made a pass at him then, he'd have thrown up. Older, he'd
grown easier—on everyone but himself. "Okay," he said.
"What the hell." At least with Sandy he'd know where he was.
There wouldn't be any surprises.

Now Sandy touches his hand on the checkered tablecloth at
Babushka's and smiles. "Don't write when you're with me—
okay? I asked you: How's Dell?"

"She's marching at Century Plaza later today. To let LBJ
know how she feels about the war."

"Of course," Sandy says. "How goes the teaching?"

"She bitches about the place all the time." Whit strips
cellophane from one of the newly bought packs of cigarettes.
"But she loves it."

"I've seen the student body standing outside when I drive
past," Sandy says, "in their fashionable rags, smoking what is
obviously not tobacco. They don't look scholarly."

The place is called the Twaingate School. It has nothing to
do with any school district. The baggy-eyed, stoop-shouldered
man who owns and runs it was kicked out of a principal's job in
Oregon or someplace for refusing to remove *Catcher in the Rye*
from the high school library as obscene. It followed that he
would hire Dell. They fight a lot because he takes in kids no
other private school will have and, wanting the money their
rich parents pay, doesn't ask them to do any work or even to
behave. Still, Dell manages to straighten a few of them out and
even teach them a little bit.

"They don't have to be." Whit lights a cigarette. "They're
kids. She doesn't like kids as much as she likes horses. But she
doesn't like anything as much as she likes horses. I could never
give her horses."

Sandy sips his wine and blinks his fox-brown eyes at Whit.
"Why didn't you give her kids?"

"Jesus," Whit says.

Sandy turns red under his freckles. "I'm sorry. I haven't any right to ask you questions like that. But you were so young, so much in love. It happened to me. I've got a son twenty years old."

Whit stares. That he looks like the tough kid on the block doesn't stop Sandy acting and sounding feminine. The most sheltered housewife in Ames, Iowa, would spot him for queer in a minute. He gets whistled at on the street. Once a bartender refused him a drink. Kenny was with them that time. He swung a fist at the man. Whit had to drag them both out of the place. To picture Sandy surrounded by dark men in hats and sidelocks under one of those flowered canopies they have for Jewish weddings, even crushing the ceremonial wineglass under foot, was just barely possible—but lifting the veil off the wide-eyed face of some teenage bride and kissing her, then crawling between the sheets with her and making a baby—? Whit says, "You never told me."

Sandy takes out his wallet and opens it to a photo and lays it on the table. The photo is of a redheaded, skinny boy of maybe seventeen, in a football jersey that hangs off enormous shoulder pads. He is squinting in sunlight, but he looks like Sandy, all right. Back of him, a practice scrimmage is taking place on a patchy green field surrounded by trees in red and yellow autumn foliage. New Jersey? That's where Sandy comes from. "He broke a leg that winter," Sandy says, "but it didn't discourage him. He's now third-string quarterback at Cornell. If he can gain twenty pounds, he thinks they may let him play."

Whit pushes the wallet back at Sandy. "What's his name?"

"Sanders Katzman." Sandy closes the wallet and puts it away. "Sanders for me, Katzman for the only father he ever really knew."

Babushka calls something from the kitchen. Whit taps his cigarette on the edge of the ashtray and drinks some more wine. "Was he on purpose?" he says. "Was the marriage on purpose? Was it supposed to go on till death did you part?"

"Who knows?" Sandy shrugs. "Why not?"

"Because that's not how you are," Whit says.

70

Babushka comes from the kitchen, still in the bloody apron, and holding loaded plates in hands covered by padded mittens, scorched and stained. She sets the plates in front of them. Chicken Kiev. Sandy must have ordered it while Whit fetched the wine. He puts out his cigarette. Babushka picks up the bottle and refills their glasses, talking all the while, but at the edge of audibility, like a radio in a far room. She laughs softly and goes back to the kitchen.

"We change," Sandy says. "You're not the same as when you married Dell. And that was only ten years ago. Do you think you're the same?"

Whit picks up his fork. The food smells good. It always does at Babushka's. "I hope not," he says. He lays down the fork. He doesn't feel like eating. He is back in the place where he lived with Dell first, upstairs in a hulking, shingle-sided house on a Hollywood back street. The walls were shingled inside too, and there were windows all around, the kind that swung out on paint-clogged hinges. Big old trees crowded the house. In summer they reached into the rooms. But the time he is remembering was gray, cold, and rainy. Winter. It was morning, they were at the kitchen table.

"Do you want to have a baby?" Dell said. She was in a faded red corduroy bathrobe his parents had given him for Christmas years before. It made her look frail. They nursed mugs of coffee while the rain blew against the window glass.

"No," he said. All the money they had was the pitiful shreds of the advance on his book that was far from finished, and Dell's unemployment checks. The publishers weren't happy about the chapters he was sending them. The unemployment payments would soon run out. "We can't even feed ourselves."

"I wouldn't have to go to a hospital," Dell said. "I could have it at home. I could breast-feed it." She wasn't arguing. She wasn't urgent. She was pointing out practicalities to him. He didn't answer. She tilted her head. "It's something else, isn't it?"

"Genes," he said.

"You are beautiful and bright," she said.

71

"But I am not as other men," he said. "I don't mind for myself. I wouldn't do it to anybody else."

The next thing he remembers about it is the woman downstairs calling him from where he sat shivering in sweaters at the typewriter by the rumpled bed to come to the phone. She stood plump in hair curlers under an umbrella at the foot of the wooden outside staircase, whooping up to him. He ran down. A man spoke through the receiver—Atkins from Cordova, the only doctor Dell trusted. Whit had colds a lot in those years. He had met Atkins, a jug-eared, raffish old goat with cropped white hair and a very red face and very blue eyes.

"What's the matter?" he cackled. "Didn't she get her mouth over it right?"

"I don't understand you," Whit said.

"I need your permission," Atkins said, "to terminate your wife's pregnancy."

"Jesus." Whit felt hollow. "She never told me."

"It's early," Atkins said. "There's no danger."

Dell took the phone. "It's all right," she said.

They both sounded cheerful. He didn't feel cheerful about it, but it was her body. It would be her pain, now or when the baby was born. And he was afraid something would be wrong with the baby because it was his. He said okay. So the only picture in his wallet is of Kenny. He used to have one of Burr too but he tore that one up and flushed it down the toilet of a service station in the Valley not far from the house where Burr's little girls played with their puppy in the yard. He had leaned his head against the plate-steel wall of the service-station men's room and cried. He hadn't cried about the baby. Now he says to Sandy:

"I sure as hell hope not."

"That's your supposed favorite." Sandy nods at Whit's plate. "Aren't you going to eat it?"

Whit numbly picks up the fork, numbly pokes food into his mouth, numbly chews. He washes it down with wine. "All I wanted was sex," he says. "You were the one who wanted lunch."

72

"Not really." Sandy pushes his own food around, looks into Whit's eyes a woebegone moment, looks down again. "I wanted to see you, to tell you something."

Whit watches the top of his red head. "Will I like it?"

"No." Sandy fills his mouth again. Chewing, he looks past Whit at the sunlit window, the cars passing on Sunset Boulevard. He swallows. He takes a deep breath. "No sex," he says. "Not anymore."

Whit gapes at him. Then he laughs. It sounds more like a bark. "So this is what they mean by the heartbreak of psoriasis."

Sandy's smile is sad. "Laugh," he says. "It's not what I want. It's what Tom wants."

"Tom?" Whit keeps smiling. "The butch-sounding one on the telephone?"

"He believes in monogamy," Sandy says. "Anyway, I'm getting old. I can't go on chasing and chasing."

"Not if you break both legs." Whit pushes his fork into the food on his plate and slaps down his napkin on the table. "You're sick in the head."

"You won't think so when you meet Tom," Sandy says. "Don't make that face. I'm serious, I tell you. This is it. In your words—till death do us part."

"Just like that?" Whit snaps his fingers. He laughs disbelief. "You're going to change, just like that? How old did you tell me you were the first time you got it on with some jock? Nine?"

"I'd sneaked into the high school locker room," Sandy says. "That's got nothing to do with this."

"It adds up to thirty years of sucking anonymous cock, no two alike. Sandy, that's not a habit you can break, like smoking. It's a habit nobody can break, like eating." He stands up, chair legs scraping the floor. "So, what comes next—'We can still be friends'?"

"That's what we always were."

"Yeah, well, sex has a way of lousing that up, you know?" He picks up the cigarette packs and sets them down. "I feel

73

sorry for poor, dumb Tom. You'll never stick with him. You don't know how."

"I've stuck with you."

"Shit. I was just another name on your list. And not that close to the top, either. I meant as much to you as a jack-off in the shower."

Babushka calls musically from the kitchen: "Chocolate mousse!"

"I have to go," Whit calls back. He lays bills on the tablecloth. "Okay," he tells Sandy. "Live out your little fantasy." He picks up the cigarettes again. He is surprised that he is so hurt and angry. He is ashamed of himself. But he can't stop. He says, "I give it six weeks. Only don't call me up afterward, okay?"

"Don't act like this," Sandy says. "Why shouldn't I have somebody permanent? You've got Dell."

"Sandy," Whit says, "you and me—it was your idea, remember? How the hell much time did it take? An hour now and then, right?"

"I'll never forget them," Sandy says.

"Dear God," Whit says, and walks out.

Bath

Sawhorses striped yellow and black blockade Berry Street. At the far end, workmen are hacking limbs off peppertrees with chain saws on long poles. The limbs splinter and crack, and the workmen back off with shouts, and the limbs come down. They bounce cushiony on their feathery leafage. The workmen are black and Mexican and wear yellow city coveralls and yellow tin helmets. Gloves protect their hands. They lift and pitch the limbs into trucks striped yellow and black. Heavier saws are sectioning the crooked trunks of trees already maimed. Vacant one-story frame houses stare through broken windows. Whit is unsettled. This is his past, and it isn't supposed to change.

He ducks under the barrier and walks up the street. The stingy lawns in front of the houses have turned brown. On one, a tricycle rusts. Surveyors' stakes, driven into the lawns, have rags fluttering off them, red bows, as if something were being celebrated. The sidewalks have been broken into tumbled chunks of cement. When they were whole, he went up and down them on a scooter made of an apple box, a board, and a roller skate. A straight scar lies where a cement strip led to the front porch. The steps are gone. He crawls up on the porch. The front door is gone. A board has been nailed across the opening. He climbs inside.

The room looks bigger without furniture. Weather has been visiting. The wallpaper is peeling. Beside the kitchen door, a strip has come down and lies like rotten ribbon candy on the floor. The paper that shows at that place is the daisies-in-a-basket pattern he helped his mother paste up on a sweaty Saturday when he was fourteen, fifteen. The sink has been ripped out of the kitchen. The cupboards have been taken away. Nails stick crooked out of the walls. A black, greasy, square outline shows where the stove stood. He did his first cooking on that stove—heating mushy canned spaghetti for his lunch when his mother wasn't home. Where he stands now, the table used to stand where he stuffed down Grape-Nuts, in a hurry to escape to school or better places.

He steps into the room where he slept. Damp trash lies in the corner where his bed was. There are books without covers. They can't have belonged to him, but he picks one up. It feels at the same time gritty and wet. Even the title page is gone. He reads a phrase, *a smile in his lifetime*. Something crawls on his hands. He drops the book. Sowbugs have nested in its moist back. He shakes his hands, wipes the crawly feeling off them. He nudges the book with the toe of his clean blue-and-white shoe. So much for the immortality of print.

He walks over stained magazines strewn on the back porch and goes out the back screen. The garage tilts more than it used to. The shed built against it, where he and Donnie Wright jacked off together for the first time, has half fallen down. He pries open one of the crooked garage doors, wanting to see the 1948 two-door Plymouth he learned to drive in. But there are only oil stains and his bicycle hanging off spikes in the wall studs. The tires droop from rust-speckled rims. The back screen door of the house makes the twanging sound it always made. He turns, expecting his mother to ask him to put oil on the push lawn mower in the shed and cut the grass. But for five years his mother has been living with her sister in Hemet. It isn't his father, either, announcing some ridiculous dish for supper—*suprême de volaille à la milanaise*—when it will never

76

be anything but meat loaf. His father is through joking. It is a man in a tin hat.

"Have to ask you to leave," he says.

"I used to live here," Whit says.

"These places are dangerous. You could fall through a floor and break your leg and sue the city."

"What's happening to the street?" Whit asks.

"New freeway dumps too much traffic onto Lemon Grove and Mountain. So we're running Berry through and widening it. Now, do you want to clear out, please?"

"I used to live here," Whit says again, but he goes.

Donnie Wright's is two blocks down. The street looks the same, the abandoned school yard across the way where they flew kites. The house looks shabbier. A fat young woman with pale hair in blue plastic curlers comes to the door. In the rear of the house, children scream shrilly. The young woman wears denims. One of the tails of her faded, flowered blouse is not tucked in. The blouse has carroty stains. Her face is bare of makeup and eyebrows, giving her a medieval North European look. A small child in saggy diapers comes shrieking from nowhere and clutches her knees. She pays it no attention.

"I'm busy," she tells Whit. "What do you want?"

"I'm looking for Donnie Wright," Whit says.

" 'Donnie'?" she says mockingly. "That's cute."

Whit feels his face turn red. "Donald," he says. "I suppose he's at his shop, only I don't know what he calls it. I just want to know where to find him. We were friends when we were kids."

The child shrieks. She slaps it absentmindedly and says, "Kevin, shut up." She tells Whit, "He's not at his shop. He should be, but his mother claims she's sick, and I've got four kids to look after, and if he wants to believe his mother is sick, then he stays home and looks after her, because that's one too many for me." She pushes open the screen door. Angrily. It almost hits him. "Come in," she says, but he doesn't know that

77

he wants to. "Well, are you coming in or not?" she demands. "Make up your mind."

He steps inside and she lets the door go so it bangs his heel. There is a smell of unwashed diapers. Children's clothes are strewn around. The furniture started out cheap and has been jumped on a lot. The white plastic is off some of Donnie's piano keys. Whit's foot kicks a metal something and it clatters off across flooring without rugs. A boy of about six, in a grubby Dodger T-shirt that hangs to his knees, runs in and picks up the toy. He glares at Whit. He doesn't look like Donnie. He says, "Watch what you're doing, man," and backs out, glowering. The fat young woman picks up the baby and it stops shrieking. She carries it away toward the back. She waves an arm. "They're in there," she says.

It's the front bedroom. The door is a little way open. He raps it with his knuckles. A woman's voice that has been droning steadily stops. A man's voice says, "Damn it, you kids." There is the feel under Whit's feet of floorboards thumped. Donnie Wright pulls the door open, frowning. He blinks puzzlement. He starts to smile, then isn't sure he ought to, then smiles. "For Christ's sake!" he says. "Is it really you?" He laughs. His gaze travels up and down Whit. He takes Whit's hands and draws him into the room, saying over his shoulder, "Peggy—can you believe who this is?"

The woman propped on pillows in the spooled maple bed takes off half-moon reading glasses, lays down a crossword-puzzle book, squints at Whit, and gasps. She smiles with false teeth that look too big for her mouth. "Whit Miller!" She holds out shrunken arms. He bends and puts a kiss on her cheek, which is webbed with fine wrinkles. They are both laughing. She lets him out of her hug. Tears are on her face. She dabs at them with Kleenex from a box on the bed. "Who'd a thunk it?" Her smile turns mournful. "But look at you! All that beautiful blond hair. What in the world happened?"

"Heredity," Whit says. "My dad was bald at twenty."

"Sit down," she says eagerly, "sit down, sit down." She was a tough little woman, self-sufficient, bossy, harsh, when

78

he knew her. Now she is frail and her eyes look defeated. The room is crowded with spooled maple furniture. She has brought much of what used to be in the living room in here. To protect it from the kids? There is plenty to sit down on, but he doesn't sit. He studies Donnie. Donnie is the one who looks as if he needs to sit down. Inside the blue work shirt, the blue work pants, he looks ganted. The shirt has JIFFY TV REPAIR stitched in red over a pocket. The hands that hang out of the shirtsleeves look too big and strong for the rest of the man. The face is still an angel's, but pain has been working on it for quite a while.

"Something wrong?" Donnie says.

"Not a thing," Whit says. "It's good to see you."

"You haven't changed," Donnie says. Mournfully. Kids run under the window, screaming. He says, "Sit down."

Whit sits down and they talk about how things used to be. They don't ask him about his life now. They are self-absorbed. Then they have run out of anecdotes. Peggy Wright begins glancing at the blank television set in the corner. Donnie keeps trying to pump the conversation up again, but it goes flat each time. Whit looks at his watch, and stands.

"I have to catch a Greyhound," he says.

Donnie jumps up. "No, no. You just got here."

"Peggy's getting tired," Whit says.

"I don't know where the old pep went," she says.

Donnie asks her, "Do you want to take a nap? Will you be all right? I'll take Whit and show him the shop."

Peggy turns her face to the window. "I won't bother Lou Ann, don't worry." Her tone is sour. "Least of all." She turns back and stretches out a rope-veined hand. "Good-bye, Whit. Cheer up, kid. I'm not dying. I just need longer and longer rests between rounds." Her smile twists and it doesn't last. She eyes her son. "If it wasn't for Donnie—" But she doesn't complete the sentence. Possibly she figures that Whit knows what she means. And she is right.

On the high, hard seat of the shaky VW van that is blue like Donnie's outfit and has the same red lettering, Donnie says,

"The doctor can't find anything the matter with her. But it's Lou Ann and the kids. She hates them and naturally they hate her, and all she wants is to get away by herself, only I can't afford it, and she won't get Social Security for another seven years."

"She looks older," Whit says. He would bet she doesn't want to get away by herself. She wants to take Donnie with her. That will be the only way she will ever go, alive. "The little boy in the baseball shirt—is he yours?"

"The top two are Lou Ann's," Donnie says. "The other two are mine—the ones that haven't learned where to shit yet. I wonder if they ever will."

"What made you get married?" Whit says.

"You know Peggy," Donnie says. "All the time after me to be a man. Music? Not on your life. Baseball, baby. Little theater? 'What kind of girlie are you, anyway?' You've heard her. Remember how she packed me off to that gym? The barbells she bought me? I kept putting it off, but nothing would do but I had to get married and make babies. Then Lou Ann came to type and keep books for me, and I felt sorry for her with two little kids to raise all alone. She already had the kids, okay? That took care of the repulsive part, didn't it? Sure, she wanted to get married. Only she wasn't about to sleep alone. She found my boy magazines—you know? I was going to sleep with her or she'd tell Peggy I was queer. So I did my husbandly duty. I nearly puked, but you can get used to anything. After a while it wasn't too bad. She wasn't fat then. She even had time to take a bath once in a while. So Peggy got her wish." Donnie laughs dolefully.

They pass the Dragon Restaurant. Whit looks at the old rose-brick front with the glass twists of dull daytime neon tubing across it. CLOSED hangs red on cardboard in the door. He peers at the upstairs windows. No sign of Chang Lee or the Dragon Lady. The van shimmies on out Mountain Boulevard and turns off at a side street. In a brown, one-story brick building, with a beauty shop on one side and a Jewish bakery on the other, is JIFFY TV REPAIR. Inside, it smells of solder and

80

short circuits. TV sets gather dust on shelves. A scarred desk is heaped with catalogues and bills. The telephone is dusty. The calendar above the desk is two months out of date. Donnie goes out through a doorway in a plywood partition.

"Come back here," he says. And when Whit does, Donnie clutches him hard in his arms and kisses him hard. Whit is surprised and his hands hang at his sides for a minute. Then he raises them and strokes Donnie's back. Donnie breaks off the kiss. "Ah, Christ," he says. Then he is crying. For a few seconds, he stands facing Whit with his face twisted and tears streaming down it. Then he drops onto a green metal stool at a workbench crowded with dismantled TV sets. He leans forward, face in his hands, and sobs.

"Hey." Whit touches him. "Don't do that."

Donnie says words, but Whit can't understand them. They come out muffled and wet. Donnie pushes himself up straight and draws a long, shuddering breath. "Sorry." He half turns away to paw around among tangles of colored wire on the bench, screwdrivers, pliers, soldering irons. There is a box of blue papers, the kind used to clean windshields in filling stations. He mops his face with one of these, and blows his nose. The shop door opens and closes. "Shit," Donnie says softly, and gets off the stool, and goes out to the counter that has gouges in its black rubberized surface. An old man in dark glasses sets an old portable on the counter.

"It gets flashes like lightning," he says.

Donnie writes out receipts and tags, sniffling, wiping his nose on his sleeve. The old man goes away. Donnie says to Whit, "This is no good. Come on."

When they get out of the van again, it is at the shabby west end of Mountain where winos sleep in doorways. They park behind another old brick building. Whit hasn't remembered there was so much brick in Cordova. They walk a few steps down a gritty sidewalk, and Donnie opens a door with BATHS gold-leafed on it in an arc. Behind this, climbs a stairway that, as soon as they're halfway up it, begins to fill with steam. Whit thinks of that rainy day with Kenny. The room at the top has glaring white walls. A muscular, fortyish man in tight white T-shirt and tight white pants takes money from Donnie and hands Donnie and Whit keys and towels. Steam drifts in the hallway. Men pass with towels around their middles. None of them is young. Whit feels old and lost. He and Donnie undress in a clean locker room. In the shower, Donnie takes Whit in his arms for a second. His cock is half hard. He lets Whit go. No one has said anything. Whit can't think of anything to say. He came for Donnie, but not this Donnie. This Donnie is like the house on Berry Street. He thinks he should put his clothes back on and leave now.

Instead, he knots the towel at his side and follows Donnie. The hallways have many doors. Most stand open. He walks along glancing inside, at men lying on their backs, on their faces, some covered, some not. When he looks at their faces, their eyes stare back at him. They have no expressions, on their faces, in their eyes. He finds an empty cubicle, turns to look for Donnie, and the hallway is empty. Whit goes into the cubicle. The cot is covered by a coarse white sheet pulled very tight over a thin mattress. Folded at the foot of the cot is a second sheet in case he wants to cover himself. There is a small, hard pillow.

He leaves the door open and lies down to wait for Donnie. He has the towel around him. Other men pass and look inside, and he turns his eyes away. He would like to smoke, but he has no cigarettes. He realizes he left all three packs on the bus. He hasn't even thought about smoking until now. What time is it? He gets up and looks along the foggy hall. But there is no clock. There's no window, either, to show him how much daylight is left. A gray-haired man with a young, hard body comes down the hall. He has a stunted leg that tilts him with every step. He smiles at Whit. Whit turns back inside the cubicle, wondering where in hell Donnie has disappeared to, and Donnie is standing there naked. He draws Whit farther inside, out of the way, closes the door, and bolts it.

When he lets Whit out of the van at the Greyhound depot, he says, "It was just like it used to be, wasn't it?"

Whit closes the tinny door. Through the open window, he lies, with a smile. "It was good. I'm glad I came."

"But you won't come back," Donnie says bleakly.

"You'll be all right," Whit says. "They know you there. You go there all the time, don't you?"

"Everybody's a stranger," Donnie says. "I get so lonesome I could die."

A bus swings in at the station driveway. Its framework creaks. Sunset light flares off its windshield. Its engine roars and gives off fumes. Passengers stare down at them.

"Say good-bye to Peggy," Whit says, and turns away.

Telegram

He shivers. He ought to have brought a jacket. It is dark, and he is climbing the last yards of the trail, which is badly lighted, the single high streetlamp at the top screened off by eucalyptus branches. More likely, Lou Ann is the lonesome one. Kids aren't company. And Donnie sure as hell isn't company. Except to Peggy. He never was. What had they been to each other, he and Whit—warm and indifferently washed adolescent bodies easy of access, stiff in their pants for each other, hurried pumping fists behind bedroom doors, in that shed gripped by pink roses where bees buzzed, in empty school washrooms late afternoons, in Donnie's narrow bed when Peggy was off someplace one weekend when they learned to do it with their mouths, between slugs of cheap wine that made them sick afterward, cheap cigarettes that made them cough? What had they ever talked about? Sex—of which they knew next to nothing. What in God's name had he expected today? He shakes his head and sadly laughs.

And somebody steps out of the dark. He stops, afraid. It is old Major Boulanger in safari shorts and a cork helmet. His voice is like the showier pipes of an organ. The accent is Britannic. "Is that you, Whit?" He raises a big, gnarly hand and comes on, waving an oblong of paper that is pale in the leaf-filtered light. "Message for you. Telegram. From New York, I think. Arrived about five-thirty." He puts the crackly envelope into Whit's hand that is starting to shake. Under the major's dauntless nose and wire-brush mustache, the grin is amiably wolfish. "Good news, I trust?"

Whit squints up at the dim light. "Dell not home?"

"She wasn't. I still haven't heard her car. Phil Farmer's, but not yours. Peace march today, wasn't there?"

"Right." Whit tears open the envelope. The fold of paper inside is caught. He tugs at it. It comes loose minus a corner. He peers at the words, can't make them out.

Boulanger says, "I was watering the plants. Saw the top of the fellow's head, heard him jingle the bells at your door, heard him knock. He called out for you. Plainly, you weren't at home. I simply stepped down the path and pretended to be you. Thought you wouldn't mind. Know how anxious you've been for news."

"Understatement," Whit says. He climbs to a ragged patch of light up the trail. He stops and holds the telegram close to his eyes. It's from Elmer Post, his agent. He reads the words. TRY TO PHONE YOU NO ANSWER. Should be TRIED. He reads the rest. His knees almost give. "Jesus!" he whispers. He turns to Boulanger and shouts, "They've taken it!" He throws his arms around Boulanger. "Twenty-five thousand bucks!" He lets Boulanger go and leaps high in the middle of the shadowy trail. He pokes his fists at the sky and shouts. Not words, just noise. He is laughing and crying. He hugs the major again, wishing it were Dell. Chuckling, the old man awkwardly hugs him back. He breaks free, slaps Whit between the shoulder blades hard enough to knock the wind out, takes his arm, and steers him toward the steep, dark slope.

"My boy, this calls for a drink."

They stumble up steps cut into the earth and propped by planks. Branches slap their faces. They hold up hands to fend them off. The major long ago strung light bulbs on poles to make this climb easy at night. Whit doesn't need to ask why they aren't shining now. The squirrels will have chewed through the wire again—the latest, squirrel-proof wire. Or they'll have stolen not merely the one bulb of this morning, but all the bulbs. "Bugger all," the major mutters. "Furry little vandals." Inside the Boulanger house, which stands propped on tall redwood posts footed in the hillside, Helen Boulanger hugs Whit at the news, and kisses him on the cheek. She was a beauty of the silent screen. Now she is a beauty of seventy.

"I knew you could do it!" she cheers, and pours Scotch.

Boulanger squats and starts a blaze in his hand-built stone fireplace that possums keep undermining. Possums also die under there, and the stink can be eye-watering. The major has some good stories about possums, living and defunct, but he doesn't tell them now. He and Helen sit in the cozy lamplight admiring Whit. Films have been their lives. They don't act anymore. They are dress extras. The closet that holds their wardrobe takes up a lot of room in the little house. They talk about Warner's buying his book, Universal, Metro. "Oh, they will, my boy. Bound to." "A hundred thousand dollars—don't you think, Frank?" "Happens all the time, my boy. Why shouldn't it happen to you? Look at the money the publishers are paying. They know they've got a best-seller, don't they?"

The whisky hits Whit hard. His stomach is empty. He ought to have eaten Babushka's chicken. Or at least a hamburger in Cordova. He is drunk as hell. He sits grinning like an idiot in the Boulangers' old chintz-covered wing chair, wagging his head and saying over and over again, "I can't believe it. I just can't believe it." He says, "Do you know how long I've waited for this? All my life."

Helen beams. "All twelve or thirteen years of it? How could you stand it?"

Whit laughs and then stops laughing and puts down his glass. "Wait a minute," he says. He frowns at Boulanger. "Didn't you say you heard Phil Farmer come home?"

Boulanger looks at his watch. "An hour ago."

Whit stands up. The whisky has made his legs weak. "But he was at the demonstration. If he's home, Dell ought to be home." He pats himself frantically. "Where's the telegram? I have to go." He turns around and around again. "What did I do with it?" Boulanger is on the floor, peering under furniture. Whit says, "Did I give it back to you?"

"Look in your pockets." Helen stands up.

"It's not there," Whit says.

She strokes his butt. "Wallet?"

He takes the wallet out and opens it. The telegram is stuffed inside in its ragged envelope. "Got it. Listen, thanks." Boulanger climbs wheezily to his feet. Whit takes their hands for a second, smiling into their beautiful old faces, the eyes soft and moist and pleased with him. "Thanks. We'll run over tomorrow, okay?"

And he is out the door and crashing down the ridge-back path in the dark. She is there. The lights are on. He grabs the smoothness of a young eucalyptus trunk and swings out in a jump that is too high. When he lands, he falls to his knees and scrapes his hands. He scrambles to his feet and bursts in at the door. Phil Farmer stares at him in a bloody shirt. Dell lies on her bed with a bloody bandage on her head. A white plastic aspirin bottle is on the table. A brandy bottle, glasses with brandy in them. She looks pale. Her eyes are closed. He stops dead.

"My God, what happened?"

"The police beat everybody up," Farmer says. "Where the hell have you been? Your wife is hurt. Don't you care?"

"I didn't know she was hurt." Whit stands staring at her blankly. He can't make himself move. "I didn't know."

Years ago, before they got this house, Chang Lee came to listen to Whit read a play he'd written. It was a warm summer night, the windows open, a big moon looking in through the trees. They drank beer and talked about the play, and Chang left late. Whit and Dell went to bed. Less than an hour later, Chang was back, pounding on the door, howling for help. Whit ran for the door, and yanked it open, and there was Chang, covered with blood. Frustrated at having to sit all night looking at Whit and listening to Whit and not being able to touch Whit, Chang had picked up a sailor. And the sailor had waited till

87

Chang's head was in his lap, and then hit him with some sharp metal thing and tried to push him out of the Dragon Restaurant truck and drive off with it. Chang had saved the truck, but it looked to Whit as if he was going to bleed to death. Dell took charge, tried to clean Chang up, discovered the deep cuts hidden by his thick hair, got him down the long stairs and back into the bloody truck, and drove him to the emergency hospital. All Whit was able to do was stand around useless.

He shakes himself now, and goes to Dell, kneels beside her and takes her hand. She jerks it away. She opens her eyes and looks at him. There is no love in the look. She is mad as hell. She wants him to feel guilty and he does.

"I tried to phone you," he says, "from the bus station, when I knew I was going to be late. Nobody was here."

"What about Polk's dinner?" she asks. "You know he eats at five. I trusted you to feed him today."

"He's a cat," Whit says. "He doesn't wear a watch. I'm not worried about him. He's tough. He'll outlive us all. It's you I'm worried about. What did they do to you?"

"Three cops about seven feet tall," Phil Farmer says, "knocked her down and knelt on her. And when she slapped one of them, he beat her on the head with his riot stick."

"It wasn't the slap." She smiles thinly at the rain-stained boards of the ceiling. "I called him a fascist pig."

"He was a fascist pig," Phil Farmer says. The brandy bottle rattles on his glass. It is so quiet, Whit hears him swallow. "They acted like this was Russia. I never saw anything like it. Charging at the people, beating them down, chasing them, dragging them in the street by the hair." He has been sitting on Whit's bed. He stands up. "Wait till tomorrow." He gives a menacing laugh. "Oh, are they going to be sorry, those hysterical bastards." He paces among the stacks of dusty magazines, his shadow traveling around the bookshelves while he lectures. "Those weren't crazies and freaks out there—they were respectable people, educated people, taxpayers. Doctors, lawyers, teachers, professors. And their wives. And their little kids." He leaves out salesmen—of cameras, like himself, of shoes, like Whit's father. But he still says *we.* "We aren't going to stand for it. Blood in the streets? This is the United States of America, for God's sake. That megalomaniac redneck Texas ignoramus!"

"Have you seen a doctor?" Whit says.

"Thanks to Phil. Nothing's broken. A slight concussion is all. What bus station?" Moving carefully, wincing, Dell pushes herself up onto an elbow. Buttons are off her shirt. The knee of her jeans is torn and the jeans are smeared with grease and dirt from the street. "Where were you?" She reaches for the brandy glass and he hands it to her.

"Cordova. I could have picked a better day, right?"

"There's lipstick on your face." She glances at Farmer as she sips the brandy. She doesn't like brandy. She thinks it is a killer drink. Whit looks at the label. It is one of Farmer's Mexican bargain brands. It probably is a killer drink. She sets the glass down and lies back. She says, "That's new and novel."

"Not really." Whit's knees hurt and he gets off them to sit where Farmer was sitting earlier. Farmer has stopped pacing and stands listening. As if he had the right. It isn't mannerly and the oddness of it is disturbing. "It's Helen Boulanger's lipstick. I just came from there."

"You went there before you came home?"

"I didn't think you were here. Frank hadn't heard the car. He met me down on the trail. A telegram came for me today, and he gave it to me, and we had a drink."

She eyes the painting over the bed—of the brave Chinese girl who went off to fight and probably got her head broken too. "How is Chang? I thought you weren't going to see him anymore. I thought you'd decided you'd outgrown him. Or did you have an unaccountable craving for Chinese food? Are you pregnant?"

"I keep trying," Whit answers mechanically. It is an old joke between them. But not one they use in front of others. What has happened? Dell doesn't even like Farmer. All of a sudden, she has no secrets from him? Whit tells her, "No—I went to see Donnie Wright. I stopped off at Berry Street. They're tearing down the house."

"Donnie Wright? Your little mutual-masturbation friend from high school? The one with the pretty curly hair and the pretty curly mouth?"

Whit won't lie about his sex life to anybody but he doesn't ordinarily volunteer information. Farmer has never shown any interest. Dell wouldn't tell him. Would she? Maybe she would. She hasn't forgotten he's here. She glances at him again. He isn't the patio-party friend who's done a neighborly good turn and now itches to be off home. He stands as if they were suddenly no longer two but three.

He says, "It was cars Frank was listening for, and he didn't hear yours because Dell didn't bring it. I took her to the hospital and brought her home. In my car. Yours is still in the parking lot at Century City. I'll drive you back to get it, if you want."

"What made you think of Donnie Wright?" Dell says.

"I'll tell you later," Whit says. And to Farmer, "I don't want to leave her like this."

"That the telegram?" Farmer nods at the crumpled paper in Whit's hand, dirty from where he fell on it when he made his excited jump. "You had a drink. So it's good news, right?"

"I told you." Whit pushes aside books, magazines, the bills he dropped this morning, and smooths out the telegram on the table. "Didn't I tell you?" If he didn't, he doesn't want to. Not Farmer. When he ran down the path, what he pictured was telling Dell, hugging and kissing her and both of them laughing, and him spinning her around, holding her so tight she couldn't breathe, and then turning out the lamps, and the two of them fucking, everyplace, on the beds, on the floor, in the bathroom, at his desk, upstairs, downstairs, on the stairs, in the kitchen, outside in back under the peppertree. Now he doesn't even want to tell Dell. He reaches out and gently touches the bandage on her head. "I'm sorry this happened. I'm sorry I wasn't here."

But she is looking at the telegram. "What's in it?"

"We ought to get the car," Farmer says. "They'll impound it, and they'll make you pay to get it out."

"Charles will do it," Dell says. "He can take a student with him. Drive the keys down to him, will you, Phil? They're in my bag, there." It is a straw bag with blood on it.

"A student from Twaingate School," Whit says, "will drive it to the moon."

"Phone Charles and tell him Phil's bringing the keys," Dell says. And while Whit gets the phone from where he left it this morning, on the floor by the front door, and while he dials and delivers the message, Dell reads the telegram. She looks at him with round eyes. But when he hangs up, it isn't to him she speaks. It is to Farmer. "A publisher has offered twenty-five thousand dollars for his book. The big one. The important one." Is awed how she sounds? She doesn't smile.

"Hey!" Farmer shakes his hand. "What did I say? Didn't I tell you just this morning—?"

Whit doesn't listen to what Farmer told him just this morning. He is watching Dell. She is looking at him in a way she never looked at him before. He doesn't know the name for what is in her eyes. If he could figure out a reason for thinking so, he'd think it was disappointment.

"You're going to be all right now," she says.

SECOND PART:
Jaime

To the central brain the individual neuron signals either *yes* or *no*—that's all. But, as we know from computers which employ binary arithmetic in which the only figures are 0 and 1, these simple elements can be formed into the most complex and marvelous patterns.

—Alan Watts, *The Book*

Beads

Foot traffic here used to be old Jews, but now it is adolescents with long, uncombed hair, vague smiles, and dirty feet in sandals. Canvas backpacks. Guitars. Castoff army fatigues, 1920s flowered chiffon dresses, greasy leather hats, wire-rim glasses, big blue beads on cowhide thongs. Behind these shop windows, kosher poulterers and bakers, tailors in black hats and thick glasses, sidelocked shoemakers and watch repairers used to starve. The six-pointed stars in flaky blue or glit have been scraped off the glass. Now flowers in fluorescent pinks, yellows, greens, grapple with drugged lettering—PEACE LOVE DOPE. Incense smoke drifts from doorways. Joan Baez whinnies from outdoor loudspeakers. Kids lean against storefronts, looking stunned.

A big tape deck is in his arms, so heavy he staggers. He has lost weight and strength. He can't even wipe the sweat out of his eyes, but the kids keep asking him for quarters. A girl in a picture hat sewn with silk roses that came out of somebody's grandmother's trunk tries to hand him a daisy. She smells of sweat and mothballs, and smears his cheek with a kiss as he passes. A thin, pimply boy gets up off the sidewalk and stands in front of him, staring at the tape deck. He is wearing a red 1776 British army coat with raveled gold braid. Pinned to it are slogan buttons. Only one catches Whit's eye. DOWN WITH PANTS. Whose? Can the kid even read?

"Excuse me," he says.

"That's beautiful," the kid says. He steps aside and lets Whit pass. But he caresses the machine. His fingernails are bitten. "Beautiful." It is a dreamer's voice.

Whit lugs the deck into the shop on Santa Monica where he bought it. It is cool. Music threads the air. The carpet is so deep he nearly turns an ankle. Between stacked amplifiers and tuners of brushed steel and glass, a mustached man in neat seersucker asks him for his sales slip, which he has lost. The man looks severe and says the warranty won't hold without it. Whit tells him to fix it anyway. The man poises a pencil. The repair department will phone him with an estimate. He doesn't need that. He doesn't care how much it will cost. He doesn't say so, because his mother taught him better, but it is a fact. He has plenty of money.

A studio has paid him two hundred thousand dollars for the right to film his book. With the publisher, he has split a half million more paid by somebody for the right to rack up paperback copies in supermarkets. A book club has added another fifty thousand. And by telephone from New York, Elmer Post, in his soft, sweet, Texas country-boy voice, keeps telling him there will be more, much more. The book won't even be published until next spring. Whit can't understand, but sometimes he can believe. This is one of the times. He tells the seersucker man what ails the machine, gives his name, address, phone number, and goes out into the heat again.

In a park across the street, trees that belong to other climates and know what time of year it is are dropping their leaves. It has been three months. He stops and shuts his eyes as if he's been punched in the belly. That is how it feels whenever he remembers, and it isn't getting better. As always, his fists clench, and he gives a cry inside himself. It is the same thin cry

96

he gave at his father's open grave. He doesn't want to hear her, but Dell says again, *You're going to be all right now.* And he starts to live again the hours that followed, when he learned what she meant. He takes a deep breath, opens his eyes, and heads back for the car. But he isn't seeing or hearing anything around him. He is back in the shack in the canyon, where he doesn't live anymore.

She looked pale and frail, asleep in the leaf-green morning light of the pine-board room. He kissed her ear and went downstairs in his jockey shorts to fix breakfast. Through the floorboards, he heard her little radio buzzing the news. When he brought her a mug of coffee, the chief of police was saying, "We proved to them that we own this city—not that rabble." "Rabble," Dell said, and snapped off the radio. He set the mug on the table, touched her shoulder, and stacked the pillows off his bed behind her so she could sit straighter. She asked, "Did Polk come?"

"And stuffed his gut. He's sleeping it off on the steps in the sun." She was wearing a faded blue sweatshirt. Between its ragged bottom edge and the skewed sheet, he glimpsed smooth, naked thigh, and started to get a hard-on. "How's your head?"

"The head's not the worst. I feel black and blue all over. Are you going to buy a Cadillac?"

"And a big cigar." He went back downstairs where the butter burned and smoked in the frying pan. He dumped it sizzling into a coffee can on the back of the stove and set the sputtering pan in the sink to cool out. He took his coffee mug to the door and leaned in the doorway smoking the butt of a cigarette from the kitchen wastebasket. A blue jay yelled at him from the peppertree. It winged to one of the big oleanders. It was not Whit he was yelling at. It was Polk, who lifted his little yellow head and half opened his eyes to give the jay a sour look. He turned around on the step and lay down with his back to the jay. The jay flew down and snatched up something in its beak and flew off with it. In the Saturday morning stillness of the canyon, its wings made a starchy sound.

Whit put out the stub of cigarette under the tap. He wiped at the hot frying pan gingerly with a paper towel, set the pan back on the stove, and cut new butter into it. He turned over the bacon slices in the other pan. He dropped slices of bread into the blackened toaster. He beat eggs in a cracked Japanese bowl of Dell's, then finished off his white coffee while the butter melted. This was the greatest morning of his life, and he was doing what he did every other morning. It seemed wrong. He started to sing. " 'I choose Je-sus when I need a friend.' " But he thought it would make Dell's head hurt and he stopped. When he opens his mouth to sing, Jesus always comes jumping out. Why does nature trust people like Margaret and Harry Miller to raise children? It never trusts them with anything else important.

Dell had a red loose-leaf binder open on her knees when he got up the gritty stairs with the breakfast plates. With a very hard, dim pencil, in very small figures, she was working algebra problems. She did this, or Latin grammar, when she wanted to shut the world out. He stood with the plates. She didn't notice. He sang, softly but jauntily, " 'I choose Je-sus, he is the best for me.' Whee!" She looked startled and hurried to close the notebook and get it out of the way. She reached out to take the plate. "Why didn't you tell me breakfast was ready?" It was her way of apologizing. Sometimes it made him mad but not this morning. He had just won the tin whistle. *You're going to be all right now.*

He sat on his unmade bed. "We can pay off the house."

She looked at him with those round, solemn eyes again. She started to answer and didn't. She pushed unhungrily at her eggs, put down the fork, bit her toast instead, a nibble. He raised his eyebrows at her. "I'm sorry," she said. "I can't eat. It must be the concussion." Polk had followed Whit upstairs and was winding his small yellow self around Whit's legs and letting it be known with loud cries that he expected bacon. His tail stuck up straight and vibrated. Whit broke off a small piece of bacon and inserted it into the pink mouth with its needle teeth. He wiped his fingers on his shorts. Dell held her plate out to him and gulped. She looked green. "You'd better take it away. I think I'm going to be sick." He stood up and took the plate, and she whipped out of bed and ran bare-ass into the bathroom.

The house was too small and the board walls too thin for him not to hear her, and he overreacts to vomiting sounds, so he carried the plates out front, Polk trying to trip him up. And here came Phil Farmer, sun glinting on his brush haircut and rimless glasses, climbing the path by the tilting white fence and red geraniums. Polk went to meet him, and he halted, as if Polk were a tiger. Cats make him swell up and sneeze. He stared at Whit in his undershorts, holding the plates of bacon and eggs and toast. He blinked.

"Dell's feeling queasy," Whit explained. He held out the plate he hadn't touched. "Breakfast?"

"Thanks." Farmer took the plate doubtfully. "We ought to talk," he said. Kenny said, *Sit down. We have to talk.* Farmer didn't go on. He and Whit stood and ate in silence. Whit heard the bathroom door. Mouth full, he called:

"Put something on."

Farmer called, "Hey, are you all right?"

She came to the front door, still barefoot, zipping up old jeans. She had taken off the bandage, washed her face, slicked back her hair with water. The sunshine made her blink. *"En plein air en slip?"* she asked Whit.

"Maybe you should see your own doctor," Farmer said.

"It's only nerves." Again her eyes held his a moment too long. "You haven't got any coffee." She looked reproachfully at Whit.

"If you were going to toss," Whit said, "I wanted to be out of earshot. Safe now? False alarm? You want to eat?"

She shook her head. "Coffee, Phil?"

"Should be champagne," Farmer said, "shouldn't it?"

Whit liked him again. "Lend me your car." He took the

empty plate from him. "I'll get some." He carried the plates indoors, set them on a bookshelf, and kicked into pants. "I have to get cigarettes anyway." He pulled on yesterday's T-shirt. It smelled of BATHS. He sat to put on socks and shoes, and Farmer picked up his wallet from the table and stuffed money into it. "Your car's down there. Here are the keys. Get half a dozen. And caviar, black. And crackers, right? I'll alert the Boulangers. Two o'clock at my place, okay?"

A teenage boy is sitting on the roof of Whit's car, playing a guitar and singing. He isn't wearing a shirt, and he is sunburned a painful red. He is rawboned, his hair is so fair it is almost white, and it gleams in the sunlight. The car is a white Mercedes sport coupe. Whit gave eighteen thousand for it on the day the check came from the film people. But the price isn't what matters. The car is new, and he wants it to stay new forever. The boy is wearing shorts made of torn-off Levi's, and Levi's have rivets, and Whit is afraid they will scratch the paint. His heart races, he lifts a hand, and starts to run. "Hey!" he says. The boy sees him, stops singing, slides down off the car. Ragged youngsters who have been loafing on the sidewalk, listening, look Whit's way, then amble into the street, making for the park. They go like cattle, disregarding the moving cars. The singer vanishes into the shop.

Panting, Whit runs his hand over the roof of the car. He doesn't feel any scratches. He bends his knees to bring his eyes to the level of the roof. He can't see any scratches. But he is upset and turns toward the shop. Its sign reads PIPELINE, and in the window stand water pipes looking Turkish. Strings of bright beads hang off wooden racks. Pot-metal amulets, peace symbols, zodiac signs on thin chains. Lopsided jars in runny brown glazes bristle with incense sticks. Glass jewels twinkle on shiny pincers meant to make possible the smoking of marijuana cigarettes down to their last spark. A pudgy, gray-striped cat lies curled up on a fan of thin, paper-covered books. He puts his face to the glass, blinkers his eyes with his hands. The books are poetry collections by unheard-of writers from presses also unheard-of. One of the books is his. He forgets about wanting to scold the guitar player. He walks in at the open shop door.

The small front room has a low ceiling. Ceiling, walls, the planks laid across bricks for bookshelves, are redwood-stained. Ferns in redwood boxes hang from the ceiling, vines that trail leafy tendrils. He has to dodge in order not to bang his head. No one is present. He reaches into the window, scratches the cat's ears, and slips the copy of his book out from under the cat. She makes a small, querulous noise, and curls up tighter. Whit opens the book, warmed by the sun and by the cat. *With good wishes, Whit Miller, May 1960,* is written on the flyleaf. To whom? Plainly someone who no longer cares. Whit is grateful, because a fire in the back room at Sandy's shop burned half the copies, and the bundles Whit had were soaked with cat piss when all of Polk's sisters, cousins, and aunts were alive. In the single copy that Whit has hung onto, the pages have come loose.

Quiet laughter and talk reach him from beyond the partition. A curtain of red and amber glass beads hangs in a doorway. He edges through it. This room is large and white. Orange crates, painted white, are stacked up and filled with books, mostly used paperbacks. Around a low table on which someone has arranged driftwood stand three rickety tin folding chairs. A scratched glass counter displays shelves of handmade silver jewelry, handmade pots, more incense, this time in bright bundles, packets of cigarette papers, more roach clips, bamboo flutes, harmonicas, envelopes of guitar strings. Copies of the *Free Press, Open City,* the *Oracle,* lie along a redwood bench where dried grasses sprout from wine bottles. To his left, wooden stairs climb to a balcony, which explains why the ceiling of the front room is so low. The ceiling back here is two stories high.

Beyond the counter, at a round, old-fashioned oak dining-room table, ragamuffins in feathers, military medals, mangy furs, torn T-shirts, tuxedo jackets, fringed leather vests sit groping beads out of big mayonnaise jars, and sliding the beads onto strings. Some of them aren't ten years old yet, most of

101

them aren't twenty. Among the jars a little adhesive-taped portable radio emits rock music, insect-thin. There is no sign of the guitar player. For a minute, no one notices Whit. Then the bead stringer who looks oldest stands up, surprised. His skin is pale brown. He has a neat mustache. A neat little beard edges his jawline. His brown eyes look as if his feelings bruise easily. Long black lashes fringe the eyes. *Infantile,* Dell says inside Whit's head, *alcoholic.* The dark brown hair would tell her the same, abundant, soft. It needs cutting. A short-sleeve shirt hangs off spare shoulders. The shirt is open, buttons missing. The chest is shallow-muscled. The pants look as if they came from a thrift shop, and don't fit the narrow hips. He is wearing nothing under them, and his cock is noticeable, long and strong. He comes around the table, smiling. His teeth are large, white, and not quite straight. Whit wants to look at him forever.

"Can I help you?" He is eager. Is he twenty-one? His voice is sixteen. "Do you want that?"

"Yes." Whit knows he is staring but he can't stop. Jerkily he holds out the book. "How much is it?"

The hand that takes the book looks hard-worked. Dell says, *Really, Whit—the stableboy?* Her Everett smile is thin, regretful. That was what she said first that night when he'd given in and climbed the stairs to tell her he was going to sleep with Kenny. He's forgotten till now. He's remembered only, *You should be very pretty together.* Which he now knows was only politeness. He winces. The stableboy who isn't Kenny says, "Five dollars?" as if ashamed to ask that much, as if ashamed to ask for money at all. "Do you know him—the poet?"

"I used to." Whit looks into his wallet. There are fifties. He carries a lot of these to remind him that all that hardcover money, film money, paperback money, book-club money, is real. Also for his father, who used to say he never owned a fifty-dollar bill in his life. But this shop won't have change for fifty dollars. Then he discovers a ten, and feels wonderful. He holds it out.

The soft eyes cloud with misgiving but the bill is accepted. "Thank you." He rummages through his pockets. They seem to be empty. He gives a little, soft, chagrined laugh and, back of the counter, opens a cigar box among cardboard flats of bright candy bars and chewing gum. Coins jingle. He winces a smile at Whit, and ambles toward the back of the place, where an old cookstove and refrigerator stand, soiled white, under high, grimy, metal-frame windows. He glances at the bead stringers, who chatter, frowning at their busy fingers. Beads patter down like rain. Chair legs scrape. Children crawl under the table, giggling.

Whit scarcely notices. He is watching the boy with the imponderable ten-dollar bill. He opens the refrigerator. The freezer compartment is a small, hanging, round-cornered aluminum box covered in snow. He keeps himself between it and anybody wanting to spy, but Whit catches a glimpse of his hand removing a wax-papered green-and-white frozen vegetable box. In a minute, the little freezer door crunches shut. The refrigerator door slams. He comes back, picks up the book off the counter where he's left it, and leads Whit into the front room. They dodge the hanging plants, and he counts into Whit's palm five cold dollar bills. He looks into the book a moment, then hands it to Whit.

"I wrecked your hiding place," Whit says. "I'm sorry."

"It isn't stealing to them," he says. "Somebody always gave it to them before—along with braces and swimming pools and their own car." He shrugs. "I'll find another hiding place. It's not your fault."

It's not your fault. The sun dropped behind the ridge. The flower patio under the big oak turned chilly. On the square red tiles, the green bottles stood around dry. The Mexican baskets held only crumbs. Black smears were all that remained of the caviar in the clay bowls. Helen Boulanger, in a muumuu printed with hibiscus blossoms, and Frank, in a yellowed Palm

Beach suit, went off chortling up their dirt steps. Dell had gone home after only a token drink. Whit's head was starting to ache. He pushed up out of the redwood chair with its flower-print plastic cushions.

"Wait, we have to talk," Farmer said. He stacked the baskets, not looking at Whit. "You know, it wasn't only the police that hurt Dell yesterday. It was you, kid."

"I never go to those things," Whit said. "She knows."

"You could have been home," Farmer said.

"I didn't know the cops would go crazy," Whit said. "You didn't know it. Nobody knew it. It wasn't my fault."

"You didn't have to go out of town." Farmer stacked the bowls. They clattered. "For sex, of all things. With some guy. That was childish."

"This conversation is childish," Whit said. "You don't know what you're talking about. Dell and I—"

"Dell and you aren't going to last much longer." Farmer gave up fidgeting. He faced Whit, red sunset light flashing off his glasses. "Not if you don't quit abusing her. Listen, kid—I'm older than you. I went through a marriage and a divorce and I know the signs, and Dell has just about had it with you."

Whit stared at him, trying to laugh. "You are unbelievable, do you know that? I hate shocking you, Phil, but Dell knew I slept with men before we were married."

"She told me. Last night. A lot of things."

"Last night she was in pain and she was scared and you can't take seriously whatever she said last night. Hell, yes, she was upset when I wasn't there. That's not a sign our marriage is going to pieces, Phil. That's a sign she needs me. Like I need her."

"You don't show it, and she doesn't think so." Farmer went around, bending, picking up the champagne bottles. "You were a kid when you married her, right?" He set the bottles on the round, redwood table. "She thought it would pass. She kept waiting for you to outgrow it."

"She never told you that. She knows better. Phil, what do you think homosexuality is—a form of acne?"

"Look, it's not your fault, I know that."

Whit unlocks the Mercedes. The smell of sun-warmed leather comes out. He tosses the book onto the passenger seat and gets in and presses the button that makes the windows roll down. The flat, pale-brown belly is at the curbside window. The knuckly hands hold the window ledge. The brown eyes look in. "It's your book, isn't it?"

"I even did the paste-up," Whit says. "All I didn't do was set the type and pay the printer."

"Those are good magazines you got into—*The New Yorker,* all those? I have poetry nights. Will you come?"

"Those good magazines were a long time ago," Whit says. "And not that often."

"You could help," Brown Eyes says. "Most of the ones who come and read don't know what they're doing." He smiles. "Me either, really." He reaches into the car. "I'm Jaime de Santos. It's on Wednesday nights."

Whit shakes the hand. It is limp. *A taker,* Dell warns him. "If I can," he says.

Spurs

The place is still strange to him, looks as if no one lives in it, and makes him want to cry every time he opens the door. He sets sacks of groceries on the sand-color carpet, pulls the keys out of the door, shuts the door. He has to start eating again. He is wasting away. He picks up the sacks and carries them around the glossy breakfast bar into the kitchen. He crosses the wide living room and starts the stereo. A late Mozart string quartet lilts out of the thousand-dollar speakers, but it doesn't fill the emptiness, not of the place, not of him. A little motor draws back the wall-width curtains. He slides open the glass doors.

"Polk?" he calls quietly.

Below, a fat man swims in the blue pool. When he surfaces at the shallow end, he blows like a walrus. He pinches his nose, shakes his head, blinks, grins, pushes thin strands of red hair off his face. He calls something to a muscular blond young man seated on the diving board at the other end of the pool. The young man doesn't notice. He is staring at young women, darkly suntanned, who lie on chaises of green webbing strung on metal tube frames. They wear outsize sunglasses and strips of bright cloth across breasts and pelvises. They drink from red tin cans. One of them reads something aloud from a paperback book and laughs.

Polk is not on the deck. It looks bare, and Whit thinks he will set plants along the rail. He empties the supermarket sacks. Into cupboards where no grit falls, where no mouse nibbles. Into a big copper-tone refrigerator that huffs each time the door shuts. He clamps a can into the electric opener, pushes the lever, and watches can and opener waltz. Claws scrabble outside the kitchen window, and Polk is on the sill, asking to come in. Whit slides the window open, Polk jumps down and starts walking in fast circles, yapping. Whit rinses a white plastic no-tilt bowl under the fancy tap where water comes out fizzing. He sets the bowl on the sleekly waxed floor, and forks food from can into bowl. Polk stops bumping his legs and eats. Whit sets the can with half its fishy contents on the refrigerator shelf. The door falls shut.

He says to Polk, "I'm not going back there."

He can think of too many places he ought never to have gone back to. He drops ice cubes into a glass. Those rooms rackety with singsong Taiwanese cousins above the Dragon Restaurant. That looming frame mansion of long porches and fat turrets, white behind dark magnolia trees, where Dell shared an apartment with another teacher. Kenny Grieve's mother's house down in the canyon. He pours Glenlivet over the ice cubes. Burr Mattox's studio above the apartment of the Weisses. He drinks whiskey, sets down the glass, and lights a cigarette. He squats, strokes the cat, who pays no attention, and sings to him a scrap of song. He changes only one word. " 'People, people who need people,' " he sings, " 'are the unluckiest people in the wo-o-orld.' " No Jesus this time. But the truth. And the way, if you were smart, and the life. He nods, reaches up for the glass, and sits on the floor, his back against the copper-tone dishwasher.

"I'm not going back there," he says again.

He went back to Dell's because of Chang. Ironically. But the first time he went there was the day he met her. She had a little office at the junior college. It was growing dark. She was too

107

busy to notice. Ghost cartons surrounded her. Ghost squares were white on the wall where maybe pictures, maybe certificates, had hung. Bookshelves gaped like mouths with teeth knocked out. She wore a school T-shirt and jeans. A bandanna bound her hair. When he stopped in the open doorway, he thought he'd got the wrong office, because she looked like a boy. She was tall enough for that, and she had those tomboy hips. Even when she turned to face him, shadowy, startled to find anyone there so late, she looked boyish because she didn't wear makeup. Dust smudged a cheek. Her eyes were cool and amused, and her handshake was firm. But her laugh was wry when he told her why he'd come.

"The school paper is not about to carry your story," she told him. "You know that, don't you?"

"They're printing the board's side," Whit said, "the superintendent's. They have to print yours."

She went back to packing her cartons.

"If they won't print it," he said, "I'll send it to *The Nation*. That'll fix 'em. The whole country will know what miserable bigots they are." He opened his notebook and leaned beside the window, so he could see to write. That was bullshit about *The Nation*. Why would they print what some school kid wrote? He said it only so she wouldn't send him away. He wanted to stay with Dell Everett the same way, earlier today, he'd wanted to stay with Jaime de Santos, looking at him, listening to him. Forever. He wrote down what she said.

When the cartons were full, he helped her stack them in the silent, empty hallway. She shut the office window, locked the office door. Matter-of-factly, as if this weren't the last time. He helped her carry the cartons out to the deserted parking lot, where tree shadows lay long in the dying red light. They loaded the cartons into the clean, empty trunk. The car was new. She said she'd have to give it back, now that she'd lost her job. He shut the trunk. "I'll ride with you," he said, "and help you unload." He got into the car quickly, before she could say no.

"It never crossed my mind to say no," she told him. It was weeks later, after the citizens' committee meeting meant to start a drive to get her reinstated at the junior college. They lay naked in the dark of her hard bed, planks and a thin pallet, a little chilly under too few blankets. The rains had come. Rain glazed the magnolia leaves outside the window in yellow street light. The leaves were stiff and the rain rattled on them. She nuzzled his belly and laughed softly. "I was too busy not believing my luck."

He smiles at his stupidity and tilts up the glass to get the last of the whiskey. He ought to have known. After they brought in the boxes and stacked them on a back porch with bulging screens and a looming hot-water heater that belched and hissed, she made him stay. In a tall old 1900s kitchen, where decades of enamel clotted gaunt tongue-and-groove cabinet doors, on a spanking new stove, she heated chili that she'd made herself. It was Texas style, and the peppers in it made him weep, but at least there was a spoon, not chopsticks. She served dark Mexican beer with it, the first he'd ever tasted. She made him talk about himself. She asked to see the poems, the play, the start of the novel. He promised, but he didn't go back. She was female, for Christ's sake. What did he want with her?

He gets up off the kitchen floor, drops new ice cubes into the glass, pours more Scotch over them. Polk's dish is empty. He picks it up, rinses it, leaves it in the sink. He walks through a wash of Mozart. The second bedroom has no bed. Handsome chairs on swivels. A big color television set. Books on modular shelves. A low table with Mexican pottery owls and stacked art books. A filing cabinet. A desk with a white telephone and a white electric typewriter. Curtains and carpet are autumn red, the walls chalk white. They need pictures but he hasn't seen a picture he wants. If he could get a picture of Jaime de Santos? Forget it. Polk is asleep on the typewriter, his favorite place. Whit isn't about to use the typewriter. All he's written on it so far are business letters. But Polk's innards are like a baby's. The hour after he's eaten is chancy. He sometimes throws up. Whit lifts him off the typewriter, carries him out of the room, and slides the door shut so he can't go back. Polk sits outside the door in the hallway and washes his tail, annoyed. Whit looks down at the swimming pool again. The fat man and his muscle boy have left, and the young women have flattened the chaises and lie face down, dozing.

None of them is as trim as Dell. She claimed the hard bed helped keep her that way. She had an athlete's body, spare and lean. Remembering it gives him an ache in his chest. It was like a boy's even with her clothes off. He was surprised that night by many things, about her, about himself. That was the first, how slim and neat she was in her flesh, economical. Margaret Miller's breasts were big and loose. The night she had held him close in bed, the night he was supposed to be dying at seven years old, their suffocating softness had panicked him. Dell's breasts weren't like that. They were firm. He was moved by them, and hid his face between them. When her hand helped him slip inside her, it was like going home. He had never wanted this surprise. He had always been frightened of it. It was the best thing that had ever happened to him.

Going home. He drinks, ice knocking his mouth, turns his back to the unreal blue water of the pool, and sits on the deck rail, feet on the lower bar. Going home was on his mind those last months of 1957. He spent his nights in a sleeping bag on a striped canvas swing hung off rusty chains on a rickety wooden porch that backed the flat above the Dragon Restaurant. Late each night, the Taiwan boys woke him, shaking the wobbly stairs, chattering, smelling of mops and buckets. It was no use asking them to be quiet. They didn't understand English. And they took their orders from the Dragon Lady, who was not Whit's friend.

At dawn, they were at it again, high-pitched, squabbling, laughing. The noise came up to him backed by rattling pans and laced with cooking smells that made him sick. Oh, he had chosen the porch himself—as the least of evils. And it was all right even when it rained, unless wind caught the rain and blew it across him. Then he crept into the disused apartment kitchen and lay on the floor between the fold-down cots, where the overworked boys snored like dying old men. Yes, he thought a

110

lot about going home. But there was no home to go to, least of all the little house on Berry Street. Margaret and Harry Miller were not his friends either, not anymore.

He gives his head a wondering shake and lights a cigarette. The last idea he would have credited, lying awake and sorry for himself those nights, and wondering what the hell was going to become of him, was Dell. He wrote the article on one of the battered machines in the school newspaper office, and mailed it off without showing it to her. They agreed to print it if they could cut it, and even then he didn't tell her. He would mail her a copy when it came out. But he had to brag to somebody. He told Chang. And when Chang got the invitation, he made Whit go with him in the Dragon Restaurant panel truck, to the meeting at Sandy Fine's shop. He didn't know why he felt afraid, sitting on the torn fake-leather seat, watching the wipers bat the hard rain off the windshield. Chang kept warning him to keep clear of Sandy.

But it wasn't Sandy he was afraid of. Once there, among the damp-haired crowd leaving wineglass rings on the new book jackets and crushing corn chips into the carpet, when he saw her again, he knew it wasn't Dell he was afraid of, either. It was himself. He looked for her the instant he stumbled inside, wiping rain out of his eyes, turning down the collar of his thin windbreaker jacket that was soaked along the shoulders because he and Chang had to run a block through puddles from where they'd parked. He didn't see her at first and his disappointment made a pain in his chest. Someone handed him paper towels to dry his hair. He just stood holding them, looking for her, looking.

"You're dripping," Chang said.

He began to dry his hair, and saw her, and felt fine. She wore a brown turtleneck sweater and new brown corduroy pants. A big gold medallion hung off a chain around her neck. The other time, a bandanna had covered her hair. Now he saw that she kept it cut short like a boy's. She had a pretty little skull. Gray-haired people surrounded her. A woman in a horse-blanket skirt and wooden beads turned away. Through the gap,

111

Dell saw Whit. She was already smiling, but now something got better about the smile. She spoke to the people, broke away from them, and came along the narrow bookstore aisle. She said to Chang that it was kind of him to come. She took Whit's hands.

"And it's you," she said. "I'm so glad."

"He's written an article about you," Chang said. He gestured at the room. "About all this. It's going to be in *The Nation*."

"So you keep promises too," she said to Whit. "Better and better." She turned. "Sandy, did you know?"

Sandy appeared from somewhere, a glass gallon wine jug in one hand, tilting him with its weight. His red hair was mussed, he looked harried. "Everyone's brought a lot of good will but not much money," he said. "Why, hello there." The fox-brown eyes unzipped Whit again. "Chang, darling, write me a big check. About your weight in litchi nuts?"

"We Chinee," Chang said, "have secret poisons of great efficacy. Come one night soon to Dragon Restaurant. You not be hungry, hour later."

"Whit's giving us national publicity," Dell said, and told Sandy about *The Nation*.

"Marvelous!" He kissed Whit, set down the wine jug, and climbed onto a desk. His foot tilted a bowl, and cheese dip ran onto his shoe. He didn't notice. He clapped his hands sharply. "Listen, everybody. Quiet, please. I've just had the most exciting news. . . ."

Dentists shook his hand, breathing mint mouthwash. Lawyers with dreamy dark eyes and razor nicks, university professors with leather elbow patches, gynecologists in three-hundred-dollar suits. Wives. A youth with blackheads who was organizing a student protest. But no junior-college instructors. Not even the one who had shared Dell's apartment. She had moved out, Dell said. Hastily.

The meeting didn't amount to much. Officers were elected. Sandy read aloud the text of an ad condemning the board for its segregationist position and for firing Dell. A lean black

112

woman from an advertising agency that was donating its services collected signatures on slips of paper to be reproduced under the text. A pair of young Mexican boys in serapes began playing guitars, and everyone else went back to drinking and munching and gossiping. Chang had to check out some old sets being repainted for a new production at the Cordova Stage. Dell asked him to leave Whit. She would run him home when the party broke up.

The new car spluttered and bucked in the driving rain along streets like ink rivers, but it got them to her place. For coffee, she said. They drank coffee from delicate old cups, Everett family stuff, in the gaunt kitchen. He had sold the article so easily, he must have talent as a writer. He'd kept his promise about the article. Why hadn't he kept his promise to show her his poems, play, novel? He promised again. It got to be midnight. When they went back out to the car, it wouldn't start. He said he could fix it, and sent her indoors. He didn't know anything about cars. In the beam of a flashlight, he poked under the hood awhile, but all he got was soaked. Back inside, he shuddered.

"You'll catch cold," she said, unzipping the flimsy jacket, peeling it off him.

"I'm all right," he said, and sneezed.

"Get out of those clothes." She pointed. "In there. I'll find you something dry. You soak in a hot tub."

He gets lamely down off the deck rail, smiling to himself. Ruefully. Rubbing his butt where the two-by-four cut into it, he returns to the kitchen for more Scotch. He was dreading the wet night ahead in the sleeping bag on the porch. Maybe that was why he obeyed her instead of hiking off through the rain to Mountain Street. He stripped in a bedroom that looked rumpled even with the light off. The pictures on the walls seemed to be of horses. A pair of silver spurs glinted off a nail.

He filled the tub in a bathroom that surprised him because no stockings and underwear were hanging up. He climbed into the tub and was lying up to his neck in the steaming water before he remembered the door. He didn't try to close it. What

113

could happen? She looked like a boy, but she was not a boy, and that was that, wasn't it? He sneezed. He almost slept. Then she was standing in the doorway, a bathrobe that looked too small in her hands. She was smiling.

"You're very beautiful," she said. "Did you know that?" He couldn't think of anything to say. She hung the bathrobe off a hook on the door. Big white towels were jammed anyhow on a rack. She pulled one down and turned to him, holding it open. She lifted her chin. "Come on. Out. I'll rub you down."

He thought he couldn't do it. He also thought she would laugh at him if he acted modest. He did it. He stood up. And right away, his idiot cock started to stretch. It didn't give a damn for what he thought or didn't think. She noticed. A smile twitched the corners of her mouth. "Come on," she said briskly. He stepped out and stood on a not-too-clean bathmat, and she put muscle into scrubbing him down with the towel. The effort made her breathing short. She said between clenched teeth, "Get the circulation. Going. Get the blood. To the surface. Warm you. Up." She was rough. Shoulders, back, buttocks. "Turn around." Chest, belly. She knelt to dry his legs. And after a minute, she wasn't rough anymore. And it wasn't the towel that was on him. It was her mouth. . . .

He thinks of her mouth on Phil Farmer and gets angry. He grabs Polk's dish out of the sink and throws it. It bounces off cabinets, the floor, hits him in the knee, settles rattling in a corner. He rubs the knee, wincing. He is on Farmer's patio again. A bouquet of champagne glasses is in Farmer's hand. They glitter in the sunset light. He is saying, "I don't have anything against it. Whatever turns you on."

"Jesus," Whit said. "This can't be real."

"But you can't expect a woman who loves you to—"

"I'm going home." Farmer's garden, every kind and color of flower, beautifully tended, deeply mulched, he had built in rock-propped terraces up the bank. Whit didn't take the flagged path. He scrambled straight up, rocks giving under his shoes and tumbling, his hands clawing plants out by the roots, flinging them behind him. He reached the ridge, Sir Edmund

Hillary of the petunias. Up there, Farmer had stuck a spidery brass TV antenna high in an oak. The flat wire hung down to trail along the ground. Whit grabbed it and yanked. A shower of dry leaves and bark fragments and dirt blinded him, and the antenna fell on him. He untangled himself from it and hurled it off the ridge. It clattered someplace below—probably on Farmer's red tile roof, but Whit hoped on the patio, at Farmer's feet. He ran home and stormed into the house.

Dell lay on her bed, face to the wall. In the poor light the shaved patch showed white on the back of her head where they'd put the stitches. He flinched for a second, feeling the needle himself. She lay very still, too still to be asleep. She was waiting. She and Farmer had mapped out this attack on him. He wanted to know how her part of it was supposed to go. He sat beside her and shook her shoulder. "Is he right?" he asked. "Have I been abusing you? I didn't know that. You always used to let me know. Why didn't you tell me. Why did you have to tell that moron?"

She didn't look at him. She said to the wall, "Because you're not going to change. You can't. It's not your fault. I made the mistake. I didn't know it would go on forever."

"I could have told you," he said. "You never asked. I thought you knew. Way back there in Cordova—you said it didn't matter, it couldn't change what we had. Look at me." He grabbed her shoulders and made her face him. She didn't look any way except tired. She blinked against the window light. "Dell, we were never going to lie to each other."

"It wasn't a lie," she said dully. "It was a mistake."

"It was a lie—letting me think something that wasn't true, backing up all this resentment. How long? Years? And then letting me hear it from that asshole." He threw his hand out to indicate Farmer's place. " 'Take it from me, kid—Dell has just about had it with you.' " He laughed hopelessly. "Dear Christ, Dell!"

She touched his face. "It's not a desperate matter."

"What?" He stood up. He sat down again. "What?"

"You don't need me, Whit," she said. "Not anymore."

He could only stare and feel sick. What she meant was, she didn't need him. It hollowed him out. Back in the time with Burr he had once imagined for hours or days maybe that he would be the one. He would say, "I'm going to live with Burr." And she would look a little bit surprised. She might even get tears in her eyes. But she would smile, anyway, and say, "I'll miss you." She always knew what to say. Nothing surprised her. Now she picked dry oak leaves off his T-shirt. She gave him a sad, gentle smile, pulled his head down, and put a light, cool kiss on his mouth. It was over before it could start. She pushed him gently away.

"No more," she said. *No more sex,* Sandy said. *I'm not going to do it anymore,* Kenny said. *And that is all we are going to have,* Burr said. Dell said, "I love you, Whit—I always did, I always will. But you never loved me. No, wait." She laid cool fingers on his mouth. "You needed me, that's all. And you don't need me anymore. You'll see. You're all right now. You're a success. You're a fine writer, and the whole world is going to say so. And you'll believe them." Her smile was wistful. "You never believed me when I said it, but you'll believe the fame, the money, the good life."

"You can have a horse now," Whit said, "your own horse."

"I want children," she said.

Children squeal in the swimming pool. He leans his head against the refrigerator and cries. With the jerking of his sobs, the ice in his whiskey tinkles. He is always doing this, standing in this expensive, empty place, drunk and crying. The good life. The crying wears itself out. The sobs turn into whimpers. Disgusted, he washes his face at the sink, dries it on a dish towel. He goes back into the workroom, switches on the television set, sits down and stares. A stagecoach is stopped by unshaven men on horseback.

"You know I haven't got an answer for that," he said.

"I'm thirty-six," she said. "If I don't have them soon, it will be too late."

"So it's a good thing this happened?" The telegram lay on

the table. He lifted it, dropped it. "Dell, I don't care about the world. You're the only good thing in my world."

"Don't you see?" she said. "That's just the trouble."

He switches off the television set. He hasn't learned how to look at it alone. They are slapping a beach ball around in the pool. He lights a cigarette and carries his drink to the deck. A boy about fourteen in little tight blue trunks that make him look like a Picasso acrobat tosses the ball to the smaller kids that swarm in the shallow end like minnows. Whit has seen the boy before—with his mother, a woman of forty who tries to dress seventeen and has a voice like a bird of prey. Whit thinks the boy is lonely but that is probably faggot sentimentality. He feels tired suddenly and goes back into the workroom and drops again into the chair that faces the blank television screen.

Going out today took effort. Just getting out of bed these days takes effort. He is always going back to it. He drinks. He sleeps. He drinks. He sleeps. But he needs the tape deck to fill in during the hours when the stations that play good music rest. Fumbling with records is too much trouble. He needs music going on all the time. He never knows when he is going to be awake. So, today, he made himself eat breakfast, shower, shave, put on clothes. It took hours—he can't say why. He unplugged the deck, but he couldn't make himself leave. He was scared. He began to sweat. He began to shake. He didn't know what he was scared of. Maybe that was the worst part. He drank and the sweating and shaking eased off, but it was still an hour before he could make himself pull open the door. After that, it wasn't too bad. What was too bad was returning to this place. It always is. Polk trots in, jumps onto the desk, and curls up on the typewriter.

"I'm not going back there," Whit says.

He stands up, but he doesn't move Polk this time. He remembers his promise to himself to eat, but he can't be bothered. It is still daylight. That makes no difference. He goes to bed.

117

Bugs

Jaime de Santos says, "You came back." He looks happy about it. The trimmed black mustache and beard frame a smile. He wears a white shirt tonight, long-sleeved, unbuttoned, clean but unironed, tails out over jeans torn off at the knee. His legs have lean, hard muscles and smooth, dark hair. He is barefoot and his toes are long. "I was afraid you wouldn't." It pains Whit to look at him, and Whit says:

"I was afraid I would."

It is plain that Jaime doesn't understand this. He looks at Whit the way Polk sometimes does when Whit tells him obscure jokes. Then, like Polk, he gives up. For the short time that this takes, Whit worries that he has hurt Jaime's feelings. But it's all right. Jaime smiles again. He won't bother with what he can't understand. "Did you bring your book?"

Whit takes it out of his hip pocket.

"That's good," Jaime says. "I want you to read."

The brown front room is crowded. Among the hanging planters, Whit counts a dozen heads. People talk, people read. On the window ledge sits a white-haired woman in black shawls. She has a profile out of a Walker Evans photograph, and she cradles a small girl-child in her lap. In a corner,

118

someone softly plays a guitar and sings, " 'The world is full of butterflies. . . .' " This is the boy who sat on Whit's car the other day, but now he wears a bulky white turtleneck, wash-faded corduroys, scuffed calfskin shoes. The sunburn on his face is peeling. Jaime de Santos studies Whit and frowns.

"Are you all right?" he says.

"Fine, thanks," Whit says mechanically.

But he knows he looks bad—white and shaken. He has seen himself in the nonstop mirrors of that vast bathroom of his. Some faggot had to have designed it. You can watch yourself jack off in four dimensions. He isn't in the mood for that. He is scared. He has never been so scared in his life. Sometime, five days ago, early in the morning, his second sleep, his third, he'd wakened, bathed in sweat, sure someone was in the room. He yelled and groped out for the lamp.

And there were bugs, black bugs, millions of them, swarming all over everything, walls, ceiling, chest of drawers, the bed, himself. He beat at them, screaming. He tried to scramble out of bed, caught his legs in the sheets, fell to the floor. He scrambled up and lunged into the hall. He slammed the door and leaned back against it. Gasping, shaking, whimpering, he kept brushing at himself. Then he guessed that he'd shut the bugs inside. Relieved, he sagged to the carpeted floor and sat against the door, panting in the dark, throat raw from screaming. When his heart slowed, he lurched to his feet. He needed a drink.

In the kitchen, he switched on the light—and there they were again, swarming all over, stove, cabinets, refrigerator. He ran screaming for the open door to the deck. But he didn't jump. His hands caught the rail and held him back. The blue pool was lighted from below. And the water wriggled with bugs. They teemed around the edges of the pool. He ran into the darkest corner of the living room and crouched down, eyes shut tight, arms over his head, and screamed and screamed. Wood splintered, voices spoke, footsteps thudded. His father held him, saying over and over that it was all right now. The

119

doctor who had cut his umbilical cord, circumcised him, taken out his tonsils, taken out his appendix, knelt, grunting, and stuck a needle into him, and he slept.

When he woke, it was red afternoon. The man he thought was his father was the muscle boy from the diving board. He sat by the bed, reading—one of Whit's Ganymede books. He wore only tight white jeans and a couple of medals on chains around his golden throat. When he saw that Whit was awake, he went to fetch the doctor, who turned out to be the fat man from the pool. He sat on the side of the bed, listened to Whit's heartbeat through a cold stethoscope, pulled Whit's eyelids wide and shone a fierce little light into them, squeezed and poked Whit's meager belly. He dropped stethoscope and light into the kit that was open on the floor at his feet, and took out a glass hypodermic syringe. While he fitted a needle to it and stuck the needle into a little bottle and sucked the contents of the bottle into the syringe, watching it carefully against the window light, he told Whit that if he didn't quit drinking without eating, worse than bugs would get him.

Now, in the brown, low-ceilinged front room of the Pipeline, Whit sees wine bottles and beer cans in people's hands, and something cringes inside him. He says to Jaime, "I haven't been sleeping well."

Jaime says, "You need some downers?" The thick lashes lower over the beautiful dog's eyes. Shy? Wary? "I mean, I don't deal, man, but if you need—"

"Thanks. I'm on megavitamins," Whit says, "and food."

The fat man rapped Whit's thigh through the sheet. "Roll over, please." He handed the empty bottle to the muscle boy. "Show me the lovely buns you're always turning to us from your deck. You see the trouble flirting can get you into?" Whit rolled over, the fat man pulled down the sheet. "Praxiteles," the fat man sighed. "Hold still, now. This will hurt for a moment, but it will start you on the road to recovery." The muscle boy said, "With Bob Hope, Bing Crosby, and Dorothy Lamour." The needle felt like a spike, and seemed to go clear to the bone. His ass still hurts.

120

"I wasn't eating right," he tells Jaime.

"What you mean is, you've been on a long drunk." It isn't Jaime who says this. It is a brown, skinny little man with a face like a dried apple. He wears an LBJ cattle-ranch hat, a strip of red cloth around his withered throat, a white satin cowboy shirt with cerise embroidery, dungarees, cowboy boots, and speaks with a middle European accent. "This is not an insult, my friend. I simply recognize the symptoms. Unhappily, in the industry, they are common."

"Abby Selzer," Jaime murmurs. "Screenwriter."

"Is the studio going to let you adapt your own book?" Selzer's sunken little eyes are bright and hard as agates. Maybe there is friendly laughter in them, but Whit thinks it is probably something else. "Or does some humble hack like myself get the assignment?"

"They asked me," Whit says, "but I told them I don't know how." He starts to make Selzer feel good by claiming screenwriters are masters of enviable skills, but he stops because of the way Selzer is smiling up into Jaime's face. Selzer chuckles, sneaks a skinny arm around Jaime's middle, and squeezes, and Whit says, "I'll leave it to a hack like you. Where's the reading," he asks Jaime, "the poetry?" He starts for the glass bead curtain, but hard, cold, little monkey fingers take his arm.

"After Jaime told me what a gifted poet you are," Selzer says, "I remembered reading your name in the trades. A friend of mine in the story department kindly smuggled out for me the galleys of your book. I've just finished reading them." His false teeth shine. "You know it will never film." Now the arm goes cozily around Whit's waist, and Whit is escorted through the bead curtain into the tall back room, where frayed adults and ragged children sit around reading, stand around talking. "The idiots bought it because everything in it is so visual. But there's no story line." Selzer peers up out of his wise monkey face. The light that glances off the white walls and white crate bookcases catches his eyes, and they are red-rimmed, blood-shot. "You know that, and I know that." He chuckles again.

121

"But the studio—they don't know that." He nudges Whit's ribs with a sharp little elbow. "Wait till they find out, eh? They made you rich for nothing."

"Just wait." Whit laughs and nudges him in return, so hard that Selzer staggers backward. "And John Huston—imagine what they're paying him. And Paul Newman." These are lies. He doesn't know who is going to direct, who is going to star. He doesn't care. Abby Selzer has let go of him and for a second can't think of anything to say, and a second is all Whit wants. He starts up the brown wooden stairs to the gallery. Just for somewhere to escape to. Halfway up, he stops, feeling sick. Jaime can't be sleeping with Selzer, can he? No one else around here looks as if they have a nickel—least of all Jaime. Could Selzer's be the money that started the shop? Did Jaime have to crawl under his rock and kiss him to get it? Whit rubs the back of a hand across his mouth to get rid of slime that isn't there. He was right. He should never have come back here.

But the fat man said he had to go out and find somebody. He was suffering from depression, a sickness. He had a bad case. The etiology was twofold—loss of a loved one, and sudden success. Either one, by itself, could immobilize. Together? The hog shoulders lifted and fell, making the blubber of the chest jiggle. He and Whit were on the chaises beside the pool, the fat man holding a glass of Dutch beer, Whit holding a can of grapefruit juice and soda that was too sweet. The muscle boy swam golden in the blue water, up to the end of the pool and back, over and over again, as if it were important to him. Together, the fat man said, they could kill. He pulled down his big dark glasses to peer blue-eyed at Whit over them, to be sure he was listening. He must cure first one, then the other. About the loss, he must stop regretting. Dell didn't want him anymore. It was a simple fact. He must find someone who did want him.

Whit turns on the steps and sees Jaime below, selling bubble gum to kids across the scratched glass counter. His smile is that of a painted plaster St. Francis in the window of a Catholic gift shop, so gentle as to be almost moronic. It is the most

122

heart-stopping smile Whit has ever seen. He tells himself to go now, down the stairs, through the bead curtain, between the hanging plants, and out the front door into the harmless night. He wants Jaime de Santos so badly his shorts are wet, so badly he hates Abby Selzer enough to kill him. But Jaime de Santos doesn't want Whit Miller. Why should he? All Whit is going to get here is hurt—as with Dell, as with Kenny, as with Chang, as with Burr, as with Sandy. But now the kids scramble off, falling over one another, unwrapping their gum, giggling. And Jaime looks up. Straight at Whit. As if he knows Whit has been watching him. He smiles. Whit smiles back wanly, touches the book in his hip pocket, and climbs the rest of the steps to the gallery.

Incense smoke is thick here, and the light is dim because black cloth hangs up, shutting off the glare of the tall white room. The dim light comes from fat, handmade candles in swirling, muddy reds and blues. A wide, arched window opens the front wall. It shows the silhouettes of big trees in the park across the street against a sky tinted with neon. The walls and ceiling of the gallery are painted here chocolate, there mustard color. Phosphorescent posters glow. Underfoot, small rugs are piled on rugs. Duffel bags, knapsacks, sleeping bags, make a khaki heap in a corner. Mattresses lie beside the walls, covered in runny madras stripes or fake fur. There are sofa pillows. A handful of anxious-looking college-age kids—long hair, Levi's, granny dresses—sit on the mattresses among the pillows, shuffling pages torn from classroom binders and written on in ball-point pen. Whit finds a spot near a candle, takes the book out of his pocket, and sits down awkwardly, cross-legged. The kids glance at him, half-smile, look away. One of the girls absentmindedly waves a stick of burning incense. The voices from below come quietly, the guitar sounds. Whit stares at the candle shadows and starts arguing in his mind with the fat man.

That first gray, rainy winter, upstairs without a phone, living off his pitiful option money and Dell's unemployment checks, in that hulking house on the Hollywood side street, when he couldn't cope with the novel and wandered around beating his

123

fists on his thighs and grinding his teeth, Dell kept trying to get him to write again for *The Nation*. She clipped the papers. She repeated to him items off the radio newscasts. In the papers, he read the comics. On the radio, he listened to "Richard Diamond" and "Johnny Dollar," detective shows. In real life—he fucked. Oh, yeah. Groggy from sleep, in the mornings, on that plank bed of Dell's that had come with them, along with barrels of Everett china, the patchwork quilts, the chests of silverware. At noon, with peanut butter and jelly in their mouths, standing up in the kitchen, pants around their ankles, butts rough with gooseflesh. At night—nothing like it to make you sleep. Oh, yeah. He shakes his head. Fucking is not the subject.

The *Saturday Review* bought one of his poems, then *Harper's,* then the *Atlantic.* He was in the magazines, and he thought that satisfied her. It only seemed that way. She stopped feeding him ideas for articles on how badly the Norwegians were treating the Lapps, but her disappointment in him rankled secretly, and never stopped rankling. He knows that now, and feels bad about it. Why did he have to keep failing her? He could have sat in bleak nighttime schoolrooms, sipping bad coffee, indignant about too few streetlights or too many liquor stores. He could have counted ballots all night, yawning in that gritty, two-car garage that was the neighborhood polling place. He could have limped down Wilshire Boulevard with ten thousand others, carrying a placard. *It wouldn't have killed me,* he tells the fat man. That he should care about politics the way she cared about politics was important to her. He says aloud, "Farmer cares about politics. Smart Farmer."

The white-haired woman in the black shawls has reached the top of the stairs, holding by the hand the sleepy little girl, who is whining and stumbling, eyes closed. The woman looks at Whit, startled, then comes and sits down beside him. She has a black cotton carryall stuffed with books, knitting, potato chips. A corner of typed manuscript, dog-eared, sticks out. The little girl falls to her knees like an exhausted runner, and tries to

124

make a place to lay her head in the woman's lap. The woman sighs, settling herself, adjusting the shawls around her. "Who's Farmer?" she asks Whit.

"The man my wife is going to marry. His testicles teem with progeny." He can't think why he wants to shock the woman. She hasn't done anything to him. Maybe he hasn't shocked her. She settles the girl-child's head, a snarl of half-braids and neglect, in her lap. She looks calmly at Whit.

"Don't yours?" she asks.

"His will fill the world with little salesmen," Whit says. "Mine would fill the world with little faggots. I don't care about the world. I care about them."

Her eyes are faded blue. "Are you a faggot?"

"It's a word like *nigger*," he says. "I get to use it—you don't."

She shrugs. "A word is only a word." She pulls black yarn and needles from her bag. "Was your father a faggot?"

He stares. It takes him a second to get his breath. "He wouldn't have told me." Whit frowns. The question makes him dizzy. He is also offended. No one calls his father bad names and gets away with it. He laughs at himself. "I never thought of it. He did some amateur acting when he was young." *Little theater,* Donnie Wright says sadly. *What kind of girlie are you, anyway?* "He was a good mimic, he could do funny accents," Whit tells the woman. "He liked to put on crazy hats." But that wasn't drag, was it? Surely that wasn't drag. "He traveled a lot." With shaky hands Whit lights a cigarette. "Jesus, I don't know. Did he hit gay bars out of town, all those years?" He laughs but it's an uneasy laugh. He tries to picture his father in a motel bed with some hitchhiking boy. He can't picture it. He shakes his head. "It would be women. The kind that would laugh at his jokes. My mother couldn't even understand them." A few feet off glints a little tin can with cigarette butts in it. He gets it and sits down by the woman again. "If he'd had a different wife, he'd probably have been an actor."

"What was he?" The woman watches her fingers knit.

"A salesman," Whit says, and they both laugh. The long

125

thing she is knitting brushes the child's face. The child paws at it, whimpering in sleep. Whit lifts the end of the knitting so it doesn't touch her. "Why black?" he says.

"I'm in mourning for the children of Vietnam," she says.

Steps have been steady on the wooden stairs, and the gallery has filled up. The sunburned boy roosts his guitar on top of the pile of luggage and sits down beside a bald man with a tangled gray beard who has with him a young woman who looks anesthetized. A thin Texas type in faded Levi's and a sweated Stetson stands with his back to the wall next to the stairs. The eye whites and teeth of a gangling black youth gleam from the smoky shadows. A plump teenage girl leans over a sketch pad in her lap, drawing and pushing back hair that hangs across her face like curtains. Jaime appears now with Abby Selzer clutching his arm and hissing. Selzer keeps darting glances at Whit as he talks. Jaime says something to him, shakes off his grip, and sits down.

"There's wine," he says, holding up a jug. "Who wants to start reading?"

For a few minutes, Whit listens hard. The writing is bad and that keeps him occupied, cutting, rewriting, changing phrases. The woman in the black shawls puts away her knitting and digs out of her black bag little plastic bottles of apple juice. She gives one to Whit. She tears open the bag of potato chips and sets it gaping between them. She nods to the rhythm of the timidly read verses, even when Whit can't find any rhythm. Now and then she hums tonelessly. A fixed, faraway smile is on her face. He smokes, takes drinks of the apple juice, and decides she is probably crazy. He decides he is probably crazy. A boy in a greasy World War II army jacket is reading as fast as he can images that jostle against each other like mail spurting from an out-of-order sorting machine. At first, Whit laughs, but there is too much of it. It goes on too long. And what he hasn't wanted to happen, happens. He isn't here. He is back with Dell.

The sun had gone entirely. Neither of them had switched on a lamp. Her face was a dim oval in the dark. "Don't you see?"

126

she said wearily. "That's just the trouble. Can't you hear me? Listen. I said you didn't love me, you only needed me. And you did. I was your safe harbor. The book went wrong, they wouldn't publish it. I was there to hold you. And after that, each time. No matter what they did to you out there in that rotten world, stupid editors, lazy agents, hateful lovers, you could come running back to me. If you cried, I'd dry your tears. I'd love you when nobody else would love you." She waited. He didn't answer. He found a cigarette. For a second, the flare of the paper match let them see each other. It was the last time. He blew out the match. She said, "I knew it was a bad world for you, mean, callous, stupid. It hurt me to see you hurt. I died for you, grinding away in that gruesome office at Rainbow Labs, tiring yourself so you couldn't get the words right at night. Then Brackett House, that awful Carmen O'Shaughnessy—what she made you write to get their dirty little checks. I wanted to help."

"Dell—you were my only help."

˒ She sorrowfully shook her head. "I kissed the hurt," she said, "but that never made it well. No matter how many times, how many years. And I'm tired of failing, Whit. And I'm tired of being the one who's wept on. I want to weep myself, sometimes, and not to have to choke it back when I see the look you get. God, if you knew that look—the pain, the bewilderment. Like a mentally retarded five-year-old. The way you scurry around, gathering pathetic little fistfuls of wilted flowers for me, trying to make up for whatever it is you've done." She laughs mournfully. "You never know what it is, never, but you're frantic to make it all right again."

"And that doesn't mean I love you?" he said.

"It means you're afraid," she said gently. "Afraid I'll go off and leave you alone to be beaten up by the bullies, with no one to run home to. Then, oh, God, what will happen to you?"

He pushed at the butts in the ashtray with the lighted cigarette, and wondered why he and Dell weren't yelling. Margaret and Harry Miller always yelled in their you-never-loved-me arguments. All Whit did was smoke the cigarette for a while. Crickets were noisy down the canyon in the warm dark. At last, he said, "I'm not a mentally retarded five-year-old. But if that's what you think I am—then, oh, God, what will happen to me? How come you don't care anymore?"

"The world has stopped knocking you down," she said. "It's picked you up tenderly and put Band-Aids on your scraped elbows and knees, and there's nothing to be afraid of now."

He went through the darkness to the bathroom. He didn't turn on the light. He dropped the cigarette into the toilet. His head throbbed, and he got aspirin from the plastic bottle in the medicine chest. He filled the toothglass at the tap. The window stood open. He leaned out, under the shaggy blackness of the peppertree, and clicked his tongue against his teeth. Polk came up the roof and stood on the windowsill. Whit washed down the aspirin and set the glass back in its holder. He picked Polk up and returned to the living room. He folded back the cover on his bed and shook his pillows out of their cases. He pushed one case down inside the other.

Dell said quietly, "What are you doing?"

Polk was bumping Whit's legs. Whit bent and picked him up and dropped him into the sack that the pillowcases made. Whit knotted the neck of the sack. Polk complained. Whit looked at Dell. "I'll take Polk with me," he told her. "Phil is allergic to cats."

She sat up. "Whit, you can't just—"

"Somebody has to," he said, "and it's your house— remember?"

The woman in the black shawls has hold of his arm and is tugging it. He blinks at her in the candlelight and incense smoke and can't comprehend. She picks up his book from the rug in front of him and puts it into his hands. He looks at Jaime, and Jaime is watching him expectantly. Has Jaime spoken his name? He seems to have heard that. He looks around. Everyone but the sketching girl, whose head is still bent above her pad, face hidden by the long hair, is watching

128

him. He tries for a smile and opens the book. The light is no good to read by, but he remembers the poems, even though he hasn't thought of them in years. He begins to recite.

With loud excuse me's, Abby Selzer stumbles to his feet and wedges through the knot of scruffy kids that has formed in the opening at the top of the stairs. He goes down the stairs, hammering them with his boot heels, and coughing loudly. Below, something crashes. Abby shouts, "Oh, Jaime, I'm so sorry. I have broken a beautiful piece of pottery, here." He comes hammering up the stairs again. "You must let me pay for it." He thrusts through the kids again, digging out his wallet. "I am so terribly sorry," he keeps repeating. "It was so clumsy of me."

"Abby," Jaime says, "Whit is reading."

"Yes." Abby nods the hat with the crimped brim at Whit. "I am so sorry to interrupt." He squats in front of Jaime, takes his hand, lays money in it. "There. I wouldn't want to leave without paying for the damages. So clumsy of me."

The woman with the shawls is knitting again. The end of the knitting covers the child's head but she is too deeply asleep to be bothered by it now. What he can see of her face is flushed, and she snores very softly. The woman says under her breath, "He did it on purpose. He doesn't like you. Why?"

"That's too easy." Whit watches Abby rise, if that's the word for somebody five feet short. Abby nods and smiles at everyone, apologizes all over again to everyone. He elbows for the third time through the kids. Whit says to the woman, "He and Jaime sleep together, don't they?"

"Jaime sleeps alone," she says. "I know. I live here."

It looks to Whit as if thirty people live here. When he finishes reading, and the college kids, the man with the tangled beard, the black, the Texan, and the agitated boy in the army jacket have left, the kids crowd in and start tearing down the mountain of khaki luggage. They unroll sleeping bags and lay them on the floor and on the mattresses. More come in from the street, the park, and trail wearily up the stairs. Smells of beer go by, of chili dogs, of sweat. Someone vomits in the washroom at the far back corner. On the round table with the driftwood, the sunburned boy sits in his undershorts with his guitar and sings about butterflies again. In the front room, Jaime weakly shakes Whit's hand.

"Thanks for coming," he says. "Your poems are good. I hope you'll come back."

"When Abby stays home," Whit says.

Food

Jaime cooks at the back of the shop. On one burner of the smoky white stove, rice bubbles in a dented aluminum saucepan. On another burner stands a big stewpot of chipped white enamel. In this red beans simmer. Jaime pulls down from the top of the smudged refrigerator a cardboard carton, and rattles out of it a flat, dented lid with a charred wooden knob. He lays the lid over the rice. He turns down the fire under the rice and asks Whit, "What time is it?" Whit reads his extravagant wristwatch and tells him. Jaime sets a crusty black cast-iron frying pan on the lid to keep in the steam. He pushes the beans around with a long-handled wooden spoon. "How do these smell?" he asks Whit. Whit bends his face over the pot. They smell like beans.

"Aren't there any onions in there?" He takes the spoon from Jaime and turns over the beans, frowning through the steam. "No meat? You need onions for flavor. You need meat for nourishment."

Jaime shrugs. "You can live without meat. Whole nations live without meat. India. In Biafra, right now, they'd give anything for beans and rice."

The plump girl who draws, and has long straight brown hair, edges between them. She squats and pulls open the oven door. Folding the grimy edge of her granny skirt to protect her fingers, she slides out a TV dinner in its shiny, crinkled tray. She closes the oven. Heat puffs up into their faces. She hurries

131

with the tray to the low, round table, and skids the tray onto the scatter she has made there of her drawings. She kneels on the cement floor and peels back the top of the tray. Out of a coarse-weave tote bag embroidered with a peace symbol and stuffed with colored marker pens and sketch pads, she brings a bent fork. She eats. Maybe it's sliced turkey. It's not rice and beans. Tim Connaught gets off the table and takes his guitar into the front room. The glass curtains chitter. Laura Sailor, seated in her black shawls on pillows under the stairs, looks up from the letter she is reading, then looks down at it again. Her girl-child, Blue Sky, has been cradling in her arms the gray-striped shop cat. Now Blue Sky gets up and goes to the table and stands staring at the eating girl. The eating girl smiles at her and goes on eating. The cat jumps up on the table and the eating girl pushes her down. The cat is not fat, as Whit thought when he saw her first, curled up in the window sunlight on the poetry books—she is pregnant. Blue Sky picks up the cat protectively, and retreats back under the stairs, where she delves in her mother's black bag, brings out the last inch of a stick of beef jerky, and gloomily chews it. Whit looks at Jaime.

"It's not a commune," Jaime says. "Carol sold some of her pictures in the park today. It's her two dollars."

"Two dollars would mean more in the pot," Whit says. "What about sleeping? She sleeps here, doesn't she? Free?"

"There's plenty of room," Jaime says.

Whit heads for the glass curtains. "I'll be back."

"I'm timing the rice on your watch," Jaime says.

"It will only take me a few minutes. I promise."

Alone in the front room, Tim Connaught bends his shaggy white head low over his guitar and tries to work out complicated fingering. Little kids crowd through the front door in an explosion of high-pitched yells. They dodge Whit, and run for the back room. The strands of beads lash with their passing, braid and unbraid themselves, rattling. Tim Connaught looks up. The peeling skin from the sunburn is gone now. His face is honey-color, smooth, young, the blue eyes innocent.

"I read about a boy," he says, "who ate the breasts off a

living girl." He laughs. "Hunger makes people crazy."

"Supper will be ready soon," Whit says. "Meantime, try to think cheerful thoughts, okay?"

He goes out. The ragamuffins stand on the sundown sidewalk. They seem to sniff the air. A straggle of them comes blindly across from the park. Auto horns blare. Tires shriek. They don't look. Their gaze is on the door of the Pipeline. The gangly black poet is leaning against the Mercedes. He is a flashy dresser. His wide-brimmed hat is at a rakish angle and there is a feather in it. When he sees Whit, he gives a sleepy smile and steps away from the car. "Why don't we put out a poem book?" he says. "All of us. I can set it. Free. Cold type. It's where I work."

"It would be a waste of paper," Whit says, and drives off.

He is stronger and steadier now, and carries the heavy grocery sacks into the shop without breathing hard or sweating. He sets them on the old oak dining table into which boards have been laid to make it long. Jaime stares. Whit finds newspaper, spreads it on the table, finds a knife in the cardboard box on top of the refrigerator, and slits open the plastic packs of wieners. He cuts the wieners into sections. He chops up onions. He drops the chunks of wiener and onion into the beans and stirs them down with the wooden spoon.

"I didn't get salt pork because that needs to cook a long while to get the good out of it."

"You didn't have to get anything," Jaime says.

"I know that," Whit says.

"I guess not." Jaime is looking at him from under his lashes again, lids half lowered, eyes dulled. His mouth moves with words not spoken. He says, "You don't understand."

"I understand hunger." Whit brings out of the bags half-gallon white plastic jugs of milk. "My father wasn't a very good provider." He holds up the jugs. "What can they drink out of?"

Jaime jerks his head at the pots on the stove. "This is yours now. You figure it out." He stamps off in his clumsy monk's sandals.

Whit catches him. "Look. Wait. I don't know what I've

133

done, but I'm sorry. I didn't mean any harm. I've got plenty of money. Why should anybody go hungry?"

"These kids had providers," Jaime says, "good providers. They don't want that. If they wanted that, they could have stayed home. You accept your old man's food, you have to accept all his other shit."

"I'm not asking for thanks," Whit shouts. "You don't have to tell them where the stupid wieners and milk came from, for Christ's sake. I don't want anything from them. I don't want anything from you." This is a lie. It isn't whiskey that makes it hard for him to sleep now. It isn't regretting Dell—at least not so much as before. Now what makes it hard for him to sleep is wanting Jaime. "Look, just feed them, when the onions get soft, okay?" He throws up his hands and heads for the bead curtain. "I didn't mean to interfere. I don't want to be anybody's old man. I don't want to tell anybody what to do." He turns back, holding out his hands, trying to laugh but crying instead. "I don't know what to do, myself."

Jaime stops sulking. He looks alarmed and sorry, and he comes to Whit. "You know what to do," he says gently. "Only not here, okay? Not again." He takes hold of Whit's hand and bends over it. Whit's heart almost stops. Is Jaime going to kiss his hand? Jaime is not. He is squinting at Whit's watch. "Is it time to turn off the rice?"

Whit looks at the watch. "Yes," he says.

Jaime sits under a tree in the park, his back against the trunk of the tree, his lean brown legs hugged by his lean brown arms. It is the last of October but it is hot. Sweat shines on the naked shoulders, arms, chest of a black youth beating bongos, a brown youth beating a tall drum. Sweat glazes the porcelain skin of a dancing white boy. Jaime isn't the only one watching. A crowd sits on the grass in a circle. Not all of them sit. Some lie. A boy and girl with arms around each other, mouths locked, appear to have fallen asleep that way. A thin boy in a swallowtail coat with no shirt under it keeps sitting up, peering into his rusty top hat, breaking into giggles, falling back helpless. Whit passes and peers down into the hat. A mirror is fixed inside its top.

Whit smoked marijuana once or twice with Burr. He smells the smoke hanging in the heat. He sits down beside Jaime, who without looking at him passes him a wine bottle in a wrinkled brown paper sack. Whit hands it back. They don't say anything. The drums are too noisy. They watch the dancing boy whose torso is bare, and whose pants are tight black satin belted with a red-and-orange silk scarf. He looks about fifteen but there is a big bulge at his crotch. He has thick, ballet-dancer thighs, a hard, muscular little butt. He is not very tall. It is a kind of gypsy dance he is trying to do, with stamps, jumps, arrogant turns of the head. But he has too many graces learned in big, bare, mirrored rooms, to the tune of *Giselle*. There is no savagery. His hands move on his wrists like the heads of flowers in soft breezes. He leaps, spins, collapses—gracefully. Applause spatters. Raggedly the drums quit. The boy gets up off the grass and comes to Jaime with the duck walk of dancers down off their points. He bends and picks up a shirt from beside Jaime. The boy is panting and gives off a sharp smell of sweat. He drops down beside Jaime, drying himself with the shirt.

"How was it?" he says.

"Beautiful," Jaime says. And to Whit, "This is Target."

Jaime comes through the shadows of the gallery, holding out in front of him a saucer. On the saucer is a chocolate cupcake, and stuck into the cupcake is a little pink candle. He shields the wavering flame of the candle with his hand. He tries not to smile. It is early for the poetry. But Whit is on the gallery. So is Tim Connaught, picking quietly at his guitar. So is Laura Sailor, seated in her spread of black shawls. She takes out of her black bag dime-store half-moon reading glasses and an envelope. Out of the envelope she takes a letter that she reads. She tucks the letter back into its envelope, and pushes it back into the bag, followed by the glasses, which make little clicks when she folds the bows. She has done this four times, wholly absorbed. She is reading the letter again, when Jaime kneels, sings under his breath, "Ta-da!" and sets the cupcake in front of her. On single strings, Connaught picks out the birthday song.

Whit is surprised and says, "Congratulations."

Laura is smiling up at Jaime over her glasses, while her fingers fold and tuck away the letter once more. "Thank you," she says. There is love with the laughter in her voice. She tells Connaught impatiently, "Stop. It's not my birthday." She has hold of Jaime's hand. She says to Whit, "I'm a grandmother."

Jaime gives her a quick, awkward little hug, and a kiss on the cheek, and gets up. She reaches for his hand again but misses. He shifts from foot to foot, shy, tongue-tied as a ten-year-old. The candlelight shows sentimental tears in his eyes. He blurts, "It's wonderful," and goes away quickly. His sandals stutter down the steps.

"Boy or girl?" Whit says.

"Come sit by me," she says. "Girl. It's always girls, poor things, in my family. I have three daughters. Back in New England. I thought I'd left all that behind. I meant to." He sits beside her and she rattles the letter in its envelope at him. "But they keep sending me dispatches."

"You don't sound pleased," he says. "But you've been reading it over and over."

"I'm not pleased," she says, and tears the letter up and stuffs the fragments angrily into the bag. The corner with the stamp lies on the rug. "I can't understand why, if you want to be left alone, you can't just be left alone. I came as far away as I could get, without leaving the country." She picks up the corner with the stamp and pushes it into the bag. "I gave those girls twenty years of my life. Why can't I have what's left of it in peace?" She tries for a smile, touches Whit's hand. "I'm sorry. Just about the time I think I've forgotten and I can be myself, there they are again."

"What about their father?"

136

"He was a man in a suit. He owned a briefcase and a law office in Boston and a large home in the suburbs and a wife who never breathed unless he told her to. He couldn't imagine why I left." Her mouth turns up bitterly at one corner. "At first he kept sending me plane tickets and money. He thought I was suffering from that commonest of middle-aged female ailments—the empty-nest syndrome." She laughs without humor. "You can't know how thankful I was to have two of those girls married and the other one off at college—out from underfoot. No man could know. Least of all Edward. He promised to be a better companion. We would do things together. God, what that conjured up. You haven't known boredom until you've known Edward Sailor."

"Twenty years is a lot of boredom," Whit says. Voices drift up from downstairs. He recognizes some of them. The poets have started to arrive. "What made you decide to put an end to it?"

"Oh, I'd been trying for a long while. I was president of the PTA. The Junior League couldn't hold a rummage sale without me. The Republican Women couldn't print a leaflet or ring a doorbell. I helped at the nursery for working mothers. I read to the blind." The small ironic smile comes back. "But it was the library that did it. I was a summer volunteer, filling in during vacations. And the new books that stacked up on tables in the back room, waiting to be catalogued, fascinated me." Her fingers flick the paper-clipped corner of the sheaf of poems sticking out of her bag. She doesn't notice. "I'd always thought I could write. Sometime. Some far-off time. Poetry."

Whit smiles. "You could," he says. "You can. You do."

"And there were half a dozen books from a little press here in L.A.—by a man named Van Meeren. No one was cataloguing. I took them along with me in the bookmobile and read them all. He put everything he was, everything he thought and felt into poems. He wasn't ashamed of anything. Words didn't make him blush and hide his face. I thought, 'Dirk Van Meeren is the most wonderful man in the world. He is everything I want to be and have never been brave enough to be.' "

Whit has read some of Van Meeren's stuff. It is sour with envy, self-pity, and beer-belly bluster. Feet begin to climb the steps now, and Whit is thankful, because he doesn't know what to say to Laura Sailor. He thinks again that she is crazy and that he is crazy for being here. He wants to jump up and run away, howling. Part of him does this, but the polite part sits and listens to the end. She is saying:

"—But I thought they'd keep looking for my body washed up on the shore, so I left Edward a note, saying I was tired of my life with him and, now the girls were grown, he didn't need me anymore, and I was going to California to live the way I wanted to, needed to. All he'd ever let me have was household money. I couldn't fly. I took the bus, slept on the bus, ate hot dogs at bus stops. When I got here, I walked straight to Van Meeren's. I knew the street name. I wandered along with my suitcases till I heard typing from an old bungalow court with the paint scaling off the stucco. I knocked on the screen door. He came, in an undershirt, with a beer can in his hand, and looked me up and down, and asked what the fuck I wanted. I told him I'd read his books and I wanted to live with him. He unhooked the screen door."

"But you live here," Whit says.

"Blue Sky is his child," she says. "His and mine."

Jaime sits on the floor in the back room. For three days it has rained, but this morning the sky is clear blue, and the sun is bright. Sunshine streams down on him from the skylight high above. He has shaved and cut his hair short. The sight of him makes Whit's knees weak. Whit stops inside the glass-bead curtain and stares with a dry mouth. He has been down on Santa Monica to get his tape deck. It lies in the trunk of the Mercedes. He ought to have taken it straight home. He ought not to have stopped here. The pain of looking at Jaime this morning is worse than at any time before. He wants to hate Jaime but he can't. He can't do anything about Jaime now. It's too late.

138

The plump girl, Carol, sits with Jaime. Around them are spread her drawings. Pencil, with timid squiggles of color that comes harsh from the fat felt tips of her marker pens but that can't keep the pictures from looking pale and afraid. And alike. They're all leaves, flowers, children. But she's never seen a leaf or a flower. And these children could never survive, with their pin heads, balloon bodies, mismatched arms and legs. She gets to her knees to reach for a far picture, and tucking her long skirt between her thighs, sits back once more, as close to Jaime as she can get without hugging him. While he talks about the picture, she gazes into his face, lips parted, eyes adoring. Jaime looks up from the picture and sees Whit.

"I'm going to give Carol a show," he says.

Jaime often rearranges the white-painted crates of books. Tonight he has made an alcove of some of them. The stark overhead lights aren't working. Candles glimmer in the big back room. Their light is feeble, and those who want to read huddle on the floor around the low table and the long bench, books close to the flames, faces close to the books. They have come in out of heavy rain and give off smells of wet clothing, wet hair. Most don't try to read. They talk and laugh and drink out of sacked cans and bottles or cracked cups. Whit works through them, looking for Jaime.

Jaime crouches at the back of the new-made alcove, a bottle of red wine in one hand, a do-it-yourself cigarette in the other. His lashes are lowered so that his eyes don't glow. He looks sulky. Tim Connaught, with his mop of white hair, squats in front of him. Whit can't hear what he says, but the set of Connaught's shoulders, straight and lean as laths inside his grimy white sweater, show that his words are urgent. Jaime says nothing. Whit wonders if he is even listening. Whatever is happening, Whit feels jealous. He steps into the alcove and, when Jaime looks up at him, raises his eyebrows and taps his watch.

"Poetry time?" he says.

Connaught makes an animal sound in his throat, jumps to his feet, shoves Whit aside, and lunges out of the alcove. Whit falls back against the crates and they totter. He grabs at them to keep them from crashing down. Connaught hurls his lanky self through the shadow poets. The round tabletop slumps off its props. Papers fly up as in a wind. A candle bumps and splutters off across the floor. There are small outcries. The front door slams. Books have fallen out of the crates. Whit crouches to pick them up and stands to put them back where they belong. He looks with raised eyebrows at Jaime. Jaime hasn't moved or changed expression.

He says, "Why do you tell me what time it is?"

Whit frowns. "I don't understand."

"You're the one who runs the poetry," Jaime says. "You don't need me. You're the one who knows everything."

"Shit," Whit says. "I thought you wanted me to—"

"I do want you to," Jaime says. "Leave me out of it."

"I'm sorry you feel that way," Whit says.

"Don't talk to me," Jaime says. "I don't know anything about poetry."

Whit takes a deep breath. He squats in front of Jaime as Connaught was doing. Jaime lifts his thick lashes for a second and holds out to Whit the raveled, handmade cigarette. Whit doesn't want it, but he takes it anyway, and sucks smoke out of it and holds the smoke deep in his lungs. Jaime looks down at his hand on the neck of the wine bottle. Whit touches the hand and the hand takes back the cigarette. Whit lets the smoke out slowly. He breathes deeply again and says, "Do you really think I come here for the poetry?"

Jaime looks up at him quickly.

Whit says, "I come here because this is where you are. I love you, Jaime."

"Oh, God," Jaime says, and shuts his eyes.

Laura Sailor taps Whit's shoulder. "I think we should start," she says. "People have come a long way in the rain."

140

Jaime, in a black rubber poncho, and Target, in soaked bib overalls, wheel a battered trash module out of the alley at the end of the block of shops of which the Pipeline is one. The wheels of the module squeak. Its cargo, from under sloped, loose-fitting lids, exhales stinks. It is late. The poets have left, and the sleepers have taken over the gallery. Laura Sailor and Blue Sky have bedded down in the book-crate alcove. A candle burns there, and Laura reads aloud quietly from a book of children's verse. Sleeping bags bulge palely across the floor of the dark back room.

No one sleeps in the front room. Among the shadows of the hanging plants there, the glint of the thick plastic that covers Carol's drawings on the walls, Whit has waited an hour for Jaime. More. Jaime didn't climb the steps for the poetry. And when Whit came down the steps, Jaime was nowhere. Now it is midnight. Whit looks out the streaming window. His car gleams white and lonely under a streetlamp by the park. Maybe Jaime is waiting until it is gone. Whit goes out into the rain, and sees them heaving and hauling the big battered trash bin. Jaime sees Whit too, and stops moving. Does he hope Whit will go get into his car? Whit doesn't care what he hopes. He starts toward him.

Jaime and Target put their shoulders against the bin and shove it to the curb. The rain beats noisily on the metal. Whit can't hear what Jaime tells Target, but Target stares at him for a minute with beggar's eyes. Jaime jerks his head, and Target looks glum, hunches his shoulders, and runs off up the street through the rain, in and out of tree shadows and streetlights, until he is gone. Jaime hikes up the edge of the streaming poncho and digs in a pants pocket. He brings out a fold of money and, peering at it in the wet yellow half-light, peels off bills. He takes Whit's hand and lays the bills in it. Whit stares—at the money, at Jaime. Jaime says:

"For the onions and wieners and milk." He tries a little apologetic smile. "It had to wait till I got paid. For emptying the wastebaskets in the offices upstairs, for hauling out the

141

trash. I can have it off the rent, or I can take cash. This time I took cash."

"Not for me." Whit tries to give back the money.

Jaime hides his hands inside the poncho. "I owe you for more than that. For the teaching you do—for helping them learn to write."

Rain streams down Whit's face. He tries to wipe it off with a hand. "This is all wrong," he says. "I told you I don't give a damn for them and their pitiful poems. I can't help them learn to write. Nobody could. They're hopeless, the whole bunch of them. Jaime, didn't you hear me? I come because of you. I love you, God damn it."

Pained, desperate, Jaime shakes his head. "No, you don't. You mustn't. I can't love anybody. Not now." He winces up at the rain as if it were the rain's fault. He takes Whit's arm and runs him across the street and into the park. It feels good to run with Jaime. They shelter, panting, in a white wooden gazebo. On a pedestal in its center stands a naked youth made of bronze. He is staring into the night, and Whit knows there is another gazebo out there, with a naked bronze maiden. They have gazed yearningly at each other across the park for years. Wooden benches line the gazebo. They sit. Jaime says:

"I was living with a kid at the beach. You heard the poem I wrote." He brings a crumpled cigarette pack from under the poncho and lights cigarettes for both of them. "Don't you remember? You said it was good."

Whit remembers. But only one line. He would say anything Jaime de Santos wrote was good. Love corrupts. Absolute love corrupts absolutely. He remembers a line about oil pumps nodding in the moonlight. That's all he remembers, because it took him back to the night he left Dell. He doesn't know and never will how he got to the beach, but that was where he ended up. He sat in the car and watched the moon rise over the oil pumps. Sometimes the wind brought him snatches of wheezy merry-go-round music from the far-off pier. He didn't feel anything. Polk had howled and struggled in the pillowcases for a while, but he'd made up his mind at last that he was going

142

to spend the rest of his days in there, and had gone to sleep. The common sense of that had reached Whit after while. He drove up a canyon into mountains. At last the houses petered out, then even the shacks with ragtag horses like Sergeant swishing their tails in the moonlight. When there was nothing but hills, rocks, brush, he drove under oaks, locked the car, and went to sleep himself. He was very tired. He didn't dream at all.

"He was beautiful," Jaime says. "But he was hooked on smack." He glances at Whit. "Horse. Heroin. It was crazy, such a waste. He was sweet and good and it was going to kill him. It kills, man. It kills." Jaime stares at the smoke from his cigarette that goes sluggishly away in the wet dark. "I got him off it." He gives Whit another quick glance. "You know how that goes? Their nose runs, they think they're freezing, they shake. They throw up. They shit a river. They kick and kick and can't stop kicking. You think they're going to fly apart like dolls. Arms, legs, everyplace." He gets up, crosses the little gazebo, and stands facing the dark. "I held him. All day, all night, all the next day, clear till sundown. And then I kept him off it. We were happy." Jaime makes a sound. Whit isn't sure what it is—if it's laughter, it is as sad as any he's ever heard. "For almost a year. Then it was quick. You build up a tolerance while you're on it. But you lose that. He forgot. Or he never knew. I had a job. I came home one afternoon, and he was on the bed. The needle and spoon. The stuff in the plastic envelope. The belt for around his arm. He was naked. We had this room with a big bay window—the light coming off the ocean. He was beautiful. And he was dead." Jaime comes back and sits down. He takes a last drag off the cigarette and flicks it away. The rain puts out the spark. "His stepfather came and got his body. They buried him in Madison, Wisconsin." Jaime looks at Whit. His eyes are wet. "I can't love anybody else. Not now."

Whit says, "Is that what you told Connaught tonight?"

"It's what I tell them all," Jaime says.

143

Plants

He doesn't know what sound has wakened him. It is cold. He is in the dark, but it isn't yet midnight—in the far room broadcast music plays. Scriabin? He lies shivering, waiting for the sound to repeat itself. *Ping,* it goes again. He can't remember ever hearing it before, but he decides it is his doorbell, and he gets up unsteadily and flaps into his bathrobe. In the dark the stereo receiver grins. He switches it off and opens the door. Plants grow below in a breezeway, lighted at night as if they were nervous children. The glow comes up and shows him Jaime de Santos in a bulky peacoat and a knit cap. He rubs his hands. His breath is visible. The skinny pants legs look like corduroy, but his feet are bare in the clumsy sandals, and he keeps lifting them and putting them down.

"I want you to come back," he says.

Whit steps away from the door so Jaime can't get a good look at him, can't smell him. He is ashamed and disgusted at himself. He hasn't bathed in a week. Or shaved. Or cleaned his teeth. "It's freezing," he mumbles. "Come in." Jaime steps inside and shuts the door. Carefully, as if he were a little scared. The only light in the living room comes through the sliding glass walls. It strikes the ceiling and is blue and wavery from the swimming pool. Jaime peers at Whit.

"You look sick." He sounds worried. "Are you sick?"

"Not anymore," Whit says. He is excited. His heart thumps. His cock stretches. But he is afraid heart and cock are wrong. He wants not to make a mistake. "Fix some coffee, will you?" he says. "That's the kitchen. I'll clean up."

His cock won't stop. It stands through shower, shave, toothbrushing. It is so stiff and the blood pounds in it so, it hurts. In the dark bedroom, he pulls on jockey shorts to keep it leashed. He picks up the bathrobe and drops it—he has lived in it too long, sweated too much whiskey and nicotine into it. He finds a clean turtleneck jersey, and tucks it into clean jeans, and goes barefoot into the glaring kitchen. He wants Jaime to notice his hard-on, but the doubter in him makes him sit down quickly to hide it.

Coffee and toast smells are strong. Jaime has shed the heavy coat and stands at the copper-tone stove, stirring eggs in a never-before-used frying pan that has a red enamel bottom. Polk bumps around his legs. "You've been drinking and not eating again," Jaime says. "Why do you want to kill yourself? Look at this place. The only other novelist I know lives in a garage you wouldn't park your car in. He's good, too. You've got everything."

"Not you," Whit says. "I want you."

"You don't even know me." Jaime lifts down plates from a cupboard. He blows dust off them. "Everything else here is spotless. How come you don't clean these?"

"I don't clean anything. Women do it." Twice a week, he thinks. In the mornings, he thinks. Young, middle-aged, brown, black, they wear uniforms, and he doesn't know one from the other. Except for what is in cupboards, the only thing allowed to go dirty here is the stunned and stumbling, bony and unshaven young man in the bathrobe, whom they shunt from room to room while clean sheets flap, the vacuum cleaner whines, and spray cans hiss. He pays for it. After the frowstiness of the canyon shack, he thought it would be worth it. It isn't. He watches Jaime spoon the eggs from the pan onto the plates. The eggs have chopped tomato in them, bits of melted yellow cheese. Jaime pours chili from another pan. He sprinkles chopped onion on the chili, and brings the plates to the table, where he has already set out forks, knives, spoons, paper napkins, a stoneware jar of imported quince jam. He fetches mugs of coffee. The table is an oval of plate glass set in white wicker. When his mug clicks on the glass, Whit looks up and says, "I mustn't want you, but you can want me?"

"To come back." Jaime sits down and unfolds his napkin and lays it in his lap. "The poetry is no good without you. Tonight was lousy." He nods at Whit's plate. "Eat."

"I told you I don't care about the poetry," Whit says.

"How you talk about it says that isn't true," Jaime says. "I'm sorry about offering you money. That wasn't right. It was insulting. I just didn't want—" But he has to find new words for whatever the next message is. A blush darkens his face. He lowers his head and eats quickly.

"You grew your beard back," Whit says. "That's good."

"I got an idea in the middle of the night." Jaime smears jam on his toast, raises his eyes to Whit's for a second, looks down again. "Beards and dope went together. So I got up and shaved it off. I don't want to wear labels."

"People put them on you, anyway," Whit says.

"People that don't matter." Jaime nods. "I saw that too." He stuffs his mouth with toast and pushes the jam jar at Whit. "Eat," he says again.

"You make me lose my appetite," Whit says.

Jaime grins. "Am I that ugly?"

"You're that beautiful." Whit knows he should not be saying these things. He fills his mouth with eggs in order not to be able to go on talking. His stomach lurches. He can't swallow. He scalds his mouth with coffee. The food goes down inside him in a lump. Right away he is talking again. "Looking at you is like looking at the sun. It gives me pain and I have to look away."

Jaime sits still with his head lowered. He doesn't move his jaws. Or his hands. He says to the plate, "What I was going to say was, the reason I offered to pay you for the poetry nights was, I didn't want to be in debt to you."

146

"For fear I'd want to collect—" Whit gets up and looks into the refrigerator. Wine bottles gleam there. He has never touched one of them. No one has come to eat with him. He hasn't invited anyone. He sets a bottle in front of Jaime where, like himself, it breaks into a cold sweat. He takes down wineglasses from a cupboard. Dust is in them. He blows out the dust, sets a glass in front of Jaime, the other at his own place. He finds in a drawer a fancy wooden corkscrew he has never used—the price tag is still stuck to the handle. He lays the corkscrew beside the bottle. "—the same way as Abby Selzer?" He sits down. "Open it, will you, please?"

Jaime stares at him. "What are you talking about?"

Whit reaches for the wine bottle. With a thumbnail, he peels the thick red plastic seal off the bottleneck. "Didn't Abby put up the money for your shop?"

"Some of it," Jaime says. "I had some of it myself." He watches Whit try to work the corkscrew. Whit's hands shake and he can't concentrate. He stabs a finger and sticks it in his mouth. Jaime stretches across to take the bottle and corkscrew and sits down and cranks the screw into the cork. "I come from a farm east of Cordova. I started reading Kerouac while I milked the cows. I wanted to go up on a mountain and I did. Nearly froze my ass. Nearly starved to death." He smiles and draws out the cork. "But I was free, wasn't I? Then they built a ski lodge in that valley. They needed boys to carry suitcases and bus the dishes, okay? You can hold out your hand when you get through hauling their skis and skates and clothes to their rooms and these kids put like ten dollars in it, twenty. The American way, you know?"

"It beat stealing acorns from the squirrels, right?"

"It was so easy." Jaime gives his head a slow shake. "I didn't know what I was getting into." He reaches across and fills Whit's glass with wine. Blowing didn't get all the dust out. It floats in a thin film on top. Whit doesn't care. He drinks half of it right off, hoping it will settle his stomach. It seems to. While Jaime fills his own glass, Whit picks up his fork and starts to

147

eat. Jaime says, "I was holed up in a cabin half burned down, chopping my own wood, talking to raccoons. Reading. Writing poems. God, it was cold! Then here's this lodge—roaring fireplaces in all the downstairs rooms, central heating for the guest rooms, all the food I could eat."

Whit grins. "You knew what you were getting into."

"No. In ten days, I was chief bellhop, then assistant manager, okay?" He glowers, his voice is bitter. "And the next winter, I'm the manager." He stops to shovel in eggs and chili, paying attention to his plate. He gets it all down, takes a drink of wine, wipes his mouth on the napkin, and looks at Whit. "Did you ever sleep with an Olympic ice skater? The dudes that do the big leaps and spins and all that? Muscles you can't believe? Throw themselves around like they weren't scared of anything? My God, what girls they are in bed. What girls."

"And Abby?" Whit says. "What's Abby like?"

Polk knocks the saucepan off the stove. It clangs and bounces and lies on its side, chili running out of it on to the floor. Polk jumps down, crouches, licks at the chili, daintily, greedily. Jaime starts to get off his chair.

"Leave it," Whit says.

"I had money saved," Jaime says, "but the shop was his idea. I had to let him invest. I couldn't stop him. What's he like? He sulks a lot, like you. I can't help it. I explained to him. I explained to you. He won't believe me. You won't believe me. I'm sick of it." Jaime walks into the shadowy living room and picks up his jacket. Whit follows and tries to help with it. Jaime shrugs away his hands. He pulls the stocking cap down hard on his thick hair. He says flatly, "Are you coming back or not?"

"For the poetry, no," Whit says. "Only for you."

"It's no use." Jaime goes to the door.

"You only said you couldn't love anybody now," Whit reminds him. "Not *never*."

"*Never* is a kid's word." Jaime pulls open the door. Cold air comes in. "Come back if you want," he says. "But I don't want to hurt anybody. If you get hurt, it's not my fault." He goes out into the dim flower-bed light and shuts the door.

Whit can't find a place to park on the street. He turns in at the alley. A small stake truck is parked behind the Pipeline. Its rear faces the open back door of the shop. A splintery plank ramp tilts down from the truck bed. Whit parks beside the truck and gets out of the Mercedes. In the cold, clear, winter morning sunlight, the grubby shop refrigerator gleams dully on the truck bed. Whit's heart gives a thump. What is happening? He starts for the door and Target's back appears there in a dirty T-shirt. He is tugging at something Whit can't see. Now it comes into view. It is the soiled cookstove, strapped to a two-wheel dolly. Jaime is pushing the dolly. Target lifts on the lowest strap, to ease the stove down the single, cracked cement step.

"What's going on?" Whit says.

"I can't feed them anymore." Jaime backs, turning the stove. "There's too many now, and more keep coming."

"I told you," Whit says, "I can buy them beans and rice. All they can eat."

"And onions," Jaime grunts. "No. And you don't mean them, you mean me. And you know I can't accept that." He lines the stove up at the foot of the ramp. Target crouches to push on the stove bottom and makes a disgusted sound and jerks away his hands. He looks at them. They are streaked with yellow-black grease. Whit moves to help.

"It's okay," Jaime says. "You'll just get filthy."

He doesn't mind getting filthy for Jaime. He puts his hands on the stove bottom. The edge is almost sharp. With a grimace and a shrug of his wide girl shoulders, Target sighs and leans his weight into pushing. Jaime heaves. The wheels turn. The stove goes up the planks. Whit's soles are slick and he falls to a knee but Target is strong and holds the stove in place and they get it up onto the truck bed. Jaime turns it again, and shoves it into place beside the refrigerator, and unstraps it from the dolly.

Whit and Target watch, holding greasy hands away from their clothes. Jaime straps the dolly upright to the truck stakes.

"Did you hear about Tim Connaught?" Target asks.

Jaime edges past them and goes down the ramp. "Come on."

They go down the ramp, Whit's shoes skidding again, so he almost falls. "What about him?"

"I wish you wouldn't talk so much." Jaime lifts the planks and slides them onto the truck bed. "Do you think he wants everybody to know?" The tailgate of the truck leans against the back wall of the shop, on whose grimy brick someone has spray-painted crookedly in white, FUCK AMERIKA. Jaime lifts the tailgate and sets it in place. He gives it a shake to be sure it is set in its holes. He turns, brushing his hands together. He tells Whit, "He'll be back."

In the washroom are a laundry set tub and a toilet. In the high, wired-glass window stands a jar of Vaseline, a can of toothpowder, a can of shaving cream. A razor lies beside the can, a toothbrush with scrubbed-down bristles. A can of Band-Aids has specks of rust on it. At the set tub, Whit and Target try to wash the grease off their hands. It isn't easy because the water is cold and the soap isn't strong. There is only a dirt-veined sliver of it. They pass it back and forth between then. Jaime is out in the front room of the shop trying to help a gray-haired woman with a little dog decide which of the hanging plants to buy.

"Where did Connaught go?" Whit asks.

"The cracker factory," Target says. "He stood out there all day." He jerks his head at the big white room. "In a corner. Just stood there. Never moved. Talk to him, he didn't answer. Most of the time, he wouldn't even look at you." He shivers. "Jaime finally called his parents and they came and got him. It's happened to him before. They put him in some hospital, and after while he's all right again. Catatonia? Catalepsy? I don't know." Target studies his dripping hands. "It's not working," he says.

"What do we dry off with?" Whit says. And when Target

brings a roll of paper towels, he says, "It's part of schizophrenia. The other part is violence."

"Scary," Target says. "The way they look at you sometimes. Out of the corner of their eyes." Target demonstrates. "Like they don't know who you are, but they want to kill you."

Blue Sky appears at the open washroom door. Her small blue coveralls are clean, her hair has been washed, combed, braided. She asks Whit, "Did you know kittens come in little plastic envelopes?"

"The kittens were born," Target says. "Couple nights ago. Jaime was up till four, delivering them. You know where she had them? In the carton with the kitchen stuff, on top of the refrigerator."

"They came out in little plastic wrappers," Blue Sky says. "There's four. I get the spotty one for me." She takes Whit's hand and tugs. "Come see."

He didn't know they were for sale—the ferns, ivy, philodendrons. Gummed yellow price tags peel off the bottoms of the redwood planters they hang in. But until yesterday, he thought Jaime had simply not bothered to remove the tags when he brought the plants here from the nursery. It has helped him make up his mind to stand plants along the rail of his deck. It will be good to see living green when he looks out. It will be like being back in the shack in the canyon. Not much, but a little. He will hang plants so they are in front of his eyes when he looks up from the typewriter—if he ever sits at the typewriter again.

The sound of music comes from a radio or phonograph on the gallery. Feet thump, making the low ceiling boards of the front room creak. Target must be practicing up there. Whit counts the plants. There are fewer than there seem to be when he has to dodge them to move around in here. Seven. Not enough. But Jaime will get more when Whit takes these away, and Whit will buy those too. He is pleased at the chance to buy something from Jaime. He has no use for beads, slogan belt

151

buckles, ocarinas. The hookahs are garish. The books are junk. Abby called the brown pottery jars beautiful the night he broke one on purpose, so Whit can't buy any of those, though he too thinks they are beautiful. He can buy plants.

The overhead music grows louder. The tempo picks up. The feet thump faster. Dust filters down from the cracks between the ceiling boards. It sparkles and drifts in the morning sunlight through the big window. He coughs and steps through the glass-bead curtain. Water drops have made a trail the length of the big back room, which looks bigger and blanker now that the stove and refrigerator are gone. The water drops go up the stairs to the gallery. Damp footprints. A girl chants to the music. Is it chanting? He raises his head. He knows the voice—it belongs to Carol, the plump girl who draws. But she is not chanting. She is loudly asking someone to watch her. The words come out jerkily because dancing is making her pant. Her voice vibrates with the drumming of her feet. But it is shrill, and he can make out the words.

"See me?" she says. "I'm naked. Aren't I pretty? Look at me, Jaime. See? I can dance too. Target's not the only one. Look at me, Jaime, watch. See what I'm doing?"

The music stops. In the middle of a phrase. The silence is startling. A thud follows. The girl says, "Please, Jaime? Let me in? I'm naked for you, Jaime. Aren't I pretty? Love me? Oh, look. Ooh! Let me—" Another thump. "No, wait. Please!" There isn't a dance now, there is a scuffle. The girl squeals. "Don't, Jaime. Jaime, I love you." She appears at the top of the stairs, wet, struggling. Her body is firm puppy fat under smooth, creamy skin, pink cheeks, pink mouth, pink nipples. Jaime has hold of her from behind. He wears undershorts gray and limp from too many washings. He lifts her ahead of him, trying to wrestle her off the gallery, down the stairs. He hasn't spoken, but he is plainly disgusted and embarrassed, and has just waked up. He sees Whit standing at the foot of the stairs and he stops.

"Ah, no. God damn it," he says to Carol. "You see? You see what your craziness has done?" He gives her an angry shove.

She clutches wildly for the rail, catches it, doesn't fall. Her wet hair is over her face. She sobs and pushes at it. Jaime tells her, "Go get your clothes on, will you, please?" He goes back out of sight onto the gallery, and Carol, trying to cover her breasts with one hand, her crotch with the other, comes quickly down the stairs. She doesn't look at Whit. She dodges past him, making a little shamed sound, and runs for the washroom, scattering water drops. Above each of her buttocks is a dimple. The washroom door slams. From behind it come long, keening wails. Jaime shouts, "Shut up!" and comes into view again, zipping up his worn corduroys. The wails turn to sobs that sound as if she is doing her best to stifle them. Jaime comes down the stairs, thumping them hard with his bare heels. He is pale and his mouth is set in a thin line.

"She must have been washing herself in there, and turned herself on," he says. "I was asleep. I didn't know." His laugh is short and sour. "They never understand, do they?"

"Not if you don't tell them," Whit says. "I thought you were open for business. The door was unlocked."

"One of the kids." Jaime puts fingertips to his eyes, rubs, draws the fingertips slowly down his face. He lets his hands fall, yawns a little, smiles. "What kind of business?"

Whit gestures. "I want to buy your plants."

Jaime tilts his head. The brown eyes study Whit. "You mean you want me to accept money from you."

Whit sighs. "You've got them. I want them. They're for sale. What's the matter with my money?"

"They're way overpriced," Jaime says. "You can get them forty percent cheaper at any nursery."

"All right," Whit says. "You've told me. I still want to buy them from you."

Jaime explains. Patiently. As to a child. "It would make me uncomfortable. Doesn't that matter to you?"

Whit laughs hopelessly. Carol comes out of the washroom. The floor-length dress she has put on is a red-and-yellow flower print, with double ruffles. Maybe she has dried herself, maybe not. She hasn't dried her hair. Or combed it. It hangs wet and

Book

A straggle of little winking Christmas bulbs hangs off the roof edge of a hot-dog stand whose window opens a yellow mouth at the late cold night on a corner across from the far side of the park. Whit has left the Mercedes near this corner. The stand breathes hot grease and onion smells into the fumes of the passing traffic. Hunched on a tall stool at the counter, the silent Texan in his weathered Levi's, Stetson pushed back on his straw hair, moodily chews French fries. Beside him, the tangle-bearded man and his stunned girl friend pass back and forth a tin saltshaker. McGriff, the gangly black poet, catches Whit's sleeve. He is cinched up in a new camel's hair overcoat, broad-shouldered, narrow-waisted. His wide brim hat is new, fuzzy, camel's hair color. Whit glimpses a pink shirt collar with long points, and the fist-size knot of a red-orange-yellow paisley tie. McGriff grins.

"Hey, man, don't you get tired of standing in line?"

The stool next to his is empty, a split in its grimy plastic cushion showing crumbled, dried-out foam rubber. Whit hikes himself up on it. He hates and fears that empty apartment after the poetry nights. He has worked his mind too hard, trying to heal too many poems, lame, halt, blind. His mind won't stop. He can't sleep. He doesn't want to drink. From a Mexican counter boy, he orders a hamburger and a milk shake. He isn't hungry, but Jaime keeps after him to eat. Jaime won't see him now, but when Whit reports next time, he won't have to lie. He asks McGriff, "What line?"

"The line we all in," McGriff says. "You and me and him." He nods toward the Texan. "And the piggie girl, and the old lady in black, and the butterfly-song cat, and the little nancy boy you wind up and he dances." McGriff's long, lean fingers, the nails pink and big as Christmas bulbs, hold a chili dog half-eaten, wrapped in orange-stained layers of paper napkin. He bites the chili dog, and says with his mouth full, "And little Rumpelstiltskin." He laughs. He chews, swallows, gulps down Coke from a big bottle. He frowns. "Come on, man. You know what line I'm talking about."

"I don't," Whit says, "but it makes a good poem."

"The line to get it on with Jaime," McGriff says.

"No," Whit says, "I don't get tired." McGriff would have had to be blind and deaf not to have noticed. But Whit is angry with him for talking about it. Whit has ignored it, made believe to himself that it didn't count. It is tough enough to fight Jaime. He doesn't want to think about fighting a crowd. The counter boy has a little gold bead in the lobe of one ear. He sets a tall, thick glass in front of Whit, and pours into it, from a frosty metal vessel, the milk shake, thick, lumpy, unnaturally white. Whit has a hard time imagining that he is going to drink that. He gives McGriff a glum smile. "Tell me—in that line, what place am I in?"

"I don't know." McGriff stuffs his mouth with the last bite of chili dog, and crushes the stained napkins into a ball that he drops into the little red plastic basket the chili dog came in. He plucks from a shiny counter dispenser fresh napkins, wipes his fingers, wipes his mouth. He swallows again. He drinks more Coke. He grins again. "But I know what place I am going to be in. I am going to be in place number one. Head of the line. Have you got a cigarette?"

McGriff never has cigarettes of his own. When Jaime served rice and beans, McGriff ate them with the ragamuffins. He

156

owns no car. He never takes buses. He walks where he goes. God knows where he sleeps. Every dime he earns he spends on clothes. He is cheerful about it. It is how he wants things to be. This shows up in his poems that he reads aloud from a grubby two-bit notebook where he writes them in pencil—pencils never new, always about an inch long. Women, grandmothers, teenagers, middle-aged, black, white, Latin, Japanese, love his wardrobe. He is a male lyrebird. The female lyrebirds screech at each other, peck each other's eyes, scratch each other's feathers out, to get to nest with him. Unless the poems are lies. Never in any of them has Whit heard a hint of homosexuality. He gives McGriff a cigarette.

"How are you going to manage that?" he says.

McGriff raises his shoulders and cups the little flame of a paper match with his pink-palmed hands to keep the wind from blowing it out. He drops the match and exhales smoke. "I am going to offer to typeset a book of poems for him. A book of poems is what he wants most in this world. Then I will hustle a paste-up man and a good printer who will work for strokes and strokes alone. I can do it. Publications people are in and out of where I work every day. I will charm a brother or sister with my wit and charisma. Or I will Uncle Tom my way, chuckling and shuffling, with a rag on my head, into the good graces of a member of the ruling white minority. Whatever it takes, I will get Jaime de Santos the most beautiful book since the Gutenberg Bible."

"And out of gratitude," Whit says, "he'll go with you?"

"And come with me," McGriff says. "We will bang together like sweet cymbals, man. And once he has banged with Andy McGriff, he will never want to bang with nobody else—not for the rest of his natural life."

One of the little red plastic baskets appears in front of Whit. A hamburger lies in it, neatly wrapped. Whit unwraps it and takes a big bite. Suddenly he is exhilarated, and it has made him hungry. McGriff is making a mistake. Whit takes a long swallow of the cold, thick milk shake. The sweetness mingles oddly but familiarly with the fried meat, onion, pickle taste of the hamburger. He swallows and says, "You may be right, that what he wants most is a book of poems, but what he wants least is to owe anybody anything. He's terrified they'll ask in return exactly what you plan to ask."

"And more terrified that he'll say yes." McGriff nods, annoyed, impatient. "I know that. You think I'm stupid? I learned the Bible at my mama's knee. I am as gentle as a dove and as cunning as a serpent. I am not some crazy nigger that can only use his head to knock people down on a football field. I have a plan—and the reason why I have waylaid you tonight is because you are going to help me with my plan."

Whit laughs. "And wreck my own chances?" He takes another big bite of the hamburger, and makes mush of it with a mouthful of milk shake. He wags his head in wonder. He is having a good time. "You really have got balls. You must think it's me that's stupid."

"What I think is, you don't have any chances to wreck." McGriff looks serious. "You never had a chance—not from the minute he found out who you are, what you've done. He thinks you are some kind of god, man. He is in awe of you. He worships you. You aren't flesh and blood. And if you aren't flesh and blood, what is there to go to bed with? Nobody goes to bed with a god."

Whit laughs again. "Jupiter did all right."

"Yeah, you think I am jiving you," McGriff says, "but you never heard him talk about you when you weren't there. He thinks you're better than Ginsberg, better than Kerouac. He wants that book, but not till you say it's a good idea."

Whit reaches past him for a napkin. It tears coming out of the dispenser. He wipes his mouth, chin, and fingers. McGriff is holding the burnt-down cigarette between thumbnail and fingernail to suck the last smoke out of it. Whit lays down the napkin and picks up the hamburger again. The wind blows the napkin away. "And my part in your plan is to say, 'Go ahead and do the book'?"

McGriff turns to him, still sucking the cigarette stub. His eyes are wide. "Will you?" he says, burns his lip, flings the cigarette stub away, and rubs his lip with a finger, while the smoke leaks out his nose. He coughs. "Will you?" He sounds and looks as if he can't believe his luck.

"Anything for a friend," Whit says.

McGriff's smile is dazzling. "Hey, man! Out of sight!" He jumps off his stool, embraces Whit, touches Whit's face with his face, this side, that side, like a French general. He is wearing a strong cologne. He stands back, holding Whit's shoulders, eyes glistening in the Christmas lights, red, blue, green. "You know, he's right? You are some kind of god."

McGriff goes off up the street, chuckling, snapping his fingers, wriggling his shoulders inside the expensive coat, and taking fancy steps in his alligator shoes, steps that are a dance and not a walk at all.

It is morning, but morning is running out. He glances in panic at his watch again. He sits in the workroom with the television set and typewriter and filing cabinet, sits at a new drafting table, in the cold light of an expensive new armatured fluorescent draftsman's lamp, and with a new T-square and new triangle of thick green plastic, lines up corners on tagboard. He makes neat tick marks with a new blue pencil sharpened in a new electric sharpener. Using a new steel ruler, he draws light lines with the blue pencil. With the keen new blade of a shiny X-acto knife, he cuts cleanly from the sensitized paper on which they are crisply printed, the poems that McGriff has typeset.

McGriff is angry at him, and has set the type only because there was no way out of it. The Wednesday night after their talk at the hot-dog stand, Jaime announced, in the candle gloom of the gallery, where a battered, secondhand electric heater rattled its fan blades and growled and warmed nobody, that it was time to do a book of poems, that McGriff had volunteered to do the typesetting free, and that Whit Miller would do the paste-up free. The only money needed would be to pay a printer, and everyone must chip in what they could.

They must all turn in to Jaime their best work so he could choose what would go into the book.

From his dark corner, McGriff popped his eyes at Whit. He made ferocious cutting motions with his hands. He mouthed threats and dirty words. He did these things only when Jaime was looking the other way. Whit told himself McGriff was playacting. McGriff wouldn't hurt anybody. McGriff was a five-year-old girl dressed up as a pimp. All the same, Whit hung around late, talking to the excited Jaime, until Jaime's eyes began to fall shut. And when at last Whit did leave, he was nervous, walking to his car. He had parked it far up the block, where big oleander bushes were shaggy and cast dark shadows. Sure enough, McGriff stepped out of the shadows. He came close, and Whit wondered about the hand he kept deep in one pocket of the camel's hair coat.

"I am going to cut you up fine," McGriff said. "You are a little old for it, but the meat will be white, and I am going to make chicken à la king out of you."

"It wasn't me," Whit said. "It was Jaime."

"You never wanted that book at all," McGriff said. "You think all the stuff we write is garbage. I knew that. I was a fool not to see where you were coming from, agreeing with me so easy. You knew I told you right—that you didn't stand a chance with him. And if you didn't stand a chance, then you were going to fix it so I didn't stand a chance, either."

"You're wrong," Whit said. "I'm not that way."

"Then how come you didn't tell me you knew paste-up?"

"I forgot. I only did it one time after I left school. I was never very good at it. I barely passed. It was required. Publications department." Whit held on hard to the car keys in his pocket. The edges dug into his fingers. "Jaime suggested it. I can't even remember when I told him I knew how. I said no, you wanted to handle the whole book." Whit started to take a step, and McGriff drew the hand out of the pocket. A knife blade clicked open. Whit swallowed and said faintly, "He wouldn't agree to that."

"You are a liar," McGriff said, "and you are not going

160

anyplace. You are going to stay right here. Piled up in sections."

"I warned you how he was," Whit said. "You told me you knew. I can't help it if your plan was transparent. He knows what you want from him. He's not stupid, either."

A car swung in at an apartment house driveway up the street. The headlight beams flashed over them on the sidewalk. The blade of McGriff's knife gleamed. The car stopped. One of its doors opened and someone called out. Someone came running down the walk. It was Target. For a second, Whit couldn't figure out what was wrong with the way he looked. Then he saw that the boy wore thick stage makeup. Beyond him, the engine of the car quit. A man in a suit got out the driver's door and stood craning to see. With big, black-edged eyes, Target stared at the knife, at McGriff, at Whit.

"Are you all right? What's going on?"

"I can cut you up too," McGriff said.

"That's my father watching you," Target said. "What are you, crazy or something?"

McGriff put the knife away and walked off down the street. Before he reached the shop, he cut across to the park and disappeared into the shadows of the trees.

"Where did you come from?" Whit asked Target.

"I live there," Target said. "My dad just picked me up. I danced tonight. Why did he want to hurt you?"

The man by the car shouted, "Come on, Sis."

"Why does he call you names?" Whit said.

"He doesn't like me," Target said. "But I guess it's okay. I don't like him either."

Whit looks at his watch again. He is worried about time because he has invited Jaime to approve the paste-up and to eat lunch with him. He is as bad as McGriff. He can't help thinking Jaime will get into bed with him when he sees the beauty of the book. Especially after a fancy lunch with a lot of good wine. He was surprised when Jaime agreed to come. That agreement he has made much of to himself. As he made much of Jaime's coming here that midnight. These actions on Jaime's

161

part are signals that he knows Whit exists, that he cares that Whit exists. He sneers at himself for getting excited over nothing. Hell, Jaime wouldn't even let him come pick him up.

"You haven't got a car."

"I'll get there, don't worry."

Whit brushes rubber cement on the big tagboard sheet and lays the last of the poems carefully in place. He smooths it down, using a clean handkerchief so there won't be finger smudges. He touches the edges of the three other poems on the board with the handkerchief, to rub away any leftover rubber cement. He gets off the new stool, tears off a length of waxed paper, lays it across the stacked paste-ups on the filing cabinet, then lays the final paste-up on top. Rubber cement has stuck to his fingers. He rubs at them and smiles at the tidily piled sheets of tagboard. He didn't think he could be so neat and accurate. His instructor at Cordova Junior College would be pleased with him—startled but pleased. Whit is pleased with himself. The doorbell rings.

His heart begins to beat fast. He goes and opens the door. He is wearing a grin. It falls off. Jaime has come, all right, in denim shorts, sandals, faded red T-shirt because, though it will soon be Christmas, it is warm. He looks fine, and smells as if he has just had a shower. What is wrong is that he is not alone. Abby Selzer is with him. In lederhosen. His spindly legs are the color and texture of beef jerky. Whit wants to push him off the walkway. He wants at least to say he is not welcome. But Abby darts past him and stands like McGriff's Rumpelstiltskin, that evil gnome, in the middle of the wide new tawny carpet and the wash of Spanish guitar music that Whit has carefully put on tape in Jaime's honor. The music sours itself, touching Abby. He turns, grinning at the room.

"How very nouveau riche," he says, and flings himself, like the shriveled corpse of a child long dead, onto the big soft brown velvet couches arranged in an open square. The couches came with the place. Whit didn't choose them. He was too drunk even to think of rejecting them. He wanted a place to sleep in out of the weather. He saw a VACANCY sign. Vacancy

162

was what he rented. He doesn't say so. He doesn't owe Abby Selzer explanations. Abby rolls on the couches. "Sexy." He laughs. "Sears Roebuck's very finest, I'm sure." He bounds to his feet, puts an arm around Whit, squeezing, chuckling. "You understand, I am only joking." He looks at the walls and his eyebrows go up. "No pictures? Uncertain about our taste, are we? Let me think. What would be most fitting. Having read your book—ah, I have it." A snap of the fingers. "Norman Rockwell, of course." He dances in front of Whit, laughing up at him. "Am I not right?"

Over his Alpine hat with its little brush, Whit tells Jaime, "I invited you to lunch. You."

"He needed a ride," Abby says. "I happened to be there." He goes out on the deck and looks down at the swimming pool that is noisy with kids because this the first warm day in many weeks.

"I offered you a ride," Whit tells Jaime.

"I couldn't help it." Jaime tries to look ashamed but his mouth twitches as if he wants to giggle. "I told him I had to go somewhere, and he wouldn't let me walk, he had to take me in his car. I couldn't shake him off. You know how he is. Look, I'm sorry." But Whit is looking, and Jaime is not sorry. He thinks it is a joke.

"I don't like him," Whit says. "You know that."

"He's an old friend," Jaime says. It is a warning.

Abby has gone into the kitchen and is peering into the oven. "Ah, a casserole. So, there is enough for all." He closes the oven door. "I was about to offer to run out for a bucket of Kentucky Fried Chicken. That would be your choice, I expect, your level of gastronomic sophistication? So thoroughly American." He winks across the breakfast bar. "I am joking, of course." He touches the candles, the place settings. "Who guided your choice of dinnerware? *Good Housekeeping*?"

Jaime says, "The food smells wonderful. I like the music. Can I see the book?"

"In a minute." Whit wants a drink. He goes into the kitchen. He mixed martinis early. He takes glasses with frost on them

163

out of the freezer. Olives on sticks are on a saucer. He pours two drinks and puts back the pitcher. He means to ignore Abby, but Abby is too quick for him. Abby picks up both glasses, hands one to Jaime, and drinks out of the other. Whit wonders how he'll get that one clean.

"Delicious," Abby says. "How happy I am that I stopped by the shop today." He winks at Jaime. "Imagine having missed this. How kind of you"—he gives Whit a little bow—"to let me share it, at such short notice."

Whit chilled only two glasses. He gets another one off a cupboard shelf. Dusty. He rinses it. He hauls out the pitcher and fills the glass. Scowling. When he sets the pitcher back, he slams the refrigerator door. Abby looks at him with exaggerated surprise. "Ah, what have I done? I thought you were not drinking. Didn't you tell me you have an alcohol problem?"

Whit opens his mouth to shout but he closes it again. Jaime is watching him, Saint Francis protecting a toad. Whit gives him a feeble smile and drinks.

"Keeping that in mind," Abby says slyly, "I brought along something different." He digs out of a pocket a clear plastic envelope and waves it under Whit's nose. Jaime's eyes open wide. It is a lot of marijuana. "A splendid high, with no addictive or damaging side effects. I hope you will share it with me. I can offer so little, and you are so hospitable."

Whit says, "Get that out of here. Don't you know who gets busted for possession? The one whose house it's found in. If I want dope, I'll get my own. Take it outside. Put it in your car."

Abby's false teeth keep their taunting grin, but his eyes grow muddy, uncertain. He looks at Jaime. Jaime jerks his head. "Go on, Abby. He doesn't think it's funny." Abby goes. Jaime says, "I'm sorry. I didn't know he'd do that. He doesn't mean anything by it. He just doesn't know where to stop."

"You didn't need to bring a chaperone," Whit says. "I'm not going to rape you."

"Let's look at the book," Jaime says.

They look at the book. Whit clears space on the drafting table, and lays the tagboard paste-ups out one by one. They

164

look handsome in the white fluorescent light. Jaime smiles but he is worried.

"Why are they out of order? Those are upside down."

"They get photographed by fours," Whit says. "After they're folded and cut and bound, they'll be in order, and all of them will be right side up."

"Beautiful," Jaime says. "It's going to be a beautiful book, isn't it? Clean. I'm glad I didn't let Carol do illustrations. That would make it messy."

Whit lifts the stack of tagboard sheets back on top of the filing cabinet. He and Jaime sit in the swivel chairs and drink. They talk about General Hershey, and Katanga, and moon rockets. Polk comes in and walks around on the drafting table. He plays with the blue pencil. It rolls off the table and lands on the rug. Polk jumps down after it. He picks it up delicately in his mouth, rolls on his back, chews the point, kicks a little with his hind feet. Whit on hands and knees reaches under the table. He picks up Polk, who drops the pencil. He puts Polk out of the room and shuts the door.

"What are you writing?" Jaime looks at the typewriter.

"I'm not." Whit sits down again. "When you come here to live with me, I'll write." He thinks he hears a thump in the bedroom. He opens the workroom door a crack. He worries that he has left the bedroom door open. He doesn't trust Polk in there, not when the bed is made. Polk likes to unmake it. But the bedroom door is shut. Whit sits down again. "If you'd sell me plants," he says, "I'd hang a couple right there, between the typewriter and the window."

"I wonder where Abby went," Jaime says.

They have second drinks, and then Whit's watch says it is time to take the casserole out of the oven. He leads Jaime to the kitchen and sits him on a white wicker chair and mixes salad dressing—olive oil, tarragon vinegar, herbs. He gets out chilled little wooden bowls of chopped lettuce and tomato and pours on the dressing. Above the squeals and splashes from the swimming pool, a woman's voice calls harshly, "Brian!" Whit has already loosened the cork of the slim, pale green bottle of expensive Liebfraumilch he has been chilling. He sets the salad bowls on the table, takes the cork out, fills the wine glasses. Jaime puts his olive in his teeth, pulls the toothpick out of it, puts the toothpick back in the martini glass, chews the olive. The woman calls Brian again, and adds, "God damn it!" Jaime gets to his feet.

"This is a big place," he says. "Maybe Abby couldn't find his way back. Maybe he didn't notice the door number."

"He can ask the manager," Whit says. But Jaime crosses the living room, steps out on the deck, looks down at the pool. Whit says, "If you go after him, the food will get cold."

"I'll be right back." Jaime pulls open the door, and a woman is standing there. She is the shrill-voiced one with the floozy yellow hair, who is the mother of the teenage Picasso acrobat. She is forty and her slacks are too tight. She comes storming in on flimsy gold spike-heel sandals. She wears big sunglasses. Her mouth is painted white. It writhes.

"Where's Brian? Where's my kid? What's he doing here?"

Jaime is so startled he hasn't shut the door. From downstairs in the echoing breezeway with the flowers come children's voices, shrill. "That's where he went. That's where Brian went. That's where the man took him." Whit comes fast out of the kitchen. He switches off the guitar music. He tells Jaime to shut the door. Jaime shuts the door, and the child voices fade a little. The woman stalks around the room. A blue bruise is on one bare ankle, where there is also a small silver chain. "Where is he? What have you done with my kid?" She gives that fish-hawk cry of hers. "Brian!"

Whit says, "There's no one here but us."

"Don't lie to me," she says. "My kid is missing. Those kids say an old man was talking to him by the pool, an old man in funny pants." She smells of gin. Her diction is slurred. "He had something in an envelope. He showed it to Brian. Then he led him up here to this apartment."

"Oh, shit," Jaime whispers. His brown spaniel eyes look at Whit, dismal and filled with guilt. "Abby."

Whit is already in motion. He flings open the bathroom

door. Mirrors. Jaime collides with him. They both lunge for the bedroom door. Jaime's nails scratch Whit's hand as they both grab for the catch. The boy is hopping around, trying to get into the little blue swim trunks. Abby is trying to climb out one of the high row of aluminum-framed sliding windows. He kicks. The lamp on the chest of drawers crashes. Whit tells the boy to go to his mother, and he grabs Abby's legs and drags him down. Abby bangs elbows and ribs. He yelps and lands in a heap on the floor. Whit jerks him to his feet. The woman is in the doorway. "Brian!" But the boy doesn't go to her. He scrambles across the bed to the far side. In the process, he loses the little trunks. They lie on the rug. He slides open a closet door, takes his twinkling little ass inside, shuts the door. The woman snatches up the trunks. She glares at the cowering Abby.

"You pervert," she says. "You rotten, wrinkled, filthy old pervert." She sniffs the air. A handmade cigarette smolders in an ashtray where lie the smoked-down butts of two more hand-made cigarettes. She picks up the ashtray and hurls it at Abby. Her hoop earrings swing wildly. The ashtray is thick green Mexican glass. It strikes the wall, ricochets, and thumps Abby between the shoulder blades. He winces and staggers as if he is killed. "Marijuana!" the woman says. "You gave my kid marijuana. You took the pants off my kid. You—"

"He took them off himself," Abby says. "Eagerly."

"Oh, God." Jaime groans. "Shut up, Abby. Just this one time, will you please shut up?" Tears start down his face. "Look what you've done. Just look what you've done."

"My kid!" The woman throws herself at Abby. Her nails are painted the same silvery white as her lips. They are long nails and they look sharp. She aims them at Abby's eyes. Whit catches her wrists. She kicks him hard in the ankle, but he wrestles her back. He wrestles her out into the hallway.

"Come on, now," he tells her. "Calm down. Everything's going to be all right. Nobody's hurt. We'll straighten the whole thing out."

" 'Calm down'! 'Nobody's hurt'? This could make a queer

167

out of him for life. Do you call that 'nobody's hurt'? This could make a dope fiend out of him for life. That beautiful little kid." But her adrenalin is lowering. She is drunker than before. Whit is relieved at that. He is relieved that her clothes don't come from some Beverly Hills boutique. They come off a rack at some cheap department store. Mainly, he is relieved that she has begun to cry. "Brian," she blubbers. "My little baby." She goes rubbery with crying. She lets him lead her to the workroom, sit her in a swivel chair.

"Take it easy," he says. "I'll get you a drink."

"Good God!" She flares one last time. "A drink! When the fucking world is coming to an end?"

"You're upset. I don't blame you. But it doesn't help. You sit tight. A drink will help." He shuts the workroom door after him. Jaime is in the hall, looking as if he doesn't know what to do. Whit pushes him backward into the bedroom. He points at Abby. "Get him out of here. Fast."

"But what if she—?" Jaime starts.

Whit says, "She won't. Get the kid into his pants and take him to the kitchen. Get him a soft drink and sit him down and talk to him."

Jaime clutches at him. "What do I say?"

"Tell him it's okay, not to be ashamed, it's not his fault. For Christ's sake, if you were thirteen, fourteen, what would you want somebody to say to you?"

Whit runs to the kitchen. Polk has taken an olive from the saucer and is batting it around the floor. Whit slops martini into the glass Abby abandoned. Jaime leads Abby to the front door. Abby looks stunned. Whit dodges them and hurries back to the workroom. She hasn't left the chair. She stares blankly at the blank TV screen. He puts the glass into her hand. She gulps down half the martini. Pushing sloppily at her hair, she glowers up at him. She hiccups.

"You're going to be sorry for this," she says. "What kind of weirdo are you, anyway? Friends like that—that—that warthog?"

"He's not a friend," Whit says.

She moons, rubbing the edge of the glass with a finger. A tear skids from under the dark glasses and drops into the martini. "Poor little kid. Father that doesn't give a damn about him. Mother alone, trying to provide for him. Edge of poverty." She says loudly, "Brian!" and tries to get up. The chair turns and almost spills her. Martini splashes her breast-bulging front. She stays in the chair and brushes at the splash. "Son of a bitch has to have lawyers after him all the time or he'd never pay. Goddamn lawyers bleed you white. What do they care you're a woman? What do they care you're a mother?" She throws back her head, drains the glass, holds it out, olive stick ticking on the rim. " 'Nother one, please?"

In the kitchen, Brian in his little blue trunks sits on one of the white wicker chairs, clutching a green can with a hole in its top. He is watching Polk jump stiff-legged at the olive that he has cornered by the refrigerator. The boy is trying not to smile, aware that this is a solemn moment, but he doesn't seem much involved. Jaime looks involved. He sits on another white wicker chair and stares at the boy. Whit empties the last drops of martini into the glass that has white lipstick on its rim. When Whit turns with the glass in his hand, Jaime looks desperate.

"I'm not a priest," he says.

"And he's not a sinner," Whit says, "so you're even."

When he gets back to the workroom, the woman says to him, "I'm going to put that old creep in jail for the rest of his life. My poor little kid." She is crying again.

"That would mean a trial," Whit says.

"He ought to have his balls cut off," she says.

Whit hands her the glass. "You're not thinking of Brian. He'd have to testify. All the details. Newspapers. Television. That's what would ruin his life. You can see that."

"Well, somebody's got to do something," she cries, and wipes her nose with the back of her hand. "It's not right. You're not trying to tell me it's right, are you? You're no pervert." She drinks, mumbling into her glass, "Not right, that's for damn sure." Her head jerks up. She drags off the dark glasses. Silvery white paint is over her eyes. One of her

Rings

Whit sees the damage from the park. The wide, arched window of the gallery is smashed out. Shattered glass lies on the sidewalk in front of the shop, glittering in the crisp morning sunlight. Passersby step around it. They step around Target, who is pushing at the glass with a wornout broom. He gets the glass into a loose heap, squats, very gingerly picks up big unsweepable pieces, and, holding them carefully so as not to cut himself, stands and drops them into a battered, galvanized trash barrel. Squatting again, managing the broom awkwardly, he pushes smaller pieces of glass onto a dustpan. When he stands and empties the dustpan into the barrel, the noise is loud. Whit waits between the bumpers of parked cars for a break in traffic, so he can cross the street and find out what has happened.

But before he can do that, a duffel bag comes flying out the shop door. And another. Sleeping bags. Red backpacks. Khaki backpacks. They bump like stuffed toys across the sidewalk, and end up against cars parked at the curb. The heavy ones lie leaden where they land. Walkers who want to pass stop and wait. A roll of strapped blankets flies out. Two more backpacks, one of them green. An old woman, in a straw hat whose brim she has folded over her ears and keeps there with a cerise ribbon tied in a floppy bow under her withered chin, halts a supermarket cart filled with brown sacks, starts to go again, stops. Two old men stare from a bus waiting bench. Jaime comes out of the shop wheeling a bicycle and leans it against the shop window. He doesn't look at the people, not even at Target, who keeps on cleaning up the broken glass. Jaime grimly piles the scattered bags against the bicycle.

The traffic eases off, and Whit jogs across the street. Jaime has gone back inside the shop. Whit asks Target what has happened, what is happening.

"Carol got wild and broke the window," Target says. He dumps another dustpan full of broken glass into the trash barrel. "She threw Jaime's radio through it."

"Wild about what?" Whit sees a jagged chunk of glass two feet long sticking up out of the gutter beside the front wheel of a parked car. He picks it up cautiously and lets it fall into the barrel. "Was she trying to get into the sack with him again?"

Target is crouching, pushing with the stub of broom at bits of glass so small that they catch in the cracks of the cement. "That was what it was really about," he says. "But it was the illustrations for the book that zapped her."

"He didn't want any illustrations," Whit says.

"Ouch," Target says, and sucks a finger.

"Here." Whit takes the broom from him. "You hold the dustpan, I'll sweep."

"He didn't tell her," Target says, examining his cut. "I don't know how she found out."

"I let it slip," Jaime says. He lays Tim Connaught's guitar on top of the stacked luggage. "Way back when the book was only a daydream, I was just talking, and I said she could do the illustrations. By the time you said we ought to do a book, and McGriff would set the type, and all that, I didn't think about it. Well, hell, yes, I did think about it, but I—"

"Didn't have the nerve to tell her," Target says.

"I don't like to say no to anybody," Jaime says.

Whit has nudged the last glass into the dustpan and Target gets up and dumps it into the barrel. As if Jaime hadn't spoken,

172

Target says, "And now it's everybody's fault but yours." He drops broom and dustpan into the barrel, picks up the barrel, and starts up the street with it, heading for the alley. "And you're throwing them all out—not just Carol, all of them."

"I'm going to love the quiet," Jaime calls after him. He watches the old woman push the shopping cart past, the rest of the walkers go by. He says almost to himself, "I'm going to love the peace. The privacy." He smiles at Whit. "My God, I can even go to the bathroom when I want. Every time I tried to jack off in there, somebody came knocking on the door."

Whit is jealous of Jaime's hand. He wants to rave. He wants to smash the downstairs window. He wants to die. Instead, he smiles and says, "Don't talk to me about your sex life, okay?"

"That's a sex life?" Jaime says.

Whit stares at him. Jaime turns his eyes away. Whit breathes in deeply. "The sun will ruin that guitar," he says.

"I don't care." Jaime is sulky. "I don't care what happens to any of their junk." He goes and kicks the heap. "I'm through worrying about them. They're irresponsible. Why should I be responsible for them?"

"I never thought you should." Whit takes down the guitar. "I'll keep it at my place," he says.

Laura Sailor crouches in her black shawls at the edge of the pond in the park. Ducks swim among tall reeds. She breaks dried bread that she has brought in a crumpled paper sack, and tosses the pieces to the ducks. They squabble for it. They are noisy feeders. They try to scramble up the short, sharp bank on their awkward yellow feet. She shoos them back, telling them to be fair and take turns. Whit stands beside her for a minute before she realizes he is there. She looks up.

"Why aren't you at the party?" he says.

"It's wrong," she says. "We're burning children with napalm every day over there. We're blowing their arms and legs off with bombs. We're killing them. We're killing their parents and they have nobody to look after them. They run the roads,

173

crying. They have nothing to eat. It's wrong. And I told Jaime so." She has broken up a lot of bread in her anger. Now she doesn't throw it to the ducks, she throws it at them. They swim in fast circles, gobbling. Their bills are egg-yolk color. Their feathers are very white, although the water looks unclean. A beer can floats in it, a Big Mac box, a condom. "He got angry at me, but I can't help it. Cookies and cake and candy." She hurls more bread at the ducks. "He may look like Jesus, but he's not Jesus. He's just as cruel and thoughtless as General Westmoreland."

"Where's Blue Sky?" Whit says.

"She's there. She's only a little child. I couldn't explain it to her. She wouldn't understand. Any more than they understand when their house burns down around them."

"Merry Christmas," Whit says.

Blue Sky and thirty other children, washed and dressed up, sit on the floor in the big back room and watch a magician turn a goldfish bowl with fish in it into a bird cage with a dove in it, turn the dove into a sash of colored scarves, the colored scarves into a torch on fire, the torch on fire back into a dove again that flutters on his hand. The eyes of the children are big with awe. So are Jaime's, who sits in the midst of them, clasping his knees. The magician is a plump young man with tightly curled pale hair and blue eyes that yearn at Jaime, while he keeps up a line of joky, poker-faced chat, and his dimpled hands link three big silver rings that chime, and unlink the rings again. Whit turns away.

The low table, the long bench, the oak table, are crowded with plates where lies the wreckage of Christmas cookies, and where glass jugs that have held apple and cranberry juice stand almost empty. Paper cups strew the floor, paper napkins. The black cloth that shut off the gallery from the white room has been taken down. Swags of dime-store Christmas green and silver loop the gallery rail, are twisted around the stair rail. Off nails hang plastic holly wreaths, bunches of gold plastic bells tied with red ribbon. The magician works near a big Christmas tree that glitters with ornaments and twinkling lights. Whit climbs to the gallery. The floor has been cleared. It is bright as never before. The tin folding chairs have been brought up here and set in a semicircle.

Now a man with a limp hauls a cello up the stairs. He is followed by two young women in glasses, shapeless dresses, lank hair, carrying violin cases and tubular cases. Out of the tubular cases come spidery music racks. The sheet music comes in the briefcase of the last of the quartet, a curly haired boy whose instrument case holds a viola. Downstairs, someone tries to play "Silent Night" on one of the fifty-cent bamboo flutes Jaime sells, gives up, begins improvising an Oriental melody, and a tambourine begins to slap and jingle. The musicians get their stands up and their sheet music on the stands and begin to tune strings. Whit goes downstairs again. Target with the tambourine is dancing in the front room, always just missing the hanging plants, among whose fronds are tucked today shiny little gold and silver balls.

The forlorn Texan is watching, the man with the tangled beard and his blank-eyed girl. And McGriff, in a new outfit, green right down to the shoes. He asks Whit:

"How come we haven't got our book yet?"

"Christmas is busy for printers," Whit says. "You know."

"I'm sorry I got mean with you," McGriff says. He holds up a limp sprig of mistletoe and kisses Whit on the mouth. "I can't be cool like you. He makes me crazy."

"The magician too," Whit says.

"Right," McGriff says, "and the crip who plays cello."

"I've seen him before," Whit says. "In a steam bath."

"There aren't that many of us," McGriff says. "By the time you're thirty, you've seen them all."

It is Jaime's birthday—number twenty-three. Whit wants to take him the book. The printers have promised it will be ready. He drives through steady rain to the big red brick plant in south Los Angeles so as to be there when the glass front doors open. But the book is not ready. It doesn't make any difference

175

what some switchboard girl told him when he called. The book has to be printed as part of a gang run—when enough little jobs like it have stacked up to make it worth gearing up the presses and they can all be run through at once. It might be next week, it might be the week after. It's the only way they can do the job at the cheap price they quoted. The man has black eyebrows and blue beard stubble. He says Whit is lucky they are printing the book at all, considering some of the words in it. They will telephone him when the book is ready.

Whit pushes a shiny cart up and down the bright aisles of a supermarket gathering eggs, cake flour, chocolate, butter, baking powder, milk, powdered sugar, shortening. If he can't take the book to Jaime, he will bake Jaime a birthday cake—a real cake, not something faked by the ton at a factory and boxed up on a production line. Wheeling the cart through the rain, through the puddles on the blacktop of the parking lot, he is pleased that he has remembered that the only cake Jaime likes is chocolate. The bag is wet by the time he reaches the car. It comes apart when he takes hold of it to shift it into the trunk. Nothing is broken. Boxes and wrappers aren't soaked through. The trot in the rain up to his apartment doesn't harm anything either. Panting, he checks his watch. If he works fast, there will be time. Four hours later, the kitchen is snowy with flour. Polk nudges and rattles chocolate-dripped bowls, pans, beaters, in the sink. With a yellow cellulose sponge, Whit mops slopped batter and frosting from floor and counters. But he has a cake. He bets he is more surprised than Jaime is going to be.

There is no space to park in when he gets to the shop. He tries the alley but that is parked up too. When it rains, people who never seem to use their cars use their cars. He keeps circling the park. At last he finds a place. It is on the far side of the park, but he doubts that he will do any better. He can't wait to find out. It is growing dark, and a birthday celebration ought to be a daytime thing. He has slid the cake, on its plate, into the carton that his record turntable came in. The carton is too roomy, but it has a slick finish he hopes will keep out the rain. He carries it at a fast walk through the park, where the trees hold the raindrops on their leaves, collecting a few before they let them fall, fat, wet, and cold.

He passes the gazebo where the naked bronze boy stands looking out. A voice calls his name. Laura Sailor sits in the gazebo with Blue Sky, who is bundled up in sweaters and holding her black-and-white-spotted kitten. Whit steps up into the gazebo. Black cloth bundles are piled around Laura's feet. She has a black woolen scarf tied over her hair. Mother and child look like subjects in an 1890s Ellis Island photograph. Immigrants. Or maybe a World War II photograph. Refugees. On paper napkins on the bench beside them lie the remains of sandwiches, two little paper milk cartons, one tipped over, and a crumpled potato-chip bag. Laura has been reading a paperback book. She pushes it into her carryall and takes off her glasses.

"Am I glad to see you," she says.

"What's happened?" Whit says. "Why are you out here?"

"I need a ride," Laura says. "To Van Meeren's. It's too far to walk and I don't have bus fare."

"Kittens don't like rain," Blue Sky says.

"But you're going to the shop, aren't you?" Laura says, staring at the turntable box. "It's his birthday. You're taking him a present."

"It's a cake," Whit says. "Why don't you come eat some?"

"He threw us out," Laura says. "This morning. We've been sitting here since nine-thirty."

"Threw you out? What for? Today? In the rain?"

"The baby died," Blue Sky says. "It got water in its lungs. Then you can't breathe and you die. It's called drownding."

Whit sets the box on the bench. "What baby?"

"My grandchild," she says. "A letter came. It drowned in the bathtub. The phone rang and Nicola went to answer it. She was only gone a moment, but it drowned."

"Dear God," Whit says.

Laura shrugs. "They're dying by the hundreds in Vietnam every day. Jaime wanted me to cry. I talked about the weather."

"He said it was our baby," Blue Sky says. "And now we'd never find out what it had to tell us, why it was born."

"I never saw him so angry." Laura's smile is wan. "He said I didn't care about the children in Vietnam. That I didn't care about anyone but myself. Is that true?"

"I'll drive you." Whit picks up the box. "Can you wait five minutes?"

"I can wait five hours," Laura says. "I've already proved that."

The shop door is locked. Whit peers through the rain-runny window. The striped cat and two of her kittens play in the front room. She lies on her side. The kittens hop over her. One attacks her tail fiercely. She lifts her head, eyes half closed, and looks at it. The other kitten comes near, she licks it twice, and it runs off into a corner chasing something only it can see. Whit told Jaime he would be here today. He props the turntable box against a hip and knocks on the door. Nothing. He knocks again, and calls out Jaime's name—loudly, because the hiss of tires on wet pavement is loud behind him. No answer. He fills his lungs and howls, rain running down his upturned face. "Jaime? It's Whit Miller." He hammers on the door. "Hey, let me in. It's wet out here." He waits, holding the clumsy box. He feels forgotten, foolish, and angry. "Jaime?" Nothing. He turns away. The door opens. Target stands there.

"Hi." He glances past Whit nervously, motions for Whit to come inside, and quickly shuts the door. The shop is dim and dead quiet and the smell of incense is strong. Target gives him a small, secretive smile. "Come on," he says, and rattles through the bead curtains, and climbs the stairs—lightly, as if merry music were going on inside his head. Whit follows, feeling heavy-footed. At the top of the stairs, Target stands aside, smiling, holding out a hand, like an usher. Unsure, a little wary, Whit steps past him.

Jaime sits cross-legged in the middle of the floor on the layers of little cheap rugs. A red and yellow cloth is tied around his hair. Swags of heavy beads hang around his neck. He wears no shirt, only ragged, faded denim shorts. Yoga fashion, his hands lie open, palms up, on his thighs. He sits inside a circle of papers, on each of them a multicolored circular design. The shop sells these in packages of six. Mandalas from India, to help in meditation, to help on drug trips. He looks up and gives Whit a beatific smile.

"Happy birthday," Whit says. "I baked you a cake."

From below, Target calls, "It better be chocolate."

"It's chocolate." Whit sets it on the floor, opens the end, slides the cake out. He carries it to Jaime and sets it down. Jaime is watching. The smile is still on his face. His eyes are wide open and glossy. Whit sits down to face him across the cake. He looks into Jaime's eyes and it is as if he is looking straight through. It isn't as if no one is in there. It is as if there is a landscape there, only he can't see it to describe it. All he can decide about it is that it is sunny and pleasant. He can't help smiling back at Jaime, and they sit there for a long minute, smiling at each other. Then Whit begins to notice a soft scuffing sound, slow, steady. He glances around. The light through the new windowpane is gray and turning dusky. But he makes out a phonograph. The table is turning. The stylus is in the end groove. "Your record's finished," he says, and starts to crawl toward it.

"Don't touch that," Jaime says. And when Whit looks at him in surprise, panic is in his eyes. "That's my contact with reality, man. That's all that keeps me here." He swallows as if he has just escaped accident or death. He smiles again but feebly. "It's my birthday," he says with a whispered laugh, half mischievous, half apologetic. "I thought I'd take a trip." He closes his eyes. "Mmm." He sighs and opens his eyes. The sunlit landscape is back. "Only you don't want to stop that." He nods at the record player. "That's where I'm coming back to. That's my radar." He touches the cake and licks frosting off his finger. "Wonderful," he says. "Thank you."

179

Whit leans across the cake, puts his hands on Jaime's shoulders, kisses Jaime on the mouth. He doesn't mean it to be a quick, friendly, happy-birthday-buddy kiss. He means it to be deep and urgent. And for a few seconds, Jaime lets it be that. Then he makes a little sound and turns his head away. "We better stop." He laughs softly. "We might be sorry."

"Not me," Whit says. His heart hammers. His cock is stiff. "I'd never be sorry."

"Target," Jaime calls. "Bring a knife. Let's cut this birthday cake."

He would like to show Jaime, but he is afraid McGriff is right, and Jaime would have an excuse to think of Whit as even less real. Dell. Her happiness for him would be genuine, and that would be too hard to take. Kenny—where is Kenny? So Whit gets down on the kitchen floor, where Polk eats breakfast, and tries to show him the jacket for his book. It is sleek and good-looking—no picture, just big, handsome lettering. His name is printed large. He can't think why. Nobody knows his name. Fake names were on his books for Brackett House, Golden Bough, and Ganymede, and almost no one read them anyway. But he does his best to feel pleased. Fate is trying clumsily to give him a happy day.

The fat man keeps telling him he must stop moping and start enjoying his success. The last time he said it was over eggnogs at his apartment Christmas day, where the muscle boy wore a gold lamé jumpsuit, and went around showing the Rolex watch Santa Claus had brought him to the crowd of fortyish lawyers, urologists, college English instructors, and their hairdresser, telephone-operator, menswear sales-clerk boyfriends. A department-store window decorator with henna bangs and a mournful nose had spray-painted and flocked white a ceiling-high blue spruce and infested it with hundreds of tiny artificial birds made of real feathers dyed bright red, blue, green, yellow. Above the relentless racket of a cocktail-bar pianist at the white baby grand in the corner, everyone cooed and chirped about the tree. And the fat man told Whit: "You'd better start smiling and meaning it. What the gods have given, they can take away, you know."

So now Whit grins and rattles the beautiful jacket at Polk, who gives it a quick, indifferent glance, and goes on eating. He appears to feel about the jacket-as-good-news the way Whit felt when the sharp jangle of the telephone jerked him out of sleep this morning when it wasn't yet daylight. He pawed out in the damp darkness, heart rattling in his chest, bumped his mouth with the receiver, and mumbled hoarsely into it. At the far end, in New York, chipper Elmer Post told him a star has been chosen for the film of his book and that right away a television network has paid hundreds of thousands of dollars for the right to show it two, three years from now. Whit's share will be hefty.

"What's his name?" Whit said.

Elmer told him and he sat up straight on the edge of the bed. He felt hit in the stomach. He also felt cold. The cold was real, and he took care of that by dropping the phone on the bed and getting into a sweater and corduroys, while Elmer called plaintively through the receiver, asking if he was still there, if he was all right, what was happening. Whit yelled at him that it was the crack of dawn, cold, rainy, and he was putting on clothes, and please to wait a fucking minute. He lit a cigarette and sat down and picked up the phone again. The actor's identity shocked him. The hero of the book is reedy, blond, quiet, sad, and thirty. The actor is swarthy, muscular, loud-mouthed, always laughing, and forty—at least forty.

Whit said into the phone, "Tell me you're joking."

Elmer wasn't joking. He knew the actor was wrong for the part but he was big box office, the biggest. His name on the marquee would mean profits astronomical. Whit hung up, stripped, and got under a hot shower. He tried to sing. None of it mattered. The book was what mattered. The book would go on for years. The movie would be forgotten. But he couldn't

181

sing. He felt bad. Nothing about the movie has been right. A month ago, two months, sometime, in a Beverly Hills restaurant with too much gilding, where waiters take telephones to the tables as often as they take food, the producer, an excitable little man with a hair transplant so new the roots looked angry, told Whit the book was beautiful, and that the now final script mirrored it exactly. The scriptwriter was there, sharing the Maine lobster—a sandy-haired, freckle-faced youth of sixty, and his every word made a liar of the producer. Whit dressed again, opened Polk's breakfast and forked it out of the can for him, and ran down barefoot in the rain to check his mailbox, where he found the envelope of jackets.

He props one of the jackets on the kitchen counter where he can see it while he brews coffee and starts sausages frying. Today he is determined to eat right. Until today he hasn't really believed he was going to have this book. But he believes the jacket—or comes close to believing. He feels both excited and scared. *You're a fine writer,* Dell says, *and the whole world is going to say so.* But maybe it won't. Maybe she was mistaken about him that way too. Reviewers never looked at his other books, or if they looked, they kept how they felt to themselves. Not only was his real name not on the other books—he wasn't standing naked inside them. The jacket will clothe this book, but it won't clothe him. Maybe the world won't love him. Maybe it will laugh. Maybe it will throw shit at him. He thinks he is a good writer. What if he is wrong? He cracks eggs into a bowl, and the door chimes ping. He turns down the fire under the sausages, and goes to open the door.

Tim Connaught says, "I came for my guitar." He wears a yellow rubber sou'wester hat and a yellow slicker. Tall, spare, broad-shouldered, he looks well, eyes clear and untroubled, creamy boy skin aglow with health. They left his shaggy white hair alone at the mental hospital. "Jaime says you rescued it for me."

"When he was throwing things out," Whit says, "everyone's stuff. I thought the weather would ruin it. I thought it would be ripped off. Come in."

182

Connaught comes in. "He can really be selfish."

Whit closes the door. "He can certainly be sudden. You want breakfast? Can I take your coat?"

Connaught sheds the sou'wester and the slicker. Whit hangs them to drip in the shower. He brings the guitar from where he has kept it, in the workroom closet. Connaught has poured a mug of coffee for himself and sits at the breakfast bar, warming his hands on the mug. "I already ate," he says, "but I'll drink some coffee with you." He lights a cigarette and watches Whit beat the eggs and pour them into the pan. He waits a while, then he says, "What excuse did he give you?"

"About what?" Whit breaks one of the sausages with the edge of a fork to see whether it is cooked. It is cooked. He forks the sausages onto a plate with the eggs and gets on the breakfast bar stool beside Connaught. "About not being able to love anyone? The same he gave you. He's grieving for the kid who OD'd at the beach."

"Did you believe him?" Connaught looks into Whit's eyes.

"Laura Sailor says he isn't sleeping with anybody. She's there day and night. Like you. Like Carol."

"She's gone," Connaught says. "I'm gone. Carol's gone. Everybody's gone. He threw everybody out." Whit eats but when he glances at Connaught again, Connaught is still staring hard at him. "Doesn't that mean anything to you?"

"Carol smashed a window. You got sick. The sleeping-bag kids were a drag. He decided Laura was a monster of detachment." Whit frowns. Connaught smiles at him with pity and contempt. Whit turns away, puts eggs and sausage into his mouth, chews, washes the food down with coffee, and says with annoyance he doesn't bother to mask, "What the hell are you getting at?"

"Who didn't get kicked out?" Connaught asks.

Whit frowns. "I don't know. Who?"

Connaught crushes out his cigarette. "Target."

Whit stares. "Target never lived at the shop. Target lives up the block, in an apartment with a father who calls him Sis. I don't know what his mother calls him."

"She doesn't call him very often." Connaught gets off the stool to pour himself more coffee. When he has filled his mug, he turns to look at Whit, glass coffee maker raised. Whit nods. Connaught slops coffee into Whit's mug and sets the maker back on the burner, where the flame is candle-size. "He's around that shop all the time." Connaught sits on his stool again. "Hadn't you noticed?"

"He's only a child." But Whit feels cold in his belly.

"He's old enough," Connaught says. "I went there this morning. To get my guitar. Front door was locked. Back door too. I climbed through the bathroom window. The guitar wasn't where I left it. I went upstairs. They were making it up there." He snorts. "Hung? You wouldn't believe me if I told you how that little kid is hung."

"Stop talking," Whit says. "Enough, okay?"

"That's why Jaime wanted everybody out," Connaught says. "So he could be alone to make it with Target."

Whit goes to the bathroom for the yellow raincoat and hat. He brings them back. "Take your guitar and go," he says.

Target

He reads his watch again. Ten-thirty. He sits in the dark
Mercedes across from the lighted shop. Rain runs down the
glass but he can see all right. Figures begin to move in the front
room. The door opens. Poets come out, tuck notebooks,
folders, under their coats, hunch their shoulders, scurry down
the wet sidewalk. Car doors slam. Whit starts the engine, lets
the parking brake go. McGriff stops in the doorway to say
something over his shoulder, then lowers his head in its
mail-order Irish tweed hat, and runs across the street. Water
explodes from under his shoes as if he ran through glass beads.
Whit taps the horn. McGriff stops so fast he skids and nearly
falls. He squints at the car, comes to the car, pulls open the
door, crouches, and looks inside.

"Come on," Whit says. "I'll drive you home."

"You got the books?" McGriff gets inside and slams the
door. He shakes rain off his fingers. "Whoo. Noah, where are
you when we need you?" He frowns. "How come you didn't
come to the poetry? No good without you."

Whit steers the car away from the curb. "Which way?"

"Right at Santa Monica," McGriff says. "I live over by
Westside College. You know where that is?"

Whit stops for a rain-blurred red light. "Where did you get your knife?"

"Some brother." McGriff cocks an eyebrow. "Why?"

Whit waits for the light to go green. He waits for two cars, then swings the Mercedes onto Santa Monica. There are still old streetcar tracks embedded here. The tires slip a little on them. He gets into the right-hand lane. "Could that brother get me a gun?"

"I don't remember who he was," McGriff says. "Have you got a cigarette?"

Whit hands him the pack. McGriff lights the cigarette, using the dashboard lighter. He hands back the pack. "What do you want with a gun?"

Whit puts the cigarettes back into the breast pocket of the calfskin jacket he has bought against the winter. From the inside pocket he takes five fifty-dollar bills, new and folded once. He glances away a second from the neon-smeared street to locate McGriff's near hand in the soft light from the leather-clad instrument panel. He turns the hand over and lays the bills in it and closes the fingers on the bills. He looks at the street again, beyond the batting wiper blades. "It doesn't have to be expensive," he says. "It just has to work. Don't tell the brother how much you've got. Keep what you don't have to spend."

They stop for another light. McGriff counts the money. Whit feels his surprised gaze without turning to face it. "What do you need with a gun? You don't have to hold up liquor stores. Here." He tries to give back the money.

Whit pushes his hand away. "I need it for protection. Spooks keep jumping out at me from the bushes, threatening to cut me up." He makes himself smile.

"You can buy it at a store. No trouble for somebody like you to get a permit. Turn here," McGriff says. "No—left, man, left."

Whit cuts across lanes to make the turn, and a horn honks angrily behind him. It is a street of old frame and stucco mansions turned rooming houses. Cars parked bumper to bumper under big dripping trees at the curbs make the going narrow. Old clunkers, new economy models, they are student cars. It is a student street. Lights are out in most of the houses, except for weak porch bulbs, piss-yellow through the rain. McGriff smokes, face against the window. One hand is on the door latch. He is tensed to jump out. He hums to himself.

"Somebody waiting for you?" Whit asks.

"A sociology major. She says she is studying me for her master's paper. In depth." McGriff chuckles. "She comes from deep delta country, and she had been itching to get it on with a black male all her life. Stop here." Whit stops. McGriff opens the door, jumps out, tosses the money onto the seat.

Whit grabs it, holds it out. "The gun," he says.

"Thanks for the ride," McGriff says, slams the door, and runs away through the rain.

Laura Sailor has brightened up. Gone are the black shawls. When she opens the door of Van Meeren's scabby stucco bungalow, in a double row of scabby stucco bungalows where lantana crowds the cracked center cement strip, she wears a white woolen poncho trimmed in reds and blues. Under it a white turtleneck sweater shows. Her trousers are red corduroy. The sagging screen door between them is grimy, but he can see these details and her smile. A typewriter clacks behind her in the room. She pushes open the door.

"Come in," she says. "Nice to see you."

Whit goes in. The room is small. A gas heater hisses. Overstuffed chairs are shrouded in worn bedspreads, but they still look as if springs would pierce your ass if you sat on them. Rickety bookcases overflow onto a floor where there is no rug. A barrel-shaped man sits at a secondhand desk by a window that streams with rain. The desk is heaped with books and papers, overflowing ashtrays, empty beer cans. The man stops typing and glares over his shoulder. He tells Laura for Christ's sake to close the door, that it is cold. His face is pockmarked and whisker-bristly. Over raveled sweaters, he wears an old

187

flannel bathrobe with cigarette burns and food stains. He grunts recognition of Whit, scrapes his chair back, and goes out through a kitchen swing door.

Laura says, "How are things at the Pipeline?"

"I don't go there anymore." Whit is studying Van Meeren's desk, wondering which drawer he keeps the gun in, the gun he has written poems about. He got the gun when a woman he had grown tired of and kicked out came back and tried to shoot him. In another poem, he writes about the five people he would like to kill with the remaining bullets in the cylinder— his father, his bookie, a queer who made a pass at him when he was young, and Whit forgets who the others are. He asks Laura, "How's Blue Sky?"

"She's in school," Laura says. "I hated to send her. There's so much stupid shit—the pledge of allegiance, all that. But I couldn't keep her cooped up here in the rain. What did Jaime do to you? He worships you. How could he throw you out?"

"He didn't. Does Van Meeren really own a gun?"

Laura gets off the arm of the bedspreaded chair and goes to the desk. She opens a drawer. She takes out a revolver. "He's an American, isn't he?" The thing looks heavy, the way she holds it, upside down, swinging off a finger by the trigger guard. It looks black and dangerous.

Van Meeren comes out of the kitchen, holding two cans of beer that foam from triangular holes punched in their tops. He hands one of the cans to Whit and tells him to sit down. To Laura, he says, "Put that away." And to Whit, "She's trying to quote one of my poems. She never gets them right. Claims to admire good writing, can't even remember it."

"I can quote it exactly." She lays the gun in the drawer and shuts the drawer. " 'Ask me about American civilization and I'll tell you: American civilization is a gun in the dresser drawer.' "

Van Meeren grunts and drops into the chair Laura left. Whit asks Laura if she doesn't want his beer. She shakes her head, murmurs something about apple juice, and disappears into the

188

kitchen. Whit sets his beer on the floor. He is not drinking at all now. He wants a very clear head.

"Next time she asks you to take her someplace," Van Meeren says, "don't bring her here." He sprawls in the chair, resting the beer can on his big belly, glowering at Whit over it. "That's some car you drive. Those are some clothes. To ask the Great American Question—what do you do?"

Whit nods at the typewriter. "Same like you."

"You must write shit," Van Meeren says. He drinks beer and belches. "Nobody who doesn't write shit makes that kind of money."

"The diplomatic corps lost a winner in you," Whit says. "You could have done a lot for world peace and understanding."

Van Meeren says, "She told me. A novel. You're the faggy one."

"That's me." Whit goes to the desk and takes out the gun. "May I borrow this?"

"Get your own," Van Meeren says. "We'll have a shootout on Hollywood Boulevard. Famous fag versus famous fucker." Whit points the gun at Van Meeren and Van Meeren looks pale, sits up straight, slops his beer. "Don't do that," he says. "It could go off."

As if in a film, Whit holds the gun up to check the cylinder and see that the empty chamber is where he won't shoot himself in the butt. Maybe he is in a film. He opens his jacket and tucks the revolver in his waistband at the back. He starts for the door. "I'll return it."

Van Meeren jumps up. He knocks the side of Whit's head with a hard, heavy blow of his fist. Whit staggers, stumbles over a stack of books on the floor. His shoulder strikes a bookcase. He is dizzy. His legs won't hold him. He falls down. Van Meeren grunts bending over him, grunts yanking the revolver out of his belt. He stamps off and drops the revolver back into its drawer. He knees the drawer shut with a bang. Laura stands in the kitchen doorway, holding a plastic bottle of apple juice, and cradling the spotted kitten in her arms. She tilts her head at Whit, who totters to his feet.

"Are you all right?" She doesn't sound alarmed.

"Cocksucker tried to steal my gun," Van Meeren says.

"I don't think he's himself," Laura says.

"I don't know who that is," Whit says, and leaves.

Whoever it is, he drives recklessly, climbs the wide, high curves of Barrymore Drive fast, and when the tires slur on the wet paving, only throttles harder. His knuckles are white on the leather-covered steering wheel, he is gripping it so hard. His teeth are clenched, the lips pulled back in a smile or a snarl. He set them that way and forgot them, and that it is raining does not prevent their feeling dry. He is in a terrible hurry. To be disappointed. He does not want to go on with this. He wants to be balked. But he is not going to be balked, is he? At the foot of the trail, in the shelter of big mountain holly bushes, where Frank and Helen Boulanger park their old green Cadillac, are only tire ruts filled with water. Frank and Helen have got work today—at Warner's, Universal, or MGM, seated in pews witnessing a wedding between stars, or laughing and holding drinks at a party, or sitting in period costumes on little velvet-covered chairs against flocked wallpaper at a ball. He is sorry.

And he can't stop. It was labor for the old Chevvy he and Dell owned to climb the trail. The Mercedes scrambles up it without strain. He noses the bumper against the flesh-color eucalyptus trunk and leaves the car. The path runs like a quick little river, as it always did. He splashes up it, keeping his footing by grabbing at the tilting white fence through which the leggy geraniums still poke their red crepe-paper faces. It is growing dark. In the house straight below, a watery yellow light goes on at a kitchen window. When he reaches the top of the path he does not look at his house and Dell's. Grabbing wet brush he hauls himself up to the ridge path. He runs along it, wet leaves slapping at him. Boulanger's small place crouches brown and forsaken-looking in the weeping dusk. He picks up a rock, breaks the glass in the door, reaches inside, and turns the lock. Standing in the familiar living room with the hand-built rock fireplace, the wing chairs, the slumping daybed under its tapa cloth in the corner, Frank's plates hanging on the wall, painted in Australian aborigine designs in black and terra cotta and white, he dislikes himself. That doesn't stop him. He wishes it would. He wishes something would.

He slides back the doors of the enormous wardrobe closet. Satins hang there, silks, laces, ghostly in the growing dark. He crouches and paws around under the hems of the garments, which smell of dry cleaning. Two hundred pairs of boots and shoes of every known period and of periods unknown. Drawers are below the closet. He pulls one open. Swords, daggers, caps, hats, spurs, medals on ribbons and in cases, pocket watches, lapel watches, cardboard boxes shapeless with age containing rings and necklaces, glass rubies, emeralds, diamonds, brooches, clips. He shuts the drawer and opens another. Rags darkly stained that smell of shoe polish, cans of shoe polish, shoe-polish bottles, shoe brushes. Spools of thread in different colors, needles in neat paper packets. Little bottles of spot remover, clothes brushes, rolls of cellophane sticky tape for getting lint off serge. Neat's-foot oil, oil-stained rags, steel rods, and guns.

His heart gives a bang against his ribs. For a second, he can't catch his breath. His fingers tremble above the guns. He picks up an automatic pistol, a big one. He peers at the maker's name, thinking he already knows it. He already knows it. Luger. He puts it down and picks up a black revolver like Van Meeren's. Colt. The cylinder is empty. He pushes the contents of the drawer around and smiles. Bullets in a little manufacturer's box. He takes one out, tries to slip it into the cylinder, and drops it. He lets it lie and tries another. It fits. He slips four more into place and clicks the cylinder closed. He shuts the drawer. He gets off his knees and shuts the closet. The costumes and props have destroyed his notion that he is in a film. This time he doesn't stick the revolver in at the back of his pants. He just drops it into a pocket of the calfskin jacket. On a basket chair by the door, he leaves ten dollars to pay for the broken glass. When he gets back to the car, he puts the gun into the glove compartment.

A tall truck with ribbed aluminum sides pulls away from the loading dock. Whit backs the Mercedes to make room for the truck to turn. Its double rear wheels go into a pothole and splash muddy water on the white hood of the Mercedes, and on the windshield. The wipers smear it. The truck lumbers off down the alley. Whit drives a short way after it, stops, reverses again, and backs up to the loading dock in the place the truck vacated. Trucks as big and bigger wait on each side of him. He feels closed in and menaced, and gets out of the Mercedes quickly. He also feels out of place and effete. But he turns the key in the trunk of the Mercedes and the lid lifts. A smell of new car comes out into the rain, a small rain now, almost lighthearted, the red light of the setting sun starting to break through. It matches his mood.

When he reached the apartment, the telephone was ringing. He was afraid it would be Elmer Post with more wonderful news about the film, but it was the girl at the printer's. Jaime's book was ready, McGriff's book, Laura's book, the book of the lanky Texan, the smoky-haired college kids, the man with the tangled beard. No—cross her heart and hope to die—it really was ready this time. She had been trying to get him on the phone since morning. He can pick it up at the loading dock by presenting the invoice. Before five o'clock. He had forgotten the book. He laughed, grabbed the invoice from the drafting table, and ran out of the apartment. Laura might say he is himself again. Maybe, though he is still scared by who he has been since Connaught came for his guitar. Now he keeps wondering how he is going to return the gun. But it makes him feel cheerful to be worrying about that. He has driven fast to

192

get here, through the rain and gathering dark. He checks his watch. He has just made it.

Loaders heave cartons and wheel heavy dollies on the dock, silhouettes against the wide, open doorway of the white fluorescent-lighted warehouse room behind them. He takes the invoice out of a pocket, unfolds it, waits to be noticed. He has glanced away, at a ragged old man rummaging in a trash bin, when he is noticed. A thickly built youth who looks part Oriental is squatting, reaching out a hand in a big work glove for the invoice. Whit holds it up. The boy takes it, goes in clumsy shoes into the yawning room, and comes back with a carton that he carries as if it weighed nothing. He sets it on the lip of the loading dock that is edged with thick plate steel to keep trucks from chipping it. He hands Whit back his own invoice and pushes at him a clipboard with a copy of the same invoice on it, and asks him to sign at the bottom. The rain smears the ball-point ink as Whit signs. The boy jumps down, slides the box off the dock, drops it into the trunk, and slams down the lid of the trunk.

"Thank you," Whit says.

"You got words in that book," the boy says, "I never even seen on toilet walls." He grins. "Everybody in the plant read it. People that never read a poem in their life." Laughing, he hikes himself back up onto the platform and picks up the clipboard with its mat of wet papers. "You know what I think? I think you got yourself a best-seller."

"If we advertise in toilets," Whit says, lifts a hand to the boy, and gets into the Mercedes out of the sifting rain. When he turns the key to start the engine, the radio starts too. Someone is playing Bach on a guitar. He drives off toward wide slashes of sunset light in the low, dark clouds over the low, dark hills, and hopes the music will keep on for a long time.

He doesn't want to take the books to Jaime at night. A picture has been in his mind from the start of how it will be. Morning, sunny, to fit with the smile Jaime will smile. Whit will

193

set the carton down beneath the skylight, and Jaime will open it there, in that shaft of sunlight. Whit knows how he will look, the rags he will be wearing, how his eyes will glisten, the pleased sound of his soft laughter. Whit wants it to be morning now. He keeps walking out on the deck to check the sky. The rain quits at seven. Wind follows it. By nine, the clouds have broken. By eleven, the sky is clear and full of stars. He doesn't want to see the TV weather report. He goes to bed, but he is too excited to sleep well. Polk complains at the way he thrashes around. He dreams.

Balloon-bellied Van Meeren is dancing in the park, wearing a big phallus made of a woman's stuffed stocking. It swings and flops. Whit wakes up. It is cold, and he puts on a T-shirt. He dreams again. Frank Boulanger is puttying glass into the frame of his front door. In the middle of the pane is a target. Whit wakes up. Polk, tired of being kicked and kneed, has curled up on the pillow. His whiskers tickle Whit, who rubs his nose hard and pushes Polk away. Whit turns over in bed. Laura Sailor writes in Oriental characters with lipstick on a men's room wall. It is the men's room of the Dragon Restaurant. Whit sighs and says aloud, "Shut up," and dreams again. Target dances in the park, naked from the waist down. His real penis is as big as Van Meeren's fake one. Carol says, "Ooh, look." Connaught says, "You wouldn't believe me." Jaime says, "It's beautiful." Jaime is leafing through a Gutenberg Bible. Whit asks, "Where did you get it?" Jaime says, "Some brother." And Whit stops dreaming and really sleeps. When he wakes up, it is morning, and it is raining again.

He showers and shaves. For Jaime. He makes himself eat breakfast. For Jaime. He puts on clothes he has never yet worn. Blue pipestem corduroys, a red wool shirt. He clips off the price tags with the X-acto knife. He locates in a drawer a tooled Mexican belt that gives off a strong tannery smell when he takes it out and unrolls it. He bought it at a vendor's stall on crowded Olvera Street not long after the book sold. Elmer Post had flown out to L.A. for some convention. Whit took him and

194

his wife to dinner at a great old smoky cave of a restaurant—festoons of painted gourds, crimson-and-gilt spoolwork gallerias, mariachis strumming guitars and dressed in huge hats and costumes lavish with embroidery. The wife writes cookbooks. When her dinner came, she tasted it, wrinkled her nose, sent it back. The scared-eyed, brown-skinned waiter brought a second plate. She sent that back. The third one she didn't even bother to taste. After dinner, they went up and down the street between the booths. She bought woven leather shoes and wrote Whit from New York that they pinched and squeaked. He has lost weight since then, and the belt is too big. He digs another hole in it with the X-acto knife, puts the belt on, buckles it. He puts on shoes that match the calfskin jacket. He checks how he looks in the bathroom mirrors. He puts on the jacket. He looks nice.

Because of the rain, no parking spaces are empty on the streets. He splashes the Mercedes through puddles in the alley. He turns in so the car points at the back door of the Pipeline. The back door is up a single step and set into the wall about three feet. In there, somebody is curled up asleep under newspapers. Whit sees the soles of shoes that don't look badly worn. Frowning, he switches off the engine and gets out of the car. The edge of the newspaper nearest the doorstep is soggy with rain. His heart thumps. Maybe what is under there is dead. He scoffs at himself. It is some wino who does this every night of his life. Whit looks for a bottle. There is no bottle. He walks over and says, "Hey." The figure under the papers doesn't stir. It's all right. He doesn't have to go in this way. He will carry the box around to the front. He opens the trunk, lifts the box out. It is a lot heavier than the boy at the printer's made it look. He balances it clumsily and slams down the car lid. The newspapers in the doorway fly apart. Target sits up and stares at him. Whit almost drops the box.

"Jesus Christ," he says. "What are you doing here?"

Target winces, moving his shoulders carefully. Plainly he is stiff and sore. He blinks against the light. The side of his face is dirty, where it has lain on the cement. Grit clings to it. He raises a hand to brush at the grit and Whit sees that the hand is caked with dried blood. "Sleeping," Target says. "Jaime threw me out." Tears fill his eyes and run down. "I love him, Whit. All I want is to live with him. Here. Him and me. That's all."

Whit leaves the box and goes to him. "You'll be sick from this. You'll get pneumonia. Why didn't you go home?"

"That's what he told me to do." Target gets to his feet. Mucus runs from his nose. He snuffles. He wipes the mucus on the sleeve of his thin windbreaker. He studies his bloodied hands. "I'm not going home. He pushed me out here. It was as close as I could get. I banged the door and banged the door, but he wouldn't let me in. So I slept here." He kicks at the papers, making a thin, sad sound in his throat. "It was as close as I could get," he says again. His face twists. "Oh, God." He hides his face in his hands, squats down in the entryway, and cries.

Whit is on the porch at the rear above the Dragon Restaurant again. In the rain. As close as he could get. He takes the box off the trunk of the Mercedes and sets it in the driver's seat. He bends across it awkwardly to open the glove compartment. He takes out the gun, slams the car door, runs down the alley, ruining the calfskin shoes, splotching the new blue pants. He runs along the building side. He runs down the sidewalk. The woman with the little dog, the one who bought a plant from Jaime, stares at him as he passes, stares at the gun. The little dog is wearing a rain protector in a houndstooth pattern. Whit tries the door of the shop. Locked. He knocks.

"Jaime?" he calls. "It's Whit. I've got the book."

He waits. The door opens. Jaime smiles eagerly, tucking shirttails into pants. Whit pushes inside and slams the door. Jaime sees the gun and stops smiling. His eyes get big. His color fades. He takes a step backward, bumps his head on a hanging plant, then turns and runs. He doesn't get to the bead curtain. Whit pulls the trigger. The noise of the shot is very loud and the gun jumps in his hand. There is a harsh smell of cordite and a little smoke. Jaime is down on the floor. Whit

196

stands over him and pulls the trigger again. And again. And again. Till all the bullets are gone and the gun only clicks. Jaime lies still.

Whit says, "Oh, Jesus, oh, God." He drops the gun. It clatters. It sounds as if it has broken on the cement. He turns and yanks open the door and runs outside into the rain. He runs to the curb, clutches a lamppost, and heaves his breakfast into the running gutter. He heaves and heaves. He sinks to his knees, heaving. Out of the edge of his vision, he sees legs beside him. He wipes his mouth and chin, and looks up, expecting a stranger. He starts to say, "It's okay, I'm all right. Something I ate." He doesn't finish. It is not a stranger. It is Jaime. There are no holes in him. There is no blood. He is just very pale.

"That was some joke," he says. "What was it about?"

Whit groans, shuts his eyes, sits on the wet sidewalk, leaning back against the lamppost. Blanks. Naturally. What the hell else would Frank Boulanger have but blanks? Frank Boulanger's whole life is a movie. Whit laughs. He has never made exactly this sound before, and it startles him so, he opens his eyes. One of the old men who, when the sun shines, always sit on the bus bench at the corner, comes shuffling toward them. He holds up a blue and green flowered umbrella. Whit tries to get to his feet. The shoes slip, and he is too weak, anyway. Jaime lifts him.

"You better come inside," he says.

Whit jerks away from him, and is so unsteady that he almost falls. He catches hold of the lamppost with both hands. The metal is cold with the rain. "No." He can't hold his head up, but he shakes it stubbornly. "No. If you want somebody inside, go get Target. He's around back. He slept out there all night." Whit lifts his head. "How can you be so beautiful and still be such a shit?"

Jaime winces. "He said if I wouldn't let him live with me, he'd tell his parents I made him have sex with me, and I'd end up in jail. I threw him out. That makes *me* a shit?"

Whit sighs. His head hurts where Van Meeren hit him. He

197

tells Jaime, "I'm sorry. I guess it's a curse, isn't it, having everybody want you all the time? But they get desperate. You have to learn to handle them better."

"I said, don't blame me if you got hurt," Jaime says.

"Yeah, I know." Whit lets go the lamppost. "It's not your fault." He feels very shaky, as if he'd been sick for a long while, but he is able to walk, and he walks away.

The bathroom mirrors show him that his eyes are swollen almost shut from crying. He turns on the cold-water tap, and the motion makes him flinch because his ribs are sore from crying. He bends to splash water on his face, and the muscles of his belly are sore. He has cried loud and hard for a long time. That came after he threw things. When he got here, he ran from room to room, tipping tables over, hurling lamps, books, the stereo, the Mexican pottery owls. The typewriter has broken a hole in the workroom wall. The drafting table lies dead on its back. The filing cabinet lies dead on its side, drawers hanging half open. In the bedroom his clothes make colored heaps on the floor. He has broken two dresser drawers and the mirror. He doesn't feel better. He splashes his face, turns off the tap, dries his face. In the workroom, he finds the telephone under splayed, torn books. The receiver hums as it is supposed to. He sits on the floor, cross-legged, and turns the dial.

"Congratulations," Charles Twaingate says. "I have your publisher's catalogue. Your book is right at the front. A two-page, color spread they've given it."

"Is Dell there?" Whit asks.

Twaingate hesitates. "Well, she's with a class."

"I have to talk to her," Whit says. "Please. Think of her health, stuck in there, breathing all that pot smoke for hours at a time."

Twaingate never jokes about such things. He refuses to admit his students are less than model, even though most of them have police records and are so addicted to dope or liquor

198

or both that even Hollywood High School has kicked them out. Half of them peddle dope, the other half sell their teenage asses on Hollywood Boulevard at lunchtime and recess and on the way home. About his students, he is like the husband of comedy since the world began—the last to know his wife sleeps with other men.

"Classes will break in thirty-five minutes," he says stiffly. "I'll have her call you."

"I'm dying," Whit says. "How would it look if I had to leave my famous last words with an answering service?"

Twaingate doesn't reply. The receiver knocks a desk top, footsteps fade, a girl giggles, a door slams. Someone calls something in a place that echoes. Whit can't make out the words. Then Dell is saying into the phone:

"It's wonderful about your novel."

"It's not wonderful about me," he says.

"When I saw that beautiful jacket design, I just hugged myself. Isn't it stunning. Phil says—"

"Ah, Christ, Dell," Whit says, "I don't want to know what silly Phil says. I thought he was dead. Why isn't he dead?" There is a long pause, and he is afraid she will hang up. "Don't hang up. I'm sorry. Dell, I need you. I'm falling apart, I'm going crazy, I'm sick, I'm thin, I can't eat, I can't write." That's what will get her. He doesn't know how he thought of it. It hasn't made any difference to him for a long time. But someone inside him knows strategy. He is so excited, he gets to his feet, clutching the telephone. He says it again. "I can't write, I haven't touched the typewriter since—" He can't find words for the rest of that sentence, and he starts over. "I can't write without you, there's no point to it. I just don't give a damn. Nothing means anything without you."

"Oh, Whit." Does she sound sorry for him, sad? "Why do you act this way? We weren't meant to go on any longer. It was over, we'd worn it out."

"You mean, I'd worn you out," he says. "Look, I understand that now. I would have understood before, only you never told me. I didn't know how sickening I was, using you to cry all over, pumping sex into you whether you wanted it or not. Dell, I didn't know. Come back. I won't be like that anymore. Just be with me, okay? Please? Look, I almost turned into a goddamn alcoholic, they almost had to cart me away screaming. I'm not making it alone. Dell, it's killing me." The rain makes it dark outside. The lamp clamped to the drafting table switched itself on when he threw the table over. It glares on him, and he sees himself reflected in the window glass. He is bent forward, shouting into the receiver. The veins stand out in his neck, in his forehead. "I almost shot somebody today. Can you believe that? Me? I can't believe it myself, but it's true, I swear it. I got a gun and tried to kill somebody. Dell, you have to help me." Now he is crying again.

"Somebody's hurt you, haven't they?" she says. "And right away I'm the one you come crying to. After eight months of silence. Darling, don't you see? Nothing's any different. Not with you." She sounds gentle and regretful, the way she sounded that last night in the sunset shadows of the knotty pine room. "There's no way you'll ever grow up. Not with me around."

The door chimes ping. He pays them no attention.

"You don't have to work there anymore," he says. "You don't have to work anyplace. Dell, I'm rich. We can have a ranch. You can have all kinds of horses." She doesn't answer. "Okay—you can have children. I don't care if they have two heads. It's all right. Whatever you want is all right with me. Even that, even that. Please, Dell."

"I'm already pregnant," she says. "Whit—don't do this again. It's over. It really is over, darling. You make up your mind to that, and you'll be all right. You'll see."

"No," he wails. "I won't. I can't." He catches his breath. "Pregnant? Pregnant! You're not even married yet." But the phone has clicked. She isn't listening. He throws the phone through the window. Some of the broken glass goes out into the rain. Some drops in big, listless slivers to the carpet. The cord from the wall is taut. Outside, in the rain, the instrument bumps the wall. Raindrops patter lightly on the white enameled metal shade of the drafting lamp. He hauls the phone inside again, slams the receiver in place, snatches it up, holds it to his ear. It hums. You can't break the damn things. He starts to dial again. He gets through all seven numbers, but then he hangs up. He is beginning to be ashamed of himself. He sets the phone on the desk, the only piece of furniture in here too heavy for him to topple. He goes to the bedroom.

He has thrown most of what hung in the closet onto the floor but not the suitcase. He gets it out, lays it on the bed, runs open the big zipper, lays back the lid. Cardboard stiffeners are inside, because the material of the suitcase is soft fake leather. He throws the cardboard strips in the air, begins snatching up clothes from where he strewed them, and slamming them into the case. Soft moans come from under the bed, cries of desolation. He gets to his knees, lifts the edge of a blanket, peers into the darkness. Polk looks at him with round, grieving, frightened eyes. Whit speaks gently to him, apologizes, lies on the carpet, stretches an arm under the bed. Polk backs up and crouches out of reach. Whit goes through the wrecked living room to the kitchen for wheat crackers. He rattles the box, gets down on the floor again, opens the box, crackles the waxed-paper lining of the box, takes out a cracker. Lying on his side, moving gently, he extends the cracker. Wheat crackers are Polk's favorite.

"Cracker, Polk," he says. "Come on, baby. It's okay."

It takes time, but at last Polk accepts the cracker and begins crunching it up. Whit goes about packing the way packing is supposed to be done, folding everything neatly, forgetting nothing. He bought the suitcase when he thought he would have to fly to New York about the book. He never had to go. Now he doesn't know where he is going. He knows only that he is going. On the way, he will stop and buy a carrying case for Polk, who dislikes riding in cars. Whit goes to the bathroom for a red and white pressure can of shaving cream, his razor, a blue and white can of tooth powder, his toothbrush. When he returns with them, Polk is curled up on the clothes in the suitcase. He lets Whit stroke him. Whit sits beside him on the bed and keeps up the petting until Polk begins to purr, eyes half shut, front paws kneading a tweed jacket that cost two hundred dollars, claws catching its threads. Whit picks him up, holds him close, scratches his ears, then sets him on the bed, tucks the toilet stuff into the suitcase, shuts the lid, and zips it closed.

He zips it open again. He has to change out of the blue corduroys that are splashed with mud below the knees, soaked at the knees, soaked on the seat. He changes. The red shirt seems all right. He lifts Polk out of the suitcase again, zips it shut again. He shrugs into the calfskin jacket, picks up the suitcase, tucks Polk under his arm, and heads for the front door. *You're not going to just walk off and leave this mess!* his mother says. *What will people think?* She never means that as a question. She believes she knows what people will think. She will go to her grave not knowing. In Hemet. If they bury people in Hemet. He will leave word with the manager about the broken window where the rain is coming in. He sets down the suitcase and opens the door. He nearly falls over Jaime, who has been sitting outside with his back against the door, and who stumbles to his feet.

"I rang," he says. "I thought you weren't here." He looks at the suitcase. "You going on a trip?"

"I didn't want you to be the last thing I saw," Whit says. "What do you want?"

"You," Jaime says. "If you still want me."

Whit stares. "I tried to kill you," he says.

"That makes me important, doesn't it?" Jaime gives him a sad little smile. "I was never that important to anybody in my life before." He raises his eyebrows. "Can I come in?"

202

THIRD PART:
Whit

Had it been foretold to me that one day I should find myself living as I do today, I should have smiled. It would not have been noticed, but I would have known that I was smiling.

—Samuel Beckett, *Malone Dies*

Rat

Sunlight streaks down hot from a glass triangle high in the front wall. This means the time is close to noon. He has kicked off the blankets and sheet and is still awash in sweat. The kid beside him has better reflexes. He has rolled to the far side of the broad bed, and the sun misses him. He breathes shallowly, at peace. He lies face down. His head is covered in silver ringlets. His skin is toasted gold. For the moment, Whit can't recall where he found him. He kisses him between muscle-padded shoulder blades, and smells his own soap, his own deodorant. So this is one of those you have to ask to shower. He can't see the face, but he doesn't need to. He knows it will be angelic. Whit chooses angels—no more dark plaster saints from Catholic gift shop windows, damaged, marked down for clearance.

Whit gets off the bed, steps across dropped jockey shorts with urine stains, an Indian cotton shirt with embroidery, a threadbare pair of jeans with flowers stitched on the back pockets, the kid's clothes. He slides back the curtains on the glass wall. Beyond a plank deck, sand stretches. Then there is the sea that today is blue and sparkles in the sunlight. Thirty yards offshore, black rocks, clumped close together, poke up out of the water. This mile of beach is called Pelican Rocks, but perched out there today are only gulls. And most days. Chemicals have decimated the pelicans, and man has moved in. No one lived here five years ago. Now, under tall, crumbling cliffs just out of reach of the tide, a dozen lean, angular houses of unpainted planks stare through sheet glass at the rocks. Whit bought one of the houses when Jaime asked him one day why he didn't live at the beach. All Jaime had to do was speak. Whit goes into the bathroom and functions. He twists the shower handles and looks out. The kid is no longer in the bed. Whit leans over a raw redwood rail and listens. Rattlings and cupboard slammings come from the kitchen.

"Shit," the kid is saying to himself aloud, "shit."

"You don't have to do anything," Whit calls.

"I do if I want coffee," the kid says. "You're going to take a fucking shower."

"If you get in it with me," Whit says.

"I can't laugh in the morning," the kid says. "Hey, I found it. Is that your cat? She wants to come in."

"It's a he," Whit says. "Yes, let him in, please." Whit goes back into the bathroom and gets under the shower. The kid comes in naked and stands at the toilet and pisses. He pisses hard and crooked to start with, half down the wall before he can aim right. He still has half the hard-on he woke up with. Ah, youth. He unrolls a streamer of toilet paper, wads it in his fist, kneels and wipes the wall, wipes the floor. He plops the wet wad into the toilet, presses the flush lever, gets to his feet. He asks Whit:

"What do you peddle?"

"Words," Whit says. He soaps his hair and scrubs it with his fingertips. "Just once in my life, I got them in the right order. And all these things were added unto me."

The boy gets into the shower with him, brushing him with a dry, smooth, firm body warm from all the sun it has absorbed along these shores this summer. Whit lays the bar of soap in his hand, ducks into the shower spray, works at getting the soap out of his hair.

The boy begins to soap Whit's back. "You're famous, right? I've seen you someplace. What's your name?"

"I told you last night," Whit says.

"I was juiced last night," the boy says. He sets the soap in the elaborate hanging chromium wire thing meant for all the gadgets it seems necessary now to take a bath with, and he begins running his hands on Whit's back. "So were you. I don't think you told me. We were at the Sea Shanty, right? You're the worst pool player I ever saw."

"You're a good back-washer," Whit says. "Thanks." He turns to let the spray slide the soap off. The boy touches his cock. Whit kisses the boy and steps out of the shower. "It's all yours." He takes down a twelve-dollar towel as big as a pup tent. He dries his hair, what is left of it, wipes steam off the mirror, combs his hair. He knots the towel at his hip, gets from the bedside stand a cigarette pack that is nearly empty, and goes down to the kitchen, where a kettle rattles on a burner turned up too high. He lowers the fire, assembles the glass coffee maker, loads it from the coffee can the kid has set out on the counter. He pours boiling water into the top section of the coffee maker, sets the kettle back on the stove, turns off the burner.

From the refrigerator, he gets out a little can of tuna with a plastic lid and, squatting, forks the meat that remains in it from last night into Polk's dish. Polk doesn't weigh much, but Whit can hear him coming, down the bare wooden stairs from the very top of the house. Whit's desk is up there, under a steeply slanted roof with a lot of glass that keeps salting up with sea spray and is a breakneck job to clean. His typewriter is there. And the typewriter is still Polk's favorite place to nap. He comes into the kitchen chatting. He eats. Since coming to live at the seashore, he has developed an appetite for tuna.

Whit drops the can into the neat, plastic-bag-lined receptacle under the sink. He lights a cigarette and leans back against the counter, thinking for an unreal moment that it is Jaime up there, showering, Jaime he has fixed the coffee for, Jaime whose breakfast he will soon start to cook. It isn't habit alone that keys off this mistake. It is the neatness of the kitchen, the neatness of the bathroom, of the entire house. Jaime was always picking up after him, shelving books, stacking magazines and records, filing away reels of recording tape, putting into order pages of manuscript, the bills and letters on the desk, emptying and wiping out ashtrays, jumping up from the table to wash the dishes before he'd swallowed his last bite of food. Whit said he would get a cleaning woman. Jaime said it would be a waste of money. So there was no stopping him, except to keep a jump ahead, to be neat first. Once Whit collected the dirty clothes and sneaked off to the laundromat in the shacky little settlement up the highway—gas station, café, grocery, bait shack. Jaime trailed him on foot, came in panting.

"What are you doing?" He looked heartbroken.

"Penance," Whit said.

"For what?" Jaime stared at the shuddering, sloshing washers. He clutched his head with both hands, shocked and grieved. "You didn't do anything wrong."

"I drove Dell crazy, following her around, picking up after her," Whit said. "Just one more offense in a long list of offenses."

Jaime looked into Whit's face, the way he always did for that brief, troubled time before he gave up trying to understand. Then he said, "You should be home, writing."

"Dear God," Whit said, and laughed to keep from crying.

He flicks ashes from his cigarette into the sink, and quickly turns on the tap to wash them away. Jaime is still only a step behind him, poised to make things spick and span. Whit wonders how long that will go on, when he will stop running the vacuum cleaner every day, polishing the endless stairs with oiled cloths, hanging off gallery rails to swipe with a broom at cobwebs among the high, angular beams. To please Jaime. Or to displease Jaime. Who isn't even here anymore, and who wouldn't know where he was if he were here. Tears sting Whit's eyes and he blinks hard. No more of that.

208

The kid comes in, wrapped in another of the big towels. It is white. He will be snatched up to heaven. When he set out the coffee can, he set out mugs. Now he picks up the coffee maker and fills the mugs. He hands a mug to Whit, who sets it on the counter and stirs in sugar, takes a cold little waxed-paper carton from the fridge and whitens the coffee. He holds out the carton, but the boy shakes his head. He blows at his coffee, tries to drink it, burns his mouth. The cigarette pack lies on the counter. He shakes a cigarette out and lights it. The lighter lies in his palm. He shuts an eye because smoke is trickling up into it, and studies the lighter. It is a square-cornered, slim little shaft of steel. He is wondering if it cost a lot of money. It did. He lays it down with a delicate click.

"Is it hard work, writing?" he wonders.

Whit sets the cream carton back in the fridge and takes eggs, butter, bacon. "It takes a long time to learn how, and you don't get paid much until you do. Sometimes you don't get paid much after you do." Skillets hang above the stove. He gets two of them down. "I got lucky, that's all."

The boy says something skeptical Whit can't quite hear. The boy crouches and pets Polk, who is at the door, meowing to go out. The door is glass panels clinched in a redwood frame. Outside it, a slatted wooden walk passes, which leads to steps down to the beach. There is a ten- or twelve-foot width of drifted sand from which sprouts tufts of dune grass. Then there is the windowless wall of the next house, with the sun turning its boards white and laying the shadow of Whit's roofs on it in a sawtooth pattern that will climb as the sun goes west, until the shadow of Whit's house fits the outline of the next house exactly. The boy says, "Shall I let him out?" Whit nods. The boy rises and opens the door a little, and Polk slips out. Polk stands blinking in the sun for a moment, before he decides to try for lizards in the cliffs in back, instead of for shore birds down at the surf's edge. Eating lizards makes him throw up, but he never even gets to eat a shore bird. They are too quick for him. Whit has laid bacon in one of the pans. It starts to sizzle. He hears the door close. The boy says, "You wouldn't say you were good, you'd say you were lucky. That's the kind of dude you are."

Whit glances at him. "What are you planning to be, a psychologist?"

"I don't have any plans." The boy comes up behind Whit and puts his arms around him. He lays his damp head on Whit's shoulder. His stout little cock is stiff against Whit's butt. "Why should I think about tomorrow? On a morning like this? After a night like last night?" He runs warm hands down Whit's chest and ribs and belly, fumbles to unknot Whit's towel, takes hold of Whit's cock, and starts squeezing. "I know it will end sometime," he says. "I'll get old. But it doesn't seem too real, okay?"

"Okay." The kid's hand is getting results. Whit sighs and lets his eyes fall shut. He sees the craggy face of the man the kid was sitting with at the Sea Shanty when Whit walked in. Handsome, in his sixties, shock of snow-white hair, an actor whom Whit has met at the fat man's, at poolsides in Beverly Hills, on sun decks in Malibu. A couple of times a week, he turns up as a banker, a lawyer, a sleek crook on television. He has to be rich. Whit says, "You don't have anything to worry about. I wish I'd been as smart as you when I was your age." He means he wishes he had been as cynical. Chang would have been lucky to hang onto Whit for one night. But Whit was far from cynical. He hopes he is nearer now, but he doubts it. He smiles to himself and takes the boy's wrist to keep the hand from moving. "If you don't stop that, we won't get any breakfast."

"Mmm," the boy says, turns Whit around, drops to his knees, takes Whit's cock in his mouth. The house rattles loudly. The boy looks up. "Jesus, what was that?"

"Rocks," Whit says. "They keep falling off the cliffs." His fingers are in the wet tangle of the boy's hair. "Don't let it worry you. They don't usually come through the roof."

The boy looks at the ceiling. "It's a dangerous place to live."

"That's how I can afford it," Whit says.

The boy studies him. "I know where I saw you," he says. "On 'Johnny Carson.'" His expression is worshipful and deeply happy. He puts his mouth on Whit again, hungrily, and his head bobs quickly under Whit's hands. He makes an urgent sound in his throat, and begins to pump with his hand to help what he is waiting for to happen quickly. Whit laughs a soft, shaky laugh, gropes behind him, and twists the stove knob so the bacon won't burn. He lifts his face to the sunshine pouring down from another of those high glass triangles. He smiles. It is make-believe time, unreal, such stuff as Ganymede paperbacks are made on. Oh, he's had other strangers here, men and boys—the beaches teem with them by day, the bars by night. But none acted like this one. Sometimes they were compliant as hell, obliging sometimes, sometimes mute objects to be shifted around like store-window dummies in the dark. None like this. For twenty seconds of a previous life, he must have done something right.

His legs grow weak. He puts his hands back against the cold enamel of the stove to keep himself upright. He is covered in sweat again. He breathes shallow and fast. It happens. He shouts, grabs the boy's shoulders, bends, jolting and shuddering above the boy. The boy clutches Whit's butt with hard, digging fingers, and it is a long, exquisitely painful moment before his mouth lets go, and he sits back on his heels, gulping, breathless, grinning. With a long sigh, he stretches out on his back on the floor, whose waxy gloss was Jaime's pride, lays an arm across his eyes to shut out the sun, and laughs to himself. Whit starts to step across him. He means to fetch the coffee mugs and cigarettes. The boy catches his ankle and kisses the sole of his foot. "Hey," Whit says, "Johnny Carson is not God, and I am not his beloved son in whom he is well pleased." He hops free, gets the mugs, cigarette pack, lighter. He sits on the floor that is cold on his ass, and leans his back against the oven door that is cold. He places the boy's mug beside him, takes the boy's hand, and guides it to the mug. The boy pushes the mug away. "My turn," he says, and with his hand calls Whit's attention to his cock. Whit lies beside him and begins to lick the soap taste off his skin.

But at last they do get breakfast, sitting up at the table, almost like people. The boy is in his limp Indian cotton shirt and wornout jeans, Whit in a terry-cloth robe with a hood that he bought for Jaime. Trying to buy Jaime anything was awkward. He entered a men's shop like a wolf being led into a cage. If Whit watched him, he would pretend to look at shirts, jackets, pants. But if Whit turned away for a minute, Jaime would be out the door. He would be in the car, smoking dope, the radio on loud to Bob Dylan, Joan Baez, Frank Zappa. Or he would have vanished, climbed aboard a bus, stuck out his thumb and got a ride—what driver existed that would refuse Jaime a ride?—or simply run off in his rotting old sandals. Then he never went far. Whit would find him at some rickety taco stand rich with brown chili-pepper smells, hunched at a splintery table, reading the book from his pocket, Corso, Ferlinghetti, Alan Watts, and washing down fried beans and cheese with orange soda pop. What was wrong with decent clothes?

"What they cost! That's indecent. Why do you want to throw money away? I know a thrift shop where—"

"You know fifty thrift shops." Whit sat down disgusted. "You are beautiful, you idiot. Why do you want to look like the garbage man?"

"If I'm so beautiful"—Jaime's eyes are lowered, he is pretending to read—"what do I need with clothes?" He looks up brightly. "You want a burrito? They're good here. My cousin owns this place."

Jaime had many cousins who owned taco stands. He claimed to have worked in all of them. "Summers. When I was a kid." The burritos were always good. Then they went to thrift shops. Now, in the shine of this sunny morning kitchen, he sees through a doorway whose frame is hung with battered old kerosene lanterns, the looming interior of one of those shops, hung with ghostly clothes on racks to the ceiling. Only one light shone inside, from a gooseneck lamp on a glass showcase where a big, black woman's hat from 1890 was cocked on a broken plaster head, where black velvet Spanish table scarves lay crumpled showing painted roses, and where tarnished jewelry lay in tarnished trays. And in and out of the circle of light, busy and so very alive among all these dead trappings, hurried a big white rat—pink nose, pink ears, pink snaky tail. Jaime fed it sunflower seeds. It sat up for them, whiskers twitching, red eyes bright in the lamplight. Nobody came to wait on them. The rat seemed to be in charge, and when he had eaten as many sunflower seeds as he wanted, he waddled off under a fold of one of the Spanish shawls. He peered out at them once, nose twinkling. Jaime wandered into the mothball-reeking shadows, and came out wearing a mangy raccoon coat so big it dragged on the ground. Whit tried to make him put it back, but he went out onto the sidewalk in it, and began to dance there, arms held out, turning slowly, dreamily, like an old Jew. Whit left a handful of dollar bills in the fold of the shawl, where he could feel the rat quivering in sleep.

"There's a shop on Fairfax run by a white rat," he says.

"You're out of cigarettes," the boy says.

"There's money in my jacket," Whit says. "And the car keys. On the couch." The boy stares at him for a minute, troubled, then goes and gets the money, the keys. He stands at the outside door, tossing the keys in his hand. Whit says, "There's a store about a mile south."

"I know," the boy says. He frowns and tilts his head. "How come you live all by yourself? You're nice, you're good-looking, you're famous, you're rich. Did somebody die?"

"Not exactly," Whit says.

"I could live here with you," the boy says. He blushes. "If you wanted me to. I like you. I like it here."

Whit shakes his head. "It never worked out for me. I'm trying to make it on my own. Thanks, anyway."

"Nobody makes it on their own," the boy says.

"Then this nobody isn't going to make it," Whit says. He smiles. "You want to get those cigarettes?"

213

The boy goes. Whit washes the dishes. He climbs the stairs and makes the bed. He shaves. He puts on clothes. He keeps listening for the car but the only cars he hears pass swiftly on the highway above. None stops. He hears the surf always, and sometimes gulls that sound like rusty hinges. The hinges of the kitchen door don't sound. The boy has gone for a long drive while he has the chance. It is the kind of car that would make that hard to resist. Whit climbs to the workroom. *He spent a long time watching from a lonely wooden tower.* It's a line from a song Connaught used to sing at the Pipeline. Whit hears it in his head each time he comes up here. The sun glares off the white sheen of the typewriter, the white matte of the papers beside the typewriter. Dark glasses lie there. He puts them on. A page is in the machine. He knows where this part of his novel is going, and he begins easily and keeps on easily.

The door closes far below, and he looks at his watch. The boy has been gone nearly three hours. Footsteps thump quickly up the stairs. The boy's shoes are grubby white canvas with rubber soles. Whit thinks of another sentence and types it, and another sentence. He hears the boy pant and feels his warmth at his back. The boy's hand lays packs of cigarettes beside the typewriter. Whit says thanks, starts to type another line, and a pillowcase comes down over his head. His arms are grabbed and yanked around behind him, behind the chairback. Rope goes around his wrists, is tugged tight. The force with which it is knotted jerks him in the chair.

"No, wait," he says. The way in which the pillowcase was put over his head has twisted the dark glasses and one of the nose pieces is cutting at his cheek. "Hold it."

But now rope is being lashed around his chest. He tries to stand up but he is pushed down hard. The rope is yanked tight. The knot-tying business jerks him again, this time pumping air in hiccups out of his lungs. He tries to kick, since his legs are free. He bangs his ankle on the steel bottom of the section of the desk that holds drawers. The pain is sharp. Now rope goes around his ankles.

"You little shit," he says.

214

But the ankle ropes are tied without comment. The motor of the typewriter in front of him stops its humming. Somebody grunts, and papers slither to the floor. They seem to be whispering secret laughter at him. The ratchets of the typewriter's platen grate. He feels footsteps go away back of him. He hears them on the steps.

"I would have given you anything you wanted," he says.

"So would I," the boy says.

Rocks clatter on the roof. Another voice says, "Jesus, what was that?"

"The cliffs are falling down," the boy says. "Don't drop that, for Christ's sake. That's a two-thousand-dollar amplifier."

There is no more conversation. He can hear them moving around. Now and then something rattles or thumps. More rocks shower down on the roof but no one remarks on it—or if they remark, the sound of the surf doesn't allow Whit to hear. What he hears comes only when the sea pauses in its breathing. He feels more than hears the kitchen door close. He feels more than hears the silence. But he does hear the engine of the car that starts on the cliff top, and it is not the engine of his Mercedes. He waits to hear that, but he waits in vain. The other car drives off with a rattling of loose valves. There is only the surf sound now, and the cries of the gulls. He yells. He hasn't thought to yell till now. Maybe he has been too surprised. He has not been afraid, which is interesting. He has only been angry and abashed. He yells, and his voice bangs back at him off the four tall windows, and down at him from the steep, reaching boards.

"Help!" he yells, and goes on yelling until his throat aches. People pass on the beach, not often but sometimes. They walk their dogs. One or two ride horses. Sometimes they stop, lay out towels, and lie on them, sunning themselves, reading, sleeping. He lunges in the chair and bumps a knee. Somehow, he lies forward on the desk, thus getting the chair off its little wheels. He hops sideways. If he can get near enough, maybe he can swing his body in such a way that the chair will smash out a window. If the noise of the breaking glass doesn't attract

215

anyone, at least his shouts will carry farther. "Help," he shouts again, and takes a big, clumsy swing with his body, and topples onto his back in the chair. He hits his head and blacks out. When he comes to, his hands feel crushed under him. He feels sick to his stomach, and hopes he won't vomit inside the pillowcase. "Polk!" he calls. What in the world does he think Polk can do? He has to laugh at that, and he does laugh, out loud and for a long time. He cries from laughing. The nausea is gone. He begins to rock the chair. He puts all his meager weight into it, and at last the chair tips on its side.

Now he can push with his feet. He pushes, and the chair slides toward the door. He pushes again, hits the door frame with his head, and wails for a minute at the pain. To straighten the chair, he twists his shoulders. He lurches to lift the chairback off the floor for a second, and at the same time pushes with his feet. And the chair, for some reason—the little bright Mexican rug that lies on the landing outside the door?—shoots off the landing, and he crashes head over heels down the stairs. Slamming his head again, scraping his elbows, jarring his knees, twisting his ankles. He yelps in surprise. And the chair wedges itself. He is hanging upside-down. He rubs his wrists together, twists his wrists, but the rope only cuts deeper into them. They feel raw. He heaves to shift his weight. He hears wood strain and crack. He doesn't want whatever is holding him to break and dump him in a long fall. He stops trying to do anything and just hangs there. His mother says, *If you lead that kind of life, you'll end up murdered,* and she bursts into tears and tries feebly to hit him with the broom. In sunshine in a rowboat, his father says, *You'll never get anyplace in life not trusting people.* Whit grins and shuts his eyes and falls asleep.

"Whit, darling, are you here? Oh, my God!"

Footsteps stutter up the stairs. Somebody jerks at the pillowcase. He knows the voice. It is Kate Schaefer, who lives next door. She owns an advertising agency and throws parties. She is whimpering.

"It's okay," he says. "Don't worry. I'm alive."

216

The pillowcase comes off, taking the sunglasses with it. They rattle below. Kate blinks at him, thrusting her face upside-down into his. Her breath smells of tobacco. She wears long false lashes. She crouches on the stairs. With fingers that have long false nails, she caresses his face. "Oh, my beautiful child. Who did this to you?"

"Get a knife out of the kitchen drawer and cut the ropes, okay? I have to go to the bathroom." He laughs.

Tears are on her face and her face is puckered with anxiety but she laughs too. She hurries down the stairs, almost falling. "It was your little cat. The poor baby was scratching at the door and meowing so pitifully." Her voice comes faintly from the kitchen. She opens and slams shut drawers there. She comes back at a knock-kneed, breast-jiggling run. "And I knew it was his suppertime, and your car was up there, so you had to be home, didn't you?" She is bending over him with a big, savage-looking Japanese vegetable chopper. Her hands tremble. "Oh, God, I'm so afraid I'll cut you."

"Just get the wrists," he says. "I'll do the rest."

"They've stolen everything," she says.

But he has a bat's-eye view. The earth-color Navajo rugs are there, the brown wicker chairs and couches with their sailcloth cushions. "Only the electronics," he says. She kneels in her elegant slacks with her butt in the air and makes little grunting noises, reaching somewhere below and behind him. He feels the cold blade on his skin. The rope gives. He shakes it loose. He brings his hands around, numb and a little blue. He rubs them and reaches up to her for the knife. He cuts the rope that binds his chest, and drops out of the chair, does a back somersault, and ends up sprawled on the landing. Kate stands with her hands clapped to the sides of her face, giving little soft shrieks. She starts down to him. "Oh, darling!"

He holds up his hands. "I'm okay." He tries to smile. "Phone the police, will you?" He looks for the knife. It is stuck into a redwood upright, as if some expert had thrown it. He dislodges it and bends to work on the ankle ropes. She isn't moving. He tells her the phone is in the bedroom and nods at the door. She scurries. She has been waiting for an excuse to get into that bedroom since he and Jaime moved here. He guesses she has never seen a fag's bedroom. It's probably the only kind she hasn't seen. He owes her that, though she is going to be disappointed. He rubs his ankles, gets to his feet, wincing, and hobbles to the bathroom. When he comes out, she is still chattering. Her voice comes and goes. She is moving around the bedroom. She gives a cry of dismay and tells the policeman at the other end of the phone connection, "His closet's absolutely empty, officer, darling. They've stolen all his clothes!"

In pain, he climbs the stairs to dislodge the chair and carry it back up to the tower. The typewriter is gone. He squats and picks up the papers the kid scattered in taking the typewriter. He stands and sorts the papers. The page he was working on when it happened is here. He reads it, frowning, chewing his lip. He lays it on the desk, reaches for a pencil, and crosses out a word.

Flowers

The interviewer is an Englishman with short arms and legs, tiny hands and feet, and a big head. Whit finds it hard not to stare at his long upper lip, which looks as if he could nibble tender leaves from thorny bushes. He does his job in a white, one-story building between tall, lacy steel towers that wink slow, lonely red lights above bare hills where oil pumps nod in the night, near the airport. When Whit got out of the Mercedes, he stood in the empty parking lot and watched jetliners roar overhead, winking red lights back at the towers. But in the boxy little studio where he sits with the interviewer, the walls and ceiling are thickly flocked with white asbestos fiber. No sound can be heard here except his voice and the interviewer's voice. And, through a raspy little speaker box on the table, the voices of lonely listeners telephoning in.

This is the second time he has been here. But it is not familiar or cozy or welcoming. It is no different from such rooms—always an anonymous engineer beyond double panes of glass turning knobs, threading tapes—in Boston, New York, Philadelphia, in Chicago, Atlanta, Denver. The talk is no different. The interviewer is sharper here and, unlike most, has actually read Whit's book. Also, unlike most, he is sober. He drinks cold tea from a big mug that has his caricature on it. He

219

has spoken the title of the book once. Whit has spoken it half a dozen times—that is why he is here, that was why his publisher paid for plane rides to all those cities, for high-rise hotel rooms in all those cities. That was six or eight weeks ago. Jaime had refused to come along. And Whit had been happy only once. In Pittsburgh. He had sat up all night looking down from the thirtieth floor at the great black rivers with the lights winking on them.

Radio shows were bad but television was worse. No one behind any desk ever seemed to know who he was, why he was in the place. Seated in high-gloss lobbies on deep velveteen couches where chrome and glass-top coffee tables held magazines no one could read, he read his watch while employees hurtled through glass doors, arguing with each other, rushing toward appointments, luncheons, dinners, elevators. Only twice was he still sitting there when the show of which he was supposed to be part went on the air in some far corner of the building without him. But so many times did this come close to happening that he lost count. It gave him diarrhea.

But the lobbies weren't the worst. The worst were the dressing rooms he was rushed to, shut up and forgotten in. The decor was always bare, television monitor, chair, couch maybe, vinyl-tile floor thick with crushed cigarette butts, makeup counter cluttered with soft-drink cans, paper cups of stale coffee, glasses holding the dregs of booze. No window. No way to prop open the door. On a mirror in one of them, someone had lettered in lipstick, HELP—I'M BEING HELD CAPTIVE BY THE MARTY GREENSPAN SHOW. Radio was less self-important, and in radio stations he occasionally encountered a human being. Not on the air, but beforehand. On the air, whether in radio or television, what you encountered were out-of-work concentration-camp directors, surgeons who preferred operating without anesthetics, torturers.

"Don't worry about them," the wispy publicity girl at the publisher's office told him. "Just take the book with you and hang onto it. And whenever that little red light on the camera winks at you, hold it up. What they say doesn't matter. The book is all that matters. Keep talking about the book, no matter what they talk about."

What they are talking about tonight is Whit's robbery. It has been in the papers and television newscasts, and the Englishman has brought it up. And the lonely callers-in are excited. A woman who sounds as if she is used to commanding troops tells him to get a big, savage dog. A manufacturer offers to give him a fancy burglar alarm system if he will mention the product name in his next novel. A boy of sixteen gives Whit detailed instructions on how to wire up his own homemade burglar alarm. A crazy man claims the crew of a Russian submarine came ashore and stole Whit's clothes for disguises, and that they are now walking among unsuspecting Californians, spreading disease from spray cans. But tonight no one thinks he is Henry Miller, and bawls him out for writing filth. And no one thinks he is Arthur Miller and wants to know what it was like to be married to Marilyn Monroe. A good many do want to talk about city council resolutions, ballot propositions, and baseball instead of Whit's book. He thanks them all, and mentions his book to them all. Then it is three minutes to midnight. A commercial slams through the monitor speakers so that Whit leaps off his chair instead of merely standing up. The Englishman takes off his headphones, shakes Whit's hand, moves his mouth in a mechanical smile and speech that can't be heard, then lunges out of the studio, waving a fistful of papers at somebody.

Whit likes driving freeways after midnight. It is one of the times when he lets himself feel a little bit romantic. The long trail of red taillights curving away ahead of him is beautiful and mysterious. He wants to know where everyone is going. It is more than wanting. He sickens with yearning to know where they are going and to go with them. He wants to walk through front doors with them into dimly lit living rooms for sleepy drinks, to follow them into bedrooms and yawn with them, watch them drowsily undress and creep between the sheets, listen to them make love and murmur to each other in the dark of where they've been tonight and what they'll do tomorrow.

He knows nothing about their lives, but they are all beautiful and terrible to him, boxed up in those dark, hurtling cars. That he can't be with them makes him ache. At the glaring interchange, where streamers of clean concrete wing this way, that way, bright green and white signs strike at him, CORDOVA, where his father will never wake up, HOLLYWOOD, where Dell bends tenderly above Phil Farmer's sleeping baby, ARANJUEZ, where Jaime sleeps drugged and alone. Whit heads bleakly for the beach.

The river at Aranjuez runs almost dry in summer. The hills are brown and dry. The hospital stands up white and new outside the shacky little town under its dusty oaks. The trees around the hospital are young, Brazilian peppers in tidy concrete boxes. Neat walks cut across lawns of tough green grass. Sprinklers loft pivoting arcs of water to keep the lawns green as paint. Rainbows form in the arcs of water. The sun glares hard off the windows and white walls of the tall hospital building. It is cool inside. The hallways are long. Patients in white starchy trousers and jackets that have ties instead of buttons wander down the hallways, always toward the tall windows at the ends of the hallways, where the light is fierce and promising, yet never seem to reach the windows, never reach the light at the end, not of the hallways, not of anything. They are always in the hallways, always walking toward the light.

Whit never found Jaime in a hallway. A few times—how long ago, now, three weeks, a month?—he found him in the recreation room. The weather was hot, and he wore only the clean, white, ill-fitting pants, which made him look like a beautiful, doomed Mexican revolutionary in an Eisenstein film. The recreation room was large, and appeared empty no matter how many patients roamed it. Scuffed boards for checkers and Scrabble lay on tables, but no one seemed to play. The floor was strewn with checkers, dominoes, playing cards. Each wall was a different pale color—pink, yellow, green, blue—and bare, except for electric outlets located high up, out of reach. From these outlets, now and then, trailed wires—to a television set, a radio, a film projector—but not often. He and Jaime were the only ones Whit ever saw sit on the couches and chairs. The patients sat on the floor, hugging their knees, chins on their knees, eyes fixed on what no one else could see. Or they walked aimlessly, or stood staring out of steel-mesh-covered windows. Now and then, someone sang loudly to himself. Some danced to music inside their heads. They never looked as if they liked what they heard.

Jaime said, "Thank you for the books. Only it's hard to concentrate. The dope they give you to keep you calm." He made an effort to smile. "I'm so calm I could scream."

"You look better," Whit said.

He kept remembering how Jaime looked the first time. He keeps remembering it. The first time was in a terrible room crowded with glittering medical apparatus. They had shaved Jaime's skull. They had shaved his beard, but stubble had started. He lay strapped to a high bed, struggling feebly, keening, scared. Drool ran from a corner of his beautiful mouth and glistened in the hard light. Whit wiped it away with his hand. He spoke Jaime's name, but Jaime didn't answer. His eyes didn't look. They kept rolling. No sunlit landscape lay at the far back of his eyes here. They held the blackness of outer space, cold, empty, endless. In the car, following its lonely headlights down a freeway nearly clear now, the smell of ocean, the chill of ocean coming through the windows, Whit feels his insides cringe. It had been hard to make himself go back.

That first time, he left the room stunned, turned the wrong way, and there sat Jaime's mother, dressed in black as if he was already dead, a priest in black beside her. She was small and big-breasted, she clutched a black handbag in her lap. Her drawn-on eyebrows, thick eyeliner, rouge, crimson lipstick, black-dyed pile of hair, only made starker her fright, helplessness, anger. Whit had met her when he and Jaime hauled her furniture out of an old stucco apartment building in Boyle Heights, where little Mexican kids in sagging diapers staggered down hallways that smelled of piss and tortillas. The furniture

223

stacked in a yellow, rented trailer, they drove it and her to a little white shack behind sunflowers in El Monte. "You sure you're going to be happy here?" Jaime touched a seam where brand-new wallpaper was already coming loose. "Because, I told you, I'm not going to move you again." It was the third time in four months. She promised she would be happy. She wasn't dressed up that day. She looked younger and prettier without all the makeup. Jaime rode in the trailer. She sat beside Whit in the Mercedes, chattering and flirting. She didn't flirt at the hospital. She glared at Whit as if it was his fault that Jaime lay in there crazy. He sat down beside her on the waiting-room sofa and tried to tell her Jaime would get better. She wouldn't answer. The plump young Mexican priest had a sparse, silky-soft mustache. He clutched a breviary the way she clutched her purse. He stared straight in front of him, expressionless.

Whit went back anyway. Because, of course, she was half right, maybe more than half. By the time he stumbled aboard the night jet, drunk because he had never flown before and it scared him, and New York was a long way off, where he was to start that stupid tour—by then, the book had already sold two hundred thousand copies in stores, and almost that many more to book-club members. Sales weren't dropping off, they were picking up. The book didn't need his help, didn't need his face, bright with brick-color makeup, on every picture tube in the country, looking wary and too young to be out without his mother. It didn't need his voice mumbling from a billion, three-hundred-twenty million radio speakers, all night, and over breakfast, and in cars droning home from work at five o'clock. The book didn't need his help, and he didn't need the book's help. No one *earned* that much money. It was making him angry and afraid. Yet he allowed himself to be badgered into taking the damned tour. And he couldn't badger Jaime. Jaime was not going. Jaime shouted. He ran from the house in his undershorts, across the sand, and swam so far out Whit was sure he wouldn't be able to swim back. He swam back. And he sulked. He tied a bandanna over his hair and bought pink spun candy in a paper cone and rode the merry-go-round all day on the Santa Monica pier.

"If you don't go, I can't go," Whit said.

"Then don't go." Jaime got out of bed.

"I have to go," Whit said. "I promised people. It was a lot of work for them to set it all up. I can't back out."

"What are they to you?" Jaime opened the glass wall of the bedroom. He was naked. It was four in the morning. Whit had waked him up to argue with him because he couldn't sleep. Jaime went out on the deck and climbed up on the wooden rail. He crouched on the rail like a runner in the blocks. He was pale enough so that starlight and a few lights along the shore reflected in the black surf let Whit see him. Whit scrambled out of bed and started after him. Jaime wobbled. Whit halted and held his breath. Jaime let go the rail with his hands, then grabbed it again. He waited a minute, let go once more, and wavered slowly upright, arms out to help him keep his balance. The wind off the sea fluttered his hair. He began to walk along the rail, teetering.

"They're nothing to me," Whit said.

"Then, if you're going to do what they want," Jaime said, "and you're not going to do what I want, I must be less than nothing to you, isn't that right?"

"If you fall off there and die, I'll kill myself," Whit said. "Does that answer your question?" He stepped on to the deck. He was naked too, and the wind made him shiver. He crossed the planks to the rail and held up his hands. "Come down from there, and stop talking like a child."

"If I talked like a child all the time"—Jaime spoke slowly, paying attention to where he put his feet—"and if it meant I was thinking like a child, and you knew I was thinking like a child"—he tilted, and it took him a second to steady himself— "with no bullshit, no manipulating, just the plain truth, then you'd believe me, and"—he started another step, tottered, waved his arms, stuck one leg out, caught Whit's hands, and fell into Whit's arms, staggering, so that Whit's arms went around him by reflex to hold him up, and he panted into Whit's

225

ear—"we'd be okay. You wouldn't do stupid things like this stupid tour, because I'd be right, and you'd know I was right." He gave off heat and was good to hold. Whit kissed his mouth.

"This isn't a child's problem," he said. "This is a grown-up's problem."

Jaime broke away from him and went back and got into the dark bed. Whit slid the glass panel closed and got in beside him. Jaime's back was turned. Whit stroked his shoulder. He shrugged Whit's hand away. But in the morning, he said gravely, rubbing steam off the bathroom mirror, peering at his face, fingering his beard, frowning, "You know what love shouldn't be?" He opened the cabinet to get little scissors, shut the cabinet, lifted his chin. *Snip,* went the scissors, *snip.* Whit finished drying off and hung up his towel. "A tug of war," Jaime said. Whit headed for the bedroom to dress. A pencil rattled lightly on the steps above. Polk was awake. Jaime called from the bathroom, "Love shouldn't be a contest of wills. You go, I'll stay."

It was settled. He acted quiet and mannerly from then on. He was frightened—that was plain from the way he clung to Whit when they made love. Once Whit awoke to find the bed beside him empty. The lights were all out. The bathroom door was open and no one was in there. No one was in the other bedroom. The kitchen and living room were empty. Whit stepped out on the deck and looked at the night beach, the ocean. There was part of a moon. The beach was barren. Waves foamed around the bird rocks but he didn't see anyone swimming. He found Jaime in the tower. He sat at the desk, moonlit in the white terry-cloth robe. His arms were crossed on the typewriter, and his head lay on his arms. When Whit switched on the light and Jaime looked up, his eyes were bloodshot. Not from marijuana this time. From crying.

"Don't do that," Whit said. "That's blackmail."

"You weren't supposed to see," Jaime said.

"You can still come along," Whit said.

"What would I do in New York, what would I do in Chicago? Wait for you. It would be a waste of money. I can

226

wait for you here." He drew a long unsteady breath, and smiled a wobbly smile. "I wanted to belong to somebody. I thought it would be easy."

"I shouldn't have let you close the shop," Whit said.

"It was too far," Jaime said. "I wanted the beach. I wanted you." He got off the desk chair. "It was a good trade-off. Anyway, the shop was over with. Things come to an end."

"Not us," Whit said. "I'll be back."

"I'll wait," Jaime said.

And that had been the only trouble he made. And Whit left him. For twenty-two days, alone with Polk, the beach house, the car, tickets to every musical, concert, play in town, and, of course, all the money he wanted to spend. He didn't want to spend any, and he didn't spend much. He didn't use the tickets. He hardly used the car. He used the house but there was no sign of that when he brought Whit back to it from the airport. It looked as if no one had breathed in it since Whit left. Whit was tired and bruised from the travel and the unaccustomed beds. It was days before he knew what time it was. Jaime was quiet and courteous. He asked Whit about the trip. He listened. He smiled and laughed and acted disgusted or surprised when he thought these were the reactions Whit expected from him. He made love dutifully. And when Whit said he was making love dutifully he made love more dutifully.

"What happened while I was gone?" Whit said. He was watching Jaime pull up the ragged torn-off shorts Whit had yanked down to get at him on the canvas cushions of the wicker couch. This was how Whit was acting. Trying to get something from Jaime that wasn't there anymore. Trying three times a day. Frantic. As if more was better when none was any good. "Why are you like this? What's wrong?"

The sun was striking through the glass wall of the living room. Jaime was a figure without detail, between Whit and the light. "When are you going away again?" he said.

"Why would I go away again?" Whit winced against the light, sat up, reached for cigarettes on the coffee table, for his lighter.

227

Jaime crouched to buckle his sandals. "You're writing another book."

"You want me to stop?" Whit reached for his own shorts on the Navajo rug. "I'll stop if you say so."

"If you stop, I'll be the one who goes away."

"Make sense." Whit put his feet through the leg holes of the shorts. "You're afraid I'll go away again, right? You don't trust me. You think I betrayed you, and you'll never trust me again, and that's why we're having such lousy sex, is that right?" He stood, jerked up the shorts, and zipped them. "And the book I'm writing is going to take me away again, but you don't want me to stop writing it. If I stop writing, you'll leave?"

"I have to go to the store." Jaime climbed the stairs.

Whit called after him, "You could have gone with me."

"I don't like being alone among a million strangers," Jaime's voice came faint from the bedroom. "What did you do with the keys?"

"You don't think I'll go away," Whit said. "That's just an excuse. You're tired of me. I know you—you get tired of things suddenly. You thought it would be nice to belong to somebody, right? The way you thought it would be nice to have a shop. Then you thought it would be nice to give food and shelter to those kids. Then you didn't think so anymore. 'Things come to an end'—isn't that what you said? You wanted the beach and me. Now what do you want?"

"I can't find the keys," Jaime said.

"On the kitchen counter," Whit said. "You've wanted out of it ever since I got back. But you don't want to hurt my feelings. You're trying to be nice about it, kind, right?"

"Look what I found." Smiling, Jaime came down the stairs. In his fingers he held up a little blue-and-white envelope. "Tickets to the ballet tonight. I'll wear my suit."

The only time Whit had seen him in the suit was the day they bought it, when he stood in front of triple mirrors while a little round bald man with tufts of white hair sticking out of his ears made chalk marks on the pants cuffs and on the shoulders of the jacket. Jaime had stood there trying not to see himself, embarrassed, fidgety. He had refused to put the suit on to see if the alterations were right. It hung in the closet with the bright shirts Whit had bought him, the new jeans, new corduroys, new shoes. Whit took the tickets and gave him a kiss. He sang when Jaime left for the store, sang so loudly he didn't hear from the shower when Kate Schaefer knocked at the kitchen door. After the shower, he went out on the deck with a drink and did a dance, and she saw him and came across the sand, breasts and hips joggling inside a flame-color muumuu.

"Who's that ugly little man?" she asked. "That friend of Jaime's? The one who kept coming here while you were gone?"

Whit stopped smiling. The happiness drained out of him. "Rumpelstiltskin," he said. "You want a drink?"

"I wish he'd go away." She narrowed her eyes between their long, thick, paste-on lashes, and surveyed the empty beach. "I don't like him."

"Go away from where?" Whit said. He felt sick.

"He hangs around," she said. "Don't tell me you haven't seen him? He's always watching us. He wears binoculars. I was changing just now, and there he was peering down from the cliff right through my windows. Mostly he's up the beach." She gave a stage shudder. "He gives me the creeps. And that's not the worst. He scares my cleaning woman."

Whit walked to the end of the deck and looked between the houses to the cement steps that climbed the cliff face to the highway. The steps were deep in crumbled rock. He lifted his gaze to the cliff top. No one stood up there, and he thought it wasn't the store Jaime had to go to. He turned back to Kate. "Next time you see him," he said, "call the police."

"He's Jaime's friend," she objected. "He was here half a dozen times while you were on your trip."

"He's nobody's friend," Whit said.

Something was wrong with Jaime when he came back with the groceries. Whit yelled at him from the minute he came in the door, carrying the brown sacks. Whit kept stepping in front of him, shouting into his face. Jaime stepped around him,

229

stowing away the cans, boxes, packages from the sacks in the cupboards where they belonged, in the refrigerator. He folded the empty sacks neatly and stowed them away neatly. He seemed not to hear. Whit grabbed him and shook him. Jaime smiled faintly. "You're acting terrible," he said. "You should see yourself. You look crazy." He pushed Whit off almost absentmindedly, as if he had something else to do, something that didn't leave him time to listen to Whit. He said, "You don't know what you're talking about. I didn't sleep with Abby. I never slept with him and I never will. So why don't you shut up?"

"Don't tell me to shut up," Whit said.

Jaime said, "You didn't say I wasn't supposed to have anybody come here."

"I didn't think you had to be told I didn't want Abby Selzer to come here, for Christ's sake." Jaime looked at him coldly for a second, turned, and left the kitchen. Whit heard him on the stairs. Whit ran to the foot of the stairs. He yelled after him, "I'll never get the place clean. I don't even want to be here now. I hate it. You've ruined it."

"You're crazy," Jaime said, and a door closed.

When it had grown late, and the light through the windows was red from the setting sun, when he had quit shaking, when his stomach had quit churning, he shook cornflakes into a bowl, poured milk on them, and ate them standing up. He fed Polk. He laid the envelope of tickets on the dresser, changed his clothes, tucked the tickets into the jacket he was going to wear. He went to the bathroom, pissed, and combed his hair. He put the jacket on and, in his shiny shoes, climbed to the tower room. He found it empty, and came down again. He looked at the closed door of the second bedroom, the one they never used. Rocks rattled on the roof. He called, "I'm going to the ballet. Are you coming?" Jaime didn't answer. Because of how fine the day had been, the home-going traffic from the beach was dense and slow. Whit was in the Mercedes with the engine running, waiting for a break in the traffic, when he heard a shout. He squinted into the rearview mirror. Jaime

230

came running, all dressed up in his suit. He looked beautiful. He pulled open the door, dropped onto the seat, and slammed the door.

"It was my idea," he said. "Of course I'm coming."

Whit got the car onto the highway. "He brings you dope, doesn't he?"

"You're crazy," Jaime said again. He was barefoot.

"You forgot your shoes and socks," Whit said.

"You're not supposed to criticize me," Jaime said. "You're supposed to love me." He sounded ready to cry.

"I love you," Whit said. "Everything's all right."

Jaime didn't cry. He talked about the ballet. The brochure had a photograph of the one that excited him. It had to do with the Olympic Games. It had only male dancers and they didn't wear much. In the crowded, tall, glass-and-steel foyer under the glittering chandeliers, no one seemed to notice that Jaime wasn't wearing shoes. He and Whit sat in the vast dark of the auditorium with thirty-five hundred other people, and stared at the bright stage. Jaime seemed all right. The orchestra played. Jaime sang softly under his breath. But not for long. He began to talk to himself. He shifted in his seat, crossed and recrossed his legs. He rolled up his program, unrolled it, rolled it up again—not idly but tightly, as if he wanted to wring moisture out of it. Heat came off him. Whit glanced at him. His face was shiny with sweat.

Whit said, "Are you all right?"

Jaime jerked, startled. He stared for an instant as if he didn't know who Whit was. Then he said, "I have to go. I'll be back."

He stood up and lunged, half-falling, over the knees of the startled, middle-aged couple seated beside them. Whit and the couple watched him hurry up the shadowy aisle. Whit gave the couple a little shrug, a little bewildered smile. He made himself sit and watch. But the time seemed long. He began to check his wrist. Five minutes. Ten. He whispered excuses to the couple and edged awkwardly out of the row. Climbing the slope to the doors, he tried to look as if nothing were wrong. Jaime wasn't in the foyer. No one was. No one was in the vast, glossy men's

231

room. He climbed to the bar. Glasses and bottles gleamed, bartenders in red Nehru jackets waited with folded arms, but no one drank. Music filtered out here like a memory. Whit ran down the staircase with its curved ribbons of flat steel railing and pushed out into the theatrically lighted night.

Great glowing glass buildings rose beyond trees, streets, fountains. Ahead of him, a plateau of cement with plantings and sculptures stretched northward. Not a human being was in sight. Not till Jaime. At the far end, in the blue water of a mirror pool, naked as a satyr on a jar. Playing in the water. Despair filled Whit, and he began to run. The mirror pool encircled the far theater whose black glass front rose sheer against a black glass sky. Jaime saw Whit coming, and ran in the water, ran away, ran around back of the theater. Whit ran after him. Was someone coming behind him? He didn't stop to look. Jaime's clothes made a trail. Whit snatched them up as he ran. Jacket, shirt, tie, trousers, underpants, all damp with sweat. He ran around the mirror pool.

"Get away from me," Jaime screamed at him. "Get away."

"Jaime, come on, put your clothes on." Whit stepped up on the flat rim of the mirror pool, holding out the clothes. Jaime was up to his ankles in the water, crouching a little, hands out like a wrestler ready to defend himself against a bear. His eyes were open very wide. White showed all around the irises. The irises looked black, the pupils had dilated so. "Come on," Whit begged. "There's nothing to be afraid of. Honest— you're just imagining things." He stepped down into the pool. Jaime turned to run, slipped, fell with a big splash, scrambled frantically to his feet again. He stumbled out of the pool. And there stood Abby Selzer in a tuxedo. Jaime clutched him.

"He's trying to kill me," he babbled. "Get him away from me. He's got a gun, and he's trying to kill me."

Whit walked through the water. Abby held up a hand. Behind him, two boys of about ten, one of them wheeling a bicycle, stopped and stared. "It's not true," Whit said, but he quit walking. He stood in the water, hugging the clothes. Abby said, "I'll handle it. I know what to do. Leave it to me."

"It's acid, isn't it?" Whit said. "You brought it to him this afternoon."

"He asked for it," Abby said. He was stroking Jaime's wet naked back. Whit wanted to vomit. "I brought it as an act of friendship." Jaime was crying. "There, there," Abby crooned to him. "I won't let him get you. You're safe with me. It's going to be all right now." He looked at Whit. "Acid can be a glorious adventure—if the circumstances are right. The circumstances between you two are not right. I never thought they would be. Throw me his clothes. No, don't come any closer."

Whit threw the clothes. Shorts and shirt fell into the water and floated, bloating. Trousers draped themselves across the rim. The jacket got there. Abby, murmuring gentleness, wrapped the jacket around Jaime's beautiful flanks and tied the arms. Jaime gave Whit a look of terror, and hid behind Abby, whimpering, cringing. Abby clucked and cooed and led him toward the escalator down to the parking garage.

"Where are you taking him?" Whit called.

The boys shrank back out of the way. "Mister," the one with the bicycle asked Abby, "do you want us to call an ambulance?" His voice was thin and piping in the stillness.

"No, thank you." Abby, arms around the shivering, whining Jaime, dropped slowly from sight.

Whit bent and picked up Jaime's floating necktie. He waded out of the water. He wanted to die of grief and rage.

"What happened to that guy?" one of the boys asked.

"He took LSD," Whit said. He sat on the rim of the pool and emptied out his shoes. The boys came and stood in front of him, watching. He wrung out his socks and put them on again. He looked at the boys. "Scary, wasn't it? Are you going to take LSD if somebody offers it to you?"

"Don't you want his clothes?" the bicycle boy said.

The other one blew a big pink bubble. It burst. He gathered in the shreds with his tongue. "Is he crazy?"

"Maybe not forever." Whit rose and pushed his feet into the wet shoes. He picked up the necktie and walked off. And those times in the hospital recreation room, he thought he had been right, that it wouldn't be forever, that Jaime was getting well. Then, one day, the nurse behind the desk sent him to another part of the hospital to find Jaime. Abby and Jaime's mother were standing in the hallway. Abby was arguing loudly with a young doctor who picked nervously at schoolboy pimples. Whit backed out of sight. He sat outdoors on a cement bench shielded by shrubbery, where he could see the exit. Abby and Rosa de Santos came out at last, and Whit went in. Jaime was in a little room with a bed, a window, and nothing else. Whit had brought flowers. Jaime didn't know him, but he took the flowers. He stood holding them for a long time, staring at them, bemused, uncertain. He turned, sat down cross-legged in a corner, his back to Whit. The light from the window shone in Whit's eyes. He couldn't make out what Jaime was doing. He took a step nearer. Jaime was pulling the flowers apart and eating them.

Strangers

The Sea Shanty, ramshackle bat and board, in need of paint, stands back off the coast road in a cleft of steep hills. The red neon letters along the ridge of its low roof are small, dim, hard to read. Cars speeding past in the night don't notice the Sea Shanty. This is how the Sea Shanty wants it. It is no place to stray into. The Iowan with his dusty camper full of wife, kids, fishing gear, if he stops, doesn't stay. Before he can ask for a six-pack or the way to the men's room, he knows he has come to the wrong place. It is a place for strangers, all right, but not his sort. He backs out, looking scared or disgusted, or both.

The Sea Shanty has regular patrons, men who can't find anything better to do with their time than sit at a badly lit bar and drink cheap beer while the jukebox raves, until two in the morning, every morning. They are young, middle-aged, old, white, black, brown. But they have one thing in common. They have given up. Proof of this is that they talk to one another. They are not the Sea Shanty's reason for being. The Sea Shanty exists for strangers, men from miles away, who come looking for men they've never seen before to spend the night with— men they hope never to see again, men to whom they will not speak if they do see them again.

Whit rolls the Mercedes onto the wanly lit stretch of gravel that fronts the place. Five other cars stand there. It has been only four weeks since he was here. It is soon to try to come back a stranger. But the place is near, and he doesn't feel like a long drive over the mountains to the Valley and the next place on his list that he's never walked into. From maybe two dozen such places, from Santa Barbara to Laguna, he has gone home with strangers, or has brought strangers home with him to be wakened startled at dawn by the clatter of rocks on the roof as trucks begin to rumble along the highway at the top of the cliffs.

He doesn't know why it is easy for him. Rarely is he recognized, a success, a celebrity. He is clean and well dressed. His car is quietly flashy. But he is not young as age is measured in these places. He is losing his hair. He is too thin. Maybe that he is bored and dislikes the places and the shrill or furtive nervousness of the men, and is poor at hiding his boredom and dislike, makes him a magnet. Whatever the reason, it is the easiness of it that lets him go on. If he had to work at it, he would stop bothering. A night is not enough. But—a night is never too much. He can grin to himself at the fright-flight in the morning. He can bear the wrench of separation and the hour's loneliness that follows. He never forgets, but he remembers without sorrow.

If a voice he last heard in a damp, laughing whisper close to his ear in the darkness of his bed or of a stranger's bed, speaks through his telephone, suggesting they ought to get together for a drink, he makes amiable excuses and hangs up. For an instant, with his hand on the receiver, he wonders if he really has to be so careful. But in the next instant, turning back to the typewriter, he knows he has done right. Give him two days or three with somebody who goes through the motions of love with him, and he will stand as much chance of survival whole as a pipe-clay doll in that shooting gallery on the pier Jaime used to love. In the sun glare of the glassy tower, behind the dark lenses, he shuts his eyes and sees the cheap hollow little dolls with their mispainted smiles fly to bits when the

236

pellets strike. The clay utters a little bell note of anguish each time. He winces. His father says, in a mock-Irish accent, *Och, I'm desthroyed!* He grins.

A choir has been singing Palestrina's music about the Garden of Love. Now it quits. He switches off the radio and gets out of the car and stands, filling his lungs with the air off the ocean that breathes on the far side of the highway, that moves out there, rustling in the dark. He listens to it for a minute. He hears the buzz of the neon tubing on top of the Sea Shanty. A string of cars streaks down the highway. He turns, crunches across the gravel, pushes the door. The noise of the jukebox hits him like a physical force, louder than Bruckner in a symphony hall. It's not Bruckner. A singer shouts hoarsely for his baby to light his fire. The place is dim under dusty, drooping fishnets. Faded ship's signal pennants are tacked to the plank walls. Circular life preservers hang off posts, peeling white paint. At the far back of the place, a pool table glows green under a dangling, hooded light. Pool cues are racked against a wall beside a poster of a motorcyclist who is young, bony, and has long, uncombed blond hair.

The five men whose cars wait outside don't sit at the little tables. They sit on stools with deep, wheezy leather cushions, at a bar whose outer edge is padded leather. A plump, middle-aged Mexican who wears a hearing aid sits next to a gnarled man in a greasy mariner's cap. They talk, and are probably regulars. The drinkers who sit apart are almost certainly strangers. They gaze alternately into the back-bar mirror and at the talking face of the Minnesota senator running for president on the gray screen of a TV set that hangs up in a corner and whose sound cannot be heard in the roar of the jukebox. The three drinkers are in their thirties. The two white ones look like high-school teachers and wear department-store suits. The black one wears Whit's two-hundred-dollar tweed jacket. Whit takes a stool beside his.

There is no need to shout. He just has to pitch his voice right. There is a trick to it. He learned it when he wrote a story for the Cordova Junior College paper about the school's auto-body repair shop. The shop was not as noisy as the Sea Shanty, but the principle holds. He sees near the shoulder of the jacket the thread loops pulled loose by Polk. He says, "That's a good-looking jacket."

The black gives him a mechanical smile. "Thank you." He studies Whit. It takes less than a second. Whit is not the stranger he has in mind. He turns back to his beer.

"Draft," Whit tells the bartender. He asks the black, "Where did you get it?"

"London," the black says. He opens the coat. "See for yourself."

Whit sees and rejoices. The little blond kid didn't even have the sense to take out the labels. "Excuse me," he says, and walks back to where a narrow hall opens off the area that houses the pool table. A battered black pay telephone hangs on the wall here, between closed doors that leak disinfectant smells and that are both labeled WHOEVER. Opposite, on a door covered in zinc, the sign reads KITCHEN IS A NO-NO. He has never known any cooking to go on in that kitchen. He takes out his wallet, slips a card from it, lifts down the receiver, drops in a dime, and dials the number on the card. It gets him the police station. The man who gave him the card isn't there, the man Kate Schaefer rang when Whit was robbed, but others are there, and they will come. Whit walks back to the bar where his beer waits. The jukebox plays "Harper Valley P.T.A." The singer is a woman with a shrill voice. A pair of girl-slim boys in T-shirts and tight jeans hovers over the pushbuttons of the jukebox, giggling. No one else new has come in, and the black has not moved. He stares at his glass, turning it in his fingers in its puddle on the bar. It is draped inside with tatters of foam. Whit climbs onto his stool. "Let me buy you another beer," he says, and holds out his pack of cigarettes, feeling like Judas. The betrayed takes a cigarette. Whit lights it for him. Whit says, "You haven't been here before, right?"

"You mean, it's a long way from the ghetto?" the black says. "That's my Cadillac outside."

"I mean it's a long way from London," Whit says.

"No, I never was here before," the black says.

Whit has suggested that the police not use a siren and they don't. They arrive like anyone else. At the Sea Shanty, when anyone pushes open the door, everyone looks to see if the stranger is arriving whom they are waiting for. The police officers, in their dark blue uniforms and caps with shiny badges, look large. They are both young, blond, and blue-eyed. One of the schoolteachers at the bar moans, the other whispers, "Shit." But neither of them moves. Their heads droop and they cling to their beer glasses. The young boys are at the pool table. They straighten up and stare. One of the officers squats and pulls the plug on the jukebox. The record slurs and groans into silence. "Hey," the bartender says. The silence is complete. The police officer's knees snap as he stands. "Mr. Miller, please?" he says.

Whit gets off his stool. He tilts his head at the black, who is saying, "Mama told me there'd be nights like this." Whit doubts it. The officers come down the room under the sagging fishnet. A sharp little electronic whine comes from up the bar. It is the hearing aid of the plump Mexican. It has fallen out of his ear. The weather-beaten man is wearing some kind of smile. Maybe it is meant to be ingratiating. His teeth are tobacco stained. One of the officers takes the arm of the black and helps him off the stool. "Would you like to step outside with me for a moment, sir? Please. Few questions?" The black is stiff with alarm. His eyes roll at Whit. They roll back at the officer. "Shit," he says. "It's about the fucking jacket, ain't it?"

"And the shoes," Whit says. They are handmade shoes. The cobbler is an Italian who talks like Chico Marx. Whit's producer recommended him. The shoes are too big for the black but they are very beautiful. "Those are my shoes too."

"The man told me somebody died," the black says. "Says he was a clerk in a law office and somebody died and left all these clothes. Had 'em in the back of his car."

"They're so hot," the officer says, "I'm surprised they're not blistering you right now. You want to walk outside, please?"

"I didn't steal 'em," the black protests as he goes. He looks

239

small and frail between the two big blonds. "I paid good bread, hard-earned bread." At the dark jukebox, the officer who hasn't spoken squats and plugs in the cord again. The box lights up. "He said he didn't know what to do with 'em. I could have 'em for twenty-five cents on the dollar." The music begins to scream again. The black and the officer who holds his arm disappear out the door. It is like the erasing of a political cartoon. The officer who has plugged in the jukebox grins.

"All right, gentlemen," he shouts, "you may resume play."

He pushes outside and Whit follows, but there is no conference on the gravel in the cold sea wind. The black in handcuffs is already inside the police car. The first officer slams the door on him and turns back to Whit, while the second officer goes around the car and gets behind the wheel. The first officer says to Whit, "Was this where you met the kid that robbed you? You didn't put that in your report." He looks at the paint-scaling wooden front of the Sea Shanty. "What do you want to come to a dump like this for?" His boy-blue eyes reproach Whit. "A man in your position?"

"You've answered your own question, haven't you?" Whit says. "What *is* in the report is a list of my clothes and the serial numbers of the television set and the stereo equipment and the typewriter. Do you want to get those back for me, now?"

"I don't know about no stereo equipment," the black wails from the car. "I don't know about no typewriter."

The officer ignores him. He tells Whit, "If you invite strangers into your home, you're asking for trouble. If citizens don't even try to protect themselves, it makes more work for us, it costs the taxpayer more money."

"Have you got the list?" Whit says.

"Yes, sir." The officer doesn't like the answer and he starts for the squad car. "We'll telephone you." Is he through lecturing? No. After he reaches the car and gives the black's head a shove to indicate that he is to move over and make room, the officer turns back. "You know, it's no secret to us what you took that kid home for." Again he gives the Sea Shanty a sour look. "We know what this place is. You

240

committed a criminal act yourself. That's right, isn't it?"

"I sure as hell made a mistake," Whit says.

The officer makes a face, folds his bulk inside the squad car, and slams the door. The car bucks forward, scattering gravel. At the edge of the highway, it jounces in a deep rut. The springs are worn out. The fenders come down hard on the tires. The howl this produces is loud in the stillness.

Whit gets into his own car and drives home.

Sandy Fine says, "Are we speaking?"

Whit has trudged across the space of sand between his house and Kate Schaefer's because she is having a party and has asked him to be there. The sun slams down. Wide plank steps lead up from the sand to Kate's deck, where men and women in white jackets and ties, in blue jeans and sandals, in dresses, in bikinis, stand around with stoneware plates on which the wind flutters paper napkins, and with drinks in their hands. At the top of the stairs, green linen slacks, green gingham shirt, copper hair shining, stands Sandy, unsure whether to smile. Whit hugs him. Sandy hugs Whit

"I'm so happy for your success."

"Right. What the hell are you doing here?"

"I lent Kate fifty feet of glorious leather bindings," Sandy says. "For a commercial. Christmas among the rich. Some revolting wine they're trying to convince viewers is good by pricing it high and showing it being guzzled in elegant surroundings." He cocks an eyebrow. "Why so thin and haggard? Isn't anybody looking after you?"

"He went crazy," Whit says. "And the electric shock treatments only make him worse. How's Tom?"

A young woman wants to know if Whit wants a drink, sir. She wears short shorts and has knotted a man's shirt under perky little breasts. She is a delicious color. Whit asks her for a Coke. She flashes a terrific smile, in case Whit or Sandy have to do with making films. She heads for the bar, wiggling her little butt. Whit watches it. *Always treat women with respect,* his

241

father says. They sit on the front steps of the house on Berry Street in the twilight. Behind them, inside the house, his mother weeps. Something Whit has done or said has hurt her. *They are God's most wonderful creation,* his father says. *They're the source of life. You must always respect that.* Sandy has been eyeing the bartender, dark, early twenties, whose puff-sleeved shirt, open to the waist, shows off a chiseled torso, brown and hairless. Sandy notices Whit watching the girl's ass. He says:

"Dell worries about you."

"Bullshit," Whit says. "I asked you about Tom."

Sandy is peevish. "That didn't last. And if you say 'I told you so,' I'll give you such a hit you'll still be hearing 'Jingle Bells' on the Fourth of July." He grins his freckle-faced kid grin, then sobers. "When your robbery was on the news, I wanted to ring you and commiserate, but I didn't know how you'd take it. I did call Dell. She was very upset. The way you're living frightens her."

"I hope you reassured her. Isn't that how all faggots live?" The girl comes with Coke in a red can, and a tall, slim glass filled with shaved ice. Whit thanks her, sets can and glass on the deck rail, hikes himself up on the rail, fills the glass from the can with sticky brown foam. "Ready at all times to have their throats slit?"

"Not at parties," Sandy says. "Not literally, anyway." He watches Whit drink. "That's new. You never used to turn down free booze."

"Booze makes me thin and haggard," Whit says. "It robs me of my rest. It makes me cry. I'm never without it. I drink it like water." He holds up the glass of Coke and marvels at it. "I can't explain this. It must be you. I always did revert to adolescence with you." He frowns. "You were never robbed, were you? Not in all these years, not with all the tricks you've turned."

"You're joking." Sandy is leaning on the rail now, squinting in the strong light, watching surfers teeter and fall in the blue waves. "I simply never told anyone. I mean, it's humiliating,

242

isn't it? And the way the police smirk. You're right—we're born victims, everybody's victims, starting with mom and pop."

"Choke, sob," Whit says. "I got all my stuff back. By crazy luck. Good as new. Sitting there waiting to be hauled away by the next pretty faker with a nifty cock."

"Well," Kate Schaefer says, "if you're going to talk dirty." Today's muumuu is a tropical forest of monster green leaves and red parrots. "Do you two know each other?"

"From Sumeria," Whit says. "We did our childish sums on wet clay tablets. Isn't that Judd Lawrence?" The craggy-faced actor has appeared in the open glass sliding door to the deck. "I want to talk to him." Whit jumps down off the rail and pushes between bodies. He says to Lawrence, "Did you know that kid you were with at the Sea Shanty last month? The stocky little curly-headed blond?"

"The one you went off into the night with?" Lawrence smiles by turning down the corners of his mouth. "No. He dropped into my car at a stoplight in Santa Monica." He sobers. "He wasn't the one who robbed you! Good Lord." The girl in short shorts hands him a julep. "Thank you, my dear." His grin is wolfish. He turns it off, takes a quick sip of the drink, and says gravely, "I got off lucky, didn't I?"

"Ah," Whit says, "it wasn't all bad news."

"I rather thought it wouldn't be," Lawrence says. "That was why I bought him an expensive dinner."

Rocks fall with a loud clatter on the roof high above and behind them. Lawrence jerks his head up. So does everyone on the deck. Some yelp. Some crouch, arms over their heads. The rocks bounce off the roof and arc over the deck and thump into the sand. Everyone talks at once. A pudgy man in a Palm Beach suit jumps the rail, picks up a pair of rocks, and turns, holding them out. Everyone knows what he means. Most of them speak it aloud. Lawrence says:

"Somebody could have been killed."

Sandy says, "Does that happen often? What about when it rains? Remember what happened in Brazil? Last June? Tons of it came down, crushed the houses, crushed the people?"

"That was mud and gravel," Whit says. "This is the continent. Everybody knows California's falling into the sea. It's only a few rocks. You get used to it."

"You get used to it if you want to." Sandy looks anxiously upward. He looks at Whit: "You live near here?"

"Next door," Whit says, and jerks his head toward his own house where Polk sleeps curled up yellow in the sun on the rail of the upper deck. "You want to see it?"

"It must be a bit empty," Lawrence says. "The police don't make any effort in cases like yours."

"They didn't have to." Whit tells about his luck at the Sea Shanty. "What wasn't in the kid's car was in his apartment. He didn't seem to know any fences. His name is Earl Hector Hoppe. He works with his twin brother, Merle."

"They'll be a treat to the other prisoners," Lawrence says. He sips the julep again. His hand is trembling, probably from the shock of the falling rocks. The sprig of mint drops off the rim of his glass. He crouches to pick it up from the deck planks. "Did you know? I'll be working in the film they're making of your book."

"It's a wonderful book," Sandy says.

Whit introduces him to Lawrence. As they shake hands, Sandy says, "We've been seeing each other for years, decades. Here and there. The Music Center, the Cordova Stage."

"There aren't that many of us." Whit quotes McGriff. "By the time you're thirty, you've seen them all."

Lawrence laughs. "By the time you're sixty, there's a whole new crop. Excuse me." He takes a deep breath, squares his old shoulders, pulls in his gut, and goes to have a word with the bartender.

"Damn," Sandy says.

Red sunset light is in the room. He has been asleep on the couch. Before the party was over, he had begun to lace his Cokes with rum. The brown-sugar taste has gone bitter in his mouth. He gropes on the rug beside the couch for his cigarettes. And he hears a sound. Somebody is in the house. He shuts his eyes, shuts his jaws so tight they hurt. Not again. Please, God, not again. He sucks in air, blows it out disgustedly, and lifts his head to peer around. He almost says Polk's name aloud and then thinks he won't. He sits up, moving cautiously, to try to keep the wicker of the couch from creaking. It creaks anyway. Feet on the floor, he sits, holding his breath, listening. It isn't Polk. What moves is bigger than that. In the kitchen. He almost calls out "Jaime" but it can't be Jaime. He wouldn't move so softly. Whit gauges the distance across the room. The glass door to the deck stands open but the screen is closed. It will take extra seconds to unlatch it, and it slides noisily. All the same, he gets off the couch and starts barefoot across the rug. Once past the screen, he can run like hell. A voice stops him:

"Oh, you're awake. That's nice. I didn't want to disturb you. You look so peaceful when you sleep. The tragic look all goes away. You look like a little boy."

It is the girl in the short shorts. Whit squints.

"Where did you come from? The party's over."

"That's why I could come," she says. "I hope it's all right. I brought food. You didn't eat. I thought you'd be hungry. I brought some wine too." She sounds wistful. "I thought maybe you'd like somebody to eat supper with. Is it all right? Kate said you were all alone."

Whit runs a hand down his face. "Everybody's all alone," he says. "It's the natural condition of man." He wants the bathroom, so he climbs the stairs. "If we all just made up our minds to that, it would solve a lot of problems." He switches on the bathroom light, empties his bladder, takes aspirin, and brushes his teeth. He rinses his mouth, splashes his face with cold water, dries his face, studies his face in the mirror, trying to see the tragic look. He shrugs. It is a child's face worn too long. It has been that for quite a time. He snaps off the light and goes back downstairs.

"I fed your kitty-cat," she says. She has found candles, set them on the table, lighted them. They show him a platter of pâté and cheeses, a basket that holds three kinds of bread, and two plates with mounds of creamy crab meat on lettuce leaves, surrounded by wedges of tomato and avocado. Wineglasses glint. Jaime never let them get dusty. Whit has kept them polished. Short shorts smiles at him across the table. It is not the flashy smile she gave everyone at Kate's party. She seems to mean this one, and he likes it. She asks timidly, "Do you want to sit down?"

He sits down. "Thank you. This is very nice." She sits down too and, like a grave six-year-old at a doll's tea party, neatly unfolds her napkin and lays it in her lap. He laughs. He wants to hug her. She has loosened the cork. He takes it out and pours the wine. "But why me?" he asks. "There were twenty men at that party."

She swallows wine quickly, shakes her head. "You were so beautiful and sad," she says. "I never saw anybody so beautiful and sad before. You made me want to cry. You made me want to make things happy for you."

"I have to do that myself." He sounds old and stodgy, saying it aloud. To her. The brightness goes out of her face. He tries to bring it back by explaining. "When I let other people try it, it doesn't work out. They get hurt, I get hurt."

"You've been hurt a lot," she says soberly. "I can tell. It's your eyes. There's so much pain in your eyes."

"I haven't been hurt more than average," he says. "I just don't manage it well." He takes a forkful of crab meat. Chewing, he gives her a smile. "It's a good thing you fed Polk before he got a whiff of this."

"The cat," she says. "I don't know where he went."

"To bed. Upstairs. On my typewriter."

"You're a writer." She tears a slice of bread with caraway seeds in it. "She told me. Everybody's reading your novel." On the scrap of bread she spreads pâté. "Not me." She looks up at him quickly, afraid she has said the wrong thing. "I don't read novels. Just nonfiction. I've got a lot to learn. But Kate says it's a wonderful book." She pops the bread and pâté into her mouth, chews, washes it down with a gulp of wine. "I guess maybe writers feel more than other people, right?"

He laughs. "They sure as hell howl more." She makes him feel good. Now she stands up, comes around the little table, bends, and peers closely into his eyes. She is concentrating and chewing at the same time. She stands upright.

"They're not really blue," she says. "They've got little flecks of yellow in them." She sits down.

"Yours are brown," he says. "That's startling, you're so blonde."

"I'm half Swedish," she says, "half Greek."

He is surprised at how he feels about her. She charms him because she doesn't seem to be trying to do that. She talks to him about her job, the crazy rich people she meets. She talks about Wisconsin in the wintertime and a pet rabbit she used to have. She talks to him about trying to get on TV and how she once cracked up an airplane in Ventura, trying to learn to fly. She is open as a little girl and at the same time aware of how funny she is. She would like to be a singer. She sang in the church choir in Appleton. He tells her about his gospel quartet in Cordova. She laughs. They eat and drink and are merry.

Then they begin to grow quiet. He simply watches her, thinking how beautifully she is made, slim and trim, like a boy. Like Dell, though smaller. Yet she is no more a boy than Dell. The neat breasts inside the thin cotton fabric of her shirt are as fetching as anything about her—maybe the most fetching. He has thought this would never happen to him again. His cock thickens, stretches. His heart beats in his cock. He feels as if he were one big smile. Then he tells himself that nothing must come of this. And with that, the brightness evidently goes out of his face.

"What's wrong?" She pours the last of the wine.

"Nothing." He forces a smile. He wants her. If he tells her the truth about himself, she will gather up her plastic food containers and go mournfully away in her caterer's truck. This will be best for them both. It will certainly be best for her. The sun has set. He pushes away his plate and lights a cigarette. "It's late," he says, and looks at his watch.

Her eyes grow round with dismay. "You're not going somewhere?" She sets down her glass. "Nobody's coming?"

He gives up trying to spare her. "I don't even know your name," he says. "Mine is Whit. It means 'an insignificant quantity.'"

"Sheri." She says it so softly it is almost a sigh. She is relieved not to be rescued. She tilts her head at him in the flickering light. She smiles. "I don't know what it means. Sheri—with an *i*."

"Well, Sheri-with-an-*i*"—he pushes back his chair and gets to his feet—"do you want to watch TV?" He holds out a hand to her.

She takes the hand and stands up. "Show me where you sleep," she says.

Friends

He walks along the night beach. It is cold, and fog has come in. Shoulders hunched, hands thrust deep in his pockets, he walks fast and hard. At first he ran. He ran until he staggered and was out of breath. He didn't fall, or even stop. He didn't let himself. He made himself go on. His legs ache, but he is still taking long strides. He is still muttering over and over to himself, "I don't need anybody, I don't need anybody." The shore is not all sand. Where creeks flow out, he wades through water. *Jaime.* Where rocks crop out into the surf, he clambers over them. They have torn his pants, scraped his knees, cut his hands. He is glad to be bleeding. He can't cry anymore.

He cried at first, during the running. She was still present to him then. Over and over again in his mind, they fucked in the three and thirty ways he thought he had forgotten—each way making him more drunk with delight in her. Her mouth on his cock was quick, clever, hungry. Her cunt was honey to his mouth. Thrust deep inside her, her legs clasped around him, he held her lightness to him and carried her, waltzing, reeling, both of them laughing, round and round the room. On hands and knees, they were happy dogs. They cried out, shuddered, caught their breath again, began again, her sly tongue, her eager fingers, waking his cock when he was sure it was past waking.

At last it was. He lay holding her under the blankets, she nestling close against him, contented, trusting, small and slight to hold, warm, soft, smooth, good to hold. She hummed and kissed his chest, the base of his throat. She whispered, "I love you." And it was over. He remembered who he was and what he had done. He remembered what he had been and all that had happened to the boy and man he had been. He remembered his promise to himself when the doctor told him at Aranjuez that to go on hoping for Jaime was a waste of time. He let her go, rolled away from her, got off the bed, yanked open drawers, jerked on corduroys, a thick sweater, sat on the bed to put on long wool socks, to tug on boots. She touched him. "What's wrong?"

"You don't love me," he said. "For Christ's sake, don't say that. You're just a kid. You don't know what you're talking about. Get out of here, and forget me."

"Why? I can't forget you. I'll never forget you."

"Then hate me, okay?" He stood up to stamp his feet down into the boots. "I did a lousy thing to you tonight. I knew it was wrong, and I did it anyway. I used you, infant. To get my rocks off, right? Right. That's all it was. It was nice, it was even wonderful, but it wasn't love, Sheri. It wasn't love, and it never can be love."

"You're not like this." She was kneeling up on the bed. Her face was turned up to him, a pale oval in the pale tangle of her hair, her eyes wide and glistening. "You're kind and sweet and gentle." Her hand groped out and pulled loose a blanket. She huddled it around her. "What did I do wrong? We were very happy here just now." Her voice quavered. "We were very happy, man."

"You didn't do anything wrong," he said wearily. "You did everything right, but I shouldn't have let you. I knew better. All I did was set you up to be hurt."

"You didn't hurt me," she yelped. "You made me very

happy. What the hell is the matter with you?" She flung the blanket away. She was a set of jerky dim insect motions on the far side of the bed. She was putting on the little shorts, the flimsy shirt—no use at all against the cold that had come. Her voice jerked as she knotted the shirt under her breasts again. She said, to his surprise, "You know what this is? This is just goddamn postcoital depression. I'll bet you never even heard of it, did you?"

"I've heard of it," he said.

"Yeah, well, sometimes it takes the form of rage, you know?" She snatches up the blanket again and wraps it around her. "Rage against the self, right? Self-contempt, self-loathing, okay?"

"Not okay," he said. "Sheri, I'm queer. Homosexual—understand? There's no future for you with me."

"Wha-at? Oh, wonderful! You must really think I'm stupid." She yanked a corner of the blanket up over her hair. "Nobody with two brains would believe that. After what we did here, on this bed, in this room, tonight? Wow, I really did mess up. I wish you'd tell me how."

"Sheri, shut up, love. It's the truth. I was going to tell you downstairs, but I didn't have the guts."

"Don't keep lying," she cried. "You were married. For ten years. Kate told me."

"Yes, well, she should also have told you that I lived here, in this house, for months, with a man. Slept in this bed with him, made crazy love with him five hundred times, doing the same things with him you and I did tonight. Him. Masculine. Yes, I was married. But I went with men then, too, okay? And everybody got hurt. And I'm not going to do that anymore. I'm sorry. But never again."

She was a dark, sad, silent little shape in the shadows. At last she said softly, "It would be all right. If you had to go with men sometimes, I wouldn't make it bad for you." He shook his head. She said, "Well, he's not here. Can't I come back for a while?"

251

"You want me to help you carry your stuff up to the truck?" he asked.

"No, thanks," she said.

Now there is a pier reaching out over the water. It is a charred skeleton. The structures on it are hollow wrecks. Up the beach, on the other side of the highway, the headlights of a car sweep the brick fronts and rusty signs of abandoned stores and pass on. The pier used to be called Tivoli. There were rides and booths. It went to seed when he was a child. Later there were fires. The smell of wet, burned wood is strong. He stands and stares.

He and Donnie Wright used to come here when the place was dying. In one of the booths, he saw his first naked woman. She had stretch marks on her belly, and her pancake makeup didn't match the lardy color of the rest of her. She seemed tired and angry. She strutted to scratchy music in red high heels, a triangle of red satin at her crotch. It worried him that this was where Jesus had come from. He felt sick the rest of that day.

There were good days, though. He smiles to himself, remembering how he and Donnie jacked each other off in the scuffed little boat that bumped through dark tunnels with sharp turns, where fake bats flapped, fake skeletons danced, a gorilla reared up with red light bulbs for eyes, where fake cobwebs brushed their faces, where ghastly laughter crackled through split loudspeakers, where they were supposed to be scared— when all they were scared of was that they wouldn't finish, that they would bang out into daylight before they could zip their pants.

He frowns and his heart skips a beat. It is very dark, but he sees movement among the pilings under the pier. Or does he? He thrusts his head forward, squinting. Nothing. Then a figure flits across an opening. Pale, furtive. He blinks. He listens. There is only the splash of waves, the hiss of surf on sand. Movement happens at the edge of his vision. He turns his head. Nothing. Then, down toward the water, another figure flickers. If it weren't so cold, Whit would think the figure was naked. Afraid, but curious, he takes a few steps toward the

252

black and hulking shadow of the pier, holding his breath, stepping softly in his boots.

What is going on? His mouth feels dry. His heart hurries. And if he doesn't know what is going on, his cock seems to. It begins to harden. He smiles grimly to himself. After all those times with Sheri? His cock is crazy. But he has always known that. He is under the pier. The stench is strong, of scorched wood, rotting seaweed, dead fish, urine, cheap sweet wine, excrement. He just misses falling over a pair of naked bodies, clutching, grunting on the sand. He mumbles apologies. A naked figure leans back against a piling like a saint in a painting, while a dark head bobs at its crotch. Someone gasps in the darkness, "Oh, Jesus, yes, deeper."

If it isn't a nightmare, it should be. He doesn't care what his cock wants. He wants out. He turns back, his foot catches, and he almost falls. He stoops, untangles his boot from dropped swim trunks. They give off a strong smell of cologne. A hand takes them away from him. He sees a gleam of teeth. A hand closes on his crotch. A voice whispers, "Ah," and fingers find the tab of his zipper and run it down. They pry inside his fly. The owner of the fingers presses naked against him, puts a wet mouth on his neck. Whit pushes him off. "No." He hears the tightness in his voice, the weakness of will, the panic. "This isn't my scene." He yanks up the zipper. "Sorry." He runs from under the pier, sweating, teeth chattering. He runs up the deep sand toward the road.

"There's one," somebody says.

"See, I told you it wasn't too cold. They don't give a fuck when they do it."

A car passes on the road. It shows Whit a figure in boots and leather jacket standing on a dune straight ahead of him. He veers, and collides with another, who grabs his arm, stops him. "Hold it. You ain't going no place." The one from the dune comes down. Another one crunches up. A light glares into his face. Only for a second. It goes out, it comes on again and rakes him up and down. A low whistle. "Shit, look at the threads the lady wears." The light goes out.

253

"Hey, miss—let's see your bankroll." Beery breath.

"Forget it," Whit says. "There are a dozen witnesses down there under the pier."

But he is shoved hard. The breath is knocked out of him. He is down on the sand. And one of them is on top of him. He flails out with fists. One of them collides with bone. His face is splattered. He tastes salt. He has made a nose bleed. A knee drives into his crotch. He yells with the pain. He is rolled onto his face. His wallet is dug out of his hip pocket. The flashlight flickers again. He hears from down at the pier a cry of alarm. From close beside him, he hears:

"Shit, man—fifty-dollar bills."

The one whose nose he damaged is heavy on him. He is having trouble breathing. He says, "Get off me." He jabs with his elbows. He is hit hard above the ear. His head rings. Circles of colored light spin in front of his eyes. He thinks of Frank Boulanger's gun lying in a drawer beneath underwear in the bedroom of the beach house. It has real bullets in it now. He bought them after the blond kid robbed him. He rarely thinks of the gun. He sees it now, sees Jaime take it out from under his poncho with a sheepish little grin. *I thought I ought to bring this back to you.* In the torn-up apartment. The first minute. Before they even kissed. *Is it broken? I thought it was broken.* He stared at it dumbly. Jaime said, *It's not broken. Why do you care? Did you want to shoot me some more?* Whit said, *I never wanted to shoot you.* He laid down the gun. *All I wanted to do was love you.*

"Five hundred bucks." Another whistle. "Shee-it."

"Out of sight," one of them says.

The pain from his crotch is still strong in his belly but he bucks, and the one that has been straddling him falls off. Whit lunges, grabs the legs of another, dumps him on his ass. And a boot drives hard into Whit's ribs. He hears them crack. He is acting like a fool. The lights of another passing car show him naked men racing up the sand. He shouts to them. "Help!" But they don't stop. They run faster. Cocks flip and flop. Then the lights are gone, and he can't see them. Automobile doors slam.

Engines start. He yells, "Help!" again, and tries to get to his feet.

He is kicked in the ribs from the other side. A rib end stabs him like a knife. He makes a sound and drops onto his face again. He tries to crawl. He is kicked in the head. He puts his arms up to cover his skull. Headlights streak across the sand, headlights from maybe half a dozen cars. "Help!" he screams to them. But the headlights swing away. He is kicked in a kidney and reflex rolls him onto his back. Something strikes him in the face, something cold and heavy, metal. Again. In the mouth. Pebbles are in his mouth. No, not pebbles. Teeth. He spits them out. Blood runs down his throat, and he gags and coughs. He gets to his knees. He can't see because blood is running into his eyes. "Hey," he says, tries to say, thinks he says, "you've got your money. What do you want to kill me for?"

"What do you want to live for, freak?"

They knock him flat again. Maybe they kick him some more. He doesn't know.

His head aches. He aches all over. He can open only one eye and not wide. The room is white. Bottles hang above him, tubes trailing out of them. He tries to turn his head but pain stops him. He turns his eye. There is a window. The light is gray. He hears a hiss and a patter. It must be raining. He shuts the eye. A minute later, or an hour later, he opens it again. Rubber soles squeak on slick flooring. Darkness passes between him and the window. Starchy cloth rustles. It has to be a nurse. He makes an effort to speak but no sound comes out of him. His mouth is numb and shapeless. The inside of his mouth is dry and tastes awful. His eyesight is not quite so blurred as it was the first time. He can make out what the nurse is doing. She is taking down a bottle and hanging up another. She touches his arm inside the elbow. He tries again to speak, and makes a sound. She bends her face close to his. She is young and pretty.

255

"Oh, you're awake," she says. "That's nice."

"It feels terrible," he mumbles, "but I guess it beats being dead."

"Don't try to talk," she says. "I'll get the doctor."

"Is it Sheri?" he says. "Are you Sheri?"

Has he seen the doctor? He can't remember. At a guess, it is another day. There is pale sunshine at the window. His vision is clear now, though he has it in only the one eye. He must have seen the doctor, because he knows that his skull was fractured, his left cheekbone broken, that he lost five teeth, but that his left eye will probably be all right. His ribs are mending nicely. He has stopped bleeding from his kidneys. It is Dell's face that bends over him this time. He moves his numb and swollen lips. He swallows. He tries to moisten the inside of his mouth with his tongue. It is not the mouth he is used to but he makes an effort to get it to work for him like the old one, to make it smile, to make it speak.

He croaks, "How long have I been here?"

"Five days," she says. "You were in a coma." And to someone else, she says, "He's awake." She is half laughing, half crying. "Get the doctor."

"Oh, bless you, Lord," Margaret Miller says. "Oh, thank you, dear Jesus." He glimpses her scurrying for the door. It sighs and clicks after her. He can't understand what she has done to her hair.

"Who's feeding Polk?" he says.

"The woman next door to you at the beach," Dell says, "the fat advertising one. What's her name? Kate Something." She gazes at him in pity and sorrow. "Whit, how did this happen?"

"How's that baby?" he says.

"Fine, just fine. Oh, darling, I'm sorry, so sorry."

"Me too," he says. "How did I get here?"

"They run tractors along the beach in the early morning," she says. "Dragging rakes. To clean up the sand before people come. The beer cans, the plastic junk."

"Which one was I?" He thinks of smiling again, but he remembers the missing teeth and decides against it. "I'll bet I'm beautiful."

"You always were to me," she says, eyes filled with tears again. She bends out of his line of vision. There is a soft rattling of small objects. That woven straw bag of hers must be beside her chair on the floor. She comes up with Kleenex and blows her nose. "You always will be. Whit, I thought you were going to be all right on your own. I never dreamed anything like this would happen."

"It's not your fault," he says. "It's the way I was born to live—sucking anonymous cocks under deserted piers at midnight, standing around exposing my pathetic self in the woods of Griffith Park, cruising Hollywood Boulevard, trying to look butch, with my shorts stuffed with old socks."

"Oh, Whit," she says reproachfully, "not you."

"No, all right, not me." He is growing tired. "With me, they have to bring a note from their mommy that it's all right, and a certificate from the doctor that they are free of venereal infection, and of sound mind." He forgets about the teeth and tries smiling. "Stop looking so unhappy. I'll be fine. I'm joking, okay?"

She gives a grim little laugh. "This was no joke. You very nearly died. Whit, it's such a waste."

"I have to sleep now." He tries to reach across himself with the arm that has no tubes in it. He means to take her hand, but pain flares in his ribs, and he drops the arm. "Thanks for coming." His eye falls shut.

"When you're well enough to leave here"—her voice seems to come from far away—"you're going home with me."

He mumbles, "Phil will love that."

His mother holds a bowl. With a spoon, she tries to slide white, gummy stuff into his mouth. At first, the tubes fed him. Lately he has been given liquids he spills. It has now been decreed that he can eat and digest again. "What is it?" he says. She

257

says, "Creamed chicken and noodles. Take another bite, now."
It is as if he were once more in his high chair in the kitchen of
the house on Berry Street. The morning sun shines through
mesh curtains stitched with tulips. His father is in the bathroom, probably shaving. The door of the bathroom is open.
His father is whistling softly between his teeth. The tune is
"The Beer Barrel Polka." Whit hears his own tiny voice piping,
" 'Now's the time to roll the barrel, 'cause the gang's all
here.' " He suspects they were the first words he ever uttered.
His mother calls irritably over her shoulder, *Can't you whistle a
gospel tune? Just listen to what the baby has learned from you.*
He opens his mouth cautiously and takes in the spoonful of
slippery, tepid stuff. "It's so you don't have to chew," she says.
What has happened to her hair is that it has turned white. The
food has no special taste. He swallows it. "That's good," she
says. "Come on." She carefully loads the spoon from the bowl
again. "See if you can finish it all up."

"This is ridiculous," he tells her.

She wipes his chin. "I hope it's a lesson to you."

"Dear Christ," he says. "Is that why you came? To see
whether I'd learned my lesson at last? You're really happy
now, aren't you? Fulfilled at last."

"I knew it would happen," she says flatly. "Here, eat this. I
told you when you were eighteen. I warned you. People who
live like that come to grief. Open your mouth. There. That's
good." She watches his mouth. He swallows. She gives a nod.
"I don't understand." She stirs the stuff in the bowl again. "We
never had anybody like that in our family." She scrapes the
bottom of the spoon on the rim of the bowl and holds the
spoon to his mouth again. "We were always decent Christian
people. No, we never had any money. We weren't famous or
important. But there was never any scandal. We knew how to
behave. Open your mouth."

"I'm planning on a long lifetime of scandal," he says. "I'm
not dead yet. I can still satisfy your expectations."

"You're not dead," she says strictly, "because your mother

has never given up on you. I pray every morning of my life that God will watch over my boy."

"Give me the bowl," he says, and reaches for it, wincing, and takes it away from her. "I can feed myself."

"You had a good wife," she says. "You never saw your father treat me the way you treated her. She looked after you. You never got into any trouble while you were married. It was a sad day when you walked out on her."

"You always hated her, and you know it." He is dog-tired again and he aches. Just the same, he shovels down the food. He is so filled with dope he half imagines he is four or five again when he learned that the only way to escape her for a while was to finish his food.

Margaret Miller says, "She wasn't our kind. All that Boston money in the family, fancy name, fancy background, Declaration of Independence la-di-da. The Millers and Whitfords were plain people—farmers, carpenters. It wasn't Everetts with their clean fingernails and their blue blood that built this country. I don't care if they are in the history books." She snatches the empty bowl from him and sets it with a bang on the metal tray. The spoon jumps out of it and dances, rattling. "Divorce, of all things! We never had a divorce in our family—either side. I don't know where you got your ideas from."

"You didn't like the Chinaman any better," he says. "His grandfather hammered down the rails for the Union Pacific. Talk about building the country."

Her blue pop eyes bulge inside their white lashes. Her neck, which time has turned stringy, goes red and blotchy. Her mouth twitches at the corners. But she is not going to talk about Chang. She hasn't spoken his name in thirteen years—not since a chilly November afternoon in 1955. She was supposed to be in the church basement with a lot of women like her, cooking food for a church supper. The house on Berry Street was supposed to be empty. For the first time, Whit brought Chang there, so they could do it in a bed for once,

259

instead of in the back of the Dragon Restaurant panel truck or, even more hastily, riskily, uncomfortably, in a dressing room at the Cordova Stage, late at night after rehearsals.

Chang was spooked. Neighbors would see him and tell Whit's mother. Months ago she had made it plain that Whit was to keep away from Chang. "There's something creepy about him." Whit said, "You think all Chinese are creepy." She said, "Nonsense—that Mr. Tek at the laundry is very nice." Whit snorted. "Sure—he comes to the back door." She said, "He has a pretty little wife and the nicest little children." Whit felt his face grow red. "What's that supposed to mean?" She said, "That he is normal, and your friend Chang is not." Whit said, "You want me to cultivate the Teks? What plays has he directed lately?" She said, "I wish you'd never gone near that theater." He said, "Dad doesn't feel that way." She said, "He sees only what he wants to see. Why can't you choose a friend your own age, your own race? What became of Donnie Wright? He's such a wholesome boy."

Whit reported this conversation to Chang. Naturally. He told Chang everything—usually over dinner at a back corner table of the Dragon Restaurant, when most of the lights were turned off, and the help was gobbling down rice with chopsticks all around them, and jabbering and giggling, and wouldn't have understood what Whit was saying even if they had tried to eavesdrop because English meant nothing to them. He told Chang everything, and so Chang was right to fear coming to Whit's house that day. For sex, of all things. And Whit was wrong to force him to come. He thought Chang was a coward. Which, of course, Chang was. But Chang also was smart about people. He knew they not only can but will do just what you least expect.

Sure enough—Whit's mother came blundering back home after some pan she'd forgotten, and there were the two of them naked in Whit's bed, naked and noisy. Here in the hospital, he grins to himself, though it hurts his mouth to grin. Chang rolled away from him so fast he fell down between bed and wall and got wedged there. Whit's mother threw herself on Whit, beating at him with furious little fists. The combined weight of the two Millers made the bed too heavy for Chang to move. Whit was too startled to push her off him, dive out the window, lock himself in the bathroom. It was more than surprise that paralyzed him. It was amazement at the things she was saying between gasps and sobs. He wouldn't have believed she knew such words. He was shocked out of his mind. Even Chang remarked about it afterward—long afterward, when they felt able to laugh, remembering.

Now Margaret Miller says, "What are you grinning at? Are you asleep?" He opens his good eye. She says, "Now, you listen to me. The doctor says, depending on your eye, you should be able to leave here before long. I want you to come home with me to Hemet, where I can look after you. I don't care how old you are. You are my child, and you obviously can't look after yourself."

"You really do want to see the end of me, don't you?" He is almost asleep. "Hemet would burn me at the stake."

Lovers

Carmen O'Shaughnessy cocks an eyebrow and bats her fur-covered eyelashes. She wears a tight scarlet dress and slick black boots. Her hair is piled high and is jet black and lacquered. She stands in the doorway of his hospital room and smiles with a mouth painted to match her dress. And her fingernails. They are long. He used to wonder how she could type with them that long. He wonders it again. She says, "You have permanently disillusioned me about the movies. Remember *The Blue Dahlia*? William Bendix beat up Alan Ladd in a cellar for one whole reel. And the next morning, Alan had a tiny abrasion on one darling cheekbone." She comes in and lets the door fall closed. "When I heard what happened on the morning news, I got right on a jet. With a bottle of Glenlivet to console you." He is sitting in a chair in the white terry-cloth robe that Sandy has fetched from the house at Pelican Rocks. She perches on the side of the bed. "They didn't even know whether you'd live."

"In my case there were three William Bendixes," Whit says.

"Ah, that explains it." She sobers. "Look, I don't mean to sound flip. Honestly, you look ghastly. Will you ever be the same? It's such a rotten shame."

"According to the doctors," Whit says, "I was hardly scratched. A lot of times when they kick you in the head you turn out to be a vegetable."

"That would be a change," she says. "From fruit?"

"Aha," he says. "Jokes. Have you got a cigarette? My

262

mother keeps lurking around. Weeds are choking out the flower beds at the church in Hemet, vines are creeping over the windows, birds are nesting in the organ pipes. But she stays in order to throw out the cigarettes friends bring me. She wants me pure again."

"She's got her work cut out for her." Carmen digs a pack of cigarettes from her black, shiny shoulder bag. She holds out the pack.

"Light it for me, please," he says. "I can't hold it in my mouth."

She lights a cigarette and watches, doubtfully, as he flinches, getting up out of the chair. He is still heavily doped but sometimes the pain cuts through. She hands him the lighted cigarette, and winces in sympathy at the careful, clumsy way he touches it to the swollen black-and-blue mess that is his mouth. She sucks air sharply between her teeth. "How can you smoke it?"

"With difficulty," he says. "Where are you working?"

"Golden Bough," she says. "Business was never better. You want to write some more books for me? I can get you a whopping thousand bucks advance."

"Maybe, after I pay the bills on all this," he says, "I'll have to."

"No fear," she says. "Last Sunday's *New York Times* book section says your sales have topped half a million."

"Money can't buy happiness," he says.

"Nor iron bars a cage," she says. "You don't look as if you're going to be fit for much for quite a while. Why don't you come stay with me till you heal up? San Diego—clean air, sparkling sea, it's lovely going through the zoo."

"In a wheelchair?" He shakes his head. "It was friendly of you to come so far. Did you bring back the Scotch?"

"They told me it would make your head hurt," she says. "So I drank it myself." This is not the truth. She digs the bottle, in a crumpled sack, out of her bag. They have a drink together, laughing about the bad old days at Brackett House. The whiskey makes his head hurt.

He has asked, so Kate has brought him his typewriter, blank paper, and, in a big envelope printed with the name of her agency, typed pages that she thinks are his manuscript, and some of which are. But maybe something important leaked out of his broken skull on the dirty sand at Tivoli pier, because he can only sit helpless with his fingers on the keys and stare at the empty page. Maybe it isn't that. Maybe it is only the painkillers. He hopes so. He doesn't want writing taken away from him. Then he really will have nothing.

"My boy, you're not going to believe this," Frank Boulanger says, "but we had a burglary of our own." Only soft lamplight glows in Whit's room. The major's white hair and bristly mustache show in the shadows. He sits on the typewriter chair. Helen, rosy-cheeked from the cold outside, has smuggled in trifle, still warm from the baking. She has spooned on Hampshire cream. They eat. It is the best thing Whit has tasted in days. He hopes he can digest it. "Fellow smashed out the front-door glass, turned the lock, walked in, and went straight to the drawer where I keep my guns. Near thing, too, wasn't it, Helen?" He doesn't wait for her to answer. He never does. She doesn't appear to mind. She only smiles, blue eyes twinkling. She is waiting to be surprised—he never tells a story twice the same way. "We must have arrived right on his heels. He'd dropped a bullet. I happened to step on it. I said to Helen, 'Someone's been going through these drawers.' Sure enough, one of my guns was missing, little Colt revolver. Then, suddenly, there the chap is. Must have been hiding in the bedroom. He's trying to cross the living room, heading for that broken door. Huge fellow. I had a gun in my hand, anyway. I pushed Helen aside and let fly with a couple of shots. Funny thing about that. Hadn't popped a pistol at a target in years. Have to put it down to natural ability, I expect. Winged the fellow. Heard him grunt. Saw him clutch at his shoulder.

264

Found bloodstains on the path afterward, but the rain soon washed those away, of course. I shouted at him to stop, and gave chase. I was out the door just in time to see him give a lurch at the top of those hillside steps of ours. And down he goes, arse over tip, crashing through the brush. I started down after him, but it was growing dark, and I caught my foot in some of those damned passion-fruit vines. Went arse over teakettle meself. He got away. I was covered with mud from head to foot. Helen had to wipe me down with handfuls of fresh straw before I was fit to go back indoors."

"He didn't steal anything else?" Whit says.

"Funny thing about that," the major says. "He not only didn't steal anything else—he left a ten-dollar bill behind. Didn't he, Helen? Lying on a chair by the door. Of course, it wasn't enough to pay for the gun. Nothing would be. Errol Flynn gave me that gun, when we were working on—what film was it? I remember we were sitting on a set of an Arab bazaar. Playing bridge. I think David Niven was one of us, as well. Anyway, a lot of camels about. Camel shat on us. Ever been shat on by a camel? No? Plays hob with whatever cards you happen to be holding. . . . No, I suspect the ten dollars was to pay for the broken glass."

"Maybe he only borrowed the gun," Whit says.

Sandy arrives with new books, shiny jackets beaded with rain. He brings anchovies, Camembert, strawberries. His coat is too big. It belongs to a houseguest. Sandy often has genuine houseguests, but he also uses the term to include young fly-by-night sex partners. They arrive on his doorstep from all over—England, Norway, Singapore, Melbourne. Sandy has friends who pass their boys along by jet. Sandy snaps the switch on the typewriter, sits down and pecks out *The quick brown fox jumps over the lazy dog*. Whit must understand that when he gets out of here, he is coming home with Sandy to recuperate. Whit tells him that all those tricks flitting in and out would make him dizzy, and he is dizzy enough as it is.

Before Sandy can argue, the nurse who would look more like Sheri if she didn't have chunky hips comes to take Whit for his walk, and Sandy goes off to his bookstore.

The nurse holds his elbow as if he were old. He is mostly steady, but he tends to fall over unexpectedly, so the staff watch out for him. The hallways of this hospital are more crowded with steel-doored food carts, with wheeled canvas bins for laundry, with gurneys, trollies, dollies holding oxygen tanks—but they are like the hallways at Aranjuez when it comes to the tall, glaring windows at their ends. He dislikes walking these hallways because they make him sad about Jaime. But walking outdoors today is impossible on account of the rain. The nurse says she is reading his book. He has noticed copies of it on this floor. She marvels that, young as he is, he can know so much about people.

"If I know so much about people," he says, "then how come I let myself get beaten half to death at midnight on the beach? Answer me that."

And a big man comes toward them, featureless against the light of the window at the hallway's end. He stops and holds out a hand. Whit squints his good eye. It is Burr Mattox. Whit takes the hand. It feels fine to have hold of it again, though it is cold from the weather outside.

"I can't believe it," he says.

"I'm out from New York," Burr says. "Shit, they really did it to you, didn't they?"

"You should have seen me ten days ago. I was blacker than you. New York? You came all that way to see me?"

"Only partly. Some dumb convention. I'm an ad company junior executive now. But I wouldn't have accepted the ticket just for that." He looks around. "Where can we go and talk?" He takes Whit's arm from the girl. He holds it firmly, the way he used to when they crossed streets. It feels good. *I wanted to belong to somebody.* In Whit's room, Burr picks him up, lays him on the bed, draws up the blankets. Whit has forgotten how very big and strong he is, how gentle. He bends and puts a kiss on Whit's mouth. He lays a hand for a minute on Whit's crotch.

"Man, I have missed you," he says. "I'm always thinking about you. We were so good together. Never knew anybody like you." He stands smiling sadly down. There are honest-to-God tears in his eyes. "Pretty," he says.

"Pretty was before," Whit says. "They broke my face."

"I can see that." Burr drags the chair from the typewriter table to the bedside. He sits down. "That wasn't the pretty I meant. The pretty I meant is inside, where nobody but me could see it." He picks up one of the books Sandy brought, and lays it down again. "Come back with me to New York. That's where it's happening, man. Where everything is happening. This is never-never land out here. Crazy people."

"I wouldn't have to walk the beach to get mugged," Whit says. "I could stay in my own apartment."

"Don't give me that," Burr says. "They did it to you at your house before. It was in *Newsweek*. It was on television. You're famous now. You'd have a ball in New York. They'd know how to treat you there." He is restless. He gets off the chair, walks to the window to look out at the rain. He is silent for a minute. He turns back. "You gone cold on me? I don't mean anything to you anymore?"

"How's your wife?" Whit says, hating to do it, wanting an answer he knows he won't get, not wanting that answer either, because even if he and Burr start out well, it will end badly, because that is the way he manages to end everything. "How are those leggy little girls of yours?"

"Not so little anymore," Burr says. "Beautiful, both of them. Start college next year." He too switches on the typewriter but he punches only one key, then turns the motor off. "Hey," he says, "it wasn't my wife got between us. It was yours. The one who forgave you everything, right? Well, I talked to Carmen. Took me some trouble to reach her. She's in San Diego now. She says you're divorced." He sits down on the little steel chair again and takes Whit's hand on the bedcovers. "That's how it had to be. Sooner or later. Isn't that what I told you?"

"That was a wish," Whit says. "Not a prediction."

"It came true." Burr laughs his chocolate laugh. "What I know is, you need somebody. I know you. You're not the kind to make it on your own. Hell, that doesn't demand a lot of perspicacity now, does it? Seeing you here, like this? All smashed up?"

Whit takes a deep breath. Tears sting his eyes, and he turns his face away. "I don't need anybody," he says.

Chang pokes his head in at the door. His eyes are wild and his hair sticks up on one side. This is because he has taken off a leather cap that he clutches in the same hand that clutches a pot of rain-wet yellow chrysanthemums. He is a lot fatter than when Whit last saw him. Understandably. It's been years. But he looks healthy. His cheeks are red from the cold outdoors. He darts fearful looks around him. He uses a stage whisper: "She's not here, is she? Your mother?"

"Sandy Fine took her to lunch." Whit gets up cautiously from the typewriter. Not on account of pain, on account of his fear of falling. "With another friend of mine, Kate Schaefer." An old reflex makes him happy that he is dressed today. He always tried to look nice for Chang. Besides, it fills him with hope to be wearing the bulky Irish turtleneck and the heavy, wide-wale corduroys. He never believed he would get out of this place while he had to keep going around in pajamas and robe. "They're trying to persuade her to go home by swearing on Bibles that they'll look after me. Come in, sit down. Put those there." His mouth has almost regained its original beauty and he gives the flowers a tight-lipped smile to keep the tooth gaps from showing. "They're my favorite flowers. You remembered that."

"I came before. The first time, they were pumping you full of secondhand blood and trying to figure out which fragments of your skull went where." Chang sits on the chair by the window. He fits the cap on his fat knee. He brushes at his hair, which he can see in the mirror on the chest of drawers. "I got a glimpse of you. I wished I hadn't. You looked like a butcher's mistake."

"Scalp wounds bleed a lot," Whit says. "You remember."

Chang blinks. "Ah—that sailor. How long ago that seems. Anyway, I kept coming back. They wouldn't let me see you. Then that awful woman was here."

"She's been waiting for this a long time," Whit says. "You wouldn't want to spoil her happiness."

"You're looking almost human now," Chang says. "The stocking cap adds a certain insouciance."

"My skull looks like a battlefield," Whit says. "They took the bandages off two or three days ago. To spare those with no interest in contour maps, I sent out for a chic head covering." Kate ran the errand. The cap is hand-knit, oatmeal color, from London via I. Magnin, Beverly Hills.

"Not all the bandages," Chang says. "What about that eye? What about that cheekbone?"

"The cheekbone they rebuilt," Whit says. "If I don't like the rugged look, they can fix the scars later. The eye may or may not be any good again. I suppose that's why we're born with two." He has been holding on to the foot of the bed, which is steel, finished to look like wood. He turns carefully, takes the necessary three steps back to the typewriter chair, turns the chair, and sits on it so he can face Chang. "An expensive specialist from Boston peered at it in a dark room yesterday. He is, as they say, guardedly optimistic."

"You walk like an old, old man," Chang says. "It breaks my heart."

"It's not pain," Whit says. "It's fear. I get dizzy suddenly. They tell me that will pass after a while. How's the Dragon Lady?"

"Not speaking to me. I'm hardly at home anymore. I'm never in the restaurant. I'm always directing in places like Ojai and Tustin. Too far away to commute from." He smooths the cap on his knee, watching his plump hands. He looks up quickly. "How did you come to go to Tivoli pier? I mean—that is sordid, Whit, squalid. That's not you."

Whit is suddenly angry. Why is it they all come at you when you're helpless? Who asked Chang here? He wants Chang to

269

go away. He says, "Hell, yes, it's me. It's you too. If you had any guts. It's what every fag dreams, tossing and turning, night after night. Isn't it? Naked bodies in the dark, cocks that belong to no one, hands that can never get hold of you for any longer than it takes to come?"

"I was mistaken about you," Chang says. "You're a lousy actor. You don't persuade me for a second. You forget how well I know you. You told me everything about yourself. Endlessly. And what you have just said is a lie."

Whit shuts his eye for a moment and sighs. "Yeah, well, if I told you how I happened to end up there, you wouldn't believe that either. Like you didn't believe me about Dell."

"You're divorced," Chang says. "What more can I say?"

"I was tired of that back porch in the rain," Whit says, as if that were the sole reason he married Dell, because that is all Chang is likely ever to believe. Then he wants to change that, and he says, angrily, his voice breaking, "You didn't cherish me enough. God damn it." He is eighteen again, when Chang was everything to him, when he had no one else, and Chang was always failing him, and each time he grew more and more afraid. "It was me or the Dragon Lady, wasn't it? And every time you said it was me, it turned out to be her. I loved you so much, so much." He is starting to cry, and he must not do that because of his eye. He bites his lip, breathes deeply through his nose, and holds the breath until he is steady again. He finishes, "And you never did one thing I needed."

Chang is expressionless. "I saved your life," he says.

Maybe. After Chang left and the screams of his mother stopped, the house on Berry Street went dead quiet. It was scary. When his father came home, and she told him what had happened, and he couldn't think of anything to say, that was when she beat Whit with the broom, screaming again, those words he couldn't believe she knew. He had never liked her. He supposes he knew that she never liked him. But she had never called him filth before. That was the word she kept coming back to. She wasn't big or strong, and the broom didn't hurt him. The broom was even comical. The word hurt him.

270

All the words. His father finally stopped simply standing in the kitchen doorway looking shamefaced, and took the broom away from her. He led her sobbing into their bedroom at the front of the house and closed the old sliding door. No one ate. The house kept silent. No radio, no television, not even a lamp in the· living room. Chang had given Whit *Finnegan's Wake,* and he opened it on the desk in his room, and forced himself to focus on the puzzles and the puns. He didn't know what else to do. He couldn't think. He could only feel, and he had to stop feeling. At last he went to bed.

In the night, she was in his room. As soon as she opened the door, he opened his eyes. In her white nightgown, backlit from the kitchen, she ran right at him. She ripped the bedclothes back and tore at his pajama pants. Something glittered in her hand. Scissors. Big sewing scissors. Making a crazy noise, half rage, half grief, she lunged at his crotch with the snapping blades. He can still hear his yell of terror. He can feel himself strike the cold, bare floor. He can hear his father speak sharply, hear the click of the switch, wince at the glare of the ceiling light, hear them scuffle, hear them go. He lay there rigid, bare-ass, for what seemed long but was probably only seconds. When he dared to lift his head, the room was empty.

He shook so, he could hardly dress. His mind was a shambles, but one thing he was sure of—he wasn't coming back. He dragged his sleeping bag from the closet, stuffed it with clothes, slung it out the window, climbed awkwardly over the sill, dropped to the ground, picked up the bag, and ran. A pay telephone waited in a wired-glass booth thick with green enamel next to a shut-up filling station on deserted Mountain Street. A few coins were cold in his pants pocket. He dropped two before he finally got one into the slot. It was hard to steady his hand enough to dial. He was blind lucky. Chang was at the black enamel desk under the cinnabar-red latticework by the restaurant doors, counting the night's take from the cash register. Chang picked up the phone.

"My father saved my life," Whit says.

"The trouble with loving anybody," Chang says, "is that it

271

gives them the power to hurt you. You called me a coward there at the end. I made her take you in. That wasn't cowardly."

"Not very far in," Whit says. "Not for long." Chang means by "her" the Dragon Lady, his mother, a taut woman with a face painted carefully as a Chinese doll's in a glass case, black, shiny hair done up like such a doll's. She wore black Chinese dresses that buttoned at the throat. She was slender and looked no more than thirty. She probably never will, not in her coffin, where he has always wished her. She spoke with a Chinese accent. In the restaurant. Nowhere else. She was born in Sacramento. So were her parents. The accent was good for business. "You never told me how you did it. What lies did you tell her?"

"That if you couldn't stay there, I wouldn't stay either. It was risky. I was scared to death of her. But I stood up to her because I loved you. I was scared of your mother too. Remember—she threatened to destroy me."

"I told you she never would," Whit says. "It would have got out that I was queer. She'd never have been able to hold her head up at church again. She's a coward too. The only one of us who wasn't was the Dragon Lady."

That night, Chang had given him money for a room in a cheap hotel at the end of Mountain Street—near the baths he went to last year with Donnie. The next day, Chang put Whit in an apartment with a greasy stove and a pissy mattress, above a garage on an alley in a rundown Mexican neighborhood. He paid the rent with a check. Two weeks later, the Dragon Lady found the canceled check. And investigated. That night unsuspecting Chang brought Whit to the restaurant for supper. The Dragon Lady flew at them. She breathed fire. The waiters and kitchen help dropped their rice bowls and fled. She screeched that Chang was abandoning her for Whit. She wept, smearing that flawless makeup. She threw dishes. She kicked at Whit with sharp-toed little shiny black shoes. He ran through the restaurant. The front doors were locked. Of course. He dodged her, skirting tables, knocking over chairs. He hurtled through the swing door into the staring kitchen, where the help cringed out of the way under the hanging pots and pans, and covered their mouths, so that the Dragon Lady wouldn't see they were laughing their heads off. Whit stumbled out into the garbage-can air of the alley and kept right on running.

She was mistaken. Chang would never leave her—not for anybody. When she dies, if she ever does, Chang will climb down into her grave. But Whit didn't know that then. He had a bad night, walking and walking, lonely, scared, not knowing what was to happen to him now. In the morning, he ought to have looked for a job. Instead he sat in the scruffy room that was the newspaper office at the Junior College, writing poems on a rickety Underwood. About how fine and special he was, and how no one understood that, no one treated him right. Chang found him there. He took him to the steamy little Armenian diner they liked near the campus, bought him a big breakfast, and told him he had straightened the Dragon Lady out. Whit was to have his own room in the apartment above the restaurant.

He had it for less than a month. Then Grandmother appeared, with a face wrinkled as a walnut, always coughing, always with a cigarette burning short at a corner of her brown mouth. Could Grandmother have Whit's room? She was sick and needed looking after. It would only be temporary. Maybe it was. Whit didn't stay long enough to find out. She was still in that room when he left to live with Dell, and that was damn near a year later. Christ, had he slept on that porch, on that tattered swing, in that semen-starchy sleeping bag of his for ten stupid months? He really had been a pathetic case. He recollects a night when hard rain blew on him from the north. He crept down the shaky stairs and crawled into the back of the panel truck. The bang of its cab door, the thrashing of its engine woke him. It drove off. He crawled forward and beat on the bulkhead back of the driver's seat. He yelled. It did no good. The truck stopped at intersections, but he couldn't get out. He was in shorts and T-shirt, and it was raining like hell.

The truck jounced and quit. He peered out the small back

273

windows. He was among long, open-sided sheds stacked with fruits, melons, vegetables, in boxes, bins, barrels. Chickens squawked in piled-up crates. In steel cages ducks were bright white and orange under big naked glaring bulbs. Men hauled gunny sacks of potatoes, mesh bags of onions on their shoulders. They wore layers of sweaters under stained aprons. They wore rubber boots. They wheeled crates on dollies, they slung crates up to the beds of trucks. The Dragon Lady strode among them, shrill, jabbing a finger this way, that way, joking, scolding, giving a fat, dirty man boxing celery a playful slap. When she opened the truck doors so the men could load the stuff in that she had bought, she pretended to be shocked to find Whit there. She got a tough, red-haired man with tattoos on his hands to haul Whit out so the crates could go in. She claimed she didn't know who Whit was. Men gathered around, laughing at him in his underwear. The crates banged on the steel bed of the truck.

"Why do you want to do this to me?" he said.

"You did it to yourself. It's not my fault." She marched to the truck and got behind the steering wheel and slammed the door. The rear doors clanged shut. The red-haired man rapped her window. "Shall we phone the cops?"

"She knows me," Whit told the celery man. "I live at her place. I'm a friend of her son. She's just mad at me."

She rolled the window down. "I don't care who you call," she said, and drove off, leaving him there.

They felt sorry for him, found him some smelly coveralls and a torn sweater, and gave him a quarter for the streetcar. Right away, he took a job busing dirty dishes in the school cafeteria to have money to rent a room. Chang was frightened and cried and begged him to come back. He would get rid of Grandmother. He promised. Whit mustn't work. Chang would give him all the money he needed. Did he want some new clothes? Chang bought him new clothes. Chang bought him a new wallet, and handed it to him over dinner, stuffed with money. But Grandmother still coughed in that room. And Whit still shivered on the porch. Sneezing, feverish, fog-voiced, Whit

274

threatened again to leave. Chang bought him a warmer sleeping bag. And an expensive watch. When these weren't enough, he promised Whit the lead in the summer play at Cordova Stage. And when it was summer, the porch was an all right place to sleep. When it rained again, that was when Whit went away for good with Dell.

"That whole thing about the porch," Whit says, "was insane. Do you realize that?"

"She wouldn't let me rent a place for you," Chang says. "And I was dependent on her. Didn't you know that? They never paid me at the Stage. I had to have the restaurant or starve. She hated my being out of her sight at any time. I made her accept the Stage. I made her accept you. I wasn't a coward, Whit."

The door opens. A shag-headed blond boy, thin, with a bony Adam's apple, looks in, worried. "They made me move the car," he says. Raindrops are on his glasses. He takes the glasses off and tries to wipe them on his damp jacket. "Are you coming pretty soon?"

Chang stands and puts on his cap. "Right now," he says. He holds his hand out to Whit. It seems a strange gesture. Whit can't remember their ever having shaken hands before. The first time they met was at a reading for a play in a gloomy, unheated theater. All Whit did then was give Chang his name when he climbed to the stage to sit under the bleak work light and read lines. After that, when they met, they kissed. Unless the place was public. Then they smiled. They never shook hands. He shakes Chang's hand. Chang says, "I hope you feel better soon."

"Thanks for the flowers," Whit says.

"I never forgot anything about you," Chang says, and goes off with the skinny kid who, Whit realizes with a wry smile, is himself at that age. Chang repeats his mistakes. This kid doesn't look like a match for the Dragon Lady either. Whit wishes him luck.

Slide

Workmen in orange metal helmets and padded orange vests use push brooms to clear from the cement steps down to the houses on the beach rubble the rain has dislodged from the cliff. The brooms have stiff, tough bristles. The workmen are young Mexicans and they put muscle into their work. And high spirits. The rock fragments go flying. They rattle against the blind wooden backside of Whit's house. Whit looks over the corroded steel-pipe handrail. The narrow space between the house and the cliff face must be three feet deep by now with rock scraps. There was nothing but sand there when he bought the place.

Phil Farmer says, "Excuse us, please?"

The workmen stand back to let them pass. One of them says shyly, *"Buenos dias,"* leaving off the *b* and the two *s*'s. Phil holds Whit's arm and steps down ahead of him. Dell has changed Phil. He has let his hair grow. His glasses have horn rims. Instead of the drab suits and strangling neckties of old, he wears a leather jacket and tight jeans. He thanks the workmen, and they smile and duck their heads a little. The rubble on the last twenty steps is deep. Phil is so concerned that Whit not miss his footing that he, Phil, turns an ankle, and has to let go of Whit and grab the rail to keep himself from falling.

"Oh, darling, do be careful," Dell says.

She is behind and above, bringing Whit's suitcase. Sandy follows her, lugging the heavy typewriter. Trailing him comes

Kate, juggling books, Whit's manuscript and notes in the big envelope under her arm. With the other hand she drags a gray canvas sack that bulges with mail from strangers, readers of his book, who want him to get well. His mother insisted on reading them to him, dime-store half-moon glasses tilted on her nose. The cards make him ashamed. These people seem to think he did something for them, and now they want to reach out and help him. And none of them can. No one can. Nobody can help anybody, and none of them seems to know that. Yet the knowledge doesn't help him, and maybe the sentimentality does help them. They will go on forever, flooding the post office with snow scenes, lilies tied to crosses with satin bows, grandmas cuddling children on their laps. And what will he go on with? Halloween is coming. He can do a skeleton dance.

"It is nice," Dell says, when they are inside the house. "But it's so cold." Beyond the front glass wall the sand lies gray and glassy, the sea is gray, the sky. Dell sets down the suitcase and crouches at the gas heater built into the wall beneath the stairs between kitchen and living room. She shivers, rubs her hands, reaches for the knob.

"Don't," Whit says. "I'll put on extra sweaters."

"Your resistance is low," she says. "You'll catch cold." But she stands, and tells Phil, "He won't use heat."

"Not air conditioning either," Whit says. "This isn't Alaska, it isn't the Sahara. It's California, damn it."

" 'It's cold and it's damp,' " Kate sings. She follows Sandy and the typewriter up the stairs that gleam. The whole place gleams—Kate has sent in her grumpy daily woman. Whit suffers Phil to steer him to the couch and sit him down. He hasn't been dizzy for days, but everyone worries. Dell makes a quick tour of the downstairs. She comes back upset.

"There's no toilet down here. Oh, Whit, you can't stay here alone. What if you get dizzy on the stairs?"

"I'll catch him." Someone has come in by the kitchen door and stands behind Dell. The light is poor, and for an instant Whit thinks it is a workman from the steps. The helmet causes him to make this mistake. And, of course, the brown skin, and the very white-toothed smile. Now the helmet, which turns out to be grubby white plastic, comes off. Whit feels dizzy and clutches the wicker couch arm. He gapes. So does Phil Farmer. He pokes his head forward, stretching his neck. He squints through his thick lenses.

"Is it Grieve?" he says. "Kenny Grieve?"

"Hi, Dell." Kenny drops his backpack, gives Dell a hug and a kiss on the cheek. He has grown stocky, thick through the middle. Once he showed Whit a dog-eared photo of his father, a potbellied, sun-wrinkled Indian holding a beer can outside some sun-bleached desert roadside bar. Kenny is on the way to looking like his father. He wears a tattered Levi outfit, short boots scuffed and run over at the heels, a grubby T-shirt. He shakes Phil Farmer's hand. "How are you, Phil?" He crouches in front of Whit. He smells of sweat and auto repair shops. He says, "I'm sorry I'm so late. I only heard what happened to you yesterday—ran into a dude who knew I knew you." He smiles. "I brag a lot about that. Your old place was empty. My mother didn't know your address. Major Boulanger did, but he said you were still in the hospital. When I got there, you'd just checked out." His eyes are filled with pity. "Christ, you look half dead."

"I'll be okay," Whit says. "Thanks for coming."

"Kenny," Dell says, "can you stay? Can you do what you said—catch him when he falls? He won't have any of us."

"Oh, Dell, for God's sake." Whit doesn't want Kenny to stay, because if Kenny stays, as Kenny will, a short while, then goes away, as Kenny always does, it will kill Whit. He feels right now as if any little thing will kill him, and that won't be a little thing. "Kenny—tell her no."

"I have to stay someplace," Kenny says. "My bike is shot. I don't have any money. Have you got room?"

"He's got plenty of room," Dell says.

"I should never have got myself into it," Kenny says. It is night. Rain whispers on the glass sliding doors, the tall panes reaching up among the shadowy rafters. Out beyond the house, the surf is heavy when it hits the beach. The earth shakes, the house shakes. Whit lies on the couch, Polk curled up asleep on his shrunken belly, waking every now and then to purr for a minute, to knead with his claws, then falling asleep again. "But I saw all this stuff that needed doing. Small stuff, stuff I could handle, but important. The fence was falling down in places, vines dragging it down, you know? And a couple of places, it was broken out. Kids, probably. Well, shit, you can't have that at a nudist camp. The buildings needed fresh paint, the faucets leaked. The old woman kept saying she'd fix it up, but she doesn't have the strength anymore. The girl can look after horses, but that's about it. She can't even cook."

"Let me guess what else she can do," Whit says. "Which is why you stayed. Not all that inviting fix-up stuff."

"I liked her. I liked the old lady, I felt sorry for them. They kept getting less and less people." Kenny shrugs, leaning forward into the circle of soft lamplight to stub out a cigarette. "I said I'd do the work free if I could have a room and meals." He laughs quietly, and settles back in the wicker chair that creaks. "It's a nudist camp, right? But she's this old-fashioned lady, just the same. Old-fashioned Mexican—the rosary, the little shrine with a candle and a plaster statue of the Virgin, lace over her head for church, the whole bit? And her granddaughter is pure, a virgin, and she's going to stay that way. She sent her to her room, sat me down with a bottle of Dos Equis, and told me if I had any ideas about Teresa, forget it, clear off. Teresa was barely seventeen, too young to marry. And when she does marry, it won't be any *vagabundo* like me, right?"

This time he laughs aloud, leans in the shadow to pick up his drink from the floor. Whit hears the tinkle of the ice. "Hell," Kenny says, "we were already doing it every chance we got. She started it. You wouldn't believe this eighty-pound skinny little sex-maniac child. Her grandmother knew about us, she had to, but she wasn't admitting it. She still won't. Teresa came to my room out in the cabins every night, and the old woman couldn't sleep worth a damn. She had to hear her sneaking out of the house. She didn't care, as long as we didn't show it in front of her."

"It sounds as if everybody was happy," Whit says.

"Yeah, that's how it sounds, doesn't it?" Kenny goes gloomy. "I figured it for a trade-off, right? Once I got the place all fixed up like new, I kept it that way—trimmed the bushes and mowed the grass, cleaned the swimming pool, fixed the beat-up old filter, screwed in light bulbs, scrubbed out toilets. Hell, I was even recreation director. I got tortillas, beans, beer, and a bed. If I got Teresa too, was that more than I was worth?" He pushes up out of the chair and picks up Whit's empty glass. "Customers began coming back. So many I had to help with the cooking. All Teresa did was burn herself every time she got near the stove." He walks to the kitchen and snaps on the light there. The rubber of the refrigerator door sucks. Ice rattles into glasses.

"No more for me," Whit says. "It keeps me awake."

"Tonight would that be so bad?" Kenny asks.

"It makes my heart thump," Whit says, "and that makes my poor broken skull hurt, all right?"

Kenny snaps off the light, comes back with whiskey and ice in his own glass, and sits down again. "I don't know what's going to happen to them alone."

"You'll go back," Whit says. "That's how you are."

"I won't go back. I'm not going to marry her. I've had enough marriages. And all the old lady will settle for now is marriage. And that's all Teresa will settle for. And one woman climbing on you all the time is plenty. Two is pure hell. Shit, I can't leave the place, can't go to town. If it's a bar, there she is. Just to get away from her, I tried motels, movies. In an hour she was in bed with me, or she's sitting next to me trying to get my cock out of my pants. She's not a movie fan. She's a cock fan." He lights a cigarette with a wooden match. "The one thing I had left that I really liked. She'd go back to her room before it got light, okay? Still pretending for the old woman.

And I'd go naked and get one of the horses and ride down to the river and swim, okay? She found out about that, and that finished it. Either I let her come along or I didn't go."

Whit lifts Polk off his belly, sets him on the floor, where he gives a big, vibrating stretch and a big yawn and makes to jump up again. Whit sits up to prevent this. "I have to go to bed," he says and peers at his watch. "Jesus, I haven't been up this late in weeks. Come on." He stands, with that little twinge of worry about falling. He doesn't fall. "Bring your backpack." He heads for the stairs. "I'll show you your room." He starts up the stairs. Kenny follows. Whit opens the door on the spare room. It smells of shut-upness, of sea damp. "The bed's made. If it's damp, I've got fresh sheets." He points to a hall cupboard.

Kenny goes in and folds back the bedcovers. He lays a hand on them. "It's not damp," he says, sits down, and begins taking off his boots. "I'm going to shower, okay?"

"The bathroom is all yours," Whit says. "Good night."

He lies in his own bed, which is so wide compared to the one in the hospital he feels lost in it. He lies in the rain-whispering dark and listens to the hot water run in the pipes and wishes he were the water. But not for long. It has been a big day. He is more tired than he knew. He sleeps. The bed moves. He grumbles awake, believing Polk is responsible. But it isn't Polk. It is Kenny. Wrapped in one of the big towels.

"You sure you want me to sleep way in there?" he says.

"Yes, because I can't start over with you," Whit says. "I couldn't take it again, Kenny. I'm sorry. When I let myself love you, I love too hard."

Kenny gets up and walks around the bed to the other side where the table is. He picks up Whit's cigarette pack and lighter. He lights a cigarette. The flame of the lighter shows Whit his black hair slicked back from the shower. The flame goes out. He hears Kenny expel smoke.

"I was never tough," Whit says. "But I was still a kid, and they have a kind of natural protection designed to last until

281

they develop common sense. I don't have the natural protection anymore. I'm trying to at least act like I've got common sense. There's nothing quite like getting beaten half to death to make you wary." He reaches up and takes the cigarette out of Kenny's thick fingers. "I don't want to be beaten up again—not outside, not inside." He takes in smoke, hands the cigarette back, blows out smoke. "And you beat me up. Every goddamn time."

"You aren't the only one who was a kid." Kenny walks to the window. Steam is on the glass, maybe from the heat he has brought from the shower. He makes a clear circle in the steam with his open hand, and pretends to peer out. "Maybe I've gotten a little common sense too? Maybe I understand better now just how much you loved me, okay? Maybe I even know exactly now. Maybe I know now just how much I love you." He turns to face the bed. Whit can see only the white towel. "Can you believe that? Will you believe me if I say I'll stay with you now? I'm not going back to Muledeer. You're the only one who ever really loved me. All I want is to stay with you."

"I believe you want to believe that," Whit says. He can't manage this much longer. "Go to bed, Kenny?"

Kenny sits beside him again. "When this guy in the bar told me what happened to you, you want to know what I thought? I thought you were going to die. I thought I'd lost you forever. I thought, if I'd been with you, nobody could have beaten you up. I thought it was my fault."

"It wasn't your fault." Whit touches him before he can remember not to, lays a hand on his arm. Kenny closes his hand over Whit's. He puts out the cigarette in the ashtray on the stand. The sparks burn small and red for an instant, then wink out. Kenny says:

"I knew you needed me, but I was always leaving you."

Whit withdraws his hand. "And you will again," he says. "Now, will you get the hell to your own bed, please?"

"No," Kenny says, and sheds the towel. He pulls back the bedclothes and slides under them beside Whit. His cock is stiff. He puts a kiss on Whit's mouth. "No."

Whit sighs and holds him. He has grown thick but not soft. Holding him is like hugging a sun-warmed boulder.

Kenny saws a neat rectangle out of the bottom of the kitchen door and trims the section he cut out and hangs it on hinges back in place. It is a door for Polk, so that he can go in and out when he likes. Whit hears from the tower the bump of the door when Kenny takes it down, hears the whine of the saw. He is filled with dread. He shrugs the dread off. He knows better than to hope. Any time Kenny spends anywhere is time running out. Whit frowns at the page in the typewriter and types words on it.

When Kenny brings the Mercedes back to the building in which a dentist has wired new teeth into Whit's mouth, boards lie tied to the roof, boards just out of the trunk. The ropes have to be undone so that Whit can get into the car. Kenny has to yank them tight and tie them again from inside. Whit helps him carry the lumber down the cement stairs from the cliff. Kenny knocks up a workbench under eaves at the side of the house. Here he works at sawing, sanding, staining, rubbing down with oil the shelves of a bookcase for the tower room. In the tower room, standing back out of the way, watching him fit the shelves into place, Whit wonders what he will do next. Work on that black, greasy, broken-down hulk of a motorcycle? Won't that signal the end? He gives his head a shake. He has to make himself not give a damn.

They get some really fine weather, sky blue and cloudless, sea blue and sparkling. One morning, three pelicans perch on the rocks for a while. Whit hopes this is a good omen. The sun is warm. Kenny and Whit swim. They lie on the sand in the sun. Kenny turns dark brown. Whit burns. One night, they rent poles and fish in the black water off the white Malibu pier. Earlier they ate lobster in a restaurant on the pier. Whit's bridgework has stopped feeling as if his mouth were stuffed with little toy automobiles. He cooks for Kenny. He enjoys it, and begins to regain some weight. They ride the gaudy bumper

283

cars on Santa Monica Pier. Kenny is afraid of the spinning, high-vaulting rides. He wants to get on the merry-go-round but Whit says no. A new booth lets you shoot at targets. Whit's eye must be as good as before, because he outpoints Kenny. He takes the target home and pins it up where he can point to it every time Kenny beats him at chess or gin rummy.

One morning, Kenny drives Whit in the Mercedes up the twisting Topanga Canyon road, under looming rock outcrops. Back in a small valley, he stops at the ranch where Sergeant spent his last years. Because strangers have the place now, they don't approach the ranch buildings, red with white trim under big live oaks. They climb through barbwire and cross uneven, dead-grass ground to the barranca. In the barranca, sycamores stretch white limbs. They have dropped most of their big, yellow leaves. A trickle of water makes its way over the rocks where the leaves have fallen. "This is where he broke his leg and they shot him. They got him out with a bulldozer and dug him a grave." Kenny walks off a few paces and stamps the earth with his boots. "Here." The earth has sunk in a little. He stands looking down. "He was a good old horse." He looks at the sky. He sighs and takes Whit's arm. "Come on—let's go."

Rain sets in. Whit goes back to writing. And Kenny reads. Never in the same place for long. If he starts in bed, soon he is downstairs in a chair, or lying on the floor, or sitting someplace on the stairs, or at the eating table, head propped on hands. He has never read any of Whit's books, though Whit has sent them to him every time he could get an address from Mrs. Grieve. *It'll come right back,* she said, ever cheerful. *He never stays any one place long enough to get more than one letter. Never lets the post office know where he's going. Doesn't know himself, half the time. The other half, somebody's after him for something he doesn't want to be caught for.* But Kenny got the books. And bragged that he knew the writer, when anybody saw them in his tackle. He just never got around to reading them. Now he does, and he marvels. "Hey, there's stuff I told you in here."

"You're my favorite character," Whit says.

He leaves on Christmas day. To Kate's party he wears a terrible satin cowboy shirt and new cowboy boots with garish tooling. He is almost savagely scrubbed and nail-clipped and combed. He is savagely beautiful and out of place. He asks Whit, "How do I look?" and Whit hasn't the heart to tell him. He knows that a suit and shirt and tie wouldn't help. Clothes do nothing for Kenny. Even small bathing trunks take away from his perfection. He is only perfect stark naked. And whatever Whit or Kate or Kate's guests might think, Kenny would never consider going to such a party naked. At Muledeer he ran around naked all day and all night presumably. This may mean he understands that clothes are not for him. It could explain why he shuns civilization and why, when he is forced to choose clothes at all, he chooses badly.

But he is excited by the party. He shows off. Outside, while the weather holds, he does handsprings, backsprings, cartwheels, on the sand. When the first spatters of rain drive the party indoors, he tucks in his shirttail, takes the center of the room, and performs card tricks. These are flashy, and he does them well, but not everyone is interested. A few men in check jackets sit around him on the floor to watch him shuffle, deal, and teach them to cheat. The cards whir in his hands. He tells them he was once a dealer in Reno. Whit thinks he is lying or exaggerating.

As a kindness, Kate has invited Whit's producer, and the producer has brought along the man in charge of publicity for the film of Whit's book. He peers out of long, shaggy black hair, a long, shaggy black beard. He is so young, he looks like an elf in a kindergarten play. He is not a lot taller than a kindergartner. He tells Whit how they intend to promote the picture. The part of the story he has seized on as the key episode, the thing that will grab attention and sell tickets, Whit

285

has to frown over for a minute before he can even remember it.

The dregs of the cheerful, red, bubbly wine grow pale pink in the bottom of the big cut-glass punch bowl. The nut bowls stand empty—no more salted almonds. The coals under the grill of the hibachi have gone out. The spicy little hot sausages have vanished, along with the smoked oysters, leaving only toothpicks behind. Cherries peer dry-eyed from the sad remnants of fruitcake. Heels rattle along the deck, guests hurrying off, heads pulled down into coat collars, squealing about the rain. Voices fade, calling, "Happy New Year." Above the thunder of the surf, car doors can be heard slamming at the top of the cliff. Cigarette smoke drifts in the empty rooms.

Whit stays behind to help Kate clean up. The renowned cleaning woman will not appear again until 1969. Whit doesn't know where Kenny has gone or why, but it is a busy hour and a half of dishwashing and the putting-away of dishes, the vacuuming-up of crumbs, the careful sponging of wine spots from the wall-to-wall carpet, before he can leave Kate standing in the middle of the house and staring around her with a weary and disbelieving smile. Polk crouches miserably by Whit's kitchen door, coat spiky with damp. It is one of those moments when he decides he can't figure out the meaning of the bit of wood that flaps for him to slip indoors. Whit picks him up, opens the door, and sees the note on the table.

He swears he will not try to bring Kenny back. But he keeps getting out of bed and putting on a jacket and going downstairs to step out the kitchen door and look at the lumpy shape of the motorcycle. It stands by the workbench, rain dripping sluggishly from the roof edge onto the stained tarpaulin that covers it. He is trying to figure out how Kenny went. Did he thumb a ride to Santa Monica, where there is a Greyhound station? He knows the location of every bus station in the West. Or did he have money for a bus? Whit can't recall when he last gave Kenny money. Never for himself—he wouldn't accept that.

286

But for tools or lumber or groceries. It is driving him crazy, not knowing. Kenny could be out there in this soaking storm, standing at the edge of some highway with his thumb out, in the middle of the night when there is no traffic. Whit goes back to bed. Kenny is not his worry anymore. Kenny is gone. But Whit can't stay in bed. At last, he dresses and climbs the cliff steps to the Mercedes, glistening white in the rain.

On a worn, torn, thumb-smudged Texaco road map from his backpack, Kenny has shown Whit where Muledeer is. It is one of those San Joaquin Valley towns surrounded by cotton fields and turkey ranches. No sidewalks. Meager, spindly houses from the 1890s, thirties and forties bungalows behind fruit trees and chain-link fences. Here and there, a string of outdoor Christmas bulbs glows red, yellow, green, blue, forgotten when the folks went to bed. Old eucalyptus trees tower shaggy at corners where sometimes a streetlight hangs, swinging slightly in the cool breeze of dawn. Main Street—farm-machinery agency, feed and grain, hardware, Woolworth's. On the dark windows of Sally's Diner, in chalky paint, Santa waves from a sleigh. MULEDEER HOTEL, a used-car lot, Tom's Tavern with a fake snowy wreath on the door, J.C. Penney, the Frontier bar and grill. All dead asleep.

Each on a broad lot, a new Legion hall faces a new Baptist church. Tall Christmas trees stand in front of both. A new filling station, two new motels, a McDonald's hamburger place not quite finished, and blocks of brand new look-alike houses. Then farmland. He watches for the sign that will appear soon. Kenny says the town is spreading out, there has been righteous talk of closing down the nudist camp. Corners of whitewashed rail fence mark the turnoff. Cutout wooden lettering: NATURE'S ACRE HEALTH RANCH. The road is narrow patchy blacktop edged by brush. It is less than a mile long.

Plank gates eight feet high loom up. WELCOME TO NATURE'S ACRE. He doesn't need the headlights to read it. The sky is growing light. He switches off the headlights, gets out, and

287

pushes at the gates. Barred. He stands and listens. Birds squabble in the brush and trees. Far off, a rooster crows. He fills his lungs to shout for Kenny, then lets the air go again. He looks in the gray half-light for a bell of some sort, maybe a string of cowbells on a rope, to let it be known that he wants in. He doesn't find anything. When they want you inside, they leave the gates unbarred. He wants only Kenny, not some old woman, not some frail little teenage girl. He doesn't want the place roused.

He turns the Mercedes around, crunching brush, and drives on back to the highway. But he doesn't make for Muledeer. He goes the other way. If there is a river, then there will be a bridge. There is. Raw cement and steel. White enamel sign. MULEDEER RIVER. He stops on the bridge and looks along the river, which is edged by rushes where redwings flash and whistle. The river curves. He gets back in the car and drives on. The first gate he comes to in a long barbwire fence has a rusty mailbox beside it and a rusty NO TRESPASSING sign. He gouges a finger, getting the loop off the post so he can open the limp gate that drags in the dirt. He drives through. Everything is weeds and thistles, dead and dry. He can see from here that the farmhouse is deserted, windows boarded up. He drives on past it, following wheel ruts almost invisible with age. He passes outbuildings, reaches another barbwire gate. The wheel ruts stop here. He leaves the car.

He trudges through an orchard of half-dead winter peach trees. The sickly sweet smell of rotting fruit rises from under his shoes. He heads for the river, guided by the cries of the redwings. Sunrise lays a pink line along the horizon. Now he is among live oaks, stepping over fallen branches, twigs crackling under his shoes. The damp of the river touches his face. Brush thickens and takes on green color. He parts a clump of brush and the river flows dark and cold-looking below him. Something white on the opposite side catches his eye. It is a cattle egret. There are two, three, stilting among the reeds in the shallows.

A noise startles them, and they rise on big white wings, long necks stretched. He watches their flight. They settle far downstream near the bridge. He hears again the noise that sent them off. It is the nicker of a horse. The light is still poor, and he narrows his eyes, looking for the horse. He sees it, dark, beneath live oaks on the opposite bank. It is saddled. Its head hangs, its reins dangle to the ground. It appears to be waiting. Then Whit sees what it is waiting for. Brown, naked Kenny and a pale little girl, fucking on a blanket. Kenny is reaffirming his manhood. He overheard someone at Kate's party say he was a faggot. He had to be, didn't he—living with Whit Miller?

Rain beats down along the coast. Traffic on the highway scarcely moves. An hour ago, he edged into the double line of rain-glistening cars, prepared to inch home with the rest— home to Frank Boulanger's revolver in the drawer with the undershorts, Errol Flynn's prop gun with the new, real, bullets in it. But, like every other driver here, he has grown impatient. Waves of horn-honking crest and subside. Now and then, a head pokes out of a car window into the rain and shouts abuse. How far have they traveled—ten miles, twelve? He laughs at himself. What does he care? If you're going to shoot yourself, you don't need an appointment. For no reason, he checks his watch. It is ten past eleven. The cars ahead of him move on briskly for a few yards. He moves on after them, and they halt again, and he halts again.

They creep past the Sea Shanty. It is 12:55. They reach the Pelican Rocks store, café, laundromat, at 1:30. And a few minutes later, he gets a glimpse of big yellow machinery up ahead in the road. It alarms him. He gets out of the car to see better. Bulldozers, dump trucks, police cars, men in shiny orange tin helmets and slickers. A landslide must have blocked the road. He drives the Mercedes onto the road shoulder, locks it, leaves it, walks, runs, the rain drenching the tweed cap he has worn, the shoulders of the tweed jacket. The bottoms of his trousers get wet and flap heavily around his ankles.

When he reaches the machinery, panting, heart knocking, he can see for himself what is going on, but he grabs a man holding an orange flag and asks him what is going on. He is told that the highway has collapsed, on the sea side. Only a narrow strip of road is left. The man is sorry for the delay.

"I don't care about the delay," Whit says. "I live down there." He points. "Down there. On the beach."

"No, sir," the man says, "not anymore, you don't."

There are yellow wooden barricades. Whit starts for them, runs into a car being led along at a walking pace by another yellow-slickered man with a flag, dodges around the rear of the car, nearly knocks down a motorcycle policeman getting off his machine, ducks under a barricade, and stands at the broken, slumping edge of the paving to stare down. Men are yelling at him, but he doesn't listen. His house has been pushed over on its front. Splintered beams and bent pipes stick out of the hunched and twisted siding boards. Electrical conduits snake around. But mostly the house is covered by rock. And great broken chunks of the cliff face steps. His arm is grabbed, he is dragged back.

"That's giving way. You can't stand there. You'll be killed. Get out of here. Get back to your car." It is a police officer with plastic over his cap and a long transparent plastic raincoat. His mouth keeps moving, but a new band concert of honking auto horns makes it impossible to hear him. There is a dimple in his chin. Whit stares at the bristles there that no razor can reach. The horns quit. The officer says, "We haven't got time for sightseers."

"That's my house," Whit says. "That's where I live."

"My God," the officer says. "I'm sorry. But honest, there's nothing you can do, see? Get yourself out of danger. That's the command car, over there. Go tell them who you are, all right? They'll look after you. Sir?" He shakes Whit's arm. Whit has turned from staring at the dimple in the chin to staring down again at the wreckage of his house. "Sir?" The space behind Kate's house is filled with rock. The house has turned on its

290

base and is tilting forward. "Sir?" the officer says again. "The rest of this cliff can go down any minute. Get back behind the barricades? Please?"

"I have to get down to my house." Whit turns back toward the bulldozers, the standing cars. "My cat." He begins to run again. "I have to find my cat."

He has remembered the place where the creek runs out. He is winded when he reaches the tumble of raw rock down to the beach, where the creek spouts foaming and muddy out of a big cement pipe far below, and roars out onto the sand. He doesn't know how to climb down there, but he climbs down there, scraping his hands, ripping his clothes, losing a shoe. He tries a jump from one rock to another near the bottom, misses, and the rushing water grabs him and rolls him crazily. The flow is very strong. His mouth and nose fill with water. He can't get his breath. Then he is tossed aside and stands up in the surf and a wave hits him in the back and knocks him down again. He struggles to stand and walk, falling, crawling, slammed down by waves, crawling again. On firm sand, he hangs on hands and knees, panting, retching. The creek water was foul. He won't have to shoot himself. He will die of dysentery.

He staggers to his feet and heads for Pelican Rocks. After some time, he realizes why he is limping, and he sheds the other shoe. The tide is high and he reaches a place where there is no sand between cliffs and sea. He does his best to wade. The pants are very heavy and he sheds them. He is beaten to his knees by the surf but he fights ashore again. He can see the houses from here. He sheds the soggy jacket and begins to run. He goes wide around Kate's house because he can hear it creaking and he doesn't want it to fall on him. He stops with the edge of the waves crawling around his ankles and stares at his smashed tower.

"Polk!" he shouts. His typewriter lies embedded in the sand. Surf sucks around it. Soggy books, soggy typing paper strews

291

the beach. He shouts again, over the noise of rain, wind, waves. "Polk! Where are you?"

From overhead, up on the broken highway, voices call. He looks up. Yellow figures wave wild arms. "Get out of there. Get out of there."

He gets on hands and knees and crawls into the tower. He keeps calling Polk. He squeezes past the desk. He heaves with a shoulder at the wedged desk chair. It budges. He gives a hard push, and it clatters away, releasing more books from the shelves Kenny built. They fall on him. He stares up at the closed door. If he opens it, will tons of rock fall on him? "Polk? Where are you?" He strains up, grabs the knob, turns it. The door falls open, hitting him, knocking him on his back. His head is covered by wet cloth. He struggles out of it—the little Navajo rug at the stair top. The stairs are out of shape, but he doesn't need the stairs. He can walk on the walls now, can't he, on the windows, like a fly. But the rooms have lost shape and he has to crawl over furniture, under beams. "Polk? Come on, baby. Where are you? Polk!" Something jolts the house with a loud bang. He squats, flinching, ready to be crushed. The house creaks and shifts but it holds. He crawls on. Much of it he can't even recognize. Only the furniture. He lies on his face for a while among broken glass and pants and cries without tears. "Polk?" He stands up, hunching, and moves into what was the kitchen, where he hears hissing and smells gas. It is dark here. The rock has blanketed it completely. He coughs on the gas and chokes out, "Polk? Come on, kid. We have to get out of here. We don't want to die, do we?" He squints, sure he will find Polk crushed, under plasterboard, paneling, a broken beam, under the stove, the refrigerator. Whit crawls on hands and knees among smashed dishes, groping around him for the feel of wet, matted fur, a cold, stiff little corpse. He stops. He hears Polk. Not moans of terror or of pain. A bright meowing. He looks up. Through a split in the siding that shows daylight, Polk is peering down at him.

"Meow," he says.